PERILOUS
PASSAGES

P. A. LYNCK

This is a work of fiction. Any similarity between characters and situations within its pages and persons, living or dead, is unintentional and coincidental, with the exception of historically significant characters, who are portrayed as accurately as possible. The major events are all historical, although some license has been taken for the purposes of the story.

Cover design by Author Packages

Copyright © 2021 P.A. Lynck
All Rights Reserved
Identifiers: ISBN: 978-1-7360008-0-9 (paperback)
ISBN: 978-1-7360008-1-6 (e-book)
ISBN: 978-7360008-2-3 (e-book)

DEDICATION

Dedicated to the captains and crew
of the Queen Mary who, during World War II,
risked their own
personal safety over and over to transport brave men
and women to the battlefront.

"Around the corners of our lives lie perilous passages that lead us into places we would not choose to go."

"We must be willing to let go of the life we have planned, so as to accept the one that is waiting for us."
-Joseph Campbell

PROLOGUE

~

Long Beach, California
June 19, 1972

A violent screaming wind louder than the screams of the men as glass crashed and the horizon tilted, threatening certain death. A torpedo skimming silently toward its target. Hiding in silence and darkness and fear. Blood everywhere as the skill of my hands was not enough. A jarring collision and hundreds of men in the icy water, gasping for a final breath, and I did nothing to help. And then my decision to break the rules with painful results.

Those fragments of thoughts kaleidoscoped across Ben Stuart's mind. He was surprised at their intensity after so many years. His eyes continued to sweep over the ship triggering more memories.

She was immobile now, but still acting as a hostess for the daily inquisitive visitors. Sadly, she could no longer feel the swell of the open ocean. The salty breeze no longer caressed her. She could never again entertain hundreds of celebrities and excited guests awestruck by her majesty, stateliness, and luxury as she conveyed them across the Atlantic Ocean. She would never again carry brave men and women through a dangerous sea to a destiny they could never have imagined. Her decks held hundreds, make that thousands, of different stories, some he shared. He stood gazing at the famous luxury liner, the Queen Mary, now permanently anchored in Long Beach, California; and just like so many years ago, her majesty captivated him.

PART I

July 1939 – May 1941

CHAPTER 1

New York, NY
Mid-July 1939

The noise of the colorful crowd clustered on the wooden New York pier, the taxicabs rumbling over it unloading their fares, and the dockworkers calling to each other as they prepared the Queen Mary for her voyage, filled the morning air. A thunderstorm the previous evening had temporarily broken the oppressive heat and resulted in the presence of many more well-wishers than might normally be present on a hot July morning, all eager to see the Queen Mary cruise ship off.

"Benjamin, quick, give me a hand here," his mother called out for the second time.

"Sorry, Mom, I didn't hear you. What did you say?"

"Benjamin, please, I need your help with these bags while I pay the driver." The heavy steamer trunks had been sent the day before and were already onboard, but Margaret Stuart had packed more items she was confident they would need. Ben quickly went to the aid of his mother, moving the final two bags away from the taxi and onto the pier.

"I don't know why we need so much luggage," he mumbled as he picked up one bag.

His mother's hearing was more attuned than Ben's and she responded to his muttering with, "Well, Benjamin, there *are* two of us and we will be away for over a month. We'll need summer as well as autumn clothes since we won't be returning until September. There will be many opportunities onboard for dinners, dancing, swimming, games, and I can't wear the same ensemble more than once. I have several new Madeleine Vionnet dresses and my hats. Your Aunt Lillian dresses so fashionably for every occasion and—"

"Mom, okay, okay," her son interrupted her. He turned back toward the huge ship. "Look at her. Did I tell you yet that this is the greatest gift ever?"

"Only a hundred times. Benjamin, you earned it." She looked at him affectionately. "You deserve it and honestly, I wanted to do this for you. You've completed medical school and internship and soon you will begin your residency at one of Boston's best hospitals. If we don't do this now, who knows when. Besides, I have wanted to visit my sister for such a long time, and—" The ship's horn gave a loud blast and drowned out the rest of her sentence.

"Come on, Mom, I think we'd better hurry. Boarding must be nearly finished," he said, gently nudging her toward the gigantic ship. With one last look at the large cruise liner, Ben handed the two bags to a porter, and guiding his Mom, he thought, *this will be a trip to remember.*

Kate stood on "C" Deck looking down at the New York pier. It was crowded with embarking passengers. Family and friends wished a bon voyage to the excited travelers as porters and taxi drivers in their tailored uniforms assisted with luggage. Food and cargo were being loaded. A small band was playing some American jazz. Excited chatter, clattering taxi wheels on the wooden pier, and dockhands calling to one another cascaded around her. She wondered if her father ever got to see this sight or if he was always too busy with the details of getting the grand ship ready for her long voyage across the Atlantic.

Her father was Captain James Hawthorne, the man in charge of the Queen Mary. He and the Cunard Cruise Line had allowed Kate to accompany her father on this voyage from Southampton in southern England to New York City. And what an exciting trip it had been. Although many times Kate had kissed her father good-bye as he left on a voyage, she had never before traveled on the Queen Mary. James Hawthorne had been the captain of the Queen Mary for several years, but this one time he had negotiated passage for Kate before her nursing training began in a few months in Southampton.

Their time together in New York was over. She had seen so much. Never had she encountered such energy and bustle. Their home in Southampton (well, really Millbrook just outside Southampton) was no comparison to life in this famous metropolis. They had visited the Empire State Building and Central Park. And what an exciting day they had spent at the World's Fair in Flushing Meadows.

One evening was spent at the theatre and they had even taken in an American baseball game. She didn't understand all of it, but the excitement of the crowd was infectious, and she learned a few things by talking to those sitting around her. Fans were eager to point out their favorite player and spout acronyms like RBI and ERA that, frankly, meant nothing to her. Some of the players' names sounded funny to her, like "Bump Hadley" and "Spud Chandler". She and her dad had a good chuckle about that. Even though the Yankees had lost 4 runs to 2 to the Cleveland Indians, they had enjoyed a wonderful afternoon. The opportunity to spend so much time alone with her father was a treasured time.

Kate resembled her mother. She had Norah's thick dark auburn hair and slender frame, but in some ways their personalities were opposites. Kate's mother, Norah, was a homebody—perfectly content to manage the details of running their home. She was efficient and derived much satisfaction from seeing that her family was comfortable and well cared for. While Kate was knowledgeable about domestic duties (her mother had properly seen to that), she longed for more than the household chores that satisfied her mother. Kate had tried to persuade her mother to come along even though she knew her mum did not like traveling—especially on a ship. For all of Kate's begging and pleading, her mother would not change her mind. She had not gone along when her brother, Robin, had gone to New York, either

"All visitors ashore," the purser called out as he passed her. She wanted to see her father one more time before he was preoccupied with navigating the huge ship through the busy harbor and out into the Atlantic Ocean. Departing guests and family members heeding the purser's announcement, pushed past her as she scurried off to the wheelhouse.

"Mom, I'm gonna' take a look around the ship," Benjamin said as he stood in the open doorway. Margaret, busily beginning the chore of unpacking, looked up distractedly.

"You won't get lost, will you?" She saw the grin on Ben's face and quickly added, "How silly of me. I suppose you wouldn't be too handy with the unpacking, dear. Run along, but when I've finished I'll need your help storing the luggage."

Ben smiled and nodded. "Sure, Mom. I'll only be gone a bit. I want to watch us pull out into the harbor." He admired his mother, but sometimes she forgot that he was over twenty-one and a medical school graduate. After Peter, his father, had died four years ago, Margaret had transitioned into widowhood with strength and determination. An inheritance from her parents, and Peter's medical practice had provided a comfortable lifestyle. Peter had taken out a substantial life insurance policy that gave Margaret and Ben great financial security, allowing Ben to continue his medical education. He heard the ship give another mighty blast.

He hurried down the crowded passageway just as a purser

announced that all visitors should go ashore. He found the elevator and took it to the Promenade Deck. Through the round windows he could see the pier and the departing visitors. The decks were still crowded with passengers waving good-by to those below. The little band was putting away their instruments. The dockhands were moving away. Columns of black smoke directed attention to the three distinctive black-capped smokestacks, also known as funnels.

As he started down a flight of stairs, he noticed his shoelace had become untied. He bent down to tie it, and the ship lurched as the big engines burst into life. He was jostled by another passenger and lost his balance. His head hit the brass railing as he tumbled down the several stairs and then, nothing.

Kate came around the corner just in time to see a young man falling down the stairs in front of her. She was first to reach him and knelt beside him. She guessed him to be about her age. He was not unattractive she noticed, except for that ugly gash on his head. His honey blonde hair matted quickly with blood and his eyes were closed. Although she hadn't officially begun her nursing training she had learned first aid, and she remembered reading that head wounds bled a lot. She knelt beside him, checking his pulse, when his deep blue eyes opened. "Can you hear me?" she asked. The young man nodded. "Look at me," she instructed. Benjamin did as he was told, looking into the face of a very earnest young woman.

"What just happened?" he mumbled disjointedly as he touched his forehead, his fingers coming away coated bright red with the oozing blood. His brain slowly focused the two images of Kate into just one. Even in his slightly dazed state he realized how attractive his rescuer was. "Why are we both on the floor of the ship?" he asked her.

"You've taken a bad fall. I want you to lie perfectly still until we know what your injuries are. We have an infirmary on board and a medical doctor. I'm going to fetch him." Taking instant

9

command of the situation she firmly instructed a passing cabin steward to stay with the young man until she returned.

"No, really I'm fine," Ben said as he attempted to push himself to his feet. A wave of dizziness took control and he slumped back deciding that maybe she was right. It didn't really matter what *he* said, though, because she had already disappeared down the ship's corridor.

"Well now young man," Dr. McHenry said with a deep Scottish brogue. "You dona' appear to have any lasting effects from your fall." The ship's doctor had done a neurological exam and cleaned and bandaged the cut on Ben's head after putting in a couple of stitches to minimize any scarring. "Aye, the dizziness is temporary and will be gone in a bit. It's best you return to your cabin and lie down, but dona' go to sleep for the next three or four hours. I've given your Mum some tablets with instructions for their use. She is to notify me immediately if any double vision, nausea or severe headache occur. Cruise lines require a report on all accidents so there will be a bit 'o' paperwork for you to sign. Wait here while I get it ready."

Ben heard his mother say "Thank you, Dr. McHenry. I'll watch him carefully." At the sound of her voice, he looked around the clean white room and saw his mother's concerned face. But he didn't see the young woman who had helped him. "Dr. McHenry, who was it that came to my assistance when I fell? I would like to thank her."

"Ah, that was Kate. Kate Hawthorne. She scurried out to the wheelhouse to see her father before he canna' talk to her."

"Can't talk to her? I don't understand."

"Oh yes, sorry, chap. The ship's captain is her father Captain Hawthorne. When we are pulled 'outta the harbor by the tugs, the wheelhouse is a busy place."

Margaret patted Ben on the arm. "Now Benjamin, we'll

properly thank her when you are feeling better and have had some rest. I knew it wasn't a good idea for you to take off on your own," she chided gently.

Ben, embarrassed by his mother's pampering, responded, "Mom, it's only a slight bump on the head. I'm fine. Really. Remember, I'm a doctor now. Well, almost."

"All the same Benjamin, until we're sure you have no serious concussion we want you to remain quiet. Agreed?"

"What a way to begin this voyage," he muttered. Obedience seemed expedient and he said, "Agreed," and closed his eyes. An image of long red curls and kind blue eyes immediately appeared but for only a minute as his mother shook him.

"Stay awake, Ben."

Ben and Margaret returned to their first class two-room suite. As he slipped off his shoes and trousers to lie down, from the adjoining room he heard, "Ben, can you hear me? Don't go to sleep." He sighed. It was going to be a long afternoon. His medical training made him aware that it probably was important to follow Dr. McHenry's instructions, but it is a well-known fact that physicians make the worst patients. After assessing how he felt he was fairly confident that he would have no lasting effects from his fall except a small scar. Maybe a niggling headache today.

This six-week long voyage was a welcome rest from the frantic pace of the past several months—years really. Graduating high school at seventeen and completing his undergraduate degree in three years allowed him to enter medical school at age twenty. Now, at age 24, he would begin his two-year family practice residency.

Even though his mother kept saying she had planned this trip for him, he knew she was just as excited to see her sister after so many years and whom Ben had met only once as a small child. His aunt's letters were filled with wonderful plans while they were abroad and he was eager to explore England.

"Benjamin, are you still awake?" his mother called from the other room.

"Yes, Mom. I'm fine." He shook his head. His dad wouldn't have hovered like Mom.

His thoughts strayed to his father. It would have been wonderful to practice together. He'd be proud. He had been stern, and so dedicated to his profession. Ben favored him in appearance, but he knew he had a long way to go to match his father's dedication.

An incident came to Ben's mind. Both of his parents knew about his boxing career while in college, although his mother very vocally disapproved. Only his dad knew about the fight that nearly got him expelled. He still felt his blood pressure rise and the anger return when he remembered the oaf who had accused him of 'having a leg up' because of his physician father. He had allowed that anger to take control and without the intervention of others he would have inflicted serious injury on the guy. And then, ironically, his physician father's influence had saved his ass. Dr. Stuart's intervention with the Dean resulted in no suspension, only a written reprimand, some additional studying, and a few hours of community service. It was his father's disappointment in him that impacted him the most. Ben knew his temper was his Achilles heel, and he vowed then to keep it under control.

His dad had never told Margaret about the incident, but he somberly told his son that he would not intervene a second time. Fortunately, there hadn't been a second time. A sudden knock on the suite door roused him from his reverie.

"I have it dear. Don't try to get up." There was a rustle as Margaret made her way to the door. "Who is it, please?"

"Katherine Hawthorne." He was immediately fully awake now and reached for his trousers, hurriedly pulling them on.

CHAPTER 2

"Come in, dear," he heard his mother say.

"I hope I'm not disturbing you, but I wanted to inquire how your son is feeling." Kate's English-accented voice carried into the adjoining suite.

"How thoughtful of you. I'm insisting he rest, but he appears to be fine. Did you want to speak to him?"

"No, don't disturb him. But if he is feeling quite well this evening, my father, Captain Hawthorne, would like to invite you and your son to join us at the Captain's table for dinner. He does not like anyone to be injured aboard his ship, and he would like to meet you and express his sincere desire that the remainder of your crossing be pleasant."

"We would be honored, that is if Benjamin is feeling like dining later." Just then Ben appeared at the suite's adjoining door, finger-combing his hair and wincing as he touched the bandage at his temple. His mother frowned at his slightly disheveled appearance.

"I don't know what all this fuss is about. I'm feeling much better and both my mother and I accept. I was hoping for the opportunity to offer my thanks for your help earlier. You will be there, too?"

"Quite all right, really, sir. Yes. We'll see you at eight then in the dining hall. Cheerio." And she was off.

"Ben, are you sure you should be up?" Margaret placed her hands on her hips and looked at her son with that same look she had used with him when he was ten and was in trouble for swiping a cookie.

Maybe this was the right time to have a talk with her, he decided. "Mom, sit down, please." Margaret eyed her son warily, and seated herself in the lone club chair.

He thoughtfully and considerately chose his words. "Mom, I was thinking about Dad while I was lying down. Ever since he died, it's just been the two of us. I know his death left a huge hole in our lives and taking care of me helped fill it." Hurriedly, "You've been there for me every step of the way and I appreciate it, really, I do." He paused, feeling his way. "When we get back I'm going to be very busy. There will be long hours at the hospital. I will be gone much of the time. Mom, it's been over four years. You're still young. You should be considering *you* now, and what you want your life to be." He stopped. Took a breath.

Margaret sat quietly for a moment and Ben was fearful he had overstepped a boundary. She looked up at Ben. "I suppose I have been a bit. . . overbearing," she admitted. "But I'm still your mother! And my life *is* what I want it to be! Now, I must finish unpacking."

"No," Ben said, reaching out and grabbing her elbow. "Not right now. I missed seeing the harbor and the send-off because of my fall. Give me a minute and then let's go up on deck and check out the view." Out of habit, she started to protest and insist that he lie down again, but he had already disappeared. She smiled to herself shaking her head. *In spite of his little speech, sometime, he still acts like he was ten.*

Four years was an acceptable mourning period. But it's so hard, she thought. *At his age he couldn't possibly understand the love she and Peter had shared for nearly three decades. Even after four years there were times when memories and tears surfaced laced with a poignancy that was at the same time comforting and heartbreaking. That wasn't something you could put in a box and place on a shelf and only take out on special occasions.*

"Hurry, Mom. Let's go," Ben called from the open door.

Margaret felt guilty admitting it, but Ben's unfortunate accident was creating the promise of an exciting evening. Her mirror image revealed a handsome woman, who had the means to care for her appearance with the finest clothes and beauty products available. She examined her reflection. The deep purple velvet gown emphasized her best features and brought out the color in her high cheeks. Ben had inherited his blonde coloring from his father, not Margaret, whose hair was the color of rich mahogany and was just beginning to show streaks of gray. She swept it up off her neck and secured it with a jeweled pin. Grabbing her gloves off the bedside table she called out. "Ben, Are you nearly ready?" He answered by coming through the adjoining doorway and making a stately bow.

"At your service, Madam." He had changed into a white dinner jacket and slacks. She looked up at him and brushed a blonde hair off his shoulder. She pushed his hair away from the newly-acquired bandage, randomly noticing that it was hiding the scar in his eyebrow received during his short boxing career. She was grateful that his straight nose had remained straight.

"There. Now we're ready." He bent down and kissed her cheek.

"You look very nice, Mom. Come on. Let's go meet this captain and daughter and show them what elegant passengers they have on board."

This was the first time they had seen the dining room. Margaret couldn't help herself. A slight gasp escaped as her eyes took in the immense size of the room. "Ben, just look at this." White-coated waiters wearing white gloves bustled around seating the passengers. Lovely floral bouquets adorned the tables. The crystal chandeliers gleamed and twinkled and the orchestra was tuning up for dancing later on.

Ben guided his mother into the room as a young steward in a white dinner jacket approached them. "May I help you, sir? Do you have a table number?"

"No, we have been invited to join the Captain's table this evening," Ben replied.

"Certainly, sir. May I have your names?"

"I'm Dr. Benjamin Stuart and this is my mother, Margaret Stuart." It occurred to him then that this was perhaps the first time he had introduced himself as Dr. Stuart, a bit premature he admitted to himself. He glanced sideways at his mother and caught her smiling.

"Please wait here, sir." He disappeared into the room.

While they waited, they surveyed the room. It was beautiful. The dining room ran nearly half the length of the ship and soared three decks high. A large map covered one wall and displayed the location of the Queen Mary in real-time as her crystal replica moved along the Atlantic routes. Another wall was completely covered with a large mural depicting an English scene of birds. The room was filling with fashionably dressed passengers chatting quietly as they, too, surveyed the room. Soft light completed the elegant mood and the subdued clinking of china and crystal could be heard as diners were seated and served. Ben had read that the ship was called the ship of woods. And now he knew why. Over 50 kinds of wood from all over the world gleamed in the soft light. It was a sight of extraordinary beauty.

"Please, sir, follow me." The steward had returned and took Margaret's elbow. They wound their way among the tables until they reached the front of the massive dining room. "Please be seated. The Captain and his daughter will be joining you soon." The steward made sure they were seated comfortably, flicked serviettes, or napkins, onto their laps with a sharp snapping sound and then left to escort and seat more dinner guests. Margaret picked up the printed menu and began scanning it as another couple approached their table.

"Well, the Brits on board are concerned and I'm worried that we will be dragged into this war or whatever it is and it's really none of our concern," the woman was saying. Their voices drew Ben's attention away from the menu. He observed the woman to be a bit older than Margaret and was carrying around a few extra pounds. To his taste her makeup was a bit overdone on her chubby face, and her sparkling rings and flashy necklace exclaimed wealth. He turned his attention to the gentleman accompanying her. He was more subdued and he impressed Ben as possibly a professor, but without the elbow patches. His tux was modest, his salt and pepper beard short and trimmed neatly, and he wore rimless glasses on his longish face.

"Poppycock, Constance, there's no chance of that," her companion replied. Turning to Ben and his mother, he gave a slight bow and said, "Please allow us to introduce ourselves. My name is Michael Breckenridge and this is my wife Constance. We received an invitation to be guests of the Captain this evening." Ben stood as Constance was seated and made their introductions as well.

"I am in total agreement with you, Mrs. Breckenridge. Europe does not need America meddling in its affairs." Margaret joined in after overhearing their discussion. Before Ben seated himself, he glanced up and saw Katherine with presumably Captain Hawthorne approaching their table.

Now that he was completely in charge of his faculties, he was really seeing her for the first time. *She isn't as tall as I thought. Must be because I'm not looking up at her from the floor this time*, he thought. Her long bright auburn hair was pulled back in an attempt to tame the wild curls. The emerald green brocade evening gown was cinched in giving the illusion of a tiny waist. She smiled at Ben as they approached and a dimple flashed briefly in her cheek. Captain Hawthorne wore a white captain's uniform and although he wasn't a tall man, the uniform gave him stature. When he removed his captain's hat it was obvious. Kate hadn't gotten her red curls from her father. His hair was a sandy brown and thinning on top. He was clean shaven and carried himself with a military posture. Ben wondered if he had at one time been in the Royal Navy. He extended his hand to the gentlemen after seating his daughter.

The two men had again stood. "Please, be seated everyone", he said. "I'm Captain James Hawthorne and this is my daughter, Katherine. She prefers Kate, however. I'm so glad each of you could join us this evening. You are Mr. and Mrs. Breckenridge from New York, correct? I trust you've gotten acquainted." Heads nodded around the table. Turning to Ben, he said, "That is rather a large bandage." Looking around the table he continued, "Dr. Stuart took a nasty fall earlier today and had to visit our infirmary." Re-addressing Ben he said, "How are you feeling? Better, I hope."

"Yes, thank you. And please, call me Ben. I'm afraid it was much ado about nothing, really. Your daughter certainly knows how to take charge of things. I didn't really get much of a chance to thank you earlier, so—Miss?—Hawthorne, please accept my thanks now."

"Call me Kate. And yes, Miss. You're very welcome. What a beastly way to begin your trip."

The wine steward arrived and Captain Hawthorne ordered wine for the table although declining it for himself. Addressing his guests, "I trust your cabin was satisfactory and everything was in order. If you need anything, please tell your room steward and he will attend to it immediately. We pride ourselves on our ability to afford our first-class passengers all the comforts of home."

"We are still getting settled in our suite," Margaret replied. "Ben's accident delayed our unpacking a bit; however, everything seems to be 'ship-shape'." She surprised herself with a slight giggle. "Captain, it was very kind of you to invite us to be seated with you and your daughter this evening. Thank you. Will Mrs. Hawthorne be joining us as well?"

Captain Hawthorne gave a slight chuckle before responding.

"Kate's Mum is not much of a traveler. She is always fearful when off dry land. No, this kind of adventure is not for her. She shouldn't have married a sea captain, eh?"

Ben turned to the Breckenridge's and asked, "You were saying something about a war earlier? I'm afraid my studies have taken most of my time and I have not thought much about events happening in Europe."

Michael glanced sideways at his wife and his expression signaled her to mind her manners. "Yes, Constance was just saying that she hopes the United States is able to refrain from interfering in European affairs. While what is going on in Europe is troubling, it really is their problem, not ours in the States."

"Perhaps, you don't completely understand what is happening." The voice was Kate's and while it was said politely, there was a glint in her eyes. "This way of thinking. . .this man. . . must be stopped. Do you know that all of the Jewish enterprises in Germany have been shut down? Do you know that Jews are fleeing Germany by the thousands to Jerusalem, and Egypt, and Greece. Do you know that a boat carrying Jewish refugees landed in Florida and was turned away by your country? I believe before it is over the United States will have a stake in this war. I believe they will see the atrocities that are being committed and will take a stand against them." As Kate spoke the passion in her voice intensified. She glanced at her father and saw the silent reprimand.

Kate impressed Ben as being very well informed, but he decided that changing the subject was a good idea. Before he could say anything, the waiter approached the table to take their dinner orders, redirecting the conversation for him.

The attention of the guests turned to the Captain as he began telling his dinner companions about the many beautiful features of the Queen Mary.

"This ship is already a legend after winning the Blue Riband just a year ago by beating the Normandie across the Atlantic," the Captain began, but was interrupted by Margaret.

"And what is the Blue Riband?" she asked.

"The word 'riband' is an archaic word for ribbon. The Blue Riband is an unofficial award given to the ship making the fastest crossing. It is awarded based on average speed and not length of crossing because ships take different routes. Also, westbound and eastbound trophies are awarded separately because currents and prevailing winds are different depending upon the direction. Last year's victory made the Queen Mary the fastest cruise liner afloat."

Ben was delighted with the change of subject and already knew a lot about this amazing state-of-the-art ship. "Yes. And it's so fast because there are 24 oil-fired water tube boilers producing a total of 160,000 shaft horsepower through four sets of single reduction geared turbines—" Ben stopped. A bit embarrassed.

"Dr. Stuart, that was very impressive."

"Thank you, Captain. I've, um, done some reading about this ship."

"Now, if you look over your shoulder you'll see the large map on the wall," the Captain continued. "That tiny crystal replica of our ship moves in real time as we cross the Atlantic. Cunard spared no expense in the construction, safety, and speed of the Queen Mary. And that is why I am proud to be her Captain." By the time the Captain had educated his guests about the intricate details of the Queen Mary and answered questions, their dinners arrived and conversation centered around the delicious food—creamed corn soup, prime rib, roasted potatoes and green apple pie à la mode—and their vacation plans.

As coffee and brandy were served, the classical strains from the grand piano ceased and the small band consisting of a cello, clarinet, bass and drummer began to play music by the likes of Count Basie and Glen Miller.

Turning to Kate, Ben asked, "Would you care to dance?" Not many couples were on the dance floor yet and Kate felt a bit conspicuous, but she agreed. They excused themselves from their dinner companions and moved to the dance floor. Ben's arm slid around Kate's waist as a two-step began to play. "Tell me about your family and your home. England, right?" Ben decided that was possibly neutral territory.

"Yes, we live in an old house outside Southampton, Millbrook, actually. I have one brother. I was born in December 1919 and he was born in January 1920."

"I'll bet that kept your mother busy raising two toddlers, what, 13 months apart? Wait a minute, that doesn't work. Was he adopted?"

She grinned at Ben as she caught his puzzled expression. "No. We're twins, actually." "I was born at 11:57 p.m. on December 31st and he was born at 12:08 a.m. on January 1st. I always enjoy the confusion until people figure it out."

"Why didn't he come with you and your father, or did he?"

"No. He came with my father on an earlier trip because he is leaving for school about the time we get back. These trips are sort of a graduation gift for us. He's attending Huntington College, studying mathematics and I will begin nurse's training in a few months."

Ben had learned that any discussion about the political situation was risky but he was curious. "What did you mean by your comments about the possibility of war?" Kate looked up at Ben's face, as they continued dancing together, unsure how to respond. After all she was the Captain's daughter and felt partly responsible for the passengers having a pleasant experience while onboard. She remembered her father's silent reprimand. Although passionate about events in Europe, she quickly determined that nothing would be gained by giving this young man an impassioned explanation. It was obvious he wasn't particularly interested, so she chose a more subdued response.

"There is no simple explanation for what is going on back home right now," she said, almost succeeding in keeping her voice neutral. "What do you know about events in Europe?"

"Um, you see, I've been too busy with my medical training to take time to understand what's happening in Europe these days." His embarrassment was obvious. "It all seems very far away to most of us in America."

Kate was having difficulty imagining how he could justify such impassiveness. It took immense discipline for her to calmly explain to Ben some of what was occurring in her homeland. She told him of rumors, some true and some not, that abounded in the press and radio; stories of an advancing German army that wanted to rid the world of Jews. Her face grew more animated and her voice louder unable to subdue her passion after all. "Hitler's army wants to 'exterminate the Jewish vermin from the world.' His words, not mine. Day by day his army grows more powerful."

Just as she spoke those words the music stopped and nearby couples glanced their way, returning to their tables. Ben was saved from displaying any further political ignorance, or ignorance in general, as they returned to their table and joined in a less serious conversation.

Captain Hawthorne watched Ben seat his daughter. He was well aware of Kate's passionate nature and how insensitive she could be at times. He understood better than she that Americans were untouched by the German offensive. He heard their comments on every crossing. Right now, it was Europe's problem.

CHAPTER 3

Kate rolled over and checked her alarm clock. Her father had arranged a first-class cabin for her while he remained in his Captain's quarters on this special crossing. She was surprised at how late it was. It was still so dark. A quick peek out the small window explained why. Fog. Thick and gray. It sought to gain entrance as it swirled around the glass. This Atlantic fog was different from the dark yellow sooty fog she had experienced in London. She showered and dressed and went up to the wheelhouse to see if her father had eaten breakfast. She wanted to experience and remember every minute of this trip and determined that a little fog wasn't going to interfere with her morning.

"Cherrio," she called as she slipped through the wheelhouse doorway. Her father nodded in her direction but appeared preoccupied with directing operations, so she helped herself to a cup of tea and waited. Looking out through the wide-open bridge windows she saw great swirls of misty fog like a great grey ghost clutching at the bow of the Queen Mary. The view gave the appearance of a large shroud thrown over the ship, separating it from the watery world surrounding it. There had been some fog on the way over, too, and she knew it created less than ideal conditions for the big ship.

Soon her father motioned for her to come to him. He slipped an arm over her shoulder and said, "Good mornin'. Sorry Kate, but I won't be joining you for breakfast. The fog. Think I'd best stay here and have something brought 'round."

Kate and her father had been able to share breakfast several mornings on this trip, but she understood that he needed to be here, uninterrupted now. "Of course. I have some things I want to do this morning. I'll come by later."

Captain Hawthorne watched her as she left. She was all grown up, he thought. He and her mother, Norah, were very proud of her. She had a good head on her shoulders and had made a wise decision about nursing. In many ways Kate and her mum were alike—decisive, passionate about their beliefs—but Kate was much more outspoken. "If only she would temper her speech," he muttered softly.

He thought about the transmission he had received earlier in the morning and wondered how much to share with Kate. The information it contained would change their lives. *It was probably right she should know and she would be a big help when I tell Norah. I just don't want to spoil this trip for her,* he argued to himself.

"Captain Hawthorne, sir," the executive officer broke into his thoughts. "The fog is beginning to lift, sir." The Captain peered across the bow and he, too, saw patches of gray water instead of the swirling cloud.

"I believe you're right," he agreed. "Prepare to increase speed to 25 knots."

Ben noticed the ship's increased speed as he joined his mother in the dining room. He bent down and kissed her cheek before helping himself to a breakfast roll and coffee in a silver carafe already on the table. A waiter immediately appeared, took his order and disappeared as quickly as he had arrived. While seating himself, he saw Kate enter the dining room alone, and motioned her over to their table.

Unlike last evening when her hair had been pulled back with a jeweled clip, this morning it was down around her shoulders. Ben smiled as she tried to manage the uncontrollable curls, and thought that the casual turquoise sweater set and white slacks she was wearing suited her. She nodded to Ben, stopped to place an order with a waiter, and approached their table.

The spark of interest in her son's eyes did not escape Margaret's notice. "Good morning, Katherine," she said as Ben seated Kate beside him. As if by magic a waiter brought Kate a cup of Earl Grey tea, and poured a bit of milk into it.

"Thank you," Kate said, turning her attention to Margaret. "Good morning, Mrs. Stuart. Good to see you again."

Margaret finished her coffee, carefully placing the china cup in the saucer. "And you as well, Katherine. I've finished my breakfast so please excuse me. I'm off to check out the library. See you later, Ben."

Kate attempted a sip of tea, but it was too hot and she set the cup back down. "I sometimes have breakfast with my father," Kate said. "But this morning when I was in the wheelhouse, the bridge to you, the fog —"

"You were on the bridge?" Ben interrupted excitedly. They actually let you go up there? I read so much about this ship. Her speed. Her size. Is it true that famous actors like David Niven and Noel Coward have been passengers?"

"Yes. It's true—and many other celebrities and dignitaries, too." She tried the tea again. "Would you like to see the wheelhouse? I can ask my father for permission. The view off the bow is really quite grand."

"Really? Of course. Who wouldn't?" He nearly choked on his coffee from excitement.

"In the meantime how would you like a tour of this magnificent ship? Have you seen the Cabin Class lounge yet? Or the swimming pool?" They hurried through breakfast as the tendrils of gray fog disappeared.

"Wait until you see this pool, Ben." Kate stepped aside allowing him to enter before her. He stopped suddenly and she sidestepped quickly, barely avoiding bumping into him.

"Jeepers! This thing is huge," he said looking down at the pool from the balcony on "D" deck.

"I recall Papa saying the pool is 35 feet long and of course filled with lots of heated seawater. It sloshes a lot in rough weather and sometimes even has to be drained. Off to your right are changing rooms, showers and the Turkish bath and massage areas. See that steward over there? He's an attendant for the Turkish Bath."

"I'll definitely be seeing him later."

His awe-filled expression amused her. "Have you noticed the different lighting?"

"Now that you mention it, it does seem darker in here."

"It's the mother-of-pearl ceiling. It diffuses the light. Something about creating a peaceful ambiance."

"You're kidding me. The whole ceiling is made from mother-of-pearl? Amazing."

They left "D" deck and took one of the lifts to the Promenade Deck. He peeked into the library with its columns of glass enclosed books and plump sofas. Didn't see his mom. Next, they took the stairs to the Sun Deck. "I want you to see the Verandah Grill. This is where the swingin' passengers gather at night." They moved aft and entered the grill. "It's much smaller than the dining room and notice—no wood walls. Just windows, to take advantage of the view. The décor is more modern. Theatrical, I think. At night the dance floor is always full and the lights change colors. It's smashing fun!" Ben noticed her passionate description and casually wondered if she was passionate about *everything*.

"I like night clubs. We danced pretty well together last evening; we should try out that dance floor sometime."

"Might be fun. We'll see."

As they walked up to the Sports Deck, Ben said, "Do I hear dogs barking?"

"You do. There are kennels on this deck. Some guests just can't bear to be away from their loveable corgis and spaniels."

A doubles game was in progress on only one of the four tennis courts. The foggy morning had deterred others. They found lounges back down on the Promenade Deck and their conversation made a logical turn from the ship to traveling.

"Have you done a lot of traveling?" Ben asked.

"Not nearly enough. "I love visiting Seté on the French Riviera. The weather is nearly perfect year-round and the coastlines are breathtaking. There are open markets selling seafood, clothing, trinkets. Always something going on." She picked up a shuffleboard cue stick left behind by a passenger. She became animated as she demonstrated the *joutes nautiques*, when boat crews joust with long poles in an attempt to knock each other into the harbor, and nearly knocked both of them out of the lounge chairs. Nearby guests joined in their laughter.

The time passed quickly. The sun had won the battle with the fog and was beginning its mid-morning dance over the surface of the water, creating glittering sparkles in the waves. The blankets adorning the lounge chairs were welcome earlier against the salty spray and chilly air; but now that the sun was in charge the air was absorbing its warm rays. Kate brushed away the blanket and stood. "I should go ask Papa about permission for you to visit. I'll catch up with you after I talk with him. Come 'round the starboard Observation Lounge at 3:00. They serve high tea there every afternoon, weather permitting."

Ben watched her scamper up the ladder to the next deck and realized how much he had enjoyed the morning with her. *Really enjoyed it,* he thought. He turned around with an improvised two-step jig and a big grin and went to share his excitement with his mother.

He found her just returning with an F. Scott Fitzgerald novel tucked under her arm. "Mom, Mom. Guess what. Kate said I might be able to visit the bridge! I've *got* to remember it's wheelhouse. This is just too unbelievable." Margaret caught his excitement and gave him an indulgent smile.

"That's marvelous. Very thoughtful of Kate to arrange it."

"She's checking with the Captain, but maybe even today. Samuel will be so jealous. When I was reading about this ship he wanted to know all about her, too." His comment gave her an idea.

"Ben, you could write him a letter. I just passed a room with writing desks stocked with ink pens and stationery embossed with the Queen Mary emblem. You could write to Laura, too. I'm sure both would be pleased to receive a letter from this ship. Oh, and there is even a post box. The letters can be posted right from here."

"Great idea, Mom."

The writing room was paneled in rich warm walnut. Underfoot was thick carpet patterned in burgundy and white. Each pedestal desk had its own club chair upholstered in a colorful leafy pattern and stocked with ink pens and the letterhead like his Mom had mentioned. Ben was sitting in one of the upholstered club chairs, pen in hand, the letterhead blank, thinking, not writing. He knew his mother was fond of Laura and happy they were a couple. Well, she thought of them as a couple.

While he and Laura had not actually grown up together, the connection between his father and hers had caused their paths to cross occasionally. Ben had thought of her as this little girl who came to some of the dinners his mom and dad had hosted. But then at his father's funeral service there she was. She wasn't a little girl any longer—that was certain. Grown to a healthy five foot six inches, filled out in all the right places, she was a lovely young woman. Although grieving the loss of his father, he hadn't failed to notice her transformation. Their paths had crossed several times since then at hospital functions, and they had gone out a few times.

The room came back into focus and he turned back to the task at hand, but instead of writing Laura and Samuel his mind kept jumping ahead to the possibility of seeing the wheelhouse. . . with Kate.

CHAPTER 4

Boston, MA
Mid-July 1939

Samuel Dressler rubbed his eyes and reached for the coffee pot on the hotplate. The coffee inside was probably bitter, but he poured a cup anyway. Remnants of his dinner cooled nearby. He took a sip while idly wondering if Ben and Mrs. Stuart were enjoying their cruise. Coffee *was* bitter. It had been a very long day and he still had much studying to do before crawling into bed. And the Jewish Sabbath would begin tomorrow.

Samuel and Ben had become good friends during the time they were attending medical school although Samuel was a year behind Ben; and it was exciting that both had accepted internships at Massachusetts General Hospital. He owed Ben and Mrs. Stuart for their generosity in allowing him to live rent-free in their small 'mother-in-law' apartment during his residency requirement. Massachusetts General was a prestigious institution and it was Ben's father's reputation that secured his residency.

The Stuarts had welcomed him as family and he and Ben decided they could carry on a compatible practice together, joining Ben's father's practice when they finished their residencies. Dr. Oglethorpe had practiced with Ben's father, but he was ready to retire. That had been the plan before the escalating events in Europe. In Lithuania.

The fact that his parents were in danger and he was safe created a conflict in his gut that made studying difficult. He had written urging them to leave their beloved Lithuania—the land of their ancestors. And for at least the hundredth time he questioned whether he should stay here in the United States or go back to Vilna and insist his parents leave?

Vilna. The city was known for its distinguished medical traditions, its Jewish newspapers and its school system. It was called the Jerusalem of the North containing the largest Jewish library in Europe. His own father was a member of the Vilna City Council and prominent in YIVO, a Jewish organization which, among other things, guided graduate students in religious research. His father's contacts had been responsible for financing his medical studies in Boston. He remembered his father's words on the day he left. "Don't forget your heritage," he had said, holding Samuel close.

He picked up his notes and told himself that a good doctor would be able to concentrate on the task at hand and not be distracted by personal issues. It was after 2:00 a.m. when he recited the Shema, his nightly and morning prayer, turned off the light and fell into bed fully clothed, his cold dinner still sitting on his desk. His dreams were full of confusion and drifted from one terrible scenario into another. He heard Foter calling to him. He heard Muter weeping. They were frightened, and lost in deep darkness. Then they were running, breathless, stomping boots chasing them. When he awoke at 6:30 he was more tired than when he went to sleep and fearful that his nightmare would become reality.

Vilna, Lithuania
Mid-July 1939

As Jonah Dressler left the synagogue where he prayed his morning prayers, he covered the yamulke on his head with his black wide-brimmed Hoiche hat. He turned right out of the synagogue heading for the postal office. Ana would be happy. A letter bearing a United States postmark was waiting for him. Samuel had finally found time to write to them. He slipped it into a pocket.

A meeting was scheduled this morning to discuss an engineering project. Soviet ground troops were moving into Vilna and inquiries had been made about local engineering and construction businesses in town. Today they would discuss the details of the project. As he neared his one-story brick office, he observed a paper tacked to his front door, again.

The Soviet presence was not Vilna's first occupation. The city's long history was a troubled one. The country had bounced around like a football between Poland, the Soviets, and Germany. Even so, he had built a successful business in Vilna he was proud of. But changes were coming soon and he sensed it. Rumors abounded. An unsettling feeling of doom had begun seeping into the city like tendrils of dark thick fog reaching into the minds and lives of the residents. Or more likely that fog was always there, hidden beneath the well-trodden brick streets, slowly escaping as a prelude to the next invasion. The current unsettled mood resonated within him causing him to have doubts about this Soviet alliance. He hoped it would be profitable, but the reputation of these Russians was not good. He had witnessed first-hand their greed and bullying and determined he would not tolerate their roughshod manner even if it meant losing the project. He was a respected businessman who refused to compromise his ethics.

He pushed open the heavy wooden door of the building, removed his jacket and wide-brimmed hat but left his yamulke on and sat down at his desk in the small office, the German propaganda pamphlet still in his hand. It was always the same message, different messengers. This time it was the Germans spreading lies about the Jews to the Lithuanians, proclaiming them to be communists. 'All Jews are communists and all communists are Jews,' the paper began. He shook his head and crumpled the paper in his fist.

Removing his spectacles from his pocket he felt Samuel's letter. Carefully he slit open the envelope, slipped out two sheets of thin paper, and quietly read to himself. His countenance darkened. "Never," he mumbled, not realizing he had said it aloud. "How could Samuel even suggest that!" He started to tear up the letter and throw the pieces away, but changed his mind, tucking it back into his pocket. Maybe he'd show it to Ana later, but there was work to be done today.

CHAPTER 5

Aboard the Queen Mary

Kate waited at the doorway to the wheelhouse for her father to acknowledge her presence. He was engaged in a discussion with two crew members and by the stern expression he was wearing—one Kate had seen on a number of occasions growing up—he was displeased about something. Maybe not the best time to ask for a favor. While she waited, she thought of Ben. She liked him but he seemed a bit shallow. He was preoccupied with his very sheltered life. In light of the uncertainty of her world, she wanted to simply dismiss him. Maybe she was jealous, she thought. His life seemed so orderly—so perfect. His wealth gave him so many opportunities. She had to admit privately, however, that there was a certain attraction. But after all, this was only a five-day cruise—four now—and she wanted to focus on this lovely time with her father before it was over.

She had almost decided to come back later, when her father took notice of her and ended his conversation. He glanced at the time.

"Kate," he said coming her way. "Just who I wanted to have a cup of tea with." And he ushered her out the door and toward the dining room, not his usual habit. Most days he had tea brought up.

A steward quickly approached, seated them, and took their

order. It was then that Kate realized the stern expression on her father's face was still there. "Is something wrong?"

"You know me too well," he said. Her father glanced around the dining room before answering assuring himself that no one was nearby. "Yes, Kate, something is very wrong." He saw the look on her face and quickly added with a flash of a smile, "But not because of you. I had a debate with myself whether to tell you this now or wait. I had decided to wait; but since you asked, I'll answer. Changes are coming, Kate, and I'm going to need your help when I tell your mum. This news I'm sharing with you will be upsetting and you can help her." He paused. "You know that I have colleagues and friends in the Royal Navy, ship captains I trust." She nodded, keeping her eyes on her father's face. "There is a very credible rumor that the Royal Navy will be pressed into active duty soon to assist in this conflict in Europe. There is also a rumor that this ship, the Queen Mary and possibly other cruise ships, may be commandeered to be used in some way, not entirely clear at this point."

"What does that mean?" Kate's tone was solemn.

"I'm not completely sure, yet. But it could mean that since I know this ship better than any other captain, and I have some Royal Navy background, I may be asked to remain as her captain as long as I am needed. I don't need to tell you that this is very confidential information and can't be shared with anyone else."

The steward brought their tea, scones, butter and jam, so their conversation lagged. Kate prepared to pour. Now she understood why they had left the wheelhouse for tea. She glanced up. "When will you know anything for sure?"

"As soon as we dock in Southampton, I will request a meeting with the President of the Cunard Line. I'm hoping he has more accurate information he can share. Kate, I don't want you unnecessarily troubled by this, but I felt it important to share this with you before I tell your mum. You know how she worries. But, promise it won't spoil the remainder of our trip together, okay?"

She nodded, lifted the china cup and took a sip of the hot tea. The Earl Grey was comforting. Steadying. Looking up at her father, she asked what she had been afraid to ask moments before. "Will this put you in danger?"

"No, no Poppet." He took her hand. "This is not a war ship. It's not outfitted with guns or torpedoes. I can't even imagine at this point how it could be used. Twenty some years ago, during the Great War, cruise liners were pressed into service as troop carriers. And that's a possibility. My meeting with the president may shed some light and we'll find out this is a baseless rumor."

But Kate, knowing her father well, knew he wouldn't have shared this with her if he wasn't reasonably certain there was truth to it. And if indeed the ship was carrying troops, wouldn't that make it a target?

He hurriedly finished the tea and rose to leave. Kate suddenly remembered why she had come to the wheelhouse in the first place. "Oh, I nearly forgot. The reason I came up to see you was that Ben—you remember the doctor who fell—was telling me he would really enjoy a visit to the wheelhouse. I told him I would ask you. Is that okay?"

"Of course. But make it later today. The weather and ocean conditions this afternoon should clear up considerably by then. The view will be much better, too." He stood to leave, then paused a moment and looking down at her said, "Kate, I'm really glad we got to make this trip together. There's a very good chance we wouldn't have had this opportunity again."

His tone was so wistful Kate was even more certain the rumor was real. She wanted to hug him close but because they were in the not-so-private dining room, she resisted. "It's been wonderful. I have memories to last a lifetime." Kate sat there alone, mulling over her father's announcement, her mind sifting it all as she finished her tea. *It's happening,* she thought. *This bloody war really is happening. It's personal now.* She placed the china cup carefully in its matching saucer and went to find Ben.

If someone had told him a week ago that he was going to be standing on the bridge of the Queen Mary, he definitely would not have believed them. But here he was. The Captain was busy, so while they waited, Ben took notice of everyone and everything. So much shiny brass. Immaculate described *everything*. It was calmer than he expected. He had imagined a ship this large would have more hubbub. With pride, the Captain explained the communication system with the boiler room. He demonstrated the echo sounding system. He introduced some of the crew members. And what a view—in all directions ocean and sky as far as the eye could see.

Afterward Kate took him to the "alley" as it was called. It ran the entire length of the ship and was off limits for most passengers. Here were the crew quarters, the laundry, the bakery and meat storage areas. One got a real sense of just what it took to run a ship this size and it was amazing. They ended their afternoon with high tea in the Observation Lounge. If he hadn't been filled with such exhilaration he might have noticed that Kate seemed quieter than earlier.

The days ticked by quickly, filled with Kate. They swam together, played shuffleboard, walked the promenade deck, and sometimes just talked. Tonight was the final night of the crossing. He was waiting for Kate in the Verandah Grill, where earlier she had said "the swingin" people gathered. The music was definitely more upbeat than the dining room and many couples were already dancing, but not the foxtrot or waltz. These couples were really "swinging", doing the jitterbug, jive and other swing dance steps. If Kate was really into dancing, he was gonna' be totally embarrassed out there.

He looked around the room and saw her and he sucked in a breath. The crepe fabric of the deep blue dress she was wearing clung to her shapely figure and fell softly to her ankles, ending in a small ruffle. The sleeves were short and the neckline deep. He let out his breath and swallowed, standing as she approached the small table.

"Ben, sorry I'm late. The time got away from me."

"The wait was worth it. You look fantastic. I'll go to the bar and order us some drinks. Pink Lady for you?" She nodded.

While they waited for the drinks, the band changed songs and Ben decided to take advantage of the slower tempo. "Care to dance?"

"Of course."

The light fragrance she was wearing was heady, and it felt like an embrace when he guided her onto the dance floor. When they danced a few nights ago, Kate had passionately voiced her opinion of European events; but tonight she was quiet. The colored lights swirled around them as they danced, until the band changed tempo again and they returned to their table. "Swing" dance steps hadn't made it to England, so Ben was off the hook. On the surface their light banter seemed the same; but underneath it was somehow different as they spent this final evening together.

The night sky was cloudless and when they left the lounge, an almost full moon was casting flecks of light across the water.

"It's so clear you could almost walk up the moonbeams and reach the moon," Kate said, resting her arms on the railing. She giggled. "Just think, Ben, someday you'll become a very famous doctor, and I can say that I knew you when."

Ben laughed. "I've still got a ways to go. Who knows—maybe we'll see one another again someday."

"Not likely."

It was drizzly and overcast when the Stuarts disembarked in Southampton. Ben commented he felt like he was in the middle of a dirty cotton ball as the low gray clouds surrounded them. It was early enough in the day that they decided to continue on to Dorchester where Aunt Lillian lived, rather than spend a night in Southampton.

They hired a livery service to transport them and their luggage to the train station where they purchased first class tickets on the Bournemouth Belle. After a short delay they were seated in a pullman car for the two and a half-hour journey.

A burping column of steam and soot announced that they were underway and presently a waiter in a white coat appeared and took their order of tea or coffee, croissants and jam. The measured rhythm of the track was noisy as they moved across Southampton, but once they had left the old brick buildings of the city and entered the more pastoral countryside the train picked up speed and quieted down. The rain had stopped but the dense sodden skies promised only a temporary respite. The steady click-clackety cadence of the train wheels had a soporific effect and lulled Ben into a trance, his mind settling on Kate.

He pictured her sitting across from him, laughing. Her dark blue gown framing her shoulders. Those wild curls continually escaping from the fiery clip. . . he drifted off.

The trip winked by quickly—make that forty winks—and the blue-clad porter was in the aisle announcing, "Dorchester, next stop." Margaret shook her son awake; her excitement infectious. She had waited such a long time for this.

Millbrook, England
Same Time

The livery car turned slowly onto the cobbled driveway and Captain James Hawthorne paid the driver, collected his bags and then stood there as the car turned and disappeared. The house lights bid him a warm welcome in the twilight. He was a lucky man. Two fine children. A solid marriage. It still amazed him that this could be his home. Norah had put so much of herself into this house—planting and tending the immaculate gardens, laughing as they placed the wrought iron bench near the tiny hawthorn tree. She had planted the tree when they first bought the house. She thought it would be funny to have a tree with the same name as theirs. Now its branches sheltered the small bench. As the tree and their family grew the bench became their "place" for talking over many things.

This was going to be difficult. With a sigh he picked up his bags and stepped onto the porch. But before he could reach for his key, the door opened and Kate gave him a big hug and a peck on the cheek. "We thought we heard a motor car out front" she said. "Mum's in the kitchen. Have you eaten?" *That could delay the inevitable for a bit,* he thought. "Not since a spot of tea and croissants earlier," he said, setting the bags down in the hall, rubbing his hands together and following Kate toward the fragrant kitchen. After disembarking, she had returned home without him while he secured the ship, thanked the crew and arranged a meeting with Cunard officials.

After hugging Norah and washing his hands at the kitchen sink, he focused on the meal before him. He decimated the shepherd's pie, practically inhaled the baked apples and was on his second cup of tea. Food aboard the Queen Mary was exceptional, but there was nothing like his wife's home cooked meals.

Norah turned from the sink and frowned at her husband. She wiped her hands on her apron and leaned back, studying him for a moment. Her blue eyes didn't miss much. Most times when he arrived home he wanted to share details of the crossing with her. Tonight he was unusually quiet. "Jimmie," (she was the only one could call him that) "You're here but you're not here. You know, a bit absent. What is it?"

He looked up. She discerned his moods so well. How many times had they sat here in this kitchen, sharing good food, laughter, friends, plans for their future. He visualized two high chairs side by side. Robin and Kate quizzically tasting mashed peas. The twins sat at this same table doing their studies. He snapped back. Now this bloody lone man in Germany had the power to totally disrupt all of their lives. Anger began to build in him. Norah was still watching him. "Norah, we'll talk later. I'm going to take the bags upstairs and change out of my uniform."

Silently, slowly bringing his anger under control, he climbed the stairs in this comfortable house that had brought such joy into his life. He heard Kate rummaging about in her room. Her door was open and he poked his head in. "Kate, could you come downstairs in a bit. I want to talk to you and your mum." Kate caught his expression and the strain in his voice.

"Did you get more information?"

He merely nodded and continued toward his bedroom. Her stomach felt suddenly tight and she crossed her arms in front of her as if that would make the feeling go away.

"Poor Mum," she whispered.

CHAPTER 6

Vilna, Lithuania
Mid-July 1939

The Lithuanian day was longer this time of year and the sun was only now pulling down the shades of night behind it as it disappeared below the horizon. The evening meal was finished and the dishes washed, dried and put away. Jonah lighted the kerosene lights, picked up his worn copy of the Torah and sat down to read.

Ana studied her husband. What was troubling Jonah? He had seemed preoccupied during the evening meal. She knew he didn't like working with the Soviets. The Lithuanian officials often frustrated him. *He'll tell me when he's ready*, she thought.

She dried her hands on her apron, untied it and placed it on the hook in the kitchen. She smoothed the folds of her long black dress, patted her hair and sat down across from Jonah. The lamps flickered across the room softening her round face. Middle age had been kind to her adding only a few pounds around her waistline. A month ago she had noticed one gray hair as she brushed her long black hair before pulling it severely back in a low bun.

Ana had made the room comfortable with hand-sewn sturdy cushions for the wooden chairs She had purchased an oval rag rug and a china cabinet from a neighbor's family when the owner had passed away. The china cabinet though not fancy was well made.

It contained the one thing that held special meaning for her. Years ago her mother had passed along to her a delicate bone china tea set. She had never told Ana how she happened to own the set and so it remained a bit of a mystery to Ana. Its lovely pastel flowers and fragility triggered imaginings of beautiful ladies, in lavish evening gowns; their long hair pulled up in jeweled clips, chatting amiably over high tea. She had never shared these imaginings with Jonah. She didn't know why, really. But he was so—well—sensible that she was afraid he would find her frivolous, somehow. Maybe even silly. She remembered one afternoon when he was away for several hours, she had taken out one of the cups and brewed herself some tea. As she sat there alone at her table, she had imagined herself in America with Samuel, sipping tea and chatting with his American family. If only they could have attended his graduation ceremonies. . .

Shaking off her thoughts and picking up some mending from the basket alongside her chair, she casually asked, "Do you think we should have had a letter from Samuel? It's been awhile."

With some hesitation he pulled the crumpled envelope from his pocket and tossed it into her lap. "He is making plans to remain over there; but he will change his mind. Wait and see. He's worried for us. Wants us to move to America to be safe, he says. Ana, we are staying right here."

Ana moved into the light of the lamp, her hand smoothing the crinkled two-page letter with a caressing motion. Samuel was consistent in writing, but still his letters were few and often lacked the details she craved. He wrote in Yiddish even though the Soviets had begun to demand exclusive use of Russian.

> *Dear Foter and Muter,*
>
> *I hope this finds you well. Ben and his mother have taken the Queen Mary to England to visit a relative. We had a talk before he left. I am considering remaining here to join his late father's practice. I've given this much thought and Ben and I have discussed*

the details endlessly. It is really what I want to do. Foter, I know that's not what you want to hear, but please understand. All of my training will be put to very good use here. When Ben returns we will work out the details of our partnership and I can tell you more then.

I am very tired by the end of my studying and hospital shift. But the hours at the hospital have taught me more than all the hours spent reading medical texts.

I am very concerned about what is happening in Germany and eastern Europe. The news here is not good and surely there are rumors in Vilna. I want very much for you to consider leaving before it becomes impossible to get passage. You can return when everything is stable again. It may only be for a little while. Ben can help with arrangements. There is much to see and do here in Boston and the synagogue is nearby. If Ben and I agree to this partnership I will have an income to take care of all of us. Please, please listen to me. It is becoming more and more dangerous for you every day.

Please answer soon. I remain your faithful son,
Samuel

Ana read the letter one more time. She tilted toward the light and a wisp of dark hair crept out from her bun. She absently tucked it back in. No wonder Jonah had been so quiet this evening and reluctant to show her this letter. She lifted her eyes to her husband's face. He had turned back to his reading. She studied him. His dark beard seemed not so dark this evening. More gray. She hadn't noticed that before. The lamplight danced in his rimless glasses making it difficult to see his dark eyes clearly, but his face looked tired. He was troubled by this letter.

Things were changing—they both knew that. But surely it wasn't necessary to take such a drastic step as this. Or for that matter would Jonah even consider it? Of course not. Her thoughts turned to her son. Really, why would Samuel even think they could leave their home, his father's business, and this land. He grew up here. We grew up here. Our parents and grandparents grew up here. Why doesn't Samuel feel the same way we do? She and Jonah were bound to this way of life in a way that Samuel did not understand, obviously. Ridiculous. They were born here and they would die here. She would write to him and try to make him understand. She would remind him of his roots and his responsibilities to his family. She folded the letter and laid it aside and vigorously attacked her mending. She glanced across at Jonah, but said nothing. Foolishness, Samuel staying in Boston.

CHAPTER 7

Boston, MA
August, 1939

Ziva Cirino was waiting for Samuel—waiting impatiently. *He always seems to be preoccupied these days. Just once, I wish someone would consider my feelings.* she thought petulantly. She caught her reflection in the window of the diner and ran her polished fingernails over her arched brows. She tugged at the slightly tight bodice of her dress and noticed a pair of male eyes browsing over her. She flirted a little, tucking her hair behind her ear and sneaking a sideways peek. Where was Samuel, anyway. It would serve him right if she got up and left—just got up and walked right out.

The waitress was hovering nearby just as Samuel pushed through the diner door. This early the diner was practically empty and he spotted Ziva at once. He slid into the booth across from her, instantly taking in the pout on her face.

Before he could explain his tardiness, Ziva said in that tone women have used down through the ages when they want to attach guilt, "You're late. . .again. I've been here so long, that man's beard over there has grown two inches—and probably yours, too." Samuel laughed at her. That was part of the attraction. She made him laugh.

"Ziva, I'm sorry," he said sheepishly, knowing his excuse for being late was flimsy. "I missed the first bus."

The waitress who had been on standby approached the table. "So, he finally showed up. Whatcha gonna' have?" Ziva ordered the diner special for the day, meatloaf and mashed potatoes, and so did Samuel. She scribbled on her order pad and walked it back to the kitchen. After she left, Samuel reached for Ziva's manicured hand, then changed his mind. He was still uncomfortable with this dating in public thing. He was trying to fit into his new culture, but Boston and Lithuania were so different. True, some of his friends back home were beginning to slyly choose partners, but parents gave the blessing on their own choice, always Jewish.

"I got a letter from Muter yesterday. She ignored my plea for them to leave. Didn't even mention it. I don't know how to convince them."

"What did you expect? They were going to get on the next boat? Samuel, we've talked about this before. There's nothing you can do right now. You are here and they are there. You told me before that your country has been through this kind of thing before. They can take care of themselves."

He responded to Ziva's harsh words with equal harshness. "You don't understand because you weren't raised Jewish and you don't know Lithuania's history. And you don't understand because this country is ignoring what is happening in Europe. My parents could be in serious danger. Life's different for us. For Jews." He paused a moment before continuing, correcting his tone. "I've always been there for my family and they've always been there for me. It was my father who arranged the scholarship and the schooling here. Even my mother encouraged me. But it was still a hard decision for all of us for me to leave. Now I'm unsure. . ." The frustration he was feeling colored his conversation. "And it's not true that I can't do anything. Somehow I have to convince them to leave. . .now!" He glanced around the diner, realizing that he had nearly been shouting. It was a good thing the diner was mostly empty.

"Samuel, please, people are looking at us," she said, growing tiresome of the talk and changing the subject.

Samuel took a deep breath to calm himself, certain that his exhaustion was the cause of his outburst. He raised his eyes to meet hers. She was three years younger than he was. and the younger sister of his English tutor, Monroe. She could have passed for being Jew with her thick dark hair worn in a short bob and dark eyes with long lashes. And her name sounded Jewish. In fact when he first saw her with Monroe, he thought she was Jewish until Monroe introduced her as his sister. She had told him her Mom saw the name Ziva in a book and liked it.

Her features were pretty, but she was not a head-turning beauty. She had experienced a bad case of chicken pox as a small girl and it had lightly scarred her complexion. Samuel really had no intention of dating her or anyone, but she was often around when he and Monroe were studying. She had flirted with him and he didn't know how to properly react. Truth was he had little extra time to spend with anyone. Curiously, he enjoyed being with her. To her credit, she made him feel needed. She was so scatter-brained, she needed someone to take care of her. When she wasn't irritated with him, she made him laugh—and sometimes, like today, even when she was irritated, he laughed.

She appeared very dressed up today, and he especially noticed how snugly her dress fitted around her and he could see—. He stopped his thoughts from going any further.

"You both had the meatloaf, right?" The waitress had returned with their food. She plunked down the plates before they could answer and returned to the kitchen. "So, how come you can eat meatloaf?" Ziva said, pointing her fork at Samuel's plate. "I thought you had food restrictions."

"My family is from western Europe. We are Ashkenazi Jews. Our food restrictions are different from other Jewish cultures." As they ate he told her more stories about his family and growing up in Lithuania.

"You speak English pretty good. How come?" Ziva asked,

spearing a lone green bean.

"My school offered an English class. I thought it a good language to learn. Monroe has helped me learn even more better."

Ziva laughed. "Yeah. He teaches more better."

Samuel paid for their dinner and saw Ziva to her door. For him kissing in public was inappropriate but Ziva reached up and pecked him on the cheek. She laughed at his obvious embarrassment as he hurried off in the warm August twilight to catch a bus to the hospital. Ziva waited until he had disappeared around the corner and then left to catch a bus in the opposite direction.

It was a short ride and darkness was still about an hour away. A brief walk brought her in front of her destination. The sign over the door read 'The Blue Room'. She hesitated. She had never been in a club before. Never been old enough to enter one; and truthfully, she wasn't old enough now. She smoothed the mauve colored dress she had borrowed. It was just a bit snug and the neckline revealed more of her breasts than usual; but the color was good with her dark hair. Because of the early hour the doorman was not in his accustomed place, so she pushed open the heavy door and slipped inside.

The room was larger than it appeared from outside with a raised stage area for a band and a few small two-top tables arranged in front of the bar. As the name suggested the motif was blue. Smoky blue. Later the interior would be hazy as patrons mingled, smoked and drank, but now only a couple of regulars sat at the bar. At a table in the back sat a man that reminded Ziva of Tweedle Dum from Alice in Wonderland. He was short, stocky, with a combover that failed to hide his baldness, instead drawing attention to it. A cigar was balanced on an ashtray to his right, smoke curls adding to the blue motif. Two fingers of Jack Daniels resided in a short glass, the rest of the bottle nearby. He was leafing through a ledger book. He didn't look up as Ziva stopped in front of him. Softly, she asked "Mr. Sergio?" He ignored her. She waited a moment, cleared her throat and tried again. "Mr. Sergio?" this time a little louder.

He picked up his cigar and said without looking up, "Yeah. Wadda' ya want?" his Boston accent pronounced.

"Camille told me to come see you."

"Camille." This time he did look up. "How do you know Camille?"

"She lives in my block and I see her at the bus stop sometimes. She said you might be looking for another hostess."

"How old are you?"

"I'll be 21 in three months."

"Close enough. Have you worked clubs before?"

"No, but Camille said if you hired me she would teach me the ropes."

He chewed on the end of the cigar and looked at her more intently, noticing her curvaceous figure. "What's wrong with your face? The scars I mean." He pointed with his cigar. But before she could answer, almost as if he was thinking out loud, he said, "Some stage makeup can fix that. Tell you what. I'll let you know. We might have an opening closer to your birthday. How can I reach you?"

"Camille knows where I live. She can get a message to me."

He dismissed her with the cigar he was holding in his hand and went back to his ledger. Ziva decided the interview was at an end and turned to leave. One of the men at the bar glanced her way and gave a low whistle. She tossed her head and scurried out the door.

CHAPTER 8

Southampton, England
Late August 1939

B en, Margaret and Lillian stood together on the dock. "These weeks have just flown by," Margaret said. The Queen Mary was being loaded for its imminent departure to New York via Cherbourg France, and good-byes exchanged. The dock looked like a field of mushrooms as dark umbrellas sprouted up among passengers, friends and family. Even though it was late August, the chilly rain dictated overcoats and hats. Dockhands were hunched behind trolleys, coats pulled round their ears, transporting luggage and goods to the Cunarder. Boarding was beginning.

The day had a distinctively different feel from when they had left New York. Instead of bright July sunshine, there was a cool drizzle with the promise of colder days ahead. Gray clouds hurried across the sky as if late for an important meeting. There was a sharpness in the air that would have been there even if the strong breeze had not shown up. The weather created a toned-down mood as well as a dark sky.

"It's damp and chilly out here, Lillian. Please go," Margaret said as she hugged her sister. "We're boarding now anyway. We've had such a wonderful visit with you and my nephews and their families. And we saw so much of England. I can't thank you enough for everything. I'll write soon. Now scoot inside."

The first blast of the great horn sounded and Ben and his mother walked briskly, crouched under the umbrella, to the loading area, waving good-bye to their English hostess.

There were no mishaps this time and after unpacking they now had gone down to dinner. "Are you going to look for bridge players this time?" Ben asked while seating his mother in the dining room. As he glanced around the lavish area his eyes widened. He lowered his head to his Mother and whispered, "Look over there. I believe that's Bob Hope and his wife, Delores. His mother turned quickly and in her excitement overturned a water glass. Before their waiter arrived to help, they began to clean up and at first were unaware that Captain Hawthorne had arrived at their table. Quickly pushing his chair back, Ben rose in greeting.

"Please, stay seated. Enjoy your dinner," Captain Hawthorne said. "I saw your names on the passenger list and wanted to say hello."

"I'm glad you did," Ben said with a smile. "I found out earlier that you were the Captain on this crossing, and I was hoping to see you. Uh, sir, is that Mr. and Mrs. Bob Hope over there?"

"Yes, it is. And he has agreed to provide a bit of entertainment later this evening."

"Wonderful! Uhm, is Kate along by any chance?" he inquired; posing his question as merely polite conversation.

"Sorry, lad. She is home with her mum. She will begin her nurse's training in a few weeks. Her recent trip to New York was a one-time gift. Cheerio. Enjoy the crossing. If there is anything you need, just ask your steward." He gave a brief salute and moved on to the next table, not noticing Ben's disappointed expression. But Margaret did.

"Mom, are you ready to go down for breakfast?" Ben was sitting on the small chair next to his bed tying his shoes. Margaret was about to answer when an announcement came through the intercom system of the ship.

"Attention all passengers and crew. This is Captain Hawthorne speaking. It is important that all passengers gather in the First Class dining room in thirty minutes. I have an important message that impacts all of you. Thank you."

"This didn't happen when we crossed to England. Do you think this is unusual?" Margaret asked.

Ben shrugged. "I guess we'll find out soon enough."

The dining room was beginning to fill when they arrived. They helped themselves to coffee and breakfast rolls and sat down with another family who mirrored their own puzzled expressions. There was a general buzz of excitement in the room as passengers guessed what this mysterious announcement might be.

It wasn't but a few minutes before they spotted Captain Hawthorne talking with several of the crew members. He quickly made his way to the band podium where Bob Hope had stood the night before, delivering his quick-witted jokes. Ben looked around but didn't spot Mr. Hope and his wife. The chattering passengers grew quiet.

Adjusting the height of the microphone the Captain began, "Ladies and gentlemen, thank you for your attendance. I have a rather serious announcement to make this morning. It is with great sadness that I tell you that yesterday Germany invaded Poland. Some cities have been bombed and there is a blockade in place. I have been instructed to put this ship on full war alert."

Gasps of astonishment filled the morning. The mood of the room suddenly changed. There were those who quickly understood the gravity of what they had just heard. Others, like Ben, were slower to grasp the seriousness of what was happening in Europe.

Margaret looked at Ben. Her brown eyes full of puzzlement.

Like Ben the events taking place in Europe had not concerned her. Peter had always kept her informed and without him she paid little attention to politics. Her sister, Lillian, had enlightened them some during their stay with her, but Lillian still felt safe. George Malcom's Daily Express was predicting '. . .there would be no great war in Europe'. "Hitler wouldn't dare invade England, of that I am sure," her sister had told them.

"What does this mean?" Margaret's question was posed to no one in particular. Ben's eyes were on Captain Hawthorne as he continued.

"Further, ladies and gentlemen, this is the last crossing of the Queen Mary for some time. When we arrive in New York this ship will be docked for an extended period of time and then sent to Australia to be retrofitted to carry troops. Those passengers who have booked a return to England aboard the Queen Mary should meet in the Lounge at 3:00 this afternoon. Cunard Lines is arranging your passage back to England on another cruise liner. I will explain everything to you at that meeting. In addition, I will be on hand around the ship this afternoon to answer questions.

"As I said, we are required to go on war alert. Lights throughout the ship will be minimal each night and you may notice staff making minor changes. Painters will be painting over the portholes for blackout purposes. There is no need for undue concern. These are merely precautions. In the meantime, the crew, the activities, and the dining room will all be at your disposal as usual. Everything will remain as normal as possible until we reach New York." The room was eerily silent as the Captain finished.

He glanced at a note that a staff member had handed him a moment before. "I wish I had time to take any questions now, but I am needed back in the wheelhouse. Please continue with your breakfast and your normal activities today." And he quickly left the room.

Slowly the usual dining room noises increased as forks and knives clinked against china and whispers became normal conversation, although a more somber mood had replaced the earlier chatter.

"Now I'm worried about Lillian and her family," Margaret said. "I know Poland is a long way from England, but still. . ."

Ben was silent. He was thinking that Captain Hawthorne knew more than he had shared in that brief announcement. After reading that note his expression had changed and he had abruptly exited. Maybe he could work out a time to speak with him privately.

For the remainder of the day the topic of conversations around the ship centered on the invasion. Snatches could be heard in passing: "I have a great-aunt in Poland. . ." "This guy Hitler or whatever he's called is going to be big trouble. . ." "Does this mean the United States will take some kind of stand?" Passengers failed miserably to carry on as before. Their solemn mood seeped into every corner of the ship, and a few prescient passengers experienced a disconcerting feeling that the luxurious ocean liner—now on war alert—somehow knew she had ferried her last load of merry vacationers for a long time.

CHAPTER 9

Later, Ben was bundled up in a lounge chair looking out across the choppy ocean. The afternoon had warmed a bit, but a steady breeze blew across the deck. Clouds skipped across the sky and the sunshine came and went as if a master switch was being turned off and on somewhere. His mind was elsewhere. He was suddenly interested in the political happenings in Europe. Only a few weeks ago he would never have believed that would intrigue him. But the earlier announcement brought the war closer. Would this invasion be contained in Poland? Just who was this Adolf Hitler character? What was his agenda? How many countries were allied against him?

He remembered the passion in Kate's eyes when she briefly discussed these events and he had sensed she wanted to say more, but held back. Now he wished he had encouraged her. When the Queen Mary was retrofitted what would that mean for Captain Hawthorne and his family?

Maybe he could find something in the ship's library that would answer some of his questions. He spent the next hour reading several recent issues of *The Daily Express* and *The Daily Mirror*, two London papers quite different in tone. One issue of *The Daily Express* had a picture of Hitler that was designed to be placed on a dartboard and another issue pictured him as a gangster on a wanted poster. But a recent quote he found from Winston Churchill, First Lord of the Admiralty and rumored to be England's next Prime Minister, stuck in his mind:

"...If the Nazi regime forces a war in the world the very existence of free government among men would be at stake. Such a struggle could not end until the reign of law and the sovereign power of democratic and parliamentary government has once again been established upon these massive foundations from which in our carelessness we have allowed them to slip."

Carelessness. That word resonated with Ben. Of course, he had been self-absorbed in his education and training and he felt that was normal, necessary, even. That's what it took to be a doctor—correction—a good doctor. But in light of these new world developments shouldn't he and others place more importance on them? Who *should* bear the responsibility for aiding in stopping this. . .this person—some said mad man? Will the United States find itself embroiled in this conflict? Lord Churchill's speech almost made war sound inevitable. But how widespread would it be? He shook his head and continued reading. He stood up to leave and caught sight of Captain Hawthorne. Now might be a good time to ask some questions. "Captain, Captain," he called. Captain Hawthorne turned at the sound. "I had a feeling you weren't telling us everything. Has something else happened?"

The look on the Captain's face was troubling, and the words he delivered to Ben were dire. "You're very perceptive, Ben. Yes, a cruise ship has been sunk. Three hundred lives lost."

The astonishment transforming Ben's face was quickly followed by a wave of fear as he repeated the Captain's words. "What are you saying? Three hundred people dead! A British cruise ship torpedoed by a German U-Boat?"

"Ben, please don't share this with other passengers yet. I chose not to announce it earlier for good reason. Passengers could easily panic and there's no reason for that."

Ben nodded, understanding about panic. He was feeling it

already himself. How could things be changing so rapidly? *I don't want to be involved in any of this. I just want to get home to my normal life where there is no talk of war and ships being sunk and innocent people dying,* he thought. Yet the experiences, the conversations of these past weeks had provoked within him a vague feeling that he was being drawn into a powerful vortex that would not let him escape.

"Were there survivors?" he queried.

"The radio transmission we received was not very detailed. She was sunk off the coast of Ireland; it appears some were rescued. I need to return to the wheelhouse. I have been answering passengers' transportation questions for over an hour and I'm needed topside again. We'll talk more later."

Captain Hawthorne's commanding presence was reassuring, but as he climbed the stairs to the wheelhouse and moved out of sight, Ben felt a shiver move up his spine, having nothing to do with the chilly ocean breeze. Looking out across the waves and thinking of them as more sinister now, his eyes scoured the water for any sign of a German U-Boat creeping up on the Queen Mary. Images of Athenian passengers—vacationers like himself—dining; playing cards; enjoying a game of shuffleboard; and all the other comforts of a cruise ship, collected in his mind. And then suddenly those images were replaced by screams and visions of passengers in the cold dark water crying for help and not finding any. And last, a vision of a fiery ship slowly sinking into dark nothingness. He shuddered again. He imagined news of the Athenia's sinking would break soon and he knew his mother would be upset when she heard. He went to find her.

Certain crew members had been informed of the fate of the Athenia and just as Ben thought, it took only a short time for word of her demise to leak out among the passengers. The panic that Captain Hawthorne had feared found residence in the mood of the ship. He made a short announcement of the disaster in hopes of quelling false stories and rumors.

Passengers, when not sheltering in their rooms, kept a watchful eye on the sea. Most had little desire for entertainment and sat quietly talking in groups, no doubt thinking of people like themselves whose lives were suddenly ended. After dinner as the sun went down and the blackout was put in place most guests retired early to their cabins. Festivities aboard the Queen Mary would not be happening for a long time.

"Oh, Ben. Those poor people. What is happening in our world? It's so unbelievable. Could that happen to us?" Margaret's words were tumbling over each other as she and Ben returned to their cabin. She was putting a voice to many of Ben's questions.

"Mom, Mom, Listen. Before we left I read all about the Queen Mary. It is a very fast ship. Much faster than the Athenia. And bigger. Plus, now everyone, military included, are on the lookout for a U-boat that might want to sink a cruise ship. I'm sure we are much safer now than the Athenia was."

His mother calmed a bit, struggling to believe that Ben was right. He put his arm around her shoulder and they sat on the edge of the bed together for several minutes picturing those souls lost in the cold Atlantic waters, both of them barely believing that anyone could commit such an atrocity. Then changing the subject, Ben said, "Mom, I think Poland is near Lithuania. I wonder if Samuel knows."

"Oh, dear. He'll be so distraught when he hears, and we're not there to comfort him."

Boston, MA
September 1, 1939

"Read it here! Read it here! Nazi Germany invades Poland! Cities bombed! The port blockaded!" The cries from the newsstand stopped him on his way to the hospital. Now he stood oblivious to the busy street around him. Emotions circulating through him like electricity through a wire. His parents. Lithuania shared a border with Poland. What did this mean for them? I *knew* I should have worked harder at getting them a visa to come here. What should I do? Is there anything I can do? Why won't they listen? I sensed weeks—more like months—ago that something like this was going to happen. Now it's too late.

Oy vey, No, No!

CHAPTER 10

New York, NY
September 1939

Ben stood on the deck of the Queen Mary as she was towed into Pier 90 for disembarking. He had eagerly anticipated this trip and all the Queen Mary had to offer. Now what was to become of her? Would she meet a fate similar to the Athenia's? The thought of this beautifully luxurious ship lying on the bottom of the Atlantic somewhere, rotting slowly away, made him deeply sad. He willed his thoughts to returning home and his future plans with Laura and left the deck to help his Mother with the final packing.

Arrangements had been made for their steamer trunks to be shipped back to Boston, but they kept a smaller overnight suitcase—although Ben chided his mom that it was too large for just overnight. Because of the late afternoon arrival, they had booked a hotel room in New York for the night returning to Boston on the morning train.

As they waited on Pier 90 for a taxi Ben noticed the activity was different from the last time they were here. Floodlights were being placed on the dock and directed at the ship. Men in New York police uniforms and U.S. Navy personnel were arriving to patrol the dock and guard the Queen Mary. Looking around he saw Captain Hawthorne signaling to him with a wave, calling his name. "Ben, wait a moment. I'd like to talk with you about something." He caught up with them, a bit out of breath. "What are your plans this evening?"

"We've booked a hotel room and are taking the train home tomorrow. Why?"

"I also have a room reserved. I was wondering if you would like to have dinner with me at my expense." Ben turned to his Mom. She gave him a quizzical shrug. "We would be honored," he said.

After checking into their rooms at the St. Regis Hotel, Ben asked his mother, "We're not far from Central Park. Would you like a walk before dressing for dinner?"

"I don't think so Ben. I didn't sleep well the last days onboard and I'm tired. That business with the Athenia was frightfully upsetting. I thought I might take a nap. But, please, go. Enjoy yourself."

It was a beautiful Indian summer late afternoon as Ben exited the hotel onto the street. September in New York. He hadn't gone but a block or two when he saw a street vendor selling bags of roasted peanuts for ten cents. He bought one and crunched the peanuts as he walked along, thinking. The blue sky. The breeze. Storefront windows. Taxis beeping. He was amazed by how quickly he could forget the events of war that only a few hours ago were paramount in his mind. Like scattered birds they flew out of his consciousness. The familiar began to replace the images of a ship shot down; of U-boats lurking beneath gentle waves; blackouts and posted guards. It became easy to feel as if it hadn't even happened.

He took in the sights, sounds and smells of this great city as he entered Central Park. A baby being pushed in a squeaky pram. Two boys on bicycles ringing the bells on their handlebars. Women in big hats walking frisky dogs. Old men playing bocce ball on the green, cheering for their team. The sweet smell of cotton candy confection and a clown selling the last of his balloons for the day. It's good to be back, he thought. I never want to leave this country.

As he turned back toward the hotel he thought about the curious purpose of the evening and quickened his stride. Could Captain Hawthorne want feedback from passengers about cruising aboard the Queen Mary? Probably not. The ship wasn't going to be cruising again anytime soon. Maybe because he might be stranded in America for a bit he wanted sight-seeing information. Sure. That was probably it.

Plans had been made to meet at the Rainbow Room, and Ben and Margaret arrived in advance of Captain Hawthorne. It wasn't particularly large or impressive. Several booths ran along the inside wall. Four-top tables with linen cloths took up the center. No maître d' was in sight but a young man in a starched white shirt and black trousers checked their reservation and seated them in one of the more secluded areas placing spotless white napkins on their laps.

Margaret had chosen a butternut brown light tweed skirt and jacket paired with a creamy blouse and her nap had revived her somewhat—that and the fact that they were no longer at sea surrounded by the threat of war. Ben was glad to shed his tux and was wearing a three-piece dark blue suit. They were home. Where it was safe. Everything was normal again.

As they examined their menus Captain Hawthorne arrived. It seemed strange to see him in regular street clothes instead of the white Captain's uniform that he wore aboard the ship. Ben started to rise as he approached.

"Please, remain seated, Ben," he said as the waiter seated him and placed a white napkin on his lap. "I'm glad you agreed to have dinner with me."

"Captain—"Ben started.

"We are no longer aboard the Queen Mary and I am out of uniform so please call me James."

"James, we are delighted to accept your kind invitation. The crossing back home was not nearly as enjoyable as the one to England. Have you heard any more about the Athenia, her captain and passengers?" Margaret asked.

"Not much. Her commander was Captain Richard Cook. It is my understanding that he survived. A number of passengers died during the evacuation of the ship. I did hear that one of the casualties was a ten-year old Canadian girl and that several were Americans. The newspapers are theorizing that those deaths may lead the United States and Canada to enter the war, although Germany is disclaiming any involvement in the tragedy."

"You don't believe that, do you? That Germany was not involved?" Ben wanted to know.

"What do I think? Something extraordinary caused that ship to go down and the crew members who survived said it was hit by a torpedo. Draw your own conclusions."

There was a pause in the conversation as the trio looked at their menus and tried not to think about Germany and war. "You said you wanted to talk to us about something?" Ben offered as a way of changing the subject.

"Well, actually just you, Ben. It will no doubt affect your mother as well. But that can wait until after we've ordered and enjoyed our dinner. I think you will like the food here. When I stay over in New York I come here. It's not fancy but the food is excellent. The veal chops are sort of a house specialty. Very tender and juicy and seasoned quite deliciously."

The meal was indeed splendid. The Captain had ordered a fine bottle of burgundy wine from Côte de Nuits. They had all enjoyed the veal chops seasoned perfectly with rosemary butter and thyme. Coffee with beads of anise had been ordered and delivered, and now the conversation changed from small talk about England and life in Boston to the purpose of the dinner.

The Captain leaned forward and placed his cup on the table. "Ben, I want you to seriously consider something. In our conversations on board and in speaking with Kate, we—uhm—I got the impression that you are an earnest young man. I realize that the events in Europe have not been a priority topic for you, but now you have seen first-hand how imminent they are. My ship is docked in the harbor and the Normandie and the Queen Elizabeth will join her soon. Instead of escorting passengers on holiday across the Atlantic, they will be carrying troops. Plans are for the Queen Mary to remain here for several weeks and then sail to Australia where she will be retrofitted to carry military personnel. As you can see it will be some time before she actually carries any troops. Some crew decisions are still pending, but I have indicated my desire to remain as her captain and because of my Royal Naval background there is a good chance that will happen. We will also need some medical personnel and that's where you come in. I would like to ask you to—"

"But sir, I haven't yet begun my residency. I haven't passed my boards. I have no real experience with patients yet and, besides, I am not even in the military."

"Whoa! Let me complete my thought, Ben. First of all, military enlistment is not a requirement. We will need nurses as well and they will not be required to have a military status. Second, it is doubtful that a high degree of medical experience is necessary. On a transport ship the typical medical issues are seasickness, dysentery, flu and colds, perhaps a cut or "bump on the head." He grinned at Ben. "Mostly close quarter issues. Plus, I think it would help to have someone near the age of the soldiers. Most of them are in their late teens to early twenties, speaking English, a good fit for you. And thirdly, the way I understand it from Kate, you haven't established a practice yet." James paused, watching Ben. But it was Margaret who spoke next.

"Capt—James. I don't mean to be rude, but that is a preposterous idea. Ben has worked hard these last several years to take over his father's practice. And I am a widow. I need Ben here with me." Realizing that she was a bit too harsh she softened her tone. "We're flattered of course that you would consider him capable, but it isn't possible. Right, Ben?"

Ben had been puzzled about the reason for this evening and had imagined several possible topics, but this, this was way out there in left field. He was too stunned to even think of a response. His thoughts were aligned with what his mother had just voiced. Of course not. Out of the question. Three hours ago he was elated at being home never wanting to leave again. Why was he hesitating? No, this wasn't something he wanted to do. He became aware of the Captain speaking again.

"I am more than aware that what I am proposing was not even remotely a part of your future only a few short days ago. Don't answer now. All I ask is that over the next few weeks you give it serious thought. If you are at all interested we can discuss it in more detail later. Now, let's change the subject. Tell me about your time in England. What did you enjoy the most?" Ben let his mother answer that one as his thoughts drifted away from the conversation imagining what living on the Queen Mary might be like.

CHAPTER 11

Boston, MA
September 1939

The taxi pulled into the driveway and Ben hopped out to pay the driver, giving an arm to his Mom. Now they were really back home. Between Samuel and Avery, a neighbor, the house had been well-cared for while they were away.

As burnished autumn replaced bright sunny summer, the elderly maple trees were transforming themselves into the reds they were famous for. Still too early for many leaves to have fallen, the trees were providing shade for the lawn and flowerbeds. Soon, though, the hibernating lawn would be blanketed in scarlet patchwork.

The house wasn't new but had new gray siding and the dormers and shutters had been painted a bright white. A flagstone walk led from the rock driveway to the wrap-around porch, in summer decorated with hanging baskets of pink begonias.

The taxi driver placed their luggage in the foyer and Ben called out to Samuel, "We're home." No answer. "He must have pulled a shift at the hospital," Ben said. Because Samuel had been living in the house there had been no need to secure it while they were away. All they had to do now was unpack the overnight luggage. The steamer trunks would arrive later today or tomorrow.

Margaret removed her hat and placed it on the Queen Anne table in the foyer, glanced at her appearance in the small oval mirror above it and fluffed her hair. They had not spoken again of their dinner conversation with Captain Hawthorne. Margaret had dismissed it completely from her mind. Now home, she was intent on getting back into her familiar routine of housework, bridge, shopping; and Ben was just as eager to get back to the hospital and begin his residency.

"Mom, I'm going over to the hospital and find Samuel. Let him know we're home. Be back in a little while."

"What about lunch?" Margaret called back from upstairs.

"I'll pick up something in the hospital cafeteria," and he was out the door. His father's car was in the garage and since Samuel had no driver's license, Avery, the neighbor, said he would drive it a few times to keep the battery charged.

The hospital was only a short distance from the house, one of the reasons his parents had selected the property many years ago. Ben returned home after college and the death of his father. Securing a residency in Boston allowed him to help his mother with the upkeep. It was the house where Ben and Claire had grown up. Funny, silly, Claire. He hadn't grown up an only child. His younger sister, Claire, had died of scarlet fever when she was only twelve years old. Ben had been fifteen. It had been a difficult time for his father—in some ways more than his mother. His father had never gotten over not being able to save Claire. The mood of the household changed after her death. The house no longer echoed with her silly, giggly, girlie laughter. Dr. Stuart worked harder, longer, as if doing penance for his self-imposed guilt. It was Margaret's strength and faith that kept their lives from crashing down around them. Ben had wondered once or twice if Claire's death was the reason his father had pushed him into medical school, hoping his son would excel where he felt he had failed.

Massachusetts General Hospital's reputation was second to none in the Boston area and Ben and Samuel had been fortunate to pull residencies here. He parked in the physician designated area and entered through the doctors' entrance.

Not knowing where in the hospital Samuel might be, Ben had him paged. When he rang in they agreed to meet in the cafeteria for a quick lunch in about an hour. Ben decided to use the time to become familiar with some new x-ray equipment that had been developed right before he left for England. It was this hospital twenty years ago that gave Dr. Francis Williams a small room in the basement to perform his x-ray examinations, eventually becoming a radiology department of five technicians. Dr. Williams continued to perfect the techniques and equipment and became a leader in radiology for medical use. As a result, Massachusetts General Hospital was well-known in x-ray technology. Ben wanted to keep abreast of the strides being made in that technology. It was changing fast.

Ben was already seated in the cafeteria when Samuel arrived. Clasping Samuel's hand with his right hand and grabbing the back of his neck with the other Ben gave him a bear hug. "It's good to be back," he grinned. "I have so much to tell you."

"Ah, Yes. Cute English girls," Samuel teased.

"Oh, let's see." Ben began ticking off on his fingers. "There was Irene, Martha, Lenore. . .and, of course, Kate." Samuel just shook his head. They went through the cafeteria line, quickly catching up on hospital matters. "How's Ziva?" Ben asked.

"Haven't spent much time with her. A quick early dinner a few times. You can still remember the grind, right?"

"When *will* you get some time away from the hospital and studying in the next couple of days?" Ben asked.

Samuel took a spoonful of his steaming lentil soup. "Hm, this is pretty good. Let's see. More labs on Monday and more studying. Maybe Tuesday morning, early? Then I get few hours off. Why?"

"So much to tell you. My visit to the bridge—oops—the wheelhouse. The sinking of another cruise ship. The blackout. The Captain's invitation." Samuel's dark eyes widened. Ben stopped. "You *do* know about Poland, right? Have you heard from your parents?"

Samuel sipped the hot black liquid labeled coffee that is the lifeblood of medical students and his face became serious. "Yes and yes. Their last letter mentioned that Russian troops had moved into Vilna, and are using my father's business to help build large fuel storage pits. I begged them to please consider coming here. But my father, very stubborn, thinks there is no danger. He says that fascist in Germany is not interested in Lithuania. Of course, his letter was written before the Polish invasion. I wrote immediately after the news broke, but it's too soon for a reply. He may have changed his thinking now. I am so very worried for them. I don't know how to convince them to leave." He had been gulping his soup as he talked and glancing at the clock. He stood gathering his lunch dishes. "Gotta' go. Can't wait to hear all about your trip. Glad you're back home. . .safely."

"Wait a sec. I'll walk out with you. I'm going by the Kensington's; see if Laura's home and let her know we're back."

"That reminds me. I need to call Ziva. Nathan invited us to his Lacrosse match later this afternoon."

Ziva sat in the worn but comfortable stuffed chair—her dad's chair. Empty now. Her mother, Rose, had moved it out of their bedroom into her small sewing alcove. It had been more than eighteen months since. . . but things had changed years before that. They changed on the day her dad's leg was mangled by that malfunctioning machinery causing him to live every day in jagged pain from the damaged nerves, dependent on pain medication which gave only partial relief. Physical therapy had not worked for him.

He had been a stern and unyielding man before his accident; but afterward, he became more and more demanding and bitter, aiming his frustration at his wife and daughter—but never Monroe. Oh no, never her brother. He was the golden boy. The demands were constant with never a please or thank you. *Rose,*

Come here. I want my lunch. Ziva bring me the newspaper. Help me downstairs. Insisting on a Ballantine's even though alcohol was against doctor's orders because of the pain medication. He made life miserable for her and Rose. Ziva had little patience for her father's self-centered attitude and Rose had little patience for Ziva's complaining.

The insurance settlement, monthly disability checks, Monroe's tutoring fees, and Rose's dressmaking income had kept them afloat. But now, the monthly disability checks were discontinued and that's why Rose had agreed to Ziva's evening job at the Blue Room. An evening job that some days left her tired. She felt drowsy, leaned back and slipped into a 'not quite awake- not quite asleep' state, reliving that dreadful day. The day they didn't talk about.

She sees herself coming in the front door. 'Monroe, we're back.' No answer. 'Mom, Mrs. Abbott loved the matching Easter dresses you made for her. Her little girl is so cute.'

'Now where has my son gone off to. Ziva, go check on your father.' Her mother heads toward the kitchen.

The staircase rises before her and this time she experiences a deep sense of dread as she reluctantly, places one foot in front of the other.

She hears her mom calling from the kitchen. 'Monroe left a note. His writing is terrible.'

She enters the room and kneels beside the bed trying to wake her father. She touches him and he is so cold.

Her mom again. 'Something about Bugsy? Needing help with his bicycle and he—'

A shrill scream fills the house and she realizes the scream is hers. Now everything begins to occur in slow motion. Her father's head rolls to one side, facing her, and foamy saliva dribbles onto his chin. She opens her mouth and screams again. She turns and sees her mom in the doorway and she knows her mom knows. She watches as Rose moves from the doorway into the room and stands beside the bed. She sees her mother discreetly slip the bottle of pain tablets into her pocket as she puts her arm around—

"Ziva!" She jumped. Her brother's voice startled her awake, her heart pounding. "Ziva, are you up there? Samuel's on the phone for you. Something about going to a Lacrosse game later?"

She rubbed her eyes and sat still a moment, her heart rate slowing as her brain quickly shelved the painful memory deep into a place she seldom strayed. She took a deep breath and rose from the chair, brushing her forehead, physically attempting to dismiss the memory. *A dream. Only a bad dream. . .this time.*

"Coming," she called. *lacrosse? What is lacrosse?*

CHAPTER 12

~——~

Millbrook, England
December 1939

"Norah. Listen to this. Some of the children who were evacuated last September have started returning home. They'll be back for Christmas." Jimmy was reading from the morning paper. "Isn't that smashing?" He was still in his maroon dressing gown in no hurry to dress since he had nowhere special to go today. He scratched his head, rubbed his unshaven cheek and laid the paper on the kitchen table next to the morning mail. His schedule with Cunard was light while he waited for the Queen Mary to be retrofitted.

Norah was pouring batter onto the hot griddle. She was dressed in pink silk pajamas with an apron tied around her waist. She had not yet pulled her thick hair up and it nestled down her back. Even after twenty-six years together sometimes just the sight of Norah raised his blood pressure.

"Jimmy, that's grand news about the children. I can't begin to imagine what those mums have gone through, separated from their little tots these months. Had to be done, I guess. They needed to be kept safe. Do you think that means Britain is safer now?"

"Would like to think so. Kate not up yet?"

"Gone. Somethin' about an early lab this morning before the winter break." Her husband walked over and nuzzled her neck snatching a bite of bacon off the platter.

"Jimmy, careful that griddle's hot!" she said, quickly turning down the flame.

She smiled at him and gave him an air kiss. "I know your're gettin' bored, Jimmy. After breakfast go upstairs and fetch some of those Christmas things. I could use the help."

"Sure thing. But right now, those pancakes and bacon smell mighty good."

Jimmy had gone to dress and Norah was washing dishes. She knew her husband made a serious attempt to reassure her that the he and the Queen would be safe. But she knew him well. He always minimized any risks for her benefit. There had to be an element of danger. A transport ship had to be a big target. She already knew England was poised for war and Jimmy would be gone for long periods of time. She wanted to share her fear with him but she also wanted him to think of her as brave. She finished cleaning the kitchen and was drying her hands on her apron when the phone rang. She answered on the third ring.

"Hello, Hawth-."

"Mum, it's me, Robin. Is Papa there?"

"Robin. Callin' us so early. Is everything okay?"

"I need to talk to you both. Right away. I'm comin' home tomorrow."

"But your classes—your finals—"

"I'll explain when I get home. I'll be on the 3:00 train. Tell Papa or Kate to pick me up." Before Norah could say more, he hung up. She stood for a moment with the phone in her hand, slowly replacing it in the cradle, unable to think of one good reason why Robin was suddenly coming home. "He's such a flighty thing," she thought and shook her head. He had been coming home for the Christmas holiday, but that was still over a week away. Maybe Jimmy would have an idea.

Suddenly, "Oh, Lordy," she said out loud. "I need to get busy."

Robin knew this was not going to go over well. Maybe his mistake was not enlisting Kate first before springing this on his Mum and Dad. Robin was sitting at the kitchen table, helping two warm Yule biscuits do a vanishing act, his leg bouncing like it always did when he was excited. Freckles, red hair and earnest blue eyes got him lots of female attention. His boyish looks served him well on campus charming the professors, but not so much with Mum. After years of exposure, she was immune.

"Robin. No. Your father and I won't hear of it." His mother was emphatic. "You are going to finish your schooling and that's that. Now take your bag upstairs."

He gave his mom a hug and a sugary kiss, "Can we talk about this more later— when Kate gets home from school." he said. "I have to run an errand in town. You know, Christmas shopping?" this said with a wiggle of his eyebrows. Grabbing another gingerbread biscuit with one hand and his bag with the other he headed for the stairs.

Norah turned to her husband, who had been listening. "Jimmy. You were quiet. We agree, don't we?" The chime from the oven timer saved him from answering, and another batch of hot fragrant treats arrived, distracting Norah for a moment. He continued crunching a warm biscuit and still didn't answer. She stopped and looked at him. "We do, don't we?"

"Norah, I don't know what to think. This is—this came from nowhere. I know a couple of years ago he talked about flying, about being a pilot. But the RAF? Give me some time. I need to think."

"What's to think about? The answer is no. It's too dangerous. You're going off in that ship soon. How dangerous is that, really? You'll be a sittin' duck target out there!" And there it was. Her fear instead of her bravery. "I can't have both of you putting yourselves in danger. No. He can't do this."

"Norah, that ship is as safe as anywhere is going to be in the near future. It is fast. It will be armed and protected. I will be fine." His tone was firm.

The front door opened. "I'm home. Did Robin make the train?" Kate called from the entry, pulling off her coat and gloves.

"Sis!" Robin called from the top of the stairs. "Don't take your coat off yet. I need you to take me to Lyons before they close. Shopping? Get it?" The wink. "Papa, can we borrow the auto?"

They found parking on the street. "So, you just wanted to talk to me alone. Is that it? You really aren't shopping?" Kate asked as they walked toward the gray block storefront of Lyons Department Store decked out in Christmas greenery and filled with shoppers.

"Well, both, really. Kate, I have an opportunity to train with the RAF. To be a pilot." Robin's excitement was palpable as he blurted out this announcement. Kate stopped walking.

"I take it Mum and Papa already know?"

"Yep. Told them before you got home. Big mistake I should have waited for you so you could help convince them. I knew it wouldn't go over very well. Mum's opposed, of course. Papa didn't say much. I know how *you* feel about this bloody tosser Hitler, so maybe we could talk to them together? Convince them?" he entreated.

"Robin, this is not a lark. Royal Air Force pilots will be Britain's first line of defense if Hitler attacks England. The Luftwaffe is . . .unbeatable. Have you really thought about this?"

"I knew Mum would be against it but I thought you'd at least be on my side, sis. Just because I'm the younger brother doesn't mean I'm not an adult. I'm doing this. I love England and it's about to be destroyed. The recruiter I talked to said that by summer we would be in the middle of the fighting. The RAF needs two or three hundred more pilots and they are bringing out a new type plane that no one knows how to fly yet. They want to train new pilots on it. I'm doing this. With or without my family's support." He pushed open the door and entered the store, leaving Kate standing outside.

Usually when Robin came home, the dinner hour was filled with laughter and catch-up conversation, typical family banter. Tonight, though, it was different. Impossibly polite. Strained. Robin's big announcement was ignored.

"Jimmy. We received a Christmas card in the post today from Ben and Margaret Stuart. Do we know them?"

"Papa and I met them when I went to New York," Kate answered. "We wrote once or twice."

"Kate, I may not have mentioned it to you, but I asked Ben to consider being a medic on the Queen after she's retrofitted for troops."

Kate looked up from her plate. "What did he say?"

"Not interested. I figured it would be a tough sell."

"Not really surprised, Papa. I thought him to be interested mostly in himself. Rich spoiled Boston socialite if you ask me. I am surprised you would ask him, though." Kate rose to place her empty plate in the sink and nudged her sullen brother.

Jimmy noticed the exchange and caught Norah's eye. He left the table and removed their coats from the cedar coat closet in the hall. "Norah, let the kids clean up. Let's go talk."

"Jimmy, it's bloomin' cold outside."

He placed the woolen coat around her shoulders, and gently guided her toward the door. "I know. But this discussion needs to happen on the bench."

A hint of daylight still illuminated the sky and an early rising moon kept the creeping darkness at bay. They settled themselves under the bare winter branches and pulled coats and scarves closer. Nothing was said between them for a time.

Then Jimmy spoke. "This is a hard time for England. I know you don't want to admit it, Norah, but we *are* at war." She started to interrupt. He placed a finger on her lips. "No, let me finish. No place will be safe and out of reach of this madman and his German army. Good men will die and have died. Innocent women and children will die and have died. Brave men need to take a stand and stop the blood bath. As much as you, maybe more, I don't want to see our only son put himself in harm's way. But by trying to stop him aren't we asking him to be less than he is? And, frankly, I believe he's gonna do this anyway. I think we should support him."

Norah knew if she let the tears fall they would freeze on her cheeks. Emotions were colliding inside her. Fear for her son. Anger at this maniac who was destroying the life they had built in this place she loved. Guilt, because she knew Jimmy was right, but wanting to argue with him. She just sat there. Rigid.

"Say something," he said.

"I'm cold. I'm going inside." She stood up and looked down at her husband. With a firm voice and blazing eyes she stared daggers into him. "I swear, if anything happens to you or Robin I will take that rifle upstairs, find that bloody Hun and shoot him myself!" She pulled her coat tighter and left him sitting alone on the bench. In twenty-six years he had never heard her swear.

CHAPTER 13

Ben's residency had started in November and his free time was limited. As he grabbed a quick meal in the hospital cafeteria, a small article in a paper left on the table caught his eye. He read:

> *"The Queen Mary left the New York harbor yesterday bound for Australia where it will undergo transformation from a luxury cruise liner to a military transport vessel. This is expected to take several months. The Normandie and the newly arrived Queen Elizabeth liner remain in the harbor temporarily. They too will be retrofitted as troop transport ships. This was the first time in history that the three largest cruise liners in the world have been in the same port at the same time."*

He couldn't help but feel some sadness. She was such a great ship. It was hard to imagine the Queen Mary as a wartime vessel. How would they change her? How would the troops be quartered? Where would she go? What about the medical staff? Is Captain Hawthorne still her captain? Occasionally, like now, a flicker of excitement at the opportunity he passed up ignited his imagination. "I'll never know," he sighed as he finished his coffee and continued his rounds.

Camille glanced at Ziva as she re-applied lipstick and checked her shoulder-length silky blonde hair in the small mirror in the ladies' room. She was more petite than Ziva and much fairer. Her green eyes were her best feature and she played up her innocent 'Alice In Wonderland' look.

Tonight was one of the few evenings they worked together. "Sergio says you are working out okay," she said. "What has it been, two months?"

"No. Over four months now. But, you know only a couple evenings a week. Thanks again for helping me."

Camille studied Ziva for a moment. "Do you like it here?"

"Most of the time. It doesn't take much smarts to smile and take drink orders. The regulars know that it's hands off, so it's okay."

"Have you told Samuel yet?"

Ziva turned away and mumbled a quick, "No. Not exactly."

Camille pressed the point. "Why?"

"Well, Samuel is always at the hospital or studying, so, we don't see each other much." Her annoyance was obvious. "And, anyway it really isn't any of his business. I just told him that I do some babysitting for people in our neighborhood. And I do —really— I do some babysitting."

Camille eyed her curiously, surprised at her tone. "Why did you want to work here anyway?"

Ziva dropped her hairbrush into her handbag before answering. A pause. A tilt of her head. "Well, I kinda' just wanted to see if I was pretty enough. You know, my complexion. And I thought the tips would be good. You seemed to do all right here. And I might meet a guy. . ." She didn't mention that her family needed the extra money.

"Ziva, this is a dump. The patrons are losers. Where I really want to work is the Cocoanut Grove. It's downtown by The Garden and it's really high class. They have a dance floor and live bands. There are cocoanut trees *inside* and a stage. I've heard that actors and actresses go there. And baseball players. A good hostess can make big money there. But it's hard to get hired. People don't quit very often."

A loud banging on the door startled them. "Girls, get out here! We got us some thirsty boys," Sergio barked through the door. As they hurriedly collected their personal items Ziva whispered, "I want to know more about the Cocoanut Grove."

PART II

March 1941 to December 1941

CHAPTER 14

Vilna, Lithuania
March 1941

Ponar Forest. The skeleton trees stood guard over the frozen landscape. Jonah had been here many times before. The Lithuanian March day was blustery and cold. He pulled his long black woolen coat tighter and pushed his hands down into its pockets. He stood with his back to the wind at the edge of a large pit waiting with another engineer for two Soviet officials to arrive.

"These are such large storage pits," They must be designed to hold an immense amount of petroleum, Jonah said."

"How many do they want?" his colleague, Azriel asked.

"Several more. That's one of the questions I have for our Soviet client—when they expect completion. We have to line each pit with rock walls which will take additional time and labor and the sandy ground has not thawed completely. It's more and more difficult to find good workers. They are afraid for their safety and are leaving. Makes for a busy time, my friend."

"Ah, yes. I have Polish relatives. It is not good there either. Many Jews have already fled. Some have lost their lives. They tell me that the Germans are moving this way, and it is possible they will invade Lithuania soon."

"I know. I hear that, too. In Kaunas I have seen the flood of immigrants from Poland." He tapped Azriel's shoulder. "Ah, but

Soviets or Germans, they will need engineers and intrastructure information, won't they. I have letters from Samuel begging us to leave and come to America. He worries. Ana worries, too. We are not leaving. We will be safe here." They turned at the sound of an armored vehicle skidding to a stop beside the deep pit. "Ah, the Soviet lieutenants have arrived."

CHAPTER 15

Kaunas, Lithuania
June 1941

T he dome of the Russian Orthodox Church glowed golden in the morning sun visible from the large rectangular window of the Japanese embassy in Kaunas. Chiune Sugihara, the Japanese Ambassador, had come to like it here. The history, architecture, food and the people in Lithuania were a stark contrast to his home in Japan; but he and his wife Yukiko and their three young children had made a decent home here and had come to appreciate the hard-working people of this country. Their infant son, Haruki, was born here. Sugihara's foreign language skills had landed the young family here ten months ago tasked with planting a Japanese consulate. Years of studying language had made him fluent not only in Japanese, but Russian, German and English.

Truthfully, there was no need for a Japanese ambassador in Kaunas. His real job here was to keep Japanese headquarters informed of the Soviet and German troop movements. The government wanted to stay ahead of any further German or Soviet invasion into the Balkan countries. They depended upon his regular reports to help them decide with whom to align themselves.

Later he would open the black iron embassy gate. Already Jews were lining up hoping to see him. He was aware the lines were becoming longer each day. He brewed a pot of his favorite jasmine tea, opened another smaller window overlooking the courtyard and pushed the assortment of paperwork aside.

Home. Japan. Gifu Province, the center of Japan. Perhaps it was the warm sunshine edging through the larger window that made him remember. Maybe it was the sound of children playing outside the embassy gate. Vivid memories of his grandmother's house high in the mountains above Yaotsu came to him. When he was five he and his older brother would go there to swim in the cool river during the warm weather. They teased him about his size but he could easily keep up with his brother and his friends. Fishermen along the river used tethered cormorants—large hand-raised birds with white cheeks—to catch trout and it was a spectacle when they swooped and dived bringing up a silvery squirming fish. To Chiune it seemed a shame that the fisherman confiscated the catch before the bird could enjoy even one tiny morsel. Often, the boys would run into the small village and buy little sweet cakes in one of the shops. When he was older he would play baseball. Oh, how he loved that. It became one of his lifelong passions. *What good memories those are*, he thought as he drank his tea. *Such innocence. And now what. Spying? For his homeland?*

He breakfasted and dressed, and although it would be a warm day he never made calls without wearing a suit jacket; so, he grabbed it, along with the keys to his big American Buick, and left the consulate. As he closed the car door and started the ignition, a smile lit up his large dark eyes. *This must be a day for remembering,* he thought.

It had happened while being assigned to the consulate in Helsinki. He always had a driver there but yearned to drive the big car himself. He talked the driver into giving him driving lessons and secretly had received a driver's license. What a hubbub he had created a few days later. Without telling his wife or his driver he had taken the car out by himself. They thought it had been stolen and they looked everywhere for him to ask him what to do. What freedom he had felt that day. Going where he wanted. Staying as long as he wanted. He smiled again when he thought of Yukiko's astonishment that he could actually drive. It had been a great day once they had forgiven him for his "thievery."

He moved his thoughts to his destination and pulled away from the consulate. The man he was going to see was well-connected in Kaunas. Many times he had provided Chiune with valuable information for his reports to the Japanese headquarters. His was but one of several influential relationships in Kaunas that Chiune had cultivated.

CHAPTER 16

Boston, MA
June, 1941

The early summer weather had enticed Margaret outside and she was kneeling on the wraparound front porch surrounded by hanging baskets, fragrant earthy mulch, and small pots of pink begonias. She was engrossed in her task of planting the baskets when the sound of the messenger boy's bicycle startled her.

"Excuse me," he mumbled, shuffling his feet—his reluctance to interrupt her apparent. "Are you Mrs. Stuart?"

"Yes, I am, she said standing to greet the boy."

"I have a cable for you. Please sign here."

Removing her garden gloves, she took the pencil and signed the small book he offered. She clutched the envelope, not opening it until he retrieved his bicycle and rode off.

Cables were rarely good news and as it turned out this one was no exception:

```
NLT MRS MARGARET STUART=
4343 RIDGEWAY LN BOSTON(MA)=

I FEAR MARTIN AND MARIE DIED
ABOARD
LANCASTRIA. LETTER TO FOLLOW.
LILLIAN
```

Margaret laid the cable on the kitchen table. Dead? How? Why? The brief message left a lot of unanswered questions. Lancastria? Was that a ship? Sounded like a ship. Why were they on a ship? They were in France.

She sat there, remembering Martin. Poor Lillian. He was Lillian's oldest. Now married, maybe two or three years. Distance had prevented Margaret's presence during Martin's childhood years; but when she and Ben were in England they were all re-acquainted. The couple had plans to go back to France where Marie had lived before their marriage. Lillian had hoped to persuade them to stay with her—convinced they'd be safer. But Marie wanted to be closer to her family.

The newspapers. Margaret saved them in the basement for several weeks before disposing of them. The cable was dated three days ago and Lillian would probably have sent it right away, so any news about a ship named Lancastria was probably within the past ten days to two weeks.

She turned on the basement light, carefully descended the steep stairs into the cool dank basement, grabbed several newspapers off the stack and scurried back to the kitchen. Nothing. A page by page scrutiny uncovered no mention of anything named Lancastria. Then another thought—the library might have something. "I'll ask Avery to drive me," she said dusting off her hands.

After returning from a fruitless trip, the two were seated on the front porch swing with frosty glasses of iced tea, the forgotten pink begonias in their tiny pots bending longingly toward the larger hanging baskets. "Thanks for going with me, Avery. I guess I'll just have to wait until I get Lillian's letter. I just feel so bad for my sister."

They drifted into a comfortable silence as they sipped the cold tea. Although different from Peter in almost every way, she felt at ease with Avery. She had loved Peter. He had been tall, handsome, and cultured. They had been a striking couple wherever they went. Avery was short and stout and always ready with a joke. His hair was thinning on top creating a fringe of light brown around his ears, but he hadn't chosen a comb over. He laughed with his hazel eyes and his laughter was infectious. He loved being with people.

"Won't you stay for supper?" Margaret asked.

"Only if you'll let me lend a hand," he said taking her hand and assisting her out of the swing.

Two Weeks Later

Dear Margaret,

This is difficult for me to write. Nothing is worse than losing a child. My heart is broken. Still no word from anyone.

As you learned when you were here, Martin and Marie were planning to return to France and they did last September, moving in with Marie's sister. The timing was incredibly bad. German forces began invading France and I begged them to leave. I was so frightened for their safety.

They wrote that they were able to book passage on the Lancastria sailing out of St. Nazaire. It was carrying RAF personnel, embassy employees and refugees out of France. I've heard a rumor that the Lancastria was bombed by the German Luftwaffe, but the radio and newspapers have reported nothing. Supposedly there were some survivors. It has been weeks now and I know someone would have contacted me if they were alive.

Not knowing is the worst. I desperately want to believe that they are safe somewhere and unable to get word to me. That's my hope, but I fear otherwise.

Ben was wise not taking that assignment on the Queen Mary that you wrote about. As long as German planes patrol the skies and U-boats roam the oceans no one is safe.

If I hear more, I will send a cable. In the meantime, please pray that Martin and Marie are alive somewhere.

Your loving sister,
Lillian

Margaret laid the brief letter aside and removed her reading glasses. "How can these things be happening?" She realized she had spoken aloud to an empty room. The day was warm and the windows were open. A songbird's warbling caused her to glance outside. A lost little breeze wafted across the solarium and went searching again.

Margaret sighed. She picked up the letter and read it again. *'Ben made a wise decision. . . Nothing is worse than losing a child.'* She felt her sister's loss and a tear escaped down her cheek. She let it go. Then an instant later a sharp anger took hold. The tears fell because of her sister's pain and the anger because an unknown man had the power to cause that pain. The two emotions tangled within her and she fought them for control. The antique clock chimed the hour reminding her it was time to get changed for a hospital benefit that evening. She tucked the letter away thinking. *When Ben reads this, he'll be certain he made the right decision.*

CHAPTER 17

Kaunas, Lithuania
Late September 1941

"Hallo, Chiune, guten morgen." Yusef greeted his friend with a hearty handshake that bordered on a hug, bending his tall frame down to Chiune's height. He spoke in German, their common language. Even after all these months Chiune hadn't become accustomed to the exuberant embraces of the Lithuanian people. His own culture was much more reserved, greeting each other with a slight bow. It wasn't that he found the greeting offensive, it was just. . .casual.

Chiune took in the smell of freshly milled lumber as he and Yusef headed for a small wooden building on the far edge of the dirt parking area. This place was one of the good memories he would take back to Japan with him.

Yusef wore a black knee-length apron over his gray shirt and trousers. His yarmulke sat atop his long black curly hair. "Come inside. We'll get a cool drink and talk, eh?" Yusef's office contained a small desk, file cabinet and an extra chair that Chiune claimed. In one corner was a tiny icebox, a pitcher of water inside. He offered some to Chiune as they sat down. An employee entered for a drink of water and they kept the conversation light until he left.

"How is Yukiko and that new little baby boy?"

"He is sleeping better and the two older boys are learning to help around the house. It is good."

"I have news," Chiune said when they were alone again. He placed the glass on the desk and leaned forward, his voice low. "I've been called back to Japan."

"When?"

"Within the month."

"Did they tell you why?"

"The Soviet Union has demanded that all foreign diplomats leave by the first of October. We haven't a choice."

"I will miss you, Chiune."

Chiune nodded. "My family has been made very welcome and we have enjoyed our station here. You have been a great help with my reports as well as a good friend. I will miss you also."

"These are increasingly troubled if not dangerous times in Kaunas. My family may need to leave soon. Already ghettos are being prepared; and soon Jews will be rounded up or worse, their property taken away." Yusef looked out the doorway. "My business has increased. Good men work here. I don't know what will become of them." The two men were silent for a moment.

"Send them to me. There is help I can give them."

"You are putting yourself and your family in great danger, Chiune. Why do you do this?"

"I see the fear in your people's eyes. I see the injustice. I know a little of your long history of persecution. And I see your faith in spite of all that. I can do little to help, but I can do something."

"You are a good man, Chiune. We are grateful." Yusef cleared his throat before changing the subject. "And the business has been good because the Soviet lieutenants have been buying up much lumber. I have also heard that Soviet Lieutenants have been meeting with engineers—here and in Vilna." The two men shared a glance and Chiune nodded in understanding, an exchange repeated many times. So maybe the Soviets and not the Germans were planning something here. That would go in his report to the Japanese General Staff. Chiune had the information he had come for and the remainder of their conversation was what two friends might share.

"This may be the last time I see you before we go," Chiune said taking his Jewish friend's hand. As they shook good-bye a paper with an official seal changed hands. Yusef started to speak, but words failed him. He pocketed the paper, gratitude in his eyes.

"I must attend to something, Chiune; but I will remember you and your family with much fondness. Thank you." He gripped Chiune's arm and strode off across the lumber yard hiding his emotion.

The unseasonably warm weather continued the next morning, and as was Chiune's habit he arose early and set about his gardening in the courtyard of the embassy building. It was his love of gardening more than anything else that had driven the location of the embassy last year. People passing by outside the gate often saw him pruning and planting and would wave a morning greeting to him. Chiune discovered long ago that working with the soil and plants gave him a peace and satisfaction unequaled by anything else.

Kaunas harbored a large district where Jewish businesses found a foothold. It was there that Chiune headed after finishing his horticultural activities and dressing for the day. A Jewish barber who liked to share gossip had a shop there. His gossip could be useful, and he always gave a good haircut. Finding a parking space for the big Buick depended upon luck, and today—not lucky. He had to walk several blocks back to the shop and the day had become windy, signaling the end of the unusually warm autumn days.

He spotted the sign with the Yiddish word for Barber. It was pronounced "sherer." His English was marginal, but he seemed to recollect that sounded like an English word about sheep. The shop was nothing more than a small cube with only one barber chair and two uncomfortable wooden chairs for those waiting. This morning there was no wait.

The proprietor, Moshe, was a small man with droopy eyes and thick dark hair and neatly trimmed beard. He had a white apron tied over his dark work shirt and trousers. Again, German was the chosen language, although Moshe sometimes slipped into his more comfortable Yiddish phrases

Moshe nodded in Chiune's direction indicating the empty barber chair. "Guten tag," Mr. Ambassador. Shave and haircut today?"

"Yes, I think both. We have a dinner guest this evening." Moshe flipped a towel over Chiune's shirt and tie and then wrapped a hot towel around Chiune's round face. He turned to the small work table and began to strop the razor and prepare the shaving lather.

"Have you heard the news from Vilna?" he asked. "Bad things are happening. My cousin in Vilna told me that Jews are being rounded up there by the Lithuanian police. But they are sure the Germans are ordering it. They were forced into a special area called a ghetto. Their homes are being looted and there are reports of murders. These are dangerous times for us. Many Jewish businessmen in Kaunas say it will get much worse, here, too." He began to unwrap the hot towel.

"They are sure it is the Germans doing this?" Chiune questioned.

"Yes, Yes. The Soviets in Vilna ordered some type of digging of great pits. I heard the pits were to store large quantities of oil and gas. But the Soviets abandoned them and now some think there is another plan for them."

Moshe began lathering his face so Chiune became quiet, thinking about the Jews he knew in Kaunas. They were such decent people. It troubled him that they had been persecuted and forced from their homes over and over. Why was there such hatred toward them? He found them very likeable. Living here among them for these months had developed admiration for their culture, their religion, traditions, and their long ancestry. He found them to be an admirable, honest, hard-working people—like Moshe—who didn't deserve the persecution they had endured for so long. Moshe finished his shave and rinsed out the tools of his trade. He picked up the comb and scissors. "Same as usual?" Chiune nodded and the snip, snip sound of the scissors blended in with the street noises and shoppers passing by outside.

Chiune returned to the embassy by mid-day instructing their cook, Keiko, to prepare a quick lunch while he opened the embassy. He looked out at the length of the line and thought back to the first time he ever met a Jewish man. He was nineteen and attending school in Harbin in Japan in 1919. Jewish refugees were arriving every day from war-weary eastern Russia. They were homeless, ragged and exhausted with no money. With the help of American Jewish representatives, travel visas were issued for thousands of Jews to emigrate to the United States. Listening to their stories made an impact on him. Today, he saw the same thing occurring here, in Kaunas. So, months ago he had frequently begun issuing travel visas, allowing thousands to escape ahead of the coming German occupation. He asked for no documents, no reasons for travel and the visa's authority covered the entire family.

Before opening the embassy gate and seating himself at the large ornate desk just inside the doors, Chiune stood at the window and again viewed the scene. The line of mostly men was longer today than ever before and wrapped around the entire embassy grounds. The wind played a blustery game with their long black coats and wide-brimmed hats. He realized he was flexing his fingers. Many days lately his hand cramped from so much writing; but he couldn't disappoint them. Some days he signed visas for six or seven hours. His travel visas could mean life or death for many of these people waiting patiently in line for hours.

Until now the Soviets were not interested in him and he hoped their indifference would continue until he and his family returned to Japan. He had diplomatic immunity, of course, but there were other ways to stop him. *But I will not stop,* he told himself. He looked one last time at the courtyard and nodded to his assistant that he was ready to begin.

He kept a log of the names, numbering each one. Today he began with number 9,271. The line kept growing and three hours later he ended with 9,347, before closing the embassy gates It hurt him to latch the iron gate and watch the remaining Jews' hopeful expressions change back again to despair, but he must see how the packing was going and dress for his dinner guest, a Mr. Stepanos Matas, owner of a large shipping company. He took some comfort knowing most of them would be back in line tomorrow. Sadly, he thought, *there were not many tomorrows left.*

Vilna, Lithuania
October 1941

"Ana, Ana!" Jonah called to his wife. He entered the small kitchen still working the buttons on his black suit. "Ana, I must make a trip to Kaunas today. If I miss the last train I will need to stay overnight. Pack a lunch for the train ride. I already have my overnight bag."

"Is it safe?" Ana's voice trembled a bit.

"I'll be fine. My services are still needed, and besides, I hold a government position. I'll be consulting with them on moving the capitol from Kaunas back to Vilna. It's the Lithuanians, not the Soviets, who are causing problems. Hurry! The train won't wait for me." Quickly Ana gathered some bublitchki, a small bag of raisins and a macaroon.

"I can buy tea on the train," he said and took the small basket.

His own concerns went unspoken to Ana as he grabbed his woolen coat and scarf, kissed her good-by and started for the train station. The winter wind whipped around him but the heavy woolen coat was made for Lithuanian winters. Even though cold, at least the day was sunny. Jonah's mind was not on the weather, however. Other events occupied his thoughts.

As part of the newly signed agreement, the Lithuanian government had allowed Soviet military bases in strategic parts of the country and Jonah's engineering business had doubled. He would like to back out of this particular contract, but his sense of ethics wouldn't allow it. The truth was that since the Soviets had agreed to return Vilna to Lithuania, trouble had begun. A four-day pogrom was organized against the Jewish population. Jewish papers reported deaths and injuries and an atmosphere of hate surrounded anything Jewish. The Soviets had intervened with tanks to quell the disturbance, but like a pot of water, anti-sematism boiled around the edges, threatening to bubble to the surface any day.

The Germans were approaching and this caused him great concern. Would the Soviets remain or would the Germans drive them out? Lithuania had been a yoyo for these two countries for generations. He had heard rumors from associates that food in some areas was becoming scarce, although he and Ana had enough to eat. He knew first hand from his board involvement with the Yiddish Institute and the Society of Friends of Science that many documents and art objects had been transferred back to Russia during the Soviet occupation. Vilna was being systematically looted. For decades it had been known as a cultural center, even being called the Jerusalem of the North. There was plenty to loot.

The preoccupation of his thoughts kept him from noticing the increased military presence on the streets this morning. He slowly became aware of soldiers' eyes trained on him, following him, as he approached the station, generating an uneasiness in him as he waited for the train.

As the train pulled away Jonah saw The Great Synagogue of Vilna came into view. Famous for its ritual ceremonial baths and richness, he wondered how long before it was looted, too. The track wound alongside Ponar Forest and the unfinished Soviet oil and gas pits. A stray thought of Samuel crossed his mind. A good thing he was in Boston—away from all of this. "Praise Yahweh. He is safe there," he whispered to himself.

The time passed quickly and soon the squeal of brakes and a swoosh of steam signaled the arrival into Kaunas. Jonah gathered his satchel and moved into the aisle his mind already on the meeting. This will be a good thing, he told himself.

The Kaunas officials and Soviets were late arriving and the meeting had dragged on ending later than he had hoped, but if he hurried he could still catch the last train. The station was unusually busy, and it was filled with mostly men. Jewish men. He had to push and shove his way through the crowd to reach the boarding area. An Asian gentleman was leaning out a train window throwing pieces of paper into the mostly Jewish crowd and they scrambled to pick them up, all the time shouting in Yiddish, "Thank you, thank you. We will never forget you. We will see you again. Thank you."

As he stood watching the unusual scene, a strong breeze blew one of the papers across his shoe. He started to ignore it but noticed it had an official looking seal on it. Curious, he picked it up and pocketed it, hurrying on to catch his own train. He used the time on the train to review information from the afternoon's meeting, the official paper forgotten.

CHAPTER 18

Boston, MA
November 1941

T he maple leaves fell; winter arrived early; and the first snow of the season covered the red and yellow carpet. Department store windows were coming alive with animated Christmas displays. Street lamps were festooned with wreaths and red bows. Ben's residency, now drawing to a close, meant long hours at the hospital and when he had any spare time he spent it working with Dr. Oglethorpe. Learning the practice. Learning the patients. Preparing for when Samuel and he would enter the practice.

But today was Wednesday. He had a few hours of free time. He and Laura were in Filene's getting an early start on shopping. It wasn't Christmas until you made a trip to Filene's Specialty Store. The familiar Christmas melodies, the smell of cinnamon and pine, the elaborate window displays every year were some of his treasured memories of Christmases past.

After Ben had declined Captain Hawthorne's request for medical help on board the Queen Mary, he had turned all of his energy to Massachusetts General Hospital and Laura. Their date nights were scattered because of his various rotations but she understood; a Wednesday afternoon was unusual.

Laura called Ben's attention to a blue patterned silk scarf. "This is lovely," she said. "Would your mother like it, do you think?"

"Well, the two of you have similar tastes. You both adore me. Hold it up." Laura's complexion was flawless. The brisk cold wind had put color into her cheeks and her brunette curls escaped from her white woolen cap onto her shoulders. The blue in the scarf was the same color as her eyes framed with those long dark lashes. "I'm not sure about Mom, but it sure looks good on you," Ben said giving her a wink followed up with a kiss. Then, suddenly, "Pay for the scarf and let's leave. I have an idea."

In no time they were shushing around the ice in the park and laughing. Both had skated often as kids, but not often together and they struggled at first finding a smooth rhythm.

"Ben, wait. My legs are shorter than yours. I have to skate faster to keep up with you." Ben let go of her hand and turning around, intending to skate backwards, bumped another skater and all three of them landed in a pile on the ice.

Ben's medical training took over and he asked, "Is everyone okay?"

"Ben, what were you thinking?" Laura sputtered while struggling to disentangle herself.

"I thought if I skated backward I wouldn't go as fast and you could keep up with me. Are you okay?" The unfortunate third skater had already righted himself and with a quick wave skated off.

Brushing ice off her gloves Laura said, "I'm fine, but I doubt if the Olympics are in our future."

"You're wrong. His arm around her waist pulled her closer and off they went again. "Just picture us gliding in front of the judges; they can't take their eyes off us. We spin. We twirl. They've never seen anything like us." And they both laughed as other skaters quickly moved out of their way.

They sat down on a bench for a moment to re-tie skates and catch a breath. "Ben, I nearly forgot. I'm supposed to invite you and your mother for dinner on Sunday. It's Mom's birthday. We're having a small celebration, nothing big. Mom can't—the wheelchair and all, well, you understand."

"I'll check the hospital schedule and let you know. I should be able to work something out."

After nearly an hour of skating the afternoon was mostly gone and the air was becoming much colder. The sun had failed to make an appearance before slipping past the horizon so daylight was departing early. To complete the picture, a few flakes of soft white snow were beginning to settle on the ice around them. It was a perfect Christmas scene. The evergreens glistening in the park as Christmas lights came on; skaters in colorful scarves and mittens; fragrant fir wreaths on the light poles lining the pond. A bonfire was beginning to cast flickering light across the ice creating a phony warmth. Ben pulled Laura closer to him, partly to keep her warm and partly to hold onto this moment. He was totally content. He felt like he had everything. His education was behind him. His career was before him. And he had Laura with him. In that moment he knew he wanted to ask her to marry him. It was perfect.

"Mom, I'm home," Ben called as he hung his coat in the entry closet. No answer. He had already dropped Laura at her house and he really wanted a talk with his mother. Where could she be? She should be here. She hadn't told him she was going anywhere. Hmmm. Not in the parlor. Not in his father's den. The kitchen was fragrant with roasting meat, but empty, too. Then he saw a note on the sideboard: *Ben, Avery took me to the market for a few things. Back soon, Mom.*

He relaxed. Avery. The neighbor. He was a widower now, losing his wife to cancer, several years ago. Lately it felt like Avery was more family than neighbor. By Boston standards, he wasn't a cultured man. He had owned a roofing company, which he sold and then he partially retired. His silly jokes and grandfatherly demeanor attracted the kids in the neighborhood, and they took bikes, scooters and other toys to him for repair.

Ben decided hot tea was a good idea and the water was just beginning to boil when he heard the front door.

"Here, Avery. Let me take your coat and I'll put some water on for tea," Margaret was saying.

"Mom, I'm in here." Water's already hot," Ben called.

"It's beginning to snow again," Avery said as he entered the kitchen with the grocery bags. Ben poured three cups of tea and they sat around the kitchen table sharing small talk. For the first time, Ben noticed that Avery was very attentive to his mom. Earlier, Margaret had placed a roast and vegetables in the oven and the savory aroma stirred hunger pangs in all of them. Avery needed little coaxing to stay for supper and they laughed, talked and dined on Margaret's delicious home cooking.

Ben waited until Avery had gone before mentioning his decision. "Ben, that's wonderful news!" Margaret's excitement was sincere. She stood on her tiptoes placing the clean dinner plates on their shelf. "She is such a lovely girl. Even after all these years I still miss having a daughter around. When are you going to ask her? Have you thought about a ring?"

"What are our Thanksgiving plans? I thought that would be a good time."

Margaret still wore her wedding band, and she twisted it around her finger. Her mind was already racing with wedding plans.

"Mom. What do you think?" Ben repeated, bending down and waving to get her attention.

"Ben, marriage is a big step. Have the two of you discussed it?"

"Well, no. Not really. I mean, we enjoy being together and have fun and all. It just seems like the next step."

"This is a pretty serious step without discussing it with her, don't you think? Do you love her?"

"Well, yeah. Sure. I mean, of course. I wouldn't be considering it if I didn't have feelings for her. I mean, you know, we've known each other for a long time and we've been dating, what, two years?"

"Some of the strongest marriages begin with friendship. I adore her and think the two of you make a lovely couple. Her father is a doctor. She knows how that commitment affects a family. She seems to have the maturity to deal with that. She's a perfect match for you. I do think you should ask her father first. It may be a bit old-fashioned, but I think your father would have insisted. Do it for him." She giggled. "I've been hoping this would happen."

"You didn't answer me. What about Thanksgiving?"

"Oh, sweetie, I think you should consider something more romantic than Thanksgiving dinner. Besides, there's some confusion about when the holiday is this year. President Roosevelt is considering making it the fourth Thursday of November instead of the third; and no one is clear whether that takes effect this year or next. I tell you, these politicians can be so frustrating at times. Give it some more thought, won't you?" The phone on the entry room table rang and Margaret left to answer it.

"Predictable. She didn't think much of my idea," he grumbled. A *Boston Globe* newspaper article from a couple of days ago caught Ben's eye. He called out, "Hey, Mom. What do you think of this? We'll have an engagement party at the Cocoanut Grove Night Club. Laura mentioned something about it being a very swanky place."

Ziva was coming down the stairs when there was a knock on her front door. She wasn't sure whether it opened before she reached for the door handle or not. Camille was moving in high gear, waving a section of the *Boston Globe* as she rushed in. Her excitement was so complete every inch of her was wiggling one way or another. She smoothed the paper on a nearby table and tapped it repeatedly so fast that Ziva couldn't get a read on it at all. "Well, what is it?" she asked trying to settle Camille's exuberance.

"Read it. Read it!"

"Well, give me a chance, then." She picked up the paper.

Boston Globe. Nov. 4, 1941. It has been reported that the Cocoanut Grove Restaurant and Night Club, 17 Piedmont Street in the Bay Village has been undergoing an expansion in order to enlarge the bar, dance and stage area. They are conducting interviews this week between 10:00 a.m. and 2:00 p.m. for qualified bus boys, waiters, waitresses, and hostesses. The club caters to adults and has been known to host the well-known movie cowboy actor Buck Jones, Charles "King" Solomon also known as Boston Charlie and the Boston Mayor Maurice J. Tobin. The present owner, Barnet Welansky, is currently a patient at Massachusetts General Hospital recovering from a major heart attack.

"Do you know what this means? This is our big opportunity. We have to get downtown tomorrow and interview for one of these new jobs." Camille was so excited she couldn't stand on both feet at the same time. Her enthusiasm was infectious increasing Ziva's excitement.

Camille was talking so fast her words were running into each other. "Please go with me tomorrow. I know you won't regret it. We can give each other moral support and speak on each other's behalf. Say you'll go? Please?"

"Camille, Sl-o-o-w d-o-w-n. I haven't had half the experience yet that you have. I doubt that they would want me. I'm not as pretty as you are and. . ."

Sternly, "Ziva, you know you want to. You're just scared. I am too, a little. That's why I want us to go together. You *are* pretty. Your figure is oo-la-la," she said making an hourglass with her hands, "and your dark hair is ravishing. You just don't see yourself as others see you. And, you're 21 now, too. Look, I'm on my way to work, but I brought a bus schedule. Quick, let's check it to see how we can get to the Garden." And as far as Camille was concerned, end of discussion.

When they arrived the next morning the line of applicants looked daunting to Ziva. Many were very young—teenagers, actually. She wished she hadn't come. Camille had worked the evening before, gotten to bed late and this was an early morning for her. *Probably, a very good thing,* Ziva thought. *She's calmed down.* Just inside the door was an older woman who was organizing the job-seekers. Busboys, bartenders and waiters to the left. Hostesses and waitresses to the right and she wrote their names down on lists.

Chairs along the lobby provided seating while each one waited to be called. Camille went in first. Ziva felt more nervous than the day she had gone to the Blue Room. Why had she let Camille talk her into this? She patted her hair and fidgeted with her skirt. The lobby seemed overly warm to her, even though the large revolving doors punctuated the room with cold air. "I think I'll wait for her outside," she said under her breath and stood up to leave when she heard her name called. She had hoped in vain that Camille would come out so she could ask her what to expect. Making a valiant attempt to get her nerves under control, she was led into a small room off the lobby. A woman, dressed very much like a secretary in a dark skirt and white crepe blouse, pointed to the lone chair. The interview was short, a few routine questions, and Mrs. Beecher told her she was hired. All her nervousness for this? She was relieved to find that Camille was also hired. They could come together for the training.

They had gotten only a small peek at the Melody Lounge and the new Broadway Lounge. The place was designed to suggest the tropics to its guests. Tall supports were camouflaged like palm trees with hidden lights. Leatherette covered the booths and bar. Their interviewer told them that the roof could be rolled back in nice weather so patrons could dance under the stars. The place looked elegant, impressive and high-class even during the day.

On the bus ride home they chatted excitedly about how much they might expect to make in an evening. Then Camille's fatigue took charge and she became more serious. "Sammy still doesn't know about your job, does he? Why, exactly haven't you told him yet? We're both gonna' be working more hours and it will take longer to get back and forth. You have to tell him."

Ziva didn't answer right away. She had been thinking similar thoughts herself while waiting for the interview. She stared out the steamy window as the bus crept along the cold slushy street between sooty brick buildings. But—after all—how serious were she and Samuel, anyway? A few dates. A few kisses. He was usually so busy at the hospital or studying it was easy to keep her secret. He'd even had to miss her 21st birthday. And his parents. Always worrying about them. She rolled her eyes unconsciously. Well, now she had a serious career. If he didn't like it, well, too bad. This new adventure was going to be very exciting.

"Ziva, did you hear me? Now you *have* to tell Sammy." Camille's voice drew her back.

She turned from the window, "He doesn't like to be called that," she said sharply. Then more softly, "I haven't told him because he's a doctor, you know. His father has. . .is important back home." She studied her gloved hands in her lap. "Maybe he'll think less of me—I don't know! I mean, you know, even though we're called 'hostesses,' we're waiting on men in a bar. But the Cocoanut Grove, well, it's a nicer place. Famous people go there so maybe it's more respectable. It might be okay to tell him, now." She glanced over at Camille. The motion of the bus coupled with her late nights had caused Camille to nod off. Ziva turned back to the window.

She shivered as a draft of cold air sneaked its way into the bus and wrapped around her feet.

CHAPTER 19

The next few days flew by for Ben. He had hospital privileges but no patients yet. He wanted to begin working with Dr. Oglethorpe, learning the patients and the details of running the practice. He visited the Cocoanut Grove to look the place over; choose the right table; talk to the bandleader. He visited Caffrey & Trott, a long-time respected Boston jeweler to inspect and price diamond rings. And he thought about how to ask Dr. Kensington.

Louise Kensington's multiple sclerosis had made her wheelchair dependent a lot of the time, but with her sister Helen and Laura they had managed a lovely birthday dinner. Dinner was over and Ben and Laura were alone, cuddling on the sofa, waiting for dessert. Ben had helped her father lay a fire in the fireplace while Laura warmed some mulled cider. They were talking about finding a Christmas tree soon. Ben nuzzled her ear and kissed her gently on the neck. She nestled closer and took a sip of cider. He had already thought about what he wanted to say and cleared his throat, but before any of the words came out, Laura turned into him and kissed him long and hard. The warmth growing between his thighs wasn't from the fireplace. Their entwinement deepened. Urges grew stronger. Ben pulled away first, his voice husky.

"Laura, uh. . ." Her beautiful eyes were on his face. She was quiet. "We've known each other for quite some time. What do you think of . . . us?" *Oh, this is really impressing her,* he thought. "I mean, do you think we were meant to be together. You know, *together?*" This was not even close to the speech he had planned. A smile played around Laura's lips, her arms went around his neck and she pulled him to her. Those smiling lips grazed first his nose, then an ear and finally ended softly, briefly on his lips.

She murmured, "Ben, I love you. I've loved you for a long time." Her words and kisses ignited a passion within him and he pulled her closer, her perfume exciting him. His mouth found hers and his pulse began to race. He was sure, had they been alone somewhere, this night would have ended differently. It was perfect.

"Hey, kids. Cake and coffee are ready in the dining room, Margaret called from the kitchen.

"Mom's timing is awful," Ben whispered in Laura's ear. "But her cake is really good," he said as he broke free from her embrace.

"Tossed aside for a piece of cake. How romantic," she said, and pushed him down against the soft sofa cushions. He struggled to get up while she raced into the dining room. She picked up a plate of cake just as Ben arrived, balanced it on her palm, and raised an eyebrow at Ben. His eyes widened and he started to duck as she turned to his mom and said, "Mrs. Stuart, thank you so much for baking the birthday cake. I would have, but you do a much better job. Just ask Ben. He was just saying that. Right, Ben? Here. Have a piece." Tentatively he reached for the plate still not completely certain what she intended to do with it; then breathed a sigh of relief when his face wasn't planted in it.

"Thank you for the compliment. I've baked that cake many times," Margaret replied.

They gathered around the dining table, serenaded Louise with *Happy Birthday* and passed the cake and coffee around. Ben, mouth full, was the first to point to an already empty plate, signaling for another piece, which was also devoured speedily.

"Ben, while the ladies are chattering, why don't you and I

enjoy a cigar?" Dr. Kensington invited.

"I've never really smoked a cigar before, Dr. Kensington. In college I smoked a pipe to look, you know, older, kind of distinguished? Smoked a few ciggies. But never tried a cigar."

"Then now's a good time. But Ben, please. I thought we settled on Dr. K. Or even Charles, if you like. But not Dr. Kensington. Feels too formal." He settled into his favorite wing-back chair with his beloved West Highland Terrier, Mitzi, beside him. He had a distinguished look about him, rather British. His full head of gray hair and healthy physique made him appear younger than he was and his casual manner put his patients at ease. He rubbed the little dog's ears and then opened an ornate rectangular wooden box on the table next to his chair and removed two cigars. "This antique humidor was my father's. It dates back to the civil war and has been in the family a long time. Allow me to instruct you on the fine art of cigar smoking."

He selected two cigars and rolled them expertly between his fingers. This, he told Ben, was to eliminate any that might have a soft spot. Next, he took a pair of what looked like large manicure scissors and cut a small piece off one end of each cigar and handed one to Ben. On the table was a strange looking lighter, called a torch lighter, he mentioned. He lit it. "This is the tricky part, Ben. You want to "prime" the tobacco by burning the end until it glows, but do not puff yet." He placed the lighter below the cigar end and turned the cigar gently until Ben saw a red glow around the edge. Dr. K placed it in his mouth and pulled gently exhaling smoke three or four times until the end was sufficiently lit. "Now, Ben you try." And he handed Ben the lighter.

Ben rather clumsily got the end "primed" but as he tried to puff the cigar he swallowed smoke and began to cough, looking rather like a buffoon, he thought. Dr. K chuckled and asked, "Are you okay?" Ben nodded and quickly began to get the hang of it. However, he thought maybe he would stick with pipes or an occasional cigarette in the future.

"That, uhm, tastes good. Nice cigar. Thank you."

Ben looked for a place to lay his cigar down and thought for a minute about what he wanted to say. "Dr. Kensington—I mean Dr. K. I admire and respect your daughter very much. I am planning an evening at the Cocoanut Grove this coming Saturday and I would be honored to have you and your wife attend." Here, he paused. His mouth was dry. He blamed it on the cigar. He stood. Dr. K waited; sensed there was more. Ben's hands felt clammy. *This is it. Big step. Take the plunge, as they say.* "Sir, I would like to ask your daughter, you know, Laura—of course, you know her—to marry me, sir; if it's okay, sir." He sat down abruptly, fidgeting with his sport jacket and tie.

Dr. Kensington took a long puff on his cigar and looked directly at Ben. His face was clean-shaven adding to his youthful appearance. His eyes were crinkly and kind, but his manner and expression had a fair amount of sternness.

"Ben, I knew your father, Peter, quite well. I had great respect for him both as a physician and as a gentleman. I watched you grow up into the fine young man you are." He put down his cigar. "Marriage is a big responsibility and should be treated as such. That said, most of us don't learn that until we are already in it. Speaking for my wife and myself we would be delighted to have you as our son-in-law and you can always come to us whenever you need us." He leaned forward and whispered in a conspiratorial tone, "Is this just between you and me?"

"Well, sir, I haven't asked her officially, if that's what you mean. I plan to give her an engagement ring on Saturday night."

"In answer to your invitation, we would be honored to attend, and, of course, I should share this news with Laura's mother." With a slightly mischievous smile he said, "Now, finish your cigar."

Ben let out the breath that he didn't realize he had been holding and visibly relaxed. The cigar was mysteriously in his hand again. Secretly, he wondered how many of Laura's other suitors had endured the "cigar ritual."

The party details came together that next week. Samuel adjusted his hospital schedule and Sabbath ended at sunset. He was bringing Ziva. Avery was available to accompany his mom. Laura's best friend Hope and her date would be there, too. That made it a party of ten. The evening would be perfect.

CHAPTER 20

"Ben, remind me of the plan for tonight?" Margaret called from her bedroom. She was finishing dressing, slipping on her low-heeled gray brocade shoes. She wore one of the dresses purchased for the cruise. It had a light gray beaded bodice and a darker gray tea length skirt. A beautiful strand of pearls circled her neck. Ben peeked around the doorframe.

"Mom. You look terrific. One more time, here's the plan. Avery will pick you up around 6:30. Laura's parents will drive themselves because they need to transport the collapsible wheelchair. Samuel's coming here from the synagogue and then we'll pick up Ziva and Laura. We should all arrive close to 7:00. Got it?"

Margaret looked up at her son with pride and love. He was wearing the tux from the cruise but the tie was giving him trouble. She stood and walked over to him, expertly tying the tie like she had so many times for Peter. Peter. If only he were here to share this moment.

She leaned up and gave Ben a kiss on the cheek. "I love you. And I love, Laura. She's perfect for you." Her eyes misted over. "I wish your father was here tonight, then both of us could wish you and Laura a happy and long life together." Not allowing Ben to see a tear escaping down her cheek, she turned away. No way was she going to spoil Ben's evening, but Ben, hugged her to him.

When he spoke his voice was shaky, too. "It's okay, Mom. I miss him, too." Pointing first to his heart and then hers he said,

"He's still with us because his memory is here." And as an attempt to change the mood he said, "Now, let's go party!" And he twirled her around the room making her laugh.

"Ziva, I have to leave now to catch the bus." Camille was reaching for her coat. "Relax. This will work. Just remember before you get to the Cocoanut Grove tonight tell Sammy that I work there. If anyone recognizes you make up something, like maybe I introduced you around one afternoon. You'll figure it out—gotta run."

"You're a good friend, Camille."

"See you in a little while." She rushed out the door and nearly slipped on the icy porch steps. Ziva caught her breath as Camille caught her balance and gave a quick wave over her shoulder.

"Was that Camille?" Monroe asked entering the room. "You haven't mentioned your new job to Samuel yet, have you. You should just tell him. I mean the Cocoanut Grove isn't some speakeasy like the Blue Room. It's very classy. I heard that a few nights ago the football players from Boston College had a rousing good time there after they defeated Holy Cross. Even the Mayor goes there. Just tell him, Ziva."

"Damn, I wish I knew what to do," she fumed aloud while slamming the door and hurrying upstairs to finish dressing. And then a fleeting thought occurred to her as she reached the top of the stairs. If she didn't have feelings for Samuel she probably wouldn't care *what* he thought; and that thought made her more nervous.

Ben dropped Laura off at the Piedmont Street entrance to the club while he parked the car in the parking lot and walked back. He escorted her through the revolving doors into the foyer and checked their coats. A hostess led them through the crowded and smoky room to their table and seated them. Ben was glad he had planned ahead.

The low lighting, the soft clink of glassware and murmured conversation took Ben back to dinners on the Queen Mary. He caught Laura's eye and smiled. "You look lovely tonight." Her dark curls were held back with a green satin ribbon. Earrings that looked like glittering bits of ice shot rainbows as she scanned the room. Her smooth shoulders were bare and the deep cut of the dress showed just a swell of what lay beneath. She had never looked more beautiful. He wanted to take her in his arms right then, but showed remarkable restraint.

She parted with one of her dazzling smiles. "Thank you, kind sir. You look very handsome, yourself. Ben, this place is fabulous. I've read about it in the papers and Hope was here once." She took hold of his hand across the table. "This is so exciting and special. What's the occasion?"

Ben was caught off guard for a moment. "It's a celebration for. . .the end of my residency. The long hours. The training. It's nearly over. Christmas is coming. Just thought it would be nice to have a special night out." The rest of the group began arriving and subsequent greetings and introductions rescued Ben from further explanation. The wheelchair was a bit of a problem at first but after moving Laura's mom to a regular chair their waiter found a place for it near one of the bars.

Ben had arranged seating in the main dining room on the edge of the dance floor. He leaned toward Laura. "Look how tall those artificial palm trees are. They have lights in them. And that dance floor is huge. I think the dance band is starting to set up." He turned his head in another direction. "You know what. I believe that's Buck Jones over there. Wonder if we could get an autograph."

"Who is Buck Jones?" Ziva asked.

"You never heard of Buck Jones? He's a cowboy-western

actor. He's worked with Carole Lombard and Tim McCoy. He's a pretty famous guy. Does a lot of his own stunts, I hear."

Samuel turned his head to sneak a peek at the actor. "Ziva. Isn't that your friend Camille over there? You didn't tell me she worked here."

"Yes I did," she lied, having neglected to mention it in the crowded car. You've been so busy you've just forgotten," she said with a forced nonchalant voice. She hoped he wouldn't press the issue.

Just then the waiter came to take their drink and dinner order and when he left Avery piped up, "Did you hear about the man who went into a restaurant and ordered a bowl of soup. He called the waiter over and asked, 'Hey, waiter what is this fly doing in my soup?' The waiter said, 'I believe it's the backstroke, sir.'"

"Avery, Bob Hope told that joke when we were on the Queen Mary," Ben laughed.

"Okay, then how about this. A man goes into a restaurant and orders a bowl of soup. He calls the waiter over and asks 'What's this spider doing in my soup?' The waiter looks and says, 'I'm deeply sorry, sir, the fly asked for the night off.'"

While the group shook their heads at Avery, Ben and Dr. K. exchanged a secretive smile. It seemed in no time their dinners arrived and talk centered around the delicious food. The band began to entertain and the dance floor filled with couples doing the rumba and foxtrot. Soon a conga line formed with everyone joining in except Louise. The line circled the restaurant before the group returned to the table, still dancing and laughing.

Ben watched Laura and Hope, their heads together laughing about something one of them had said. He looked at his watch, then caught the eye of the bandleader. They exchanged nods, a signal it was time for their prearrangement. The bandleader ordered a drum roll, and Ben pushed back his chair and stood. He was scared he would fumble this. Maybe drop the ring. Overturn a drink. Guests at the nearby tables turned to see what was happening, as did Laura and Hope.

Laura's expression grew puzzled as she saw Ben standing and looking at her. And suddenly it became clear what was happening. He walked over to her, said a little prayer, knelt down in front of her and took her hand. Her other hand covered her mouth.

"Laura, would you do me the honor of becoming my wife?" Without the fumbling he had feared, he pulled the ring box from his pocket. The dining room was quiet as patrons collectively held their breath. When Laura nodded and said yes, the band broke into their rendition of Jimmy Dorsey's 'Two In Love', and the place erupted with a loud cheer. The ring would have to be sized later and their kiss was a bit shy in front of so many witnesses, but when Ben pulled her up and the newly engaged couple entered the dance floor congratulations came from all directions. It was perfect.

With a lilt in her voice and the excitement of a new bride Margaret said, "Well, Louise, it looks like we have a wedding to plan. I'll call you." Then she touched Avery's arm. "I think maybe it's time to go and leave the rest of the partying to the younger crowd."

"I'll get our coats," and he was helping her up from her chair just as the happy couple exited the dance floor arms entwined, faces glowing.

"I think we'll call it a night, too," said Dr. Kensington. "Louise tires easily." He signaled the waiter to retrieve the wheelchair.

Everyone hugged everyone and the satisfied parents left, feeling like they were the winners tonight. Laura and Hope giggled and talked for a few minutes then excused themselves to use the powder room and check out the ring in better light. Ziva was out on the dance floor with Samuel trying to teach him the rumba. Fred Astaire needn't worry. Earlier in the evening, when Ziva realized none of the dining room staff recognized her, she had relaxed and began to enjoy herself. She worked mostly in the Melody Lounge with different waiters. Even if someone did see her she looked very different with her hair pulled back and wearing a borrowed black embroidered cocktail dress.

Downstairs, below the main dining room, in the dark Melody Lounge a sailor and his girlfriend were getting real chummy. They had been exploring one another for a while now. A false ceiling of blue satin fabric stretched overhead absorbing what light there was in the room, but still the sailor had reached up at one point and unscrewed the light bulb from the palm tree overhead providing more darkness. The couple were just a bit inebriated and they decided to find a place that provided even more privacy for their explorations; but in their state they were having difficulty replacing the light bulb. They summoned a teen-aged waiter to do it for them.

"Of course, sir. I can take care of that for you," he said and pulled a chair alongside to stand on. In order to see better as he inserted the bulb he lit a match giving off a tiny spark. Within seconds the entire false ceiling was ablaze. It happened so fast it was as if a bomb had gone off in the lounge. The leatherette seats and bar caught fire next creating a blanket of dense black acrid smoke.

Guests ran screaming and running for the one exit. The fear and resulting panic were so strong most guests didn't have a chance of finding the door. Sounds of coughing replaced calls for help as lungs filled with smoke. Guests fell underfoot and if not trampled, quickly died of smoke inhalation. The fireball burned through the ceiling in a matter of minutes.

Upstairs Ben waited for the girls to return to the dining room and watched Ziva and Samuel's Latin moves. She was demonstrating and he was trying to follow, but it didn't resemble any rumba step he had seen.

"Someone must be smoking a big cigar nearby," he thought

aloud. It's quite strong. But the thought got lost as the lights went out and screams of "FIRE!" "FIRE!" were heard all around him. Within a minute the fire erupted through the floor. Many were unable to get away quickly enough and the flames caught pants legs and skirts. Almost immediately, Ben caught the scent of burning hair and flesh. Tables and chairs crashed as panic-stricken partygoers ran for the doors. Pain-filled screams filled the room. Ben was immobilized. The immediate chaos and panic disoriented him. He lost sight of everyone he knew. The revolving doors at the entrance were being rushed by a crush of hundreds of people. A dam of bodies was piling up as many reached the revolving door, unable to make it move fast enough and eventually not at all.

A thick cloud of black smoke swirled around the room filling lungs and stinging eyes. In minutes it was impossible to see across the room. "Laura! Laura! Where are you?" Ben screamed. He grabbed a handkerchief from his pocket, doused it in a water glass and covered his mouth and nose. Suddenly, someone was pulling on his arm. Ziva. He grabbed cloth napkins off the table and pressed one to her face.

"Ben come with me! I know a way out!"

"Have you seen Laura?" he yelled through the handkerchief, but smoke still found its way in triggering a wracking cough.

"There's no time. We need to leave, NOW! She'll find her own way out."

"I can't leave her! I'll find her."

Samuel came alongside and with Ziva directing him began moving Ben toward a back wall of the stage where a curtain was hanging. It covered a service entrance and a number of the crew and the orchestra were crowding through the open door. Ben struggled against the two of them. "Let me go!" he shouted above the din of screams as fiery debris rained down around them. "I have to find her!"

Samuel and Ziva tightened their hold on him and pushed him out the service door onto the street behind the nightclub. All three collapsed onto the sidewalk with spasms of coughing, expelling the thick caustic smoke from their lungs. The screaming sirens were loud. People were nearby, some who had escaped the inferno and some gawking at the burning building.

As the cold night air cleared their lungs, it also cleared Samuel's brain. "Ben, we're doctors. We need to try and help if we can." Samuel helped Ben up and the three of them stumbled around to the front of the building. What they saw was a scene from hell. Utter chaos.

Flames were shooting from the roof and windows. A few club-goers had made it through the revolving door, exiting the club with clothing and hair on fire and screaming for help. Some collapsed as soon as they cleared the building. Ambulances, sirens blaring, had started arriving lining up waiting to carry survivors to nearly hospitals. Attendants wheeled gurneys as fast as possible through the meleé, triaging as they went. Firemen and trucks had begun arriving, spraying water onto the flames with little effect. Black water hoses were coiled in front of the building. Dark vipers attacking the conflagration. Firefighters were shouting to one another and pulling charred bodies and pieces of bodies from the revolving door, laying them on the street in front of the Cocoanut Grove. Police were putting up barriers to keep onlookers at a safe distance. People with massive burns, probably from the basement level, appeared among the survivors—some burned so severely they would not be listed among the survivors. Everyone was in shock. Some, like Ben, called out for friends and family, hoping futilely that they would find them in the chaos.

"Do you see Laura anywhere?" Ben's voice was scratchy and weak as they searched around for her. Two emergency personnel approached them and guided them toward the back of a waiting ambulance. Ben stopped him. "No, wait. We're looking for someone."

"First, let us check you out." The young man speaking was dressed in a white jacket and pants, already stained in places with soot. "We'll give you some oxygen and check for any burns." A sudden loud explosion made them all duck as something inside exploded.

"No. There are far more seriously injured people who need this ambulance. We're okay. We're doctors." Samuel told him. "Go." He addressed Ben who seemed more in control now. "Do you think we can really help here? Or should we get to the hospital. It's being flooded with patients. We're not really equipped to give first aid."

Ben was still searching the scorched blackened faces willing his eyes to see Laura. "I can't leave until I find her. Until I know if she—" he stopped, sat down on the curb and pushed his hair back from his face coughing again. The recent memory of Louise's birthday celebration, the smell of the cigars and the coughing crossed his mind which seemed ludicrous to him given the dreadful scene before him.

Samuel sat down beside him, placed his arm on his shoulder. "Ben. We can't do much good here, but we can be a big help at the hospital. If Laura did survive this the best way you can help her is to be there when they bring her in."

A tear slid down Ben's soot-covered face. He was numb. In shock. Part of him knew Samuel was right, but he couldn't get his brain to respond. He stood and looked back at the building. The fire department was making headway on the fire and some of the burn victims had been transported. The crowd was larger, but screams of anguish were fewer as the fire claimed more lives and others were taken away. Piercing ambulance sirens continued to add their falsetto notes to the macabre scene in the Melody Lounge. Still he did not see Laura. He turned anguished eyes to Samuel. "This is my fault. My idea to come here," he said, his throat sore and voice croaky and dry from the smoke. "Oh, God." And he buried his face in his hands again, shock taking hold.

CHAPTER 21

When they arrived at Massachusetts General the scene before them was beyond belief. They hardly recognized the hospital. The number of gurneys was inadequate for the number of patients, and victims were lying on the floors in the corridors. All staff had been called in to treat the injured and they were having difficulty maneuvering around victims and corpses. Some patients, like Ziva, arrived suffering only from smoke inhalation and required only minimal care. Others were in line for skin grafts. surgical removal of charred, blackened skin or even amputations. All those arriving with burns needed pain medication and supplies of morphine were running low.

Instead of treating burns with tannic acid, Massachusetts General had been using gauze and petroleum jelly with good results. Two surgeons on staff had pioneered a fluid resuscitation procedure and quickly showed Samuel and Ben how to administer IV and Murphy drips. Massachusetts General was a pioneer in treating burn injuries with penicillin and staff made calls to request supplies from neighboring hospitals. Ben and Samuel worked well into the early morning helping stabilize and triage hundreds of burn and smoke inhalation patients, always watching for Laura. Time was blurred by the continuous influx of moaning, sobbing, mostly young revelers many of whom were military. The Grove was popular among the young soldiers and navy recruits.

When Ben stood up to stretch out his back, a young female nurse caught Ben's eye. The man standing in front of her was stabbing a fat finger at her and his tone was insolent.

The Cocoanut Grove was a popular nightclub with the wealthy, upper crust populace of Boston. Some family members had arrived demanding special attention which only added stress and confusion to the workload of the medical staff. He was tired of these pompous asses interfering with the staff who were attempting to do the impossible.

He noted her nametag and motioned for her to leave. She rolled her eyes, mouthed a thank you and rushed off to help in another direction. He walked over and tapped the man on the shoulder.

"Sir, I'm Dr. Stuart. May I be of assistance here?" The man turned and that's when Ben recognized the mayor of Boston. He was paunchy, slightly balding, and shorter than Ben. He extended his hand, caught a whiff of smoke, noticed Ben's stern expression, and withdrew it.

His haughty attitude became a bit more conciliatory as he said, "Yes, doctor, you most certainly can help me. My niece was brought here and I want her put into a private room immediately. That young nurse said she can't do that, but I expect you can. Marta's somewhere in here on the floor with these other people. I would like her moved now."

Ordinarily discussions with agitated family members were conducted in private. Tonight, however, Ben had no choice but to confront the Mayor where they stood.

By now Ben had escaped from the fiery inferno himself, had probably lost his fiancée, had been treating serious wounds for many hours, and had not slept. He wanted to believe that this man was simply motivated to do everything possible for his niece and was not trying to use his title as leverage; but the tone he had used earlier with the nurse gave him doubts. Ben had little patience with someone interfering with the emergency treatment of these gravely ill people, even if that someone was the mayor.

With a gravelly voice that had little life left, he said, "Mr.

Mayor, Miss Blackstone was correct. We cannot give special treatment under these conditions. We are assessing the most seriously injured first. We are transporting some to other nearby medical facilities, and we are releasing those who are less seriously injured.

As you can plainly see we have a chaotic crisis here. I sincerely hope your niece is not among the most seriously injured, but the best way you can help her is to stop interfering with those who are providing care. Now if you will excuse me, I have much more important work to do here." And before the Mayor could respond, he walked away to assess the next victim, totally unaware of the surprised and indignant look on the Mayor's face. *Maybe they took Laura to Boston City Hospital,* was his hopeful thought.

Sunday morning

After leaving the Cocoanut Grove, Avery had escorted Margaret to her door and thanked her for the evening. She had gone upstairs, undressed and climbed straight into bed. It had been an exciting evening, but she quickly fell asleep. The phone downstairs in the entry woke her and she looked at the bedside clock. 5:30 a.m. Who could be calling so early on a Sunday morning? She grabbed her robe off the bed, hurried downstairs and answered the phone. Before she could say hello she heard Ben's raspy voice. "Mom, I'm alright. I just have a minute. Have you seen the morning paper yet?"

"No, dear. You woke me with the phone call. Where are you?"

"At the hospital. I don't know when I might be home. Read the paper. You'll understand. We'll talk later. And Mom, please call Dr. and Mrs. Kensington," and he was gone. Puzzled by this strange conversation, Margaret slipped into her robe, went into the kitchen, filled the percolator with water and coffee and lit the burner. The frigid morning air greeted her as she opened the front door and picked up the paper. The headline was right there and her knees weakened beneath her. "Oh, dear God," she breathed.

CHAPTER 22

Three Days Later

Ben opened his eyes. The bedside clock read 4:45. Was it morning or evening? What day was it? He couldn't tell. He still had his clothes on. This was the first real sleep in his own bed since when? Last Friday night? Three nights ago. He had been able to grab a few hours here and there at the hospital but that was all. The fire. He turned over wanting desperately to go back to sleep. *Maybe if I wake up again these past days will only be a horrible nightmare. Actually, they are a horrible nightmare*, he thought. There were things he could never un-see—never un-feel. Laura was gone. The only item identifying her was the new engagement ring found with her remains. And Camille and Hope. They were among the 492 people who perished. Thankfully, his mother, Avery, and the Kensington's had left only minutes before the fire broke out.

The dream he had been having lingered in his consciousness. Maybe it was the voices downstairs that had pulled him back to the present. *4:45. Voices. It must be evening*, he thought absently. He showered, changed and went downstairs.

The mood was somber. "How is he doing?" It was Samuel. Ziva was with him. Margaret started to answer just as Ben walked into the kitchen.

"Ben, dear, you're up. Are you hungry?" He sat down, pushed a folded newspaper aside, and nodded knowing that would please his mother. She set about fixing plates for him, Samuel and Ziva. "I was over at the Kensington's earlier," she said as she took warm rolls from the oven. "I took a pie over. Laura's brother has arrived from upstate New York for the funeral. They are still making final arrangements, but it will probably be Friday morning at St. Paul Episcopal Church. Louise wanted to combine the service with Hope's family since the two girls grew up together." Margaret continued talking as she mashed potatoes and finished the string beans. "Their faith is strong and they will get through this, but right now they're devastated. Laura took a lot of responsibility for caring for her mother. They may need to hire a caregiver now. Ben, maybe you know a nurse at the hospital that would like to do private nursing? Poor Louise, instead of planning a wedding, she's planning a funer—." Her eyes darted to Ben becoming aware of her thoughtless chatter.

"I'll ask around. . .about a nurse," Ben answered as Margaret set a cup of coffee in front of him.

The fire had replaced the war news over the past several days. They ate and talked about what the newspapers had been reporting. Was it started by a bus boy changing a light bulb? Or a sailor unscrewing a bulb for privacy to kiss his date? Either way the very flammable methyl chloride was the culprit, firefighters said. They called it a flash-over. Freon, now in short supply, was replaced in the air conditioning system with the highly flammable methyl chloride. Over 1,000 revelers had been crowded into the club designed for under 500. In addition, some doors had been locked to prevent party-goers from skipping out on their bills. The club had hired many under-aged bus boys whose short lives ended tragically Authorities were involved in the investigation and new fire codes and regulations and litigation would be a certain result. *Too little, too late*, Ben thought.

Ben barely touched his food. The conversation lagged. "Ziva, that night is such a blur. Did I ever thank you and Samuel for pulling me out of there? If the two of you hadn't absolutely dragged me away. . . You were the one who kept your wits when I was frozen in place. Frozen. In the midst of a fire. Ironic, huh. Ziva, how *did* you know about that door, anyway? You saved our lives."

Ziva knew this question was coming sometime. A week ago she would have made up a story about visiting Camille there, following her out that door, etc. But going through what she went through. Seeing what she saw. In some ways the Ziva of a week ago died in that fire along with Camille. She didn't want to lie. Somehow it would be like dishonoring Camille's memory. She took a deep breath and answered. "I was working there. Part-time," she added hastily. "Camille—" her voice failed her, and she swallowed. "Camille helped me get hired. That's how I knew. It was an employee exit." Then in a rush, "I know, Samuel, I should have told you, and I'm not sure why I didn't. Just. . . I didn't think you'd approve. Anyway, it doesn't matter anymore. There is no job." They looked at Samuel. He put down his fork and paused a moment before he spoke.

"You are right. I would not approve." Ziva's face fell. "Where I come from, girls are not allowed to work in a place like that. It would be. . ." he searched for the right English word gave up and used the Yiddish word 'degreyding.' But here, things are different. I know. And, of course, you don't need my approval. But I think you can do more. You are funny and smart and pretty. But, yes, we are very glad for you to know that door." He threw a glance at Ben. "Sorry—you know what I mean," apologizing not for his grammar but his thoughtlessness.

"It's okay guys. Laura was. . . You did what you thought was right. I wish we could have done more."

Ziva was touched both by Samuel's words and thoughts of her friend, Camille, and her eyes filled with tears. "Camille was the one so excited about the Cocoanut Lounge. She died and I survived. It isn't fair. She should be here, too. I miss her. "

As the conversation moved around the table punctuated by the quiet clink of glasses and forks, Ben looked at the faces of his two friends. *Our relationship is different*, he thought. *Not sure exactly how, but it's different. We've gone through hell and back together and that has changed us. The images ingrained during that awful night will bind us together for a long time. Shared grief creates a strong bond that runs deep.*

An article in the folded newspaper caught Ben's eye and for the first time he read an account of the fire and the violations the night club was facing. His anger grew as he learned more and more about the way the club was managed and the underaged busboys. *Don't lose control,* he told himself. But his loss—all of their losses—the horror he had experienced these last few days, and his exhaustion all conspired against him. He could feel his heart pounding and his fists tightening. It wouldn't be good for his rage to erupt during a hospital shift. And he knew it would. The article mentioned that the club's owner was still in the hospital recovering from a heart attack. Jumping up suddenly he announced, "Please, finish your supper. I'm going back to the hospital." He grabbed his coat and keys and rushed out.

It wasn't right that this man could get away with what he had done. His greed had caused enormous grief and pain. Ben slammed the car door, not bothering to lock it and turned toward the hospital. He knew he shouldn't be here. He knew the righteous anger seething inside on the quick drive over was compromising his professionalism, but his impulsiveness ruled. He easily found Mr. Wilansky's room. Dinner was over and the nursing shift had changed. The patient was listening to a radio program when Ben entered his room.

"Mr. Wilansky?" Ben asked. *Calm down,* he told himself.

The man in the bed turned toward Ben. He was pale with deep set dark eyes. Even though he had been in bed for days his expensively styled dyed hair was neatly in place and he wore pressed pajamas. He looked up as Ben spoke his name. "Yes?"

"I'm Dr. Stuart. I'd like to talk to you."

"I haven't seen you before. Are you some new kind of

specialist?" He reached for the radio and turned it down.

"I'm not here about your medical care." Ben walked further into the room. His fists clenched and unclenched at his side. "I understand you are the owner of the Cocoanut Grove night club."

The pain medication Wilansky was on kept him from picking up on Ben's tension, tone or the anger on his face. "Yes. That's correct."

Ben drew out the words slowly. "I just wanted you to know that I lost my fiancée, her best friend and another acquaintance in the fire. Because of your poor management, your greed or negligence, or whatever, I worked for three days and nights trying to save lives—trying to put bodies back together—trying to console relatives and loved ones." Any calmness was long gone. "And it wasn't just me, this entire hospital worked their butts off exhausting our resources to save a relatively few. Maybe someday you will realize what the cost really was. You are fortunate to be here where you are well-cared for by a staff that values life. Every life. Even yours. I just wanted you to meet face to face one of the people your actions deeply affected. That's all I wanted to say. I am a physician and I have a professional standard to maintain so I'll leave now before I forget that." With a tinge of sarcasm, "Have a pleasant evening, Mr. Wilansky."

As Ben left the patient furrowed his brow, shook his head, and turned the radio back up.

CHAPTER 23

Six Days Later

Christmas was the main topic of conversation everywhere he went: Have you finished your shopping? What are your kids asking Santa for this year? Where are you spending Christmas day? Ben was standing in Filene's Department Store, where he and Laura had stood only a few weeks ago; the excitement of Christmas all around him. Bright red poinsettias and gold Christmas ribbon decorated the columns. Sprigs of holly with red berries filled silver vases placed all around the store. A group of carolers was singing 'Deck the Halls' just inside the revolving doors. He remembered back to when his sister had died and how Christmas that year had such a hollow feeling. And then when his father had died. This year felt the same. In many ways worse.

He was staring into a snow globe. The scene inside was a church with little pine trees and a small deer. He seemed to recall something about the snow globe inventor being a surgical instruments inventor, too. He shook it and the snow came to life obscuring the tiny scene. As he turned the globe over and over in his hands the memory of that foggy morning aboard the Queen Mary surfaced. That's how he felt now—separated from everything around him as if in a fog. The funerals were over but the mourning would go on for a long time.

Guilt had a stranglehold on him. Two-fold guilt. Why was he still here? So many had perished that night. Why not him? Why

Laura? And then there was the other guilt. Could he have done more to save her? He should have died trying. Had he saved himself at her expense? Had her death been his fault? He had gone immediately back to work at the hospital, but everything was mechanical. He put in the hours, went home, ate and slept. Repeat. Repeat. And the questions had no answers. He was still staring at the snow globe when he heard his name.

Dr. Kensington signaled to him as he called out, "Ben. Over here." As Dr. K approached, Ben reached out his hand but Laura's father surrounded him in a hug instead of a handshake and sudden tears came to their eyes. Pulling away Ben looked into the anguished gray eyes of his once future father-in-law and said, "How are you, sir?"

"Coping. The grief and related-stress have aggravated Louise's MS. And now the holidays. . . But for you, too. Could you come by the house for some eggnog or brandy or both. Maybe a cigar?" *Was that a stab at humor?* "I'd really like to have a talk with you. We're very fond of you, Ben, and you've stayed away much too long."

"Please, Dr. K. I'm not good company these days. I . . .my schedule—"

"We'll expect you the first afternoon you have off." He tipped his hat, clapped Ben on the shoulder as he walked away. Ben watched him disappear among the shoppers and then remembered he was still holding the snow globe. The snow had settled, revealing the church again.

As it turned out, it was only a couple of days later that Ben's schedule permitted him an early day at the hospital. He hadn't forgotten about Dr. Kensington's invitation or request or whatever, but the guilt he felt about Laura's death had not lessened, and he thought going to see the Kensingtons ranked right up there with a root canal, even more painful in some ways.

So, here he was with the phone in his hand working up his courage to call them. This meeting would inevitably happen sooner or later he told himself. His mother had made several trips to see them over these past days, suggesting he should visit them, but he always made some excuse for not accompanying her. The phone call was brief. They would be home. No more excuses. "Mom," he called up the stairs. "I'm going out. To visit the Kensingtons." And then he mouthed the words, "That should make you happy."

He stood at their door. The bright green holly wreath had been replaced with a wreath made of black ribbons alerting visitors to be respectful, because a death had occurred in the household. He turned his eyes away to avoid looking at it. Louise Kensington's new caregiver answered the door. "Hello, Dr. Stuart," Mrs. McGinty smiled. "Thank you for the referral. Dr. and Mrs. Kensington are very lovely people."

"I'm glad it is working out for all of you," Ben replied. She took his coat and scarf and ushered him into the parlor to wait while she collected the doctor. Fortunately, the wait was brief or the lump in his stomach would have grown to the size of a boulder.

The doctor's distinguished voice preceded his appearance. "Ben, greetings. Please, let's go into my study. This parlor business is way too stuffy for me." The doctor settled into the wing-backed chair motioning Ben toward the only other chair in the room. The little white terrier, Mitzi, found her spot on his lap and everyone was seated.

Ben had decided on the snow globe now artfully wrapped by his Mom and he set it on the table next to the antique humidor. He glanced sideways at his host, hoping he wouldn't offer a cigar.

"You're looking well, sir," Ben said. Dr. K was dressed casually in a dark gray wool cardigan and black slacks, but still wearing his usual tie—for now . . .black.

"And you are not," Dr. K said. "Louise's new caregiver, Mrs. McGinty, is bringing coffee in a bit, along with some brandy. Thank you for finding her for me. She has helped Louise a great deal. Between the grief and the MS, the days are very difficult for her. But let's talk. What's going on, Ben?"

The abruptness caught Ben off guard and his response was reactive. "What do you mean? Everything's good. I'm back at the hospital . . .working."

"No, Ben. Everything isn't good. Your mom is worried about you. She asked me to talk to you. She noticed—"

The coffee arrived just then and while it was being poured, brandy and cream added, Ben used the interruption to consider the doctor's words. His mom had talked to them about him? Why? His annoyance grew. Couldn't she understand he wasn't her 'little boy' anymore? Apparently not. He sipped the coffee but it was hot and burned his tongue so he set the cup down. Mitzi had jumped down and scampered off somewhere when the coffee arrived.

Quietly, "Ben, do you think we blame you for Laura's death?" *Really. This man should look up the definition of subtle.* "Maybe. How can you not?" A pause. Sip the coffee again. Still hot. The silence nudged him and his anger surprised him. "But it doesn't matter because I blame myself." And then as if the force of his words had cracked a dam deep inside him an explosion of words came gushing out—barely making any sense. "I tried . . .I'm a doctor for God's sake. . .they pulled me . . .I couldn't see . . . the smoke. . ." The overdue stream of tears, sorrow and guilt rose to the surface searching for absolution. His head was in his hands and Dr. Kensington remained silent until the purge had finished. Ben removed a handkerchief from his pocket. Used it to wipe his eyes and nose. He was embarrassed—both at his angry tone and loss of control.

The doctor's eyes were moist, too and he cleared his throat before he spoke. "We've lost a beloved daughter much too soon. And, Ben, I could ask myself the same question I asked you. Do I blame myself? What if we had stayed twenty more minutes? Could *we* have saved her? Could we have saved anyone? I'm a physician, too, don't forget. Can you see the futility of the what ifs? We'll never have those answers. I've known you for a long time, Ben. If there had been any way, *any way at all*, you would have gotten Laura out of there. There just wasn't.

"If my years of being a physician have taught me anything it's that death is a part of life. I've held the hands of dying old men and I've comforted the mothers of young children and babies. Your own father lost a daughter much younger than mine. Do I understand why God allows these horrible tragedies to happen? That question has been asked for centuries; only God has the answer to that one. But when we stop believing that God is intrinsically a good God, we are lost. What other religion has at its core a God who would suffer and die for mankind? That's why I don't blame you—because God doesn't blame you. There was nothing you could have done to save her. That fire was over in just 15 minutes.

"Ben, God has a plan for each of our lives and the Good Book tells us that He knows the number of our days. He has a plan for your life, too." Ben heard a small yip and looked up as Mitzi bounded into her master's lap snuggling in beside him again.

As Dr. Kensington spoke, Ben felt the cloud he had been under begin to lift. His body actually felt lighter, if that was possible. Neither spoke for a bit until Ben broke the silence. "Thank you, sir. Your understanding and forgiveness mean a lot."

"As important as that is to you, Ben, it's more important that you forgive yourself."

Ben didn't respond to the comment, instead he reached for his coffee, drinking most of it, and gestured toward the wrapped box. "I brought a little Christmas gift for the two of you. I hope you like it." He rose from the chair. "I should go. Please, give my regards to Mrs. Kensington." Mrs. McGinty had slipped in to ask about more coffee and was sent to retrieve Ben's coat instead.

Laura's father stood as well. "One last word, Ben. Sometimes God's plan for your life isn't the same plan that you have. I'll tell you a story about that someday," and with a hand on Ben's shoulder, he walked him to the door.

Ben had not been near the remains of the Cocoanut Grove since the fire and he didn't know why he turned the car toward Piedmont Street now. He parked nearby. The little bit of afternoon warmth was vanishing along with the transparent sunshine. The naked trees shivered as the frostbitten wind sought refuge in their bare branches for the night. Ben's shoes made a hollow sound on the cobblestones and he pulled his coat collar higher successfully warding off the cold. But there was no way to ward off the memories.

The scene was dramatically different from when he was here over a week ago. Instead of the chaotic array of ambulances, firemen, coils of hoses and charred bodies, barricades were in place and a policeman remained on sentry duty to keep people away from the burned out remains. Instead of sirens, screams, and the roar of the fire, only reverent silence now. Ben reached into his pocket for the new pack of cigarettes, took one out and struck a match to it, watching it glow. He had bought a pack after the fire thinking they might help him cope.

He looked around. The wind stirred up the ash, the cold smell of charred wood and an indefinable something else that swirled around him. He stared at the cigarette and match for a moment and dropped them both grinding them into the pavement with his heel. *Bad idea.* He never wanted to smoke again, cigars or cigarettes. They both had become a reminder of his loss. A loss, he realized, that was more than Laura, Hope, Camille. He had lost so many other patients that night. Death had defeated him over and over. He had lost his temper first with the mayor, and then again when he let anger guide his visit to Wilansky's room—the same anger he had promised his father he would control. What kind of physician was he, anyway? Maybe he wasn't cut out for this after all. *Laura, I miss you so much. I had our lives all planned out. Now, what?*

The dam had burst at Dr. K's house leaving his eyes dry for now but not releasing all of the pain inside. Even with Dr. K's sincere forgiveness there was still an emptiness inside that mirrored the burnt-out shell of the Cocoanut Grove before him. His failures bore down on him, driving away his confidence. *I'm losing sight of who I am*, he thought. The cold seeping into his bones finally turned him away.

CHAPTER 24

Boston, MA
Late November 1941

Margaret was concerned about Ben. She had voiced those concerns to Dr. Kensington and she hoped their visit had helped Ben work through his grief. She needed to keep busy so she had just placed the first tray of Ben's favorite Christmas cookies into the oven when the doorbell rang. Wiping her hands on her apron, she hurried to the door and peered through the small side window. A young messenger dressed for the weather in a dark woolen coat, cap, gloves and boots was holding an envelope. His bicycle lay at the base of the porch steps.

"May I help you?" Margaret said after opening the door.

"I have a telegram for Dr. Benjamin Stuart. Please sign here?" She signed the notebook he handed her. "Merry Christmas," he said retrieving the notebook and handing her the envelope. She closed the door as he picked up the bike and pedaled away.

She stood in the hallway, debating with herself. *Should I open it? No. He should be back soon.* It wasn't often that a telegram arrived and it was usually bad news. Her curiosity was winning, though. She picked up the letter opener. *It must be important.* She hesitated. *No. If he calls I'll ask him if he wants me to open it. Or maybe I'll—Oh no! The cookies!* The smell of burning cookies decided it for her. She hadn't set the timer.

Ben snacked on an unburnt cookie as he read the brief telegram out loud to his mother:

```
NLT DR BENJAMIN STUART=
4343 RIDGEWAY LN BOSTON(MA)=
ARRIVING IN BOSTON ON 12/02. QEM
IN FOR HULL REPAIRS.
WILL CALL YOU J HAWTHORNE
```

Ben scratched his head, perplexed. *December 2nd. That was only a few days away. Why does he want to see me now?* It didn't take Ben long to come up with a reason.

"How nice that he wants to see you, Ben. Maybe he could come by the house for dinner." She bent down to take more cookies from the oven.

Behind her back he mouthed, "If you had figured it out you wouldn't be extending that invitation."

"How is Kate and the rest of your family? We read about the bombings in Southampton but Millbrook wasn't mentioned. Did your house survive?" Ben asked. He noticed the Captain looked tired—dark circles residing under his eyes that hadn't been there on the trip back home from England. The two men were seated in the restaurant at the Parker House. White tablecloths and clinking china were subtle reminders of the recent horrible night at the Cocoanut Grove. He shielded his eyes.

"Kate and her Mum are fine. I'll tell her you asked. Cunard Lines helped evacuate them to Australia, near Sydney actually, just weeks before the bombings began. I have a sister there. The Queen has made several trips to Australia for troops, plus I've had time off to be with them. Still miss them, though."

"As for our house, I haven't been home for a while, but word is we have only minor damage. That hawthorn tree that Norah loves better still be standing. It's practically a member of the family. Three residents were reported killed, but everyone we know is either safe or has evacuated. So far, that is. Southampton is another story. A spitfire factory was taken out and over a hundred were killed. There has been complete devastation in that area.

"What about Kate's nursing studies?" Ben asked.

"Kate graduated before the bombing and the evacuation, but Robin, her twin, is another story. He quit school and joined the Royal Air Force. Got his training with the British Commonwealth Air Training Program and finished just in time to fly during the Blitz. He's wanted to fly ever since we can remember. He got his chance. Says he loves the Supermarine Spitfire. His mum was— how should I say—opposed? But now that all our lives have been turned upside down and our beloved England is suffering immense death and destruction, she has accepted Robin's decision. That doesn't mean she isn't fearful every day that bad news might catch up with her. She tries to be brave." He paused, noticing Ben's silence. "And you, Ben. How are you? How's the residency going?"

"I've finished my residency." It struck him that the Hawthorne family was experiencing deep losses, too, like himself. "I doubt that you know about the fire here in Boston. My fiancée died, and her best friend that night." He spared the Captain most of the horror. But he shared how helpless he had felt. He grew silent again.

"I had no idea, Ben. I knew *our* world had descended into a hell like no other; but I had no reason to believe yours had as well." The Captain cleared his throat. "You must be wondering why I wanted to see you. Do you remember our talk in New York?" Ben nodded attentively. "We're still finding it difficult to enlist physicians for the Queen Mary. We've made thousands of miles of troop transport trips and worn out several medical staff volunteers.

"While the ship is here briefly for repairs, I'm recruiting. The war with Germany is certain to drag on. Many British doctors have enlisted and been assigned in various capacities in England to care for those wounded by the bombings or to serve in field hospitals. Several have declined to be aboard a ship for an extended period of time believing they are more urgently needed elsewhere. And, face it, some are just too old for the job. It's a bit of a problem, Ben. For all the reasons we talked about earlier, you are uniquely qualified. Are you at all interested?"

Ben was prepared for this question. It was the only possible reason the Captain had requested this meeting. "Captain, a month ago my life was all planned out. I was going to complete my residency, take over a medical practice, and marry a wonderful woman. Now, everything's changed. *I've* changed. This summer my cousin and his wife perished aboard the Lancastria when it was sunk. We had a great time with them while we were in England. Now they're gone. They were close to my age."

"I'm sorry, Ben. The tentacles of this war are extending everywhere."

An urn of coffee was nearby and Ben re-filled their cups just as their waiter brought two pieces of Boston Cream Pie, the restaurant's signature dessert. "The fire, the Athenia, the Lancastria, all made me aware of how unexpectedly life can end. The night of the fire, I saw so many families overcome with the sudden and senseless death of loved ones—relatives and friends who only hours earlier were dancing, laughing and full of life—just like Laura. Life holds no guarantees." He paused and sipped the coffee. "There were so many victims that night that died on my watch. I tried—we all tried— but we couldn't save them. All the combined training and experience that we had. . . didn't help. I'm not sure I'm cut out for this. It made me question everything."

The Captain watched Ben as he talked, recognizing changes in him since their dinner in New York. Tragedy, and its companion grief, bookended him. His naïve confidence had been replaced with doubt and confusion about his abilities and purpose. But he was searching. That was good.

"I haven't said anything to anyone, but I've been considering walking away from the hospital temporarily to figure things out. Maybe being aboard the Queen Mary would help me do that. I'll think about it. You said that advanced medical skills were not usually required. Right? I've had limited surgical training."

The Captain nodded. "That's correct." He laid a hand on Ben's shoulder. "Kate was wrong," he said. Ben raised an eyebrow. "She told me you'd decline straightaway. But I saw you in the library in deep thought after the sinking of the Athenia. I had a strong feeling about you. Now it appears that the circumstances in your life have done what I couldn't do with words. I'll contact you with the logistics and timing as soon as I'm given that information. Think about it; but, Ben, don't take too long."

Ben rose, extended his hand and they shook on it. "This will affect several other people, too. And, of course, Mom and I haven't discussed it. If you remember our dinner conversation, you know how that's gonna' go." He made a face.

"Given Robin's new career, she and Norah will have something in common, then," Captain Hawthorne said with a slight smile. "I anticipated you might have questions if you said yes, and I prepared this information for you." He handed Ben several sheets of typed paper. "I'll be in Boston a few more days and you can reach me here, at the Parker House. Read this and if you have any other questions, call me. It is a paid position, not volunteer; but, sorry, not much pay. Each duty lasts six months, give or take, and if the ship still has need, you can sign on again. Ben, Britain is grateful." They shook hands. The Captain headed for the elevator and Ben pushed his way out through the lobby doors wondering if this might be the stupidest decision of his young life.

CHAPTER 25

Boston, MA
Saturday, December 6, 1941

He had been skating in the park. The same park he and Laura had gone to just a few short weeks ago. The tumble they took, their 'Olympic performance', were treasured memories that this park would trigger for a long time. A tear trickled down his cold cheek and he blamed it on the winter breeze. He had made his decision, but it would be a hard sell.

His mother was out when he got back home providing a short respite from his planned announcement. He ran water into the percolator, placed fresh coffee in the basket and turned on the burner. The house was warm and smelled of pine needles. Because of the recent death, they had decided not to decorate a Christmas tree this year. Instead Margaret had purchased a fresh pine wreath and a long mantel garland that were both filling the house with their woodsy fragrance. She had unpacked and arranged some Christmas decorations that had been a part of Christmas ever since Ben could remember. As he listened to the burp of the perking coffee he thought about when he and Claire had strung raw cranberries and popcorn for the tree. They had thrown the popcorn at each other trying to catch it in their mouths, failing miserably. Dad had placed the porcelain angel on the top of the tree at the very last. The angel was now sitting on the table in the entryway in the midst of some greenery and fake snow that his mom knew how to make.

Ben poured some coffee, sat down at the kitchen table and retrieved the papers Captain Hawthorne had given him. He read through them and laid them aside resting his chin in his hand. How could he explain his improbable decision to Mom in a way she would understand? Was that even a remote possibility? She was unaware of his current state of mind. Couldn't blame her, though. He'd been less than honest around his family and friends lately. Withdrawn and closed off. He gazed off into space gathering his thoughts, considering his words, nodding his head at times.

He picked up the typed pages again and sipped his coffee. Although they contained few specifics, they did summarize what his responsibilities would be while aboard the Queen Mary. He read the typed pages while savoring the fragrant brew.

The sound of the foyer door opening interrupted his reading. Here we go, he thought. Mom first.

"Mom, I'm in the kitchen," he called out. "Want a cuppa?"

"That's a switch. You waiting on me for a change," she called back as she hung her coat in the entry closet and removed her hat and gloves. "Hot coffee sounds wonderful." Her cheeks were bright pink from the cold and she rubbed her hands together efficiently warming them.

"Where were you?" Ben asked.

"Guess I forgot to mention it this morning. I walked down to the church to help with a quilting group. Very nice ladies. How was your meeting with Captain Hawthorne?"

Ben placed the coffee cup in front of her and sat down opposite. Gently, he said, "Mom, that's just what I wanted to talk to you about."

She tuned in to Ben's tone and expression. "This sounds serious," she said spooning sugar into the steaming liquid.

And he told her. He told her about the offer. He told her about his recent doubts and confusion. He told her that something like this might be just what he needed. "Here, listen. I'll summarize the duties for you. I won't be military. I'll actually be an employee of Cunard. The commitment is only for six months. And the ship is fast, Mom, that's why they're using it. And you remember how Captain Hawthorne described the job in New York, right?"

"You and Avery have become good friends. If I go he'll be here for you, I'm sure; and, of course, Samuel will still live here." He was working it all out as he spoke. A pause. "Mom, Mom. You are listening, right? Captain Hawthorne is convinced the danger is minimal. They've made twelve crossings and not been shot at once."

Margaret's knuckles were as white as the porcelain cup she held while Ben talked. "Ben, this is foolishness. Once you stop and think this through you'll realize that. You have a career and a life here that you've worked hard to build. Why would you ever think of abandoning that for something this dangerous?"

"Mom, I'm not abandoning it. I'm just walking away from it for a while."

She pushed her chair back and walked the cup to the sink emptying it. Ben sat quietly for a minute watching her rinse the cup, allowing her the distraction. "I *have* thought this through over the past few weeks. Not about the ship, exactly, but taking a break. The fire made me realize how short life is. How little time we really have to do something important. I've felt like such a failure these past weeks. I'm not sure *what* I want to do with my life now. I've been reading more about conditions in Europe, in England. The German army has already affected Aunt Lillian and her family. She lost a son and had grandchildren evacuated, remember? Samuel's distraught about his parents. And what about the loss of life aboard the Athenia? All of these things have touched us in some way. I can't believe this opportunity isn't here for a reason—that this is all some weird coincidence."

Margaret turned from the sink to view her son. "I know you would like me to give you my blessing. To applaud your valor, bravery. . ." she paused, searching ". . .patriotism. But I can't. This isn't our war. It isn't our concern. I can't pretend to be pleased if you decide to put yourself in harm's way. I've lost one child and a husband. I'm not going to risk losing you too." She dried her hands on the dishtowel she was holding and with a stubborn demeanor she left the kitchen.

Ben's coffee had grown cold while he talked and he rose and poured the remainder into the sink. He stood staring out the window at the snow-covered backyard. Inner conflict was not his favorite thing and this was a big one. *It would be so easy to say I need to stay here, for Mom—safe and secure. Use her as an excuse. But there's a strong impulse, pushing me into uncharted waters that I can't ignore. No pun intended,* he thought wryly.

He pulled up the memory of their days together on the Queen Mary. How carefree he had been. How unconcerned about events in Europe. How confident. . .until the fire. Regardless that his Mom thought this was a rash and impulsive decision, he knew better. He saw this as an opportunity to volunteer his training and use the time to figure things out. The experience and the adventure would be a good thing. Maybe it had been pulling at him all along. She'll see. There was time. Days, possibly weeks before the Queen Mary would leave again. Maybe something would happen to change her thinking. *Give her a little time,* he thought.

Ben knocked on the door to Samuel's room. "Are you in there? He heard a light shuffling sound, as the door opened and Samuel was standing there bleary-eyed in his pajamas, his dark hair tousled. "Did I wake you? Sorry. I forget, residents sleep when they can. May I come in? Samuel nodded. He brushed past Samuel into the small room. It was a one-sided conversation as Ben explained this radical change of direction. Samuel struggled to clear away the fog of sleep and reached for his robe.

When Ben took a breath Samuel said," I understand more than you what the stakes are. Father"—he pronounced it fa•tur—

"and *muter* try to spare my concern, but I know things." His head bobbed. Talking about the war agitated him. "Germans are in Lithuania and they will do terrible things to Jews there, and he *still* won't leave! *Farbisn*—stubborn. Of course I understand." Samuel was thoughtful for a minute. "We should talk with Dr. Oglethorpe."

"No time like the present," Ben said. "This afternoon?"

Saturday afternoons the doctor was usually home with family and together Ben and Samuel met with him and the last piece fell into place. The doctor's sister-in-law had just come to live with them while she regained strength from a tuberculosis infection. She had recently undergone a pneumothorax procedure at a sanatorium in Saranac Lake and appeared to be dramatically cured. Dr. Oglethorpe was very interested in studying this procedure, so he was quite willing to postpone his retirement. No one discussed what the plan would be if Ben didn't return. Because like Ben said, the risk was minimal.

CHAPTER 26

Sunday, December 7, 1941
Boston, MA

"Ben, hurry up. Avery will be here any minute," Margaret called from the foot of the stairs. She pinned her hat in place, checking it in the mirror as she always did. She had put yesterday's discussion out of her mind, treating it as a frivolous notion. *God knows I understood what grief feels like. Maybe I didn't understand Ben's feelings of helplessness and failure, but that will pass, given time. He'll get through this. He's strong.* These were her thoughts as she moved to turn off the radio. Her hand reached for the dial but instead of turning it off, she—like millions more on this Sunday afternoon—couldn't believe what she heard:

> *"We interrupt this program to bring you a special news bulletin! This morning at 7:53 a.m. Japanese planes attacked the United States Naval Base at Pearl Harbor, Hawaii Territory, killing an estimated 2,000 Americans with a final casualty count still to be determined. The U.S.S. Arizona was completely destroyed and the U.S.S. Oklahoma capsized. Twelve ships are confirmed sunk or beached in the attack and nine additional vessels were damaged. More than 160 aircraft were destroyed and reports are*

still coming in regarding additional damage and loss of life. Ladies and Gentlemen, it appears that the United States has now entered the war in Europe. President Roosevelt will address the nation in a few hours. Please keep your radios on and remain alert for updates to this national emergency.
We repeat, this morning at 7:53 a.m. . . . "

The shock on Margaret's face took Ben by surprise as he came down the stairs just in time to hear the bulletin repeated. They looked at each other not saying anything as their conscious minds made a valiant effort to absorb the reality of the words they were hearing.

The war had come to America.

Yesterday's discussion—the one she had shrugged off—no longer seemed frivolous. *If Ben doesn't serve in the relative safety of the Queen Mary, he might be required to serve in . . .* She stopped her thought. Margaret looked up at her son and as the first tear left her eye she breathed, "I know, Ben. I know."

The telephone in the foyer rang. The first of many calls that afternoon. Ben's voice was shaky as he answered. It was Captain Hawthorne, his voice thick with sorrow. He understood the shock and pain Ben and his family were feeling. His own city had been bombed; his family relocated; his country in turmoil; and the Queen Mary a troop transport now. "Ben, I just wanted to tell you how sorry I am that your country is suffering such a great tragedy. This changes everything for both our countries. A few minutes ago I got word that your president and Mr. Churchill have talked and that immediately the United States government will be in charge of the Queen Mary. From now on she will be transporting American soldiers into the battlefields of Europe."

Ben was listening to the Captain, but his eyes were on his

mother as he spoke the words that would change their lives. "Thank you, sir, for your kind words. We are in shock like the rest of our country. If I had any doubts before, they're gone now. I need to do this." Their conversation was brief. When he replaced the receiver, Margaret wrapped her arms around her son realizing this might be the final time she would hug this young man she loved. Because war changes people. It changes boys into men. It changes men into leaders. It creates cynics and heroes; damages bodies and souls. The ones who return can never go back to being who they were before they witnessed this unspeakable depravity of the human race. Once home again, survivors might think their wartime experiences and images are stowed away deep inside and forgotten; but unbidden, the horrors unexpectedly surface as dreams and flashbacks that are as real as the day they happened. So, as she hugged Ben, in some unconscious way, she knew that when this was over, if—no! when he returned, he would be different. The Ben she hugged today would be gone forever.

She released Ben and said, "I should call Avery."

The next day President Roosevelt's words were broadcast: *Yesterday, December 7, 1941—a date which will live in infamy— The United States of America was suddenly and deliberately attacked by naval and air forces of the Empire of Japan. As Commander-in-Chief of the Army and Navy, I have directed that all measures be taken for our defense. With confidence in our armed forces, with the unbounded determination of our people we will gain the inevitable triumph, so help us God.*

By early January thousands of men and women were either enlisting, being drafted or hired into wartime factories. New auto sales were ordered ceased. Japan had conquered the rubber-producing areas in southern Asia and stopped rubber imports, so rubber tires were severely rationed. Gasoline rationing allowed only three to four gallons per week per household and rationing of sugar and other foodstuffs would follow in the weeks to come. Every household sacrificed in varying degrees. America had refrained from aiding Europe, but with the Japanese attack on Americans at Pearl Harbor, restraint was no longer an option. The nation stood behind her President and rallied to the cries of war.

PART III

February 1942 – May 1942

CHAPTER 27

Vilna, Lithuania
February, 1942

Ana was home alone when they came. Two Lithuanian policemen dressed in dark brown uniforms, holding big guns. Their manner menacing. "Take what you can carry," they told her. "We'll wait." She started to protest—to tell them that her husband was an important man—to tell them that they were making a mistake. And they pointed their guns at her. She stood there. Terrified. Not certain what she should do. They shouted at her and took a step closer, their guns advancing first. "Beeilung, hurry. We haven't all day. We have more kikes like you to round up."

Her voice quivered as she asked, "Please, go get my husband, Jonah Dressler. He will explain. You have made a mistake." Quickly she wrote out the address for them. The larger soldier, seemingly the one in charge, snatched the scrap of paper from her hand and quickly glanced at it. "I know this address. We'll get him and bring him here. While we are gone, pack; and put this on." And with a final intimidation of firepower they were gone.

She collapsed into a nearby chair. Ana had heard horrible stories. She knew terrible things were happening in Vilna. But she had thought because of her husband's prominent position, his Lithuanian contacts and the engineering business they were safe.

Maybe Samuel was right after all. She reached down and picked up the armband decorated with the yellow Star of David the soldats had thrown at her feet. All Jews were required to wear one at all times.

Her eyes wandered around the small house that had been their home, Samuel's home. The rag rug and china cabinet. The chair where Jonah sat in the evenings and read the Torah. She stared at the worn pattern on the wooden floor that recorded the many visits of family and friends. So many memories. Would they ever live in this house again? Oh Jonah, help me! Her heart pounded in her chest and she placed a hand there as if to keep it from escaping. Tears blurred her vision as she moved into their bedroom. She grabbed a photo of Samuel he had sent them and kneeling beside their bed, dragged out two large satchels all the while struggling to focus on what they might need in the coming days.

Jonah removed his black woolen coat shaking the snow off as he hung it on the stand in the corner of his office. He was thinking about making a cup of tea when he heard loud voices in the front of the building. Removing his spectacles and laying them on the dark wood desk, he started toward the entry. Two Lithuanian policemen barred his doorway, shouting in Lithuanian. "Come with us, now. Lock your office. You may bring your coat and hat. NOW!"

"What is this about?" Jonah asked even though he knew this same thing had been happening to other Jews in Vilna, many he was acquainted with. He had relied on his business, his city contacts and knowledge of Vilna's infrastructure to keep he and Ana safe. "I can't leave now. I have employees here. We have work to do." The loud voices had drawn one of Jonah's draftsmen near the office. The larger of the two policemen turned and without so much as a blink shot the draftsman in the head. "You have one less employee now, kike."

This wasn't happening. He was frozen in place staring as the blood pooled around Elam. Earlier they had shared lox and a bagel and they had laughed together about how Elam's oldest son had teased his younger brother about his futile attempts learning to tie his shoes. They would never laugh together again. His trance was broken when one of the policemen poked his gut with the rifle. "Move, now!"

"We can't just leave him. There are Jewish burial laws. What about his family?" Jonah was stunned by their violence.

The one with the rifle poked him again, moving him along. "We'll see to his burial. He will be thrown into a pit with the others."

Anger suddenly colored Jonah's voice. "You are making a big mistake. I—"

"No mistake," the same man interrupted. "You are working for us now."

Jonah had lived through much political upheaval in Vilna over his lifetime. He was not unprepared for this day. He knew it could come. The two soldiers were involved in searching Elam's body for money, a watch, whatever they could keep or sell. Quickly, Jonah went to his desk and retrieved a packet containing papers for him and Ana and some cash. Grabbing his long black coat, he stuffed the items into the secret pocket. The soldiers were finished with Elam and gave his still warm body an unnecessary kick with their heavy boots.

"What is taking you so long! Get your coat we are taking you back to your house where your wife is packing. Go!"

Ana! Oh, dear God, Ana. He grabbed his black hat and gloves and at the last moment remembered his eyeglasses lying on his desk and ran back for them. He had to pass Elam's defiled bloody body. *What kind of monster shoots an innocent in cold blood. What was it they had said?* 'You are working for us now?' *I will never work for you, swine,* Jonah resolved. *We will find a way out or die trying.*

CHAPTER 28

~

Ana woke gasping for air. Shivering both from the cold floor and the icy fear that had invaded her world. At any moment, day or night, German soldiers or Lithuanian police could storm into the ghetto apartments waving those terrible guns, shouting orders in German, or worse, marching fellow Jews away to be shot and thrown into a pit somewhere outside the city. Whenever she heard the sound of boots on the stairs her stomach tightened and her heart began to pound. Fear thrived among all of them.

They had been moved to an apartment in one of the ghettos in Vilna. The flat she and Jonah were assigned to they shared with two other families: Soske and her small daughter, Rebekah; a doctor, his wife and two grown sons who all worked at the hospital. She reached for Jonah but he wasn't there. "Jonah," she whispered hoarsely as she raised herself on her elbows. The spot next to her on the thin sleeping mat was empty. Her fear grew. Then in the gray dawn she saw him picking his way across the room avoiding the other bodies asleep on similar mats. He lay down beside her. "Where did you go?" she whispered again.

"Klozet," he said. Toilet. It was an outhouse in the courtyard. She clung to him grateful for the warmth of his body and the security she felt when he was near.

"I had a dream. They killed you."

"Shhh, bubbala. They need me. That's why we are here and not dead in one of those pits. I am still of some use to them." The wool blanket he crawled back under was one of the few things Ana had packed for them. "It is not yet daylight. Go back to sleep."

After a moment she whispered, "Jonah, maybe Samuel was right about what he wrote in his letters. Maybe we should have listened?" His light snoring signaled Jonah had drifted off; or maybe he was avoiding the questions that troubled her.

Across the room, three-year old Rebekah raised up, whimpered softly and snuggled back against her *muter*; her long dark tangled hair hiding her face. Ana had helped with the child yesterday, soothing and rocking her while Soske, her mother, rested. Helping out with the small child kept her from thinking about hers and Jonah's own uncertain future. She and Soske had talked while sitting on the floor leaning against the wall and she learned that Soske didn't know where her husband was. The Germans had taken him at gunpoint and she was certain they had killed him. Her words had carried no depth of emotion; neither did any show on her face or in her eyes. Ana could see that Soske was giving up—giving the Nazis another victory.

Ana knew they were in an older poorer Jewish section of Vilna. She had been hearing stories since last September. The Lithuanians and Germans had been clearing it out in order to bring the wealthier Jewish population here. 'Clearing it out' she was told meant they had killed most of the people who lived here. Only a few were able to escape. The room they were in now was for sleeping. The only other room they had was a small kitchen, not nearly large enough to feed this many people, and certainly not like her own kitchen where she had cooked many meals for her family. From what she had seen of food rations, there wouldn't be a lot of cooking anyway. During the day the sleeping room became the unfurnished living area. Privacy didn't exist. But to preserve as many of the Jewish laws as possible, the doctor brought sheets from the hospital and strung them across the room partitioning the room for men and women.

Dr. Milavetz, had also smuggled in some lye soap. Lice were

a problem in most of the ghettos. They shared the soap when they were able to use the bath house. It worked. As yet, no one in their apartment was itching from head lice.

The two large satchels Ana had packed were now stored beneath the one window near their sleeping mats. She glanced toward the window. Forty years of their lives were now stored in those two satchels. The delay while the policemen had gone for Jonah had given her time to calm her fear and focus on what might be needed. Warm clothes and coats, heavy shoes, two of her thickest warmest blankets. And a cup and saucer that she had wrapped carefully in a thick scarf. She allowed herself that one small item from her *muter's* treasured china. She had grown up in a Lithuania that yo-yoed between occupation forces. It changed hands between Imperial and Soviet Russia, Germany, and Poland multiple times. But never had she faced what was before her now.

During the first few days in the ghetto the tears had flowed. Privately, of course. She grieved for her treasured family heirlooms and the comfort, privacy and safety of her home. She grieved for friends and neighbors that were either dead or in a mad race for their lives; lives that would never be the same; lives taken away by these monsters. It was an unbearable pain that she pushed away and replaced with anger. She wanted to spit a curse on all of them. Then the niggling fear would find its way back into her stomach, completing the emotional circle. *What is to become of us?* she wondered. A new thought made her sit upright. *Samuel! He doesn't know what is happening to us. But if he doesn't hear from us, he will worry. Oy Oy. We should have listened to him.*

CHAPTER 29

Boston, MA
February, 1942

Avery and Ziva were at the Stuart's and they were all sitting around the kitchen table, laughing. Too much time had passed without the sound of laughter in the house. Ben had passed his medical board examinations and was now officially an M.D, and a celebration was taking place. With Ben being away for extended periods of time, Margaret had decided that Samuel should get his driver's license. He had been both nervous and excited about driving the big car that first day. Clutch in. Shift. Ease clutch out. Accelerate. Jerk! Jerk! He thought he'd never get the hang of it. "This is harder than medical school," he lamented. "I'll never get this."

"You'll get it," Ben had encouraged, looking away and rolling his eyes thinking maybe his friend was right. But Samuel's persistence paid off. Massachusetts was one of the few states that required an exam and Samuel missed only one item on the test.

"Ok, Samuel. Tell us again why you had a problem knowing left from right?" Ben was goading him and they all knew it.

"I told you once already. A patch of ice made the auto skid. The agent said turn left. Turn left. Nobody was hurt. I stopped the car and he said I did a good job of recovery."

"Yes, true. But you turned the wheel to the right."

"I was nervous, ok? I forget about turning *into* the skid. I corrected, ok?"

"And then what happened?" Uh-huh, come on tell us. Is that all he said?" Ben again.

Samuel glanced sideways at Ziva. "He said maybe I should review the English words for "right" and "left" and in the future be very aware of ice. But honestly, Ben, I think I would rather take the bus most of the time." And besides I do know right from left" he said, first holding up his left arm and then his right just to see if they were paying attention. That brought more laughter. He looked around the table at his American family and tried to picture his mother and father here, laughing with them. These were the times he missed and worried about them the most.

Margaret had left the kitchen for a moment but was now standing beside Ben. "Ben, for Pete's sake! He found the brake. Hmm, that rhymes doesn't it." A groan circulated around the table, but at least she had their attention. "Ben, I have a present for you," she said as she placed a long black box on the table beside him. "I've been saving this for you and now is the perfect time to give it to you." Ben carefully removed the lid from the box that held his father's stethoscope. "Your father had several of these, but this one held special meaning for him. Do you remember?"

Ben gently removed the medical device. A picture appeared in his mind. He and Claire sitting Indian style on the floor. Wrapping paper and a bow nearby. Claire giggling and him shussing her. He was what—maybe ten, Claire seven. It had been their unanimous decision to give their dad a new stethoscope for Christmas that year. After Claire's death a few years later, that stethoscope was the one he used most of the time.

"I remember. Seeing this again makes me feel like Dad and Claire are here with us, laughing and celebrating." He reached out and took his mother's hand. "Thanks, Mom."

"One more thing," Margaret said gesturing toward the sideboard. "Tonight there's cake for everyone, but who knows after the sugar gets rationed. So, enjoy it while you can."

"Margaret, that was quite a celebration you put together for Ben and Samuel this evening," Avery said as the last of the cake plates and silverware were washed and put away. They were alone in the kitchen. "He's going to be leaving very soon, now. Do you want to talk about it?"

"Not tonight Avery. I want this evening to end remembering the laughter and fun we just had. I don't want to think—" Her thought was interrupted as Samuel entered the kitchen.

"Mrs. Stuart. Please, may I ask a favor?"

Margaret dried her hands on a nearby dishtowel. "Certainly, Samuel. What?"

"Uh, getting my driver's license was to help you. Petrol is not plentiful with rationing. But I was—am—asking if I could use the automobile to take Ziva home. Her house is close." Hastily he added, "We ride the bus but it is late and there is no bus back here—"

"Samuel. It's alright. Yes, you may borrow the car. I'm going to need your help around here in the coming months. And Ziva, too. The roads are clear this evening, but be careful. Show me your right hand again?" she said teasingly.

Margaret was right, the roads were safe. The night air was cold and clear and the sky glittered with a billion ageless stars. The car's heater barely kept the cold at bay on such a short trip. Ziva shivered and pulled her heavy coat tighter around her shoulders. She glanced sideways at Samuel. His concentration couldn't be more intense. His hands were locked onto the steering wheel as if in a vice. He hadn't spoken but two words since they left. A startling revelation came to her. A few months ago—before the fire—she would have been annoyed at Samuel's lack of attention to her. Tonight it amused her. It made her proud that he was driving her home. This relationship was definitely different from those created by her obvious flirtations. She loved spending time with the Stuarts, and Avery. She peeked at him again. He was still concentrating.

Samuel knew he was neglecting Ziva but he didn't yet have the cavalier confidence to drive and converse at the same time. He took his eyes off the road to glance at her. She was smiling at him. *That's good, I guess. She looks like she's cold.* Quickly, he turned his eyes back to the road. *Sometimes I feel so protective of her. Sometimes I just enjoy her laughter and crazy outlook on things. And sometimes. . .* His thoughts trailed off as he brought the car to a stop at her house.

"Here we are. Will your mother be worried about you being out so late?" he asked.

"Not a chance. Honestly, she likes you *and* trusts you with her only daughter. Can't say that about every guy I've gone out with. Besides, our times together are not really "date" dates. You know what I mean? They're mostly times with the Stuarts or friends from the hospital."

"Ziva, now that the Cocoanut Grove is gone, have you given any thought to what you want to do?

"About?"

"Well, work or more school?"

"Monroe's enlisting and that means I need to be here for Mom. Anyway, girls aren't supposed to have "careers." She tried to make quotes in the air with her mittens but that didn't work. "Maybe there's something I can do."

"Like what?"

"I don't know yet. Can we go inside? I'm freezing!"

His initial intention was to stop her shivering. He slid from behind the wheel and pulled her close. She snuggled into his shoulder and without benefit of planning he kissed her. This wasn't their first kiss, or second. But it was a more intimate kiss. He pulled away. "What's wrong?" she asked. "I'm ok with a little necking."

"Necking? What is necking? Oh. Yes." *So like her*, he thought. "Nothing is wrong. We have more rules in my country. I don't want to disrespect you. Listen, Ziva. My residency is beginning soon. Ben is leaving and I will be busy w—"

"That's just your excuse. It's more than that, isn't it?" she insisted, interrupting. "It's because I'm not Jewish, and because my father. . ." she stopped. "Because I'm not Jewish you think I'm not good enough for you." She pulled further away from him, brow furrowed, eyes straight ahead, arms folded. "Do you want to stop seeing me?" she said, her tone sullen.

He ignored her last question, patiently explaining instead. "I could never think of you as not good enough. Don't you think like that either. Right now, across the ocean, some madman is killing us because he hates us; because he thinks we are . . . what is the word. . . inferior. So, no. I could never think of you—or anyone— as not being good enough." A silence fell between them for a minute. "Ziva, what I am wondering is if my Jewishness is more of a problem for you instead of me. How do you think of me?"

She was taken off guard for a moment by his question. She turned to look at him. "I just see you as Samuel. A guy who laughs with me—or sometimes at me. Someone who works really hard. A man I can talk to. You dress a bit weird, I'll admit. Someone who has a close connection to his family. I guess I'm jealous of that. I don't know who you were in your own country. I only know the American version."

The honest child-like simplicity of her answer touched him. "You're cold. We'll talk more another time." It was a silent walk to her door on the icy surface; his hand on her arm for protection. She turned toward him expecting a kiss.

He touched her cheek instead. "Go inside. Get warm."

Ziva didn't go inside immediately. She waved and watched until the auto rounded the corner. Their unusual conversation had unexpectedly dredged up unpleasant memories of her father, which made no sense to her. He had been the very opposite of Samuel. As she had so many other times, she wished for someone she could talk to. Someone who would understand and not judge.

CHAPTER 30

Boston, MA
February, 1942

T he repairs to the damaged hull of the Queen Mary had taken several weeks and the transition from the British Navy to the American Navy had been completed during that time. The Queen Mary was ready to carry her first load of American soldiers and would leave Boston soon.

The wind blew across the frigid pale water in the Boston harbor creating small peaks on its surface and its bluster whipped Ben's plaid scarf across his face and colored his cheeks bright pink. He placed his hand on his woolen cap securing its placement. It took him a moment to zero in on the Queen Mary. The transformation of the ship was startling. Every inch was now painted gray. Even the enormous black letters of her name were completely obliterated by gray paint. The three iconic red funnels now matched the gray smoke that would soon bellow out of them. In fact, England had dubbed her the 'grey ghost'. 'Grey' because of her color, 'ghost' because of her elusive ability to escape detection by the German U-boats.

He was meeting Captain Hawthorne for an orientation tour. All work on the hull damage was completed and the gangway was down. The Queen was days from leaving for Australia via New York and Rio de Janeiro. The papers were calling it the '40 days 40 nights journey'. It was a mystery how the papers knew the itinerary in light of its supposed secrecy. 'Loose lips sink ships' was a recent popular phrase that didn't seem to apply to a former cruise liner. He stepped on board and seeing no one, began wandering around.

Even though over two years had passed, he still remembered the ship. The stairway he had fallen down was just ahead. The round portholes were covered and bolted shut. He headed to the main dining room up a couple of decks. The empty decks, cold and windswept, gave him an eerie feeling. Even wisps of snow swirled around. No warm sunshine. No people laughing, lounging on the decks, sporting their colorful summer cruise wear.

As he continued walking, he noticed that the rich carpeting in the corridors had been removed exposing the bare floors. The expensive artwork on the walls was gone. The dining room opened before him. He took in a sharp breath. The first time he saw this room the opulence had made him catch his breath. The dramatic changes he saw now made him catch his breath again. All of those beautiful original paintings had been removed. The richly colored Persian carpets covering the parquet floor were gone. The parquet itself was covered over with what looked like a layer of ordinary large thin wood slabs. Ben recalled dancing with Kate that first night across this same floor. The tables and chairs, fine linens, fresh flowers and the crystal chandeliers were all gone, as well as most of the shiny brass. The only thing remaining that he remembered was the large map that marked the passage of the ship across the Atlantic. He continued climbing the silent stairs. It felt like a totally different ship to him now.

The Queen Mary had already been transporting British and Australian troops for over a year and the evidence of so many passengers was apparent. The remaining brass that had glowed from hours of polishing was dark with the oily tarnish of countless hands. The wood covering the dance floor had pieces of dried mud scattered among the scuff marks made by thousands of military boots. During the time in the harbor the crew was able to make headway on cleaning but there was wear and tear on the ship that would never go away. And more to come, he thought.

As he stood there his brain attempting to reconcile one picture in his mind with a completely different one in front of his eyes, Captain Hawthorne approached him from behind echoing his thoughts. "She's a different Queen, isn't she now," he said softly. He placed his hand on Ben's shoulder. He was no longer dressed in the white captain's uniform. He wore a heavy dark blue woolen uniform with two rows of white buttons down the front and rows of white stripes on the sleeves. His captain's cap matched.

Ben turned. "Hello, Captain." His astonished expression said it all. "I had no idea how different the ship would be. She is . . .unrecognizable."

"That was the plan. Come with me. I'll show you the medical quarters. I apologize for the delay but we are very short staffed just now. Most of our British crew returned to England when we docked in New York." They walked along the corridors, took the lift up to the Sports Deck with Ben shaking his head all the way at what had been done to this majestic ship.

"We have converted some of the engineer's quarters to be medical staff rooms. These rooms will be separate from the crew and the soldiers. Most of them are two to a room and most have their own head, uh, toilet to you. Bunk beds have been set up for the nursing staff in several of the suites. The first group will come on board in New York." They proceeded up another deck. "This is the infirmary"—he glanced at Ben, letting forth a slight chuckle—"which you may remember. And down this way is the isolation room."

"Isolation?" Ben quizzed

"It is a requirement on a ship this size. It's rarely used, but is there if needed. There are four beds available for quarantine should the need arise. The infirmary is well-equipped with the most common supplies—antibiotics, first aid, motion sickness and intestinal medicines. There is even surgical equipment, but not as complete as a hospital operating room."

"How many of us will there be?" Ben asked.

"Quite a large complement of nurses—maybe 20 or 25—all of them continuing on. Not as many physicians, like yourself. Probably only three of you. Most of the time it can be rather boring. There's something else I want to show you." They continued topside toward the bridge and wheelhouse and the scene that opened before Ben stopped him in his tracks. Along both sides of the ship were guns. Big guns and smaller guns. It had not occurred to him that the Queen Mary would be armed. He turned to the Captain. Again, his astonished expression said it all.

"Those big guns fore and aft are 40 mm cannons. Those 24 smaller guns are single-barrel cannons. Mounted near the aft funnel are two anti-aircraft launchers, 20mm and 50 calibers. Down below are depth charge bombs for those damn submarines and on both sides at the water line are torpedoes. Nobody's sinking *my* ship." Ben was still staring at the menacingly large cannon. The Captain drew his attention to three men working near the wheelhouse. "They are installing a medium range surface-search radar unit." The Captain walked over to the men, leaving Ben alone for a minute. The sight of all that firepower made him weak in the knees. Its presence brought him some comfort and then instantly took it away. If the crossings were as safe as he had been told, why was so much firepower necessary? *What would Mom think. . . if I tell her,* he thought. He swallowed. Besides weak knees, his stomach was queasy.

"Ready to go Ben?" the Captain had finished his conversation. They took the lift down to D Deck and were looking into the swimming pool. Instead of water it was filled with bunk beds stacked in layers six deep with narrow spaces between the rows for access. "These are used in shifts. There are more sleeping areas around the ship, but this is quite a sight, no?" the Captain said.

"Must get pretty noisy when hundreds of guys are snoring," laughed Ben.

The Captain laughed with him. "Aye. Add to that the maritime aromas of sweat, vomit, and cigarettes, and it can be most unpleasant around here. The Queen has always had a tendency to roll, but in the rougher winter waters she's worse. Even seasoned shipmen 'shoot the cat'." Ben looked puzzled. "Sorry chap. That's British slang for vomit."

Ben had a few more questions and then Captain Hawthorne walked him back to the gangway.

"We leave on February 21ˢᵗ at 0800 hours, Ben. We'll dock in New York and that's where we will load the first American soldiers and nurses and two more doctors plus our crew and staff. I'll save the rest of your indoctrination and you can hear it at that time. Our route, our destinations and arrivals, and who's on board cannot be disclosed to anyone, including family. All written communication will be censored. Between embarkations you will be allowed to contact family, if communications exist." He extended his hand. "Welcome aboard Dr. Stuart."

February 21, 1942

A sharp wind tossed around a few snowflakes that were leading the pack. The weather and the early hour had not kept curious Bostonians from watching the Queen Mary depart. A few newspaper reporters and, of course, family members and friends stood on the pier. Ben could still see Margaret, Samuel and Avery huddled together and he waved a final farewell. His eyes misted over remembering their earlier poignant goodbyes.

His emotions were swirling like the snowflakes in the air as the Queen Mary was readied to leave the Boston harbor. He loved his family and this had been a tortured decision. But once made, he knew it was the right one. *Mom will be alright. Yeah, she'll be okay. She has Samuel and Avery.* He was surprised at the sense of adventure and excitement building in him. It felt like the adrenalin rush from college just before a boxing match. He had been asked if he was afraid. He answered *No. Not really*. With all that firepower and such a fast ship he had complete confidence that the Captain and the Grey Ghost would bring him home again.

The Queen was pulled away as the rest of the snowflake pack caught up and began descending on the Boston skyline shrouding it in a white blanket. Even the familiar lighthouse appeared ghostly. Ben looked back as the great ship began her first journey as an American transport ship. "Forty days, forty nights," he whispered to himself.

CHAPTER 31

T he meticulous precision of the military was everywhere on
Pier 90. Berthed on one side of the Queen Mary was a
battleship and on the other was a destroyer. Planes could
be spotted overhead as they patrolled the New York harbor,
another layer of protection for The Queen Mary and her
entourage. Army trucks, one after another, bloated with supplies
crisscrossed the docks. Procurement had been working night and
day calculating and purchasing adequate provisions for forty days
for over 9,000 troops and nearly 1,000 crew. Over the course of
the afternoon Ben watched as truck after truck unloaded 15,000
pounds of bacon and ham, a ton of cheese, 90,000 pounds of
potatoes and so much coffee that when brewed he was certain it
would fill the swimming pool. One truck pulled up loaded with
stack upon stack of life vests. Hundreds more crewmembers came
on board, settled in and received instructions and work schedules.
Nearly all of the activity was on the lower decks, leaving the upper
decks relatively quiet.

As Ben was returning to his room, he saw a large man staring
at a paper in his hand and shaking his head. He appeared lost. He
caught Ben's eye and approached asking, "Excuse me sir, can you
help me?"

"I can try," Ben answered. As he walked closer he could see

the man was maybe fifteen or more years his senior. His appearance, though clean, was a bit shabby. Run down shoes, ill-fitting overcoat. And he was black. The dark eyes behind the rimless glasses looked kind enough but perplexed at the moment. "What seems to be the problem?"

His diction was good, but the southern accent was obvious. "Sir, I'm unable to locate the deck this room is on," and he handed Ben the paper repurposing that hand to rub his closely cropped frizzled hair.

Giving the paper a quick glance, Ben said, "There must be a mistake. These are the medical rooms and you probably want the crew quarters. Follow me I'll show—"

"Young man." Pulling himself to his full height of over six feet and looking Ben straight in the eye, he said, "My name is Dr. Joseph Elias Ramsey and I am indeed looking for the medical rooms."

Embarrassment causes the sympathetic nervous system to widen the blood vessels in the face. It's part of the "fight or flight" reflex. Ben's fair complexion was a perfect canvas for this phenomenon. The pink began in his ears then spread to his cheeks finally traveling down his neck. Attempting a brave recovery, he managed, "I'm on my way there right now. Please, follow me. . .sir. . .Dr. Ramsey."

"You're not the first and probably not the last," grumbled the doctor under his breath as he bent down and picked up his baggage.

"Uhm, maybe I should introduce myself?" Ben queried as they moved toward one of the elevators.

Dinner was served at 1900 hours. Days ago when Ben had viewed the immense dining room in Boston it had been empty. Now long rows of tables filled the room leaving only enough room between them to pass through. Troops would be arriving tomorrow so dinner tonight was a relatively quiet affair including just deck stewards, management, the Captains, the bridge crew and the medical staff. The majority of the crew took their meals on the lower decks on a strict schedule.

No flowers. No candles. No silver or china. No menu choices. Everyone was served the same meal. Ben discovered that each one aboard was responsible for keeping and cleaning his own table service. Special equipment had been installed in nearby lounge areas for troops and staff to assist the kitchen staff by washing their own dishes.

Captain Hawthorne was speaking. "Tomorrow when the troops arrive I will address everyone and explain regulations and lifeboat drills." He was still wearing the dark, navy blue woolen uniform with the white buttons down the front. He turned to the older man on his right wearing an identical uniform. "I'd like to introduce you to Captain Merriwether. He and I will share the captain's duties during this long voyage. I'll let him tell you a little about himself."

"Thank ye', Captain. Most people call me Merry," he said addressing those around him. "I'm a Scotsman bloke through and through from a long line 'a seafarin' men. If the name doesn't sound like a Scot to you that's because me great-grand pappy left England for Scotland in his youth and stayed. Confirmed bachelor, I am. Hired on with Cunard about eight years ago and worked my way up to the bigger ships. This's me first time with the Mary. She's a mighty one, she is. And brave. It's an honor to be her Captain during these ominous times."

The Scottish accent brought to mind Dr. McHenry, the physician who had treated him after his trip and fall. *Maybe he's the third physician joining us,* he wondered. "Merry" had a smile to match his name, Ben noticed, and his stubby hands were never still. They rearranged the silverware; they strayed to his long sideburns, giving them a loving touch; and they tried but failed to tame his thick eyebrows. He had an unidentified quality that reminded Ben of Laura's father.

The two captains left early, but others remained, getting acquainted, new staff posing questions, veterans giving answers, each man pondering the days of work ahead.

Ben turned his attention to Dr. Ramsey. He was sipping the last of his coffee. Ben cleared his throat. "I'm very sorry about earlier. It's just that I—"

"—have never seen a Negro doctor before. Correct?" Dr. Ramsey finished for him placing his cup in front of him.

Ben nodded, then asked, "Where did you get your medical degree?"

"I went to school in Savannah, but completed my internship and residency in a small hospital in the Florida panhandle. It took longer than usual because I was working in between saving money to finish."

"I've always wanted to visit Florida. Where were you working before coming here?"

"I converted a small house next to mine into a hospital. I left it in capable hands. It isn't easy being a Negro doctor in the South. White folks don't trust your abilities, so you treat mostly colored folks, and most are glad to have a Negro doctor. But they whisper among themselves that maybe I'm not trained as well as a white doctor. Colored folks are uncomfortable around me because I'm 'edjeecated'—their word," he said with a laugh. "And the white folks see me as part of the colored community. Either way, people never let me forget my race. It can be very lonely at times."

Ben was watching Dr. Ramsey as he told more of his story, recognizing that this proud man had led a complicated and difficult life. Ben's life in the social structure of Boston had not included people of color. He had read about the history of the south; but they were just stories to him—read and forgotten. This man had lived them, and not forgotten.

"I didn't intend to ramble on so. Guess I should head off to bed. Early day tomorrow," Dr. Ramsey finished. He pushed his chair away from the table, stood and stretched his thick arms and neck.

Ben stood, too. "Dr. Ramsey—"

"Please, call me Dr. Joe. That's what my patients call me."

"Dr. Joe, then. I'm glad we'll be working together." The two doctors shook hands. Ben felt like he should say something else, but didn't know what it was, so he simply said, "Try to get a good night's sleep."

"Right. Don't think sleep will be a problem. It was a long trip getting here. Good night." He was yawning as he left the dining room.

There were no windows in Ben's room, so when he opened his eyes he didn't know if it was morning or the middle of the night. He felt disoriented. Checking the windup alarm clock beside his bed he discovered it was 6:10 a.m. There were two beds in the room and he rolled over to see if his roommate was still sleeping. The bed had not been slept in. Puzzling.

He was fortunate to have a private head—bathroom—and quickly completed his morning hygiene. His stomach rumbled and he started to leave in search of breakfast, returning immediately to retrieve his tableware. "Gotta' remember that," he said out loud, placing them in his white medical jacket pocket.

He opened his door, stepped into the corridor and it felt like a movie reel that had gone berserk. To his untrained eye the scene was chaotic. Clattering carts were pushed along, piled with toilet paper and various supplies. Stewards and Deck Supervisors, voices raised, were giving instructions. He dodged crewmembers carrying armloads of towels and washcloths to be distributed around the ship. Placards and charts were being put in place. Canteen areas were designated and stocked where soldiers could buy anything from shaving cream to Coca-Cola. Every square inch of the ship was being readied for the trainloads of passengers en route.

He grabbed coffee and a sweet roll from the dining room buffet and drifted to where he could see the dock. The morning was cold, but clear, and the sky had brightened considerably. Gangways were down at every ship entrance, surrounded by stacks of bright orange life vests. Red Cross workers were passing out donuts. Crewmembers, some sipping hot coffee, were milling around each entry point with boxes of red, white, and blue colored buttons at their feet. He remembered seeing a large blue poster on the wall by the swimming pool. He saw no soldiers, but based on the level of activity he surmised they were due to show up soon.

"Ah, there you are, Ben." The voice behind him belonged to Captain Hawthorne. "I thought you might be here. I need to tell you something," he said, then stopped to answer a question from the dining room manager. "We've had a bit of bad luck. Do you remember Dr. McHenry? He planned to join us yesterday. It seems he slipped in his hotel room and broke his hip. He's in hospital and will have a bit of recovery ahead of him and definitely won't be aboard for this little jaunt."

"Who's replacing him?" Ben asked.

"Well, that's just it, isn't it. Sorry, old chap, it's much too late to find a replacement. It will be just you and Dr. Ramsey. We will have a bevy of Army nurses on board to lend a hand. These things happen. If you see Dr. Ramsey before I do, could you let him know? Carry on." Ben stood there speechless as the Captain hurried off to deal with another problem.

"Great. Just great," he grumbled and realizing how unprofessional that sounded—after all it was an accident—he looked around to see if anyone had heard him.

The first busload of the 9,000 plus troops began arriving an hour later. All day large buses shuttled between the railroad station and ship delivering sons, husbands, fathers and sweethearts to fates unknown. They trudged up the gangplank, each with a musette bag on his back; a gas mask dangling around each neck; and a canteen crisscrossing each chest. Before embarking every man was given a life vest and a colored button indicating which of the ship's zone he was berthed in, red, white or blue. They were told to wear the button at all times and NEVER enter a different zone.

It was near the end of the day and Ben had been watching for several minutes when he noticed a young woman struggling up a gangway with a heavy metal suitcase. In addition to the gas mask and musette bag, she had a brown purse slung over her shoulder and a flashlight was attached to her web belt. Behind her were six or seven other young women working their way aboard. Must be some of the nurses, he thought.

The public address system came to life with a sharp crackle calling everyone to attention. "Gentlemen and Ladies, this is your captain. Please give me your attention. Welcome aboard the Queen Mary, the finest luxury ship to ever sail the Atlantic. We seem to have overbooked this voyage by several thousand"— laughter spread around the ship—" and that will require some changes. You are going to have the rare opportunity to help manage the day to day operations on this big ship. More about that in a minute.

"You were given a life vest—or as you refer to them a 'Mae West'—and a red, white or blue button before boarding and were directed to one of those colored areas. The life vest is to be worn at all times during the day and kept by your bunk while sleeping. Keep your canteen filled and your survivor rations with you at all times. Your zone color is to be displayed at all times and you are to remain in that zone except for meals or on deck for fresh air. All other colored zones are strictly out of bounds. And don't even think about switching buttons with someone else. If you did not receive or—sadly—have already lost your button, see one of our crewmembers stationed throughout the ship. They will assist you.

"After the embarkation is completed, we will conduct a required safety drill. Boat drills can be called by the klaxon at any time of the day—every day. You must go to your designated areas as quickly as possible. You will never know when it is the real thing. Now, a word about the lifeboats. Because of our 'overbooking', the demand exceeds the supply. But you needn't be concerned because this ship is so fast German U-Boats cannot catch her. She is so fast she can even outrun their torpedoes." A loud cheer went up. "And, of course, you will have that lovely orange life vest on and your canteen full. We've been making these runs for many months now and haven't been shot at once." Another loud cheer. "And we intend to keep it that way. That's why the following regulations are mandatory.

"The Queen is a 'dry' ship. No alcohol will be served on board and none allowed to be brought onboard. There will be no swearing, obscene or profane language used while on my ship. Gambling is also forbidden." Groaning and moaning replaced the earlier cheers.

"A blackout will exist every night we are at sea. That means no smoking. No flashlights. No light of any kind. And no radios. Also, German U-boats have been known to watch for debris left behind by transport ships. So *never* at any time throw anything overboard. No cigarettes, no paper of any kind and no people. This ship will not stop for anyone going overboard. We will not risk the safety of thousands for one whose chance of surviving a 50-foot fall into icy water is unlikely.

"Now let's talk about something more pleasant. Food. Our culinary staff is here to cater to your every desire, twice a day. Yes sir, that's true. Just as long as your desire matches what's on the plate. Along with your zone designation card you also received a smaller colored button. That is your mealtime color. You must wear it to the dining room. Charts are on display around the ship with mealtime details. Now, think about this, my fine folks. Our kitchen must prepare at least 20,000 sometimes as many as 30,000 meals each day we're at sea for as many as 2,000 at one time. It becomes obvious that your meal times must be strictly adhered to in order to get everyone fed on schedule. Again, no switching buttons. In addition to your dining pleasure, Canteens have been set up in each zone stocked with Coca-Cola, snacks and limited personal hygiene items. These are available for purchase.

"As I mentioned a moment ago, previous guests aboard the Queen Mary only got to lounge around, listen to music, play shuffleboard, etc. But you, lads and lassies, will have the pleasure of *working* while on board. There will be no mess hall this evening because of the embarkation; so, you get this evening off. In the morning you will be given tableware. It will be your responsibility to bring it to the dining room on C Deck, clean it afterward and store it in your bunk area. If you share your bunk area, work it out. Shifts from each of the three zones will be organized and those fatigues will assist the kitchen and cleanup crews. Your bunk area is to be cleaned each morning and ready for the daily inspection by 0700 hours. You will still have considerable free time to play cards, read or write letters. Mail will be censored, of course. Movies will be shown on occasion and if any of you have a talent you would like to share, let us know. In the past we have had impromptu entertainment.

"There is a barber shop on board with five barbers. Our infirmary is well stocked and is located on "B" Deck. If you feel ill or are injured you will need permission from your appointed Deck Commander to leave your zone and you must be accompanied there by a nurse or physician. Physicians and nurses are nearby at all hours of the day and night.

"One last thing. I call upon all officers and men to obey my orders to the letter. My job is to bring this ship and you men safely to port. The enemy will do everything in its power to bring down this ship. Submarines will trail us and aircraft will hunt for us. We've seen it on previous trips and expect to see it on this one. That's why these regulations must be adhered to with no exceptions.

"This announcement will be repeated again after embarkation

is complete and at that time you will be instructed where to go for the safety drill. Welcome aboard, everyone, and thank you for cruising with us." That last comment generated a few grins and chuckles.

Everyone was on board by 1900 hours. The safety and boat drill was over and The Queen Mary's massive engines came to life. Thousands of men and women of the United States Armed Forces remained on deck waving goodbye with high-spirited cheers and whistles that the wind whisked away into the cold night. As Ben stood there, shoulder to shoulder with these young men, he was overcome with a deep sense of pride. He looked around the packed deck. In spite of the boisterous atmosphere and the pretense of fearlessness, one common unspoken thought hung in the air like a hovering gray ghost. *Which of us will not be coming back? Am I one of them?* As the great ship gained speed, catching starlight in its wake, those thousands of souls grew silent as they watched the darkness slowly engulf the Statue of Liberty. Now it felt real.

The second night out, Ben had fallen asleep, finally getting used to the small bed and rolling motion of the ship when a loud boom penetrated his slumber. He jerked awake, stubbed his toe getting out of bed in the darkness and hopped around putting on his shoes. *My God, we've been hit!* he thought. He searched for his Mae West in the dark —finally found it and fumbled it on. Throwing open his cabin door he rushed into the corridor only to bump into a room steward. "What happened? Are we going down?" he shouted.

Reuben (he found out later) calmly took his elbow and led him back into his room. "Sir, Sir, calm down. It's alright. They regularly fire the cannon to test and clean it. That's what you heard. Everything's fine." Reuben closed the door and left. When his knees stopped shaking, Ben wondered: *Why in the world do they do it at night?"*

CHAPTER 32

Vilna, Lithuania
February, 1942

"No! No! You can't take him!" Ana screamed. A meaty hand forcefully slapped her across the face and she slammed against the wall.

"Ana, Ana," Jonah said and helped her to her feet. "They just want to ask me some questions. I'll be back. It's okay. It's okay." She wrapped her arms around his waist but, again, the German soldat brusquely shoved her aside.

"*Sich Beeilen!*" Hurry up! the German grunted and propelled Jonah with the butt of his rifle through the door. Ana sank to her knees, sobbing. Certain she would never see her husband again.

What should have been familiar sights to Jonah as the German car sped through the streets were instead alien. Jewish men and women were no longer allowed on the streets. Businesses were shuttered and closed. German soldiers in their gray uniforms and black jackboots smoking their beloved cigarettes, rifles nearby, loitered in doorways and on corners, watching. Schoolyards were deserted. German vehicles dominated the streets. Jonah had asked but his escorts refused to tell him where they were going. He had reassured Ana, but he knew that many Jewish men had been taken away and executed.

The Horch 901 pulled to a stop before a two-story brick building. The warm air hit him in the face as he was led into the building. It felt good in spite of his uneasiness. They followed the corridor to a back corner office and went inside. A large white flag emblazoned with the symbol of German nationalist pride, the Hakenkreus, or hooked cross, better known throughout the world as the swastika, hung on the wall behind an ornate wooden desk. A very large man was seated there and looked up as they entered. Jonah's escorts snapped their heels and gave the German salute, "Heil Hitler!" The German officer returned his attention to the papers before him. He wrinkled his nose as if the black mustache was tickling it and tapped the page as he read. The patches on his uniform revealed to Jonah that he was a Major and the assignment of an office indicated he had significant authority over Vilna.

Ignoring the courtesy of an introduction he said, "You are Jonah Dressler?" Jonah nodded. "Speak. I did not hear you."

"Yes, I am Jonah Dressler."

"Are you the Jonah Dressler who was head of an engineering firm in Vilna?"

"I am."

"What kind of engineering did you do?"

Jonah was considering what this man's purpose might be. There wasn't a hair on his head or bearded face that wanted to help these men, but he was astute enough to know that his knowledge of the infrastructure of Vilna might save his and Ana's life. After all the Germans were living here now and needed sewage and water and roads for their vehicles.

"We designed most of the sewage system, did structural design of many buildings, bridges, built roads. We worked with the Soviets when they dug the huge pits in Ponar Forest for gas storage." The Major studied Jonah as he talked, and Jonah studied the Major as well, detecting if not a flicker of respect at least less hostility than usual.

"We will move you. There is a camp on Subacious Street. We have placed many workers there such as yourself. It is run by a Wehrmacht Engineering Unit. We may have need of your services or possibly other work you can do. Are you married?"

"Yes."

"Children?"

"No." *Fortunately, far away from here*, he thought.

The Major addressed the soldiers in the room. "Take his family, too."

The probability that his employees had been killed was strong, but if he could give them a chance. . .so he asked, "If I give you the names of my workers could you have them moved there, also? They are hard workers." The flicker Jonah saw a moment ago was gone.

"We already have their names, Herr Dressler." Addressing the men beside Jonah he said, "Return him to his flat and wait while they pack their belongings. Then take them to HKP 562. That is all."

As they climbed into the vehicle, Jonah prayed that this move would be good thing.

Ana heard Soske stifle a sob. The woman's depression was worse. She fluctuated between crying and sleeping. Ana scooted on the floor next to her and gently touched her shoulder. "Can I help?" she asked. Soske shook her head and turned away drying her eyes on her full skirt. The large brown sweater she wore was long and fell below her waist. A dark red kerchief was around her head. Ana had a suspicion. "You are with child?" she whispered. Soske's hands flew to her mouth. Her eyes full of fear furtively swept the small room. "No, don't say that!" she shouted in a whisper. Ana knew it was true. And she also knew why Soske had denied it. A few weeks ago the Germans had posted a decree forbidding any births in the ghetto. Pregnant women were forced to obtain abortions at the hospital. If a baby was found, it was killed along with the mother.

"When?" Ana persisted.

Soske's searching brown eyes reached the depths of Ana's

heart. Mother to mother. Soske placed Ana's palm against her belly as she felt for the baby's kick. It was futile to deny it. If Ana had guessed. others would, too. Soske drew a quivering breath. "Soon. Maybe a few weeks. You won't say anything? I did not show much when we came. But now. . ." The tears overflowed again creating tiny rivers in the deep worry lines that were out of place on so young a face. "What am I to do? No husband to help me. No one."

"Shush," Ana said pulling Soske into her arms. She desperately wanted to reassure her that it would be okay, but Ana could not see how. The Germans controlled every minute of their lives. The two women sat there on the cold floor rocking each other. And that's where they were when Jonah returned.

"Ana, we must gather our clothes and bags. We are being moved to another camp. They are waiting for us."

"Why?" Where? Just us?" Ana's questions came in a flurry.

"Ana, hurry! They are waiting for us. I'll explain later."

"Jonah, listen. I can't leave now. Soske is. . . I can't leave her. I can't."

"Ana. We don't have a choice about these things. They say go, we go."

"She can go with us then. I'm not leaving her." Ana's lips formed a firm thin line, her arms still around Soske. Her husband was well aware that when his wife's stubborn will took over, reasoning with her went out the window. Soske was watching him, tears still staining her cheeks; Rebekah clinging to her mother's skirt. Hadn't he just made the same plea for his own workers?

"Let me think while you gather our things." He looked at the young girl leaning against his wife. "Soske, you too."

He scratched his beard, deep in thought. They had lost so much. Their home, his business, their freedom and security. And now this: Ana asking him to put their lives at risk for a young girl they barely knew. . .and she had a child. Ana the rescuer. He looked at Ana then, who had begun collecting their clothes, blankets, personal items. Was he a good husband if he deliberately put her life in danger? But wasn't she the one asking him to do that? And weren't they already in danger every day anyway? He knew her. There must be something she hadn't told him.

One of the German soldiers appeared in the doorway. "What is taking so long? Sich Beeilen!"

Jonah knelt down to help the women and whispered in Yiddish. "Soske, pick up Rebekah. When we start toward the door, follow us. But don't say anything." Jonah stood and confidently faced the man. "We are ready." And the three of them, Soske carrying Rebekah, walked toward the door.

"What is this? You were asked about family. Only the wife is permitted to go with you."

Jonah moved closer. "The Commandant said to take my family. This is my wife's sister and child. I wasn't asked about them, but they are family." Jonah looked the German in the eyes as he lied to him. *The Torah taught that God had permitted lying at times to save lives*, he thought. He held his breath. Jews had no rights now. If this soldier decided Jonah was lying, they could all be shot where they stood. The Nazi standing before him had all the power. He could make Soske stay in the ghetto and maybe Ana, too and force Jonah to leave alone with him. This was dangerous ground. They were taking a huge risk. Thousands had been shot to death for no reason. The soldier stood his ground, his boot-clad feet spread. At first he seemed undecided about Jonah's demands. Then Rebekah began to whimper, her small hands clutching her ragged cloth doll closer. The German's mouth tightened, his head tipped and he slowly raised his rifle toward the group. He stared at Jonah for a full minute all the time training the rifle on Jonah's head. To Ana's credit she remained steady and moved closer to her "sister". Then suddenly their military escort raised his rifle and used it to motion the group through the door. The Major had given instructions that family could accompany this man and he was trained to follow instructions. "Gehen! Go. Keep the child quiet or I will silence her permanently."

The two soldiers rode in the front and the three adults were in the rear, Rebekah on Ana's lap, her head pressed into Ana's shoulder partly to shelter her against the biting wind and partly to muffle her crying. All of their meager belongings were either tossed in the back or on their laps. Jonah was thankful for his woolen coat and buttoned the top button as the cold air rushed around them. Soske kept her head bowed, not daring to say a word. The pounding in her chest began to lessen. She wasn't certain she wanted to go where they were going, but she was certain she didn't want Ana to leave her alone. Ana's presence comforted her; so, she kept quiet, fearful if she said anything at all it would give the German a reason to shoot all of them, including Rebekah.

As the car navigated the brick roads, they were astonished at the changes. The only people on the streets or in horse drawn carts were Lithuanian residents or German soldiers. Jewish residents going about their daily business were nowhere to be seen. As the car sped along through the ghetto they saw apartments designed for families of six or eight crowded with hundreds of Jews. Mothers with small children huddled together in the frigid morning waiting to use the outside toilets and the communal bath. Most of their male relatives had either been shot or forced into labor camps.

Jonah spoke in Yiddish to Ana and Soske. "I was told that a five-member *Judenrat*, demanded by the Nazis, was established weeks ago." The vehicle noise and wind prevented the two Germans in the front from hearing him even if by some chance they understood Yiddish. "This governing council is controlling sanitation and food rationing in the ghettos. I've heard that one of the doctors has been producing vitamins for the children. I'll try to get some for Rebekah."

"Vitamins? How?" Ana asked as the wind carried her words sideways.

"The doctor sharing our flat told me they're made using waste from a local brewery."

"So the children get 'shickered'?" Ana gasped.

187

In spite of their situation, Jonah smiled at his wife. "No, Ana. The vitamins do not cause children to be drunk." They were passing a small wooden building. Smoke was pouring out a vent in the tin roof. "What is that place?" Ana asked.

He knew about this building. "That is one of six 'teahouses'. The Sanitary-Epidemiological Section created by the council has established them. They provide hot water for cooking, cleaning, laundry and washing children. You can also get a cup of hot tea there. If we survive long enough we may be visiting one ourselves."

The car slowed and a strong vile odor caused the passengers to catch their breaths. A horse-drawn cart piled high with human excrement was exiting one of the apartments. The driver pulled up on the reins stopping the horses just as the motorcar passed. The outdoor toilets in these old apartments were not designed for the sudden increase of human waste and garbage and had rapidly become a health hazard. The *Judenrat* had ingeniously devised a plan with nearby non-Jewish farmers to remove the waste and garbage and use it as manure and livestock feed.

Around the next corner the military car jerked to a sudden stop in front of a brick apartment building similar to the one they had left. Their escort jumped down. "Aussteigen!" Get out." he said as he opened the door. Ana handed Rebekah to Soske and began lugging their belongings from the car. They were here. It's just they didn't know where 'here' was. Or why.

CHAPTER 33

~~~~

Aboard the Queen Mary
March, 1942

The Statue of Liberty had disappeared three days ago and the long boring days at sea stretched ahead like the blue horizon. At this moment the Queen Mary was headed for Trinidad and the sparkling azure water, clear skies, and balmy breeze were straight out of a travel brochure.

The two doctors met with the group of nurses who were traveling to various battlefields. While on board the ship they would be on duty to help treat the troops, so the group had worked out a schedule.

With Captain Hawthorne's permission Ben and Dr. Ramsey were now enjoying the spectacular view from the wheelhouse. They watched a large tanker about eight miles astern moving away from them. Ben was excitedly sharing his limited knowledge of the equipment and procedures of the bridge, intentionally giving Dr. Ramsey the impression that he could fill in for a crewmember anytime they needed him. He explained the communication system between the wheelhouse and the crew on the lower decks. He pointed out the navigation maps and charts and the immaculate brass machinery. Ben's attention was so focused on giving Dr. Ramsey the "royal" tour that he failed to notice Captain Hawthorne's concentration as he read over a wireless transmission.

Ben turned to ask the Captain a question and caught his stern and thoughtful expression. After a brief discussion with his First Officer and the navigation officer the Captain signaled to Ben.

"We have a bit of a problem. We just had reports of considerable U-boat activity in and around Trinidad so your visit here must be cut short." He directed his next comments to his First Officer. "I have decided to change course. We will sail west of Cuba then east into the Caribbean and enter the wide Atlantic via the Anegada Passage. We'll then pick up speed. I'll make one quick announcement before maintaining radio silence until we're safely out into open water." He reached for the switch and turned on the ship's communication system. The now familiar crackling of the intercom system signaled news coming and the soldiers paused to listen.

"Attention, please. This is your Captain. Several U-boats have been sighted nearby. I'm not particularly concerned because our ship is considerably faster than any German U-Boat and their torpedoes. However, there is always the outside chance they could get lucky. In addition to our normal sentries, all passengers should spend some time on deck scanning the water for enemy U-Boats. Try to remain as silent as 10,000 passengers can. Remember the rules we went over earlier. If you see anything suspicious point it out to a crewmember who will communicate the information to the wheelhouse. Be alert. The life boat drill that was scheduled for this morning has been cancelled."

Craps games, letter writing, etc. were abandoned in light of this news. The boredom that had been settling in was replaced by the excitement of actually seeing a U-boat. The surface radar was searching and soon hundreds of men and women, eyes straining into the blue waters, crowded on deck, hoping to see a submarine. But not one caught sight of the two U-Boats following the Queen Mary as she made her way toward the wide Atlantic Ocean.

An incoming Morse code alerted the bridge. At the same time three flares could be seen off the stern. The Communications

Officer translated aloud the message before handing it to the Captain. He said:

> *'Pan-pan, pan-pan, pan-pan. All stations, all stations, all stations. This is the BTC British Emperor. Position is 21.4550 o N and 71.7990 o W. Sustained moderate damage to bow. Minor injuries to crew. Returning to Key West. Suspect U-Boat attack. Maintain extreme vigilance.'*

The Captain nodded to the Communications Officer and immediately he shouted into the communication tube to alert the boiler room. "Pour on the juice. Full speed ahead." For the next several hours as the great ship gathered speed and circled through the Caribbean islands, sentries stood lookout with powerful glasses. Machine guns and cannons were manned continuously. Hundreds of soldier passengers scoured the waters with binoculars or used their hands to shield their eyes from the sun as they searched in vain for U-boats on the prowl. An ally ship had been fired upon. They were no longer onboard waiting *to go* to war. It was here. The day had become less boring.

Ben and Dr. Ramsey were exiting the wheelhouse when they heard the message. It occurred to them at the same moment. The tanker that had passed them a few minutes earlier was the same one issuing the distress signal. Once again Ben was reminded how the beautiful panorama they had enjoyed moments earlier could quickly become menacing. He had felt like this when he heard about the sinking of the Athenia. The Queen Mary was a large and politically valuable target considering her speed and precious cargo of vast numbers of soldiers. Germany would score big if they could sink her. He had assured his Mom before he left Boston that the risk to the British ship was really quite small. But was it?

Six days Later

It was a busy morning in the infirmary treating a case of conjunctivitis, or pink eye. While generally not a serious condition, which clears up on its own, any outbreak would bear watching. If bacterial in nature, blindness could occur.

The ship was docked in Rio de Janeiro, Brazil, and Ben and Tom had gone ashore to pick up medical supplies—a liberty not extended to the other crew members. Ben took a deep whiff of the salty sea breeze so welcome after the stench aboard the ship. The two doctors didn't realize just how unpleasant the smells aboard the ship had become until they walked down the ramp into the early morning unspoiled Brazilian air. The Queen Mary had been sailing for days now with thousands of men and women denied the luxury of bathing and changing clothes. A slight flaw in the design of the ship made her pitch unmercifully, causing hundreds of soldiers to hurl over the sides of the ship—if they were lucky to make it to an open deck. Cruise ships are designed with an adequate ventilation system for the usual number of passengers and crew, but these voyages far exceeded *usual*. When the body odors of thousands of sweaty, closely packed humans mingled with stale cigarette smoke and other delightful fragrances, the result was unpleasant. Maybe the term 'rank and file' was more accurately 'rank and vile.'

The two purchased some medical supplies and had them delivered back to the ship. Then, it was a short bus ride to Mount Corcovado where the nearly 100-foot high statue of the Christ the Redeemer resided, built ten years earlier. They bought empenadas and pastels from a street vendor and drank *caldo de cana,* a sugarcane juice drink as they strolled along one of Brazil's most beautiful beaches, becoming known as Ipanema.

Joseph Ramsey had grown up on the Gulf of Mexico, living

in the Florida panhandle for several years. He had already experienced white sugar sand and warm turquoise water. Ben's childhood memories were of the eastern seaboard with rocky cliffs, crashing surf and icy water. This looked like paradise to him. A March day in Brazil signaled autumn, but the day was still very warm and sunny. The two walked barefoot along the pristine beach, pant legs rolled up leaving behind footprints in the warm sand whose brief lives vanished in the gentle surge of seawater. They walked and talked sharing stories.

"What made you decide to leave the clinic and do this?" Ben asked.

"A couple of reasons. There are many Negro soldiers going to war, fighting for this country but feeling they are only 'half-citizens'. In June of last year President Roosevelt issued an Executive Order saying that *there shall be no discrimination in the employment of workers in defense industries or government because of race, creed, color, or national origin.* I wanted to test that new rule. And then in some ways the plight of the Jews is not unlike what colored folks have faced in the South and still do today. Jews are killed for being Jews. I have family members who were killed for no reason other than they had black skin. Blacks have been used as slaves until they dropped dead from heat exhaustion pickin' cotton in white men's fields. Their hands raw and bleeding, many as young as ten years old. This country already went to war once over slavery, doubt if they're gonna do it again, even though injustice and murder because of skin color still exists. Now the United States has gone to war to fight injustice and the murder of Jews. Maybe someday this country will wake up to the fact that the United States is not 'lily white' when it comes to race and begin treating the Negro race as equals just as the founders of our country declared over 160 years ago. If I can't fight for my own race, thought I could help in the fight for the Jews. Sorry, but you asked."

"I had no idea those things still existed in the South," Ben said.

The two were quiet then. The warm sun on their faces, the

silky sand on bare feet, and the salty breeze flavored with the tropical fragrance of the sea filled their senses as they continued along the beach.

The glorious day made Ben wish for Laura, and a deep sigh escaped. The stubborn ache refused to heal. Maybe it never would, he thought. He had grieved when his sister, Claire, had died. He was much younger then. In retrospect, his parents' grief may have affected him as much as his own. It was upsetting to see his father cry. And then came the loss of his father. Although it had been over six years now, sometimes without warning he'd feel the loss again, like now. There was so much he wanted to tell him. Each loss unique—faceted by age, relationship and circumstances. And always faced alone.

"Everything okay, Ben?" Dr. Ramsey asked, catching Ben's sudden mood shift. "I'm sorry if I put a damper on our day."

Caught off guard, Ben rubbed his hand over his eyes. "Huh? Oh, no. It's not you. Something else. I'll tell you about it sometime."

Joe Ramsey understood pain very well—not just physical pain but emotional pain as well. He saw it flicker in Ben's face just now. "Whenever you want," he said kindly and the two of them continued their leisurely stroll along the white sandy beach.

While on the ship the war was on everyone's mind every minute of every day. But here, on this beach, to the two doctors, it seemed a million miles away. But it wasn't.

The Italian Count Edmondo di Robilant sat at his ornate desk in his office in the Brazilian capitol. One of his aides had delivered a cup of sweet fragrant Brazilian espresso. The Count's dark Italian features were full of amazement as he scanned the document in front of him. "Unbelievable," he breathed in Italian. As he continued to read it became clearer that this was a bit of luck he could turn into a financial windfall.

"I need to relay this immediately," he said to the empty

room." He thought back to the interception of a coded message several weeks ago. It had resulted in the sinking of a merchant marine ship carrying supplies out of Rio de Janeiro, Sao Paulo and Recife. "But that is small potatoes compared to this. This is big. The German espionage ring operating here included this notable Italian and they were going to be very happy when they heard from him." He sipped the hot espresso and pressed the buzzer on the corner of his desk. "Frederich, get me the German ambassador immediately. I have some very good news for him."

Robilant stared out at the Rio street scene as he waited to be connected to the German embassy. In the distance he could see a large favela. He had little compassion for the hundreds of poor Brazilians crowded into these makeshift communities. "Good afternoon, Ambassador." After a few brief pleasantries Edmondo arrived at the purpose of his call. "You won't believe this. I have in my possession the itinerary of the Queen Mary and it appears to be accurate since there is a very large gray ship now anchored in the Rio port as indicated in this document. According to this paper, she is scheduled for departure at 22:00 tonight. Can you radio the information *immediately*? I have knowledge of a "wolfpack" trolling the waters just off the coast."

"Good work, comrade," said the ambassador. You are correct. There *is* a fleet of U-Boats nearby. We keep a line of communication open to them at all times. I'll radio them without delay. We've got her this time."

Thirty minutes later on board the Queen Mary, a Morse code message began its staccato transmission. The Communications Officer sat down to transcribe it. His heart was pounding as he raced to the captain's quarters and knocked on the door. "Captain. Are you in there? We have an urgent message."

The door swung open and the Captain stood there in his underwear. Both captains had been getting extra rest while in port. He reached for his trousers, slipping them on in one quick movement. "Read it to me."

The officer caught his breath and read the transcribed message: "Allied intelligence intercepted coded message to German U-boat commander. Queen Mary itinerary has been compromised. Leave immediately."

Captain Hawthorne finished dressing while listening. His instructions were brief. "Find out if they are finished loading supplies and fuel. Oh, and check to be sure the wounded Australians are on board. We will depart within the hour. Contact the port authority and make arrangements."

"Sir. What about the crew who went ashore?"

"They are required to be back on board by 18:00 hours. If they are not we will leave them behind. Now, go!"

At 19:00 hours The Queen maneuvered around a large oil tanker and pulled out of the harbor three hours ahead of schedule. The Captain had chosen not to share with everyone the reason for the early departure. They encountered no danger as the ship gathered speed, its bow pointing toward open water, its wake spreading far behind them beginning the long six or seven boring day voyage to Cape Town, South Africa, then Sydney Australia, returning injured soldiers back home. The Cunard ship was traveling alone without a convoy.

The two doctors were back on board with little time to spare before the early departure. After dinner that evening as the Queen Mary left the Rio de Janeiro harbor, Ben opened his expensive leather journal, an extravagant gift from Samuel considering his limited budget, and wrote for a bit. He still wasn't sleepy so he wandered back on deck. An uncommon sight greeted him. Off the starboard side of the ship he saw a shimmering brilliant electric-blue patch of water, generated by thousands of bioluminescent creatures. The glow ebbed and flowed with the waves, changing shapes and intensities. Ben was mesmerized and didn't hear the Captain approach. "Beautiful, isn't it?" he said.

"Not like anything I've ever seen," Ben responded. They

stood in silence, taking in the spectacle for a few minutes.

"Are you curious why we left Rio early, instead of 22:00?"

"I kinda' figured it was to keep the Germans off-balance."

"Our itinerary was compromised. We got word to leave immediately. A few minutes ago I received another message. The oil tanker berthed next to us was also scheduled to leave at 22:00. It was sunk by a German U-boat. There were no survivors." The Captain patted his shoulder and walked away. Ben was stunned, giving an involuntary shiver. This had been a close call. He looked back out across the water, but the luminous display had faded.

The following morning the crackling of the intercom system interrupted the first breakfast seating. "This is your captain speaking. This announcement is for passengers and crew. The bridge has just received notification that Adolf Hitler—who is also known by some other more colorful names—has placed a bounty of 1,000,000 Reichsmarks or approximately $250,000 on the Queen Mary. This will be paid to any submarine crew who can sink her. While on the surface—no pun intended—this may appear to be an incentive for the German submarine crews, they will never collect it. Because they can't catch The Queen! Right!" And then because they had distanced the ship from the Rio harbor over the night, he added, "It's okay. Go ahead. Make some noise." From the crews in the boiler room and the 8,000 plus Americans on board all the way to the crew on the bridge, a mighty '*Long live The Queen*' rose into the morning air.

Captain Hawthorne chuckled at what he had *not* announced. Also contained in the message about the bounty was the news that the Germans were claiming that a U-boat off the coast of South America had sunk the great ship. *Perhaps that U-boat Commander thought he would claim the 1,000,000 Reichsmarks,* he mused. Turning to his Communications Officer, he said, "Let's not let the troops know we've been sunk. It might worry them."

CHAPTER 34

Vilna, Lithuania
March, 1942, At about the same time

Ana opened her eyes. What sound had awakened her? She lay quietly for a moment adjusting to her surroundings. This new apartment was not much different from the last one. It was warmer. But that might be a result of the weather growing warmer. It was just as crowded as before. Jonah was now working long days. A bus transported the men to a vehicle repair building every day. The physical labor was exhausting him. There. The sound again. A sharp moan. Ana sat up. She could see a dark shape nearby. As her eyes adjusted she could see someone sitting, bent over. Soske. Quickly she went to her. "What is it?"

"It's not time. It's not time," was all she could get out of the girl. Soske stiffened as a new pain grabbed her and she stifled a deep moan.

"The baby is coming?" asked Ana.

"It's not time," Soske repeated.

In the dark room Ana's hand touched something warm and sticky on the girl's skirt and she identified the coppery smell. Blood. She kept her voice low. "Soske. What is happening?"

"I don't know. I haven't felt the baby move for many days. This doesn't feel right. Not like when Rebekah was born." Again, she clutched her abdomen.

"I will help you, but you must be quiet. The soldats cannot

know what is happening."

Soske clamped her lips tight to avoid making noise.

Ordinarily, Ana would have called a midwife. Soske would have had privacy and some herbs to ease the pain. They would have had instruments to help in the delivery. But here. . .

Rebekah was asleep near her mother hugging the ragged doll that gave her comfort these days.

"We will have to make do with what we have," Ana whispered. She looked around the room. "Can you walk?"

Soske nodded her head.

Ana had grabbed her small blanket when Soske's distress awakened her. She moved to a corner of the room and spread it down on the cold floor. Something small and hard was in the way and she brushed it aside. She motioned for Soske to come. "I want you to lie here." When Soske was adjusting herself on the blanket, she cried softly. "I need to push, Ana." Ana reached up Soske's skirt and felt a small head. Almost immediately a tiny baby began to appear. There was no cry from either Soske or the infant. It must have perished days ago in the womb and now Soske's body was expelling it. Ana looked around for something to cut the cord with. The hard object on the floor lay within reach and she pulled it toward her. It was a small piece of glass that had fallen from the cracked window. She used it to free the dead baby from its mother's womb.

Ana was spared from telling Soske that she had given birth to a stillborn. Soske had already guessed. Ana reached down and wiped the tears from the young woman's face. There was nothing to say to comfort her. This had to be for the best. There was no way Soske could have kept a live baby a secret. "When you feel stronger we need to clean up." Although others in the room had stirred in their sleep, no one paid them attention. Ana wrapped the tiny lifeless body in one of Soske's scarves and her mind was busy planning what to do next. They could clean up, but what to do with the baby? If the Nazi soldiers see it they will kill Soske and

Rebekah. I can make excuses for Soske that she is ill, but. . . She realized then that there was blood on her hands and she was still holding the piece of glass. That gave her an idea. "Soske," Ana whispered. "As soon as it is daylight I will pretend that I have been badly cut because I laid my hand down on a piece of glass. I will ask to be taken to hospital. I will ask for the doctor who was in our apartment in the ghetto. He will help us. The hospital performs abortions. They have ways of disposing of. . ." She stopped. "You rest now."

"Thank you, Ana. . .for helping me." Soske was drifting between wakefulness and sleep and just before sleep won she asked, "Was my baby a boy or a girl?"

"You had a son, Soske," Ana whispered.

She sat on the floor beside Soske as the girl slept, the scarf bundle cradled in her lap. This is for the best, she thought again. Who would want to raise a child in a world such as this. She touched the scarf. Gently, she let a corner fall open. Her eyes took in the baby's face. Tiny eyelashes. Eyebrows beginning to form. There is no one to lift a prayer for this life that might have been, she thought. She kept a Jewish prayer book hidden in her undergarment. Looking around the room she carefully removed it. It was barely light enough to make out the words as she turned to the prayer for the dead. She laid her hand on the baby and mouthed the words and quickly returned the book to its hiding place.

Her hand remained on the still body. This son will never experience the loving hand of his mother. He will never laugh or cry or taste his mother's warm milk. Soske will never experience the joy of hearing his voice and watching him learn to stand, walk and run. He was denied growing up, blessing Soske with grandchildren. A tear formed in her eye and she whispered the Jewish blessing for a son. It is for the best, she told herself again. It is God's will. She sat there with the dead baby, unaware of the time, thinking of her Samuel so far away. As the room grew brighter she realized the day was approaching. It was time to put her plan into motion. She inched back toward Jonah to wake him and explain what they must do.

This time Jonah agreed with her. She was right. The infant must be smuggled out; if found, they could all be in danger. "The soldiers will be coming soon to take us to work. We will do it then. They can drop you off near the hospital."

Ana reached into one of the large satchels they had brought with them and retrieved a bag with a drawstring. She emptied it of the few items. The other Jews in the room were awake now and moving around. Some leaving to use the toilet in the courtyard. Some preparing food before leaving for their workday. When she was certain no one was watching, she opened the bag and gently placed the baby inside still wrapped in the scarf and pulled the bag closed. Soske remained asleep in the corner. She wanted to let her say good-bye to her baby, but there was no chance now. The sound of the bus arriving, its brakes squealing as it came to a stop caused Ana and Jonah to look at each other. He nodded to her. Taking the piece of glass in her right hand and pressing very hard, she made a large cut across her palm into her wrist. Fresh blood began oozing out. She had saved a piece of the bloody skirt and wrapped it around her hand. Throbbing pain began wrapping itself around her hand as it bled into the fabric.

Jonah grabbed her, pushing her toward the door and the bus outside. One of the soldiers was just coming through the door. Jonah held up Ana's bloody hand and said, "We need to take my wife to hospital. She has badly cut her hand. Can she ride in the bus until Konarskio Street? She can walk the rest of the way."

"How is that possible? The cut I mean?" the man asked.

"She was looking for something in the dark on the floor and placed her hand on a piece of glass. The bleeding will not stop. Please. The hospital can bandage it and give something for pain."

The other Jews in the room were crowding past Jonah, ignoring them, making their way to the bus. Not waiting for the Nazi soldier to reply, Jonah guided Ana out the door with the others. The guard made no movement to stop them as the group stepped on board. "Does it hurt badly?" Jonah asked her when they reached the back of the bus.

"Some," she said. Then in a soft voice. "Do you think Soske will be okay?" When they come to take her to work in the kitchens, I told her to claim she was ill, but they may make her go anyway. I am frightened for her."

"Ana, you have done all you can for her," Jonah whispered back. "She must help herself now."

"But she still has Rebekah to take care of and I am not there to help."

They were silent then as the bus rocked along. "How will you get back?" Jonah asked her after a few minutes.

"I don't know." She pulled the bag with the drawstring closer to her. A young Jewish man leaned in and said quietly, "We know what is happening but we will never breathe a word to these *szkops!* We are sorry for the young girl. Blessings on you for helping her."

The bus rattled on and soon lurched to a stop with a grinding sound. The Nazi guard signaled to Ana to get off and with one last glance at Jonah, she made her way to the door and stepped off the bus. It groaned and rattled away leaving her alone in the street. This was the most dangerous part. Jews were not allowed on the streets at all and she didn't know what would happen if she was discovered, especially with a dead baby. It was still early and the street was fairly deserted.

It was not far to the hospital, but dread surrounded each step she took. Any moment she expected to hear a loud voice commanding her to stop. The constant throbbing in her hand had increased and she walked faster. She turned a corner, seeing the hospital ahead. A military vehicle was bearing down on her and she knew he must hear her heart pounding. As the car approached she could see by the uniform that the driver was a Lithuanian policeman. Catching sight of her he slowed the vehicle, coming to a stop.

"You are not allowed on the streets," he shouted at her. "Get in."

CHAPTER 35

A na's heart raced. She held up the bloody hand. "I am injured and have permission to seek aid from hospital." Her voice quivered more than she had hoped, but she prayed the policeman would think it was because of the pain. He appeared to be in a hurry and, thankfully, he allowed her to proceed, gunning the auto and paying no more attention to her. Her heart rate slowed and she reached the hospital without seeing anyone else.

She had never been in the hospital before. Samuel had been born at home with the help of a midwife and the three of them had never needed hospital care. She didn't know what to expect as she opened the door with her good hand. The smell hit her first. It reminded her of her grandmother's house after her grandfather had become ill. A mixture of antiseptic, urine and feces. A few chairs were lined along one wall, none of them empty. A young girl sat at a small desk opposite the chairs, writing. On the remaining adjacent wall was a large door.

The first apartment in the ghetto had been shared with a doctor and his family who worked at the hospital. She remembered his name and walking to the desk asked for Dr. Milavetz, showing the girl her bloody hand.

"No! You cannot request a doctor. You will be seen by whoever is available. Take a seat," she said, fully aware that they were all occupied.

"Please," Ana said. Tell him that Ana Dressler must see him.

It is urgent. He will understand." The girl made no effort to call him and turned her attention away from Ana, who stood there for a full minute, uncertain about what to do. Resolve took over, however. She hadn't endured pain and risk just to be ignored by this young girl. Only one doctor could help her. She thought of something. It had worked before. Leaning over the desk giving direct eye contact she said to the girl, "I am his sister. He will want to see me."

The girl continued her haughty attitude and made no effort to contact the doctor. But Ana could tell her lie was working when the girl said, "He won't be available. Go sit. When I am finished with this paper, I will try to find him." Then she dismissed Ana with a wave.

There was nothing Ana could do but wait with the tiny deceased infant and a bloody hand which was throbbing quite painfully now. No seats had been vacated and she had been standing for what seemed like a very long time. The girl left the desk and disappeared through the one large door. *Where is she going?* Ana wondered. *To find the doctor? Or has she forgotten about me?* The wait wasn't as long this time when the girl returned. Following her was Dr. Milavetz. Before he could say anything, Ana rushed to him. "Bruder. I am so glad you are here. I have badly cut my hand. Please help." Ana's eyes implored him to understand.

Her greeting puzzled him, but he said, "Yes, of course, Ana. Come with me." He held the door open for her and led her down the corridor into an examination room. When they were alone she told him of the stillborn infant, why her hand was cut, her dangerous walk to the hospital and how she claimed to be his sister so she could see him. As she got to the end of the story large teardrops dripped down her cheeks and heaving sobs followed.

Dr. Milavetz allowed her to release the morning's stress and tension before saying. "You are very brave, Ana." He examined the wound. "First, I'll clean and bandage your hand and give you something for the pain. I'm guessing the bag contains the infant? I can take care of that. I can also get you back to your apartment."

Relief flooded Ana at the doctor's words and her sobs quieted. "Thank you. I didn't know what else to do." Dr. Milavetz bandaged her hand and gave her some tablets for pain.

"You put yourself in great danger, Ana. The mother was fortunate you were there. I've given you some tablets for her, too."

The hospital laundry truck stopped in front of the ghetto depositing Ana into the courtyard, then drove away. She climbed the stairs to the second story apartment suddenly feeling the long night and the stress of the morning.

The apartment was empty. Soske and Rebekah were gone. The men were at the vehicle repair facility. The other women had been taken to the kitchens and laundry existing for the benefit of the German soldiers. She removed her scarf and laid down on her skimpy mat quickly falling asleep, in spite of the pain in her hand. Footfalls on the stairs woke her some time later as her tired female compatriots returned to the cramped and crowded quarters. She sat up, placing her mitpachat on her hair again and looked around for Soske. She wanted her to know that everything was taken care of and ask how she was feeling. Minutes passed and the young mother and Rebekah did not appear.

One of the women Ana worked with in the kitchens knelt down beside her. "I am so sorry, Ana," she said. The man with the Wehrmacht boots came to the kitchen and took Soske and Rebekah away this morning. He was very rough with her and somehow I think they knew about. . ." she lowered her head and stopped, looking around then continued. "He told us, 'they won't be coming back.'"

Ana choked back a sob. "No! Not sweet Rebekah. Not Soske. How could the *szkops* have known. We were so quiet. So careful," she whispered. She hadn't given Soske's name to Dr. Milavetz and he hadn't asked.

A shot of adrenaline ratcheted up her heart rate. If they knew about Soske, did they also know what she, Ana, had done? And now it seemed the risks she had taken during the past 24 hours were for nothing. Soske and Rebekah were. . .

"Could she have told anyone else?" the woman asked.

Ana shook her head. "I don't know," the tears beginning a slow trickle down her cheek.

"Maybe someone at the kitchens noticed something. Said something."

The two were startled as their German guard entered. He wore a sterner than usual expression and looked around the room. "We know what happened in here today. And we know that it was forbidden. Lies and secrets are also forbidden. The matter has been dealt with." His eyes settled on each woman for a moment, focusing intensely on Ana. Then he spun around and left.

No one spoke. Ana's eyes strayed toward the corner where Soske had given birth just a few hours ago. Her satchel stuffed with Rebekah's clothes, shoes and hairbrush was still propped against the wall, no longer needed by the small child. Rebekah's worn rag doll was gone. She always took it with her to the kitchens every day staying close to her mother. She wondered if the khazers—pigs—murdered the doll too. It was an insane thought and Ana wondered if that was where she was heading. She continued to sit trancelike as the others in the room busied themselves, allowing her a bit of privacy and grief. They also felt the loss and feared the day that soldiers wearing the Wehrmacht boots would take them away, too. And Ana's thoughts echoed theirs. *Are they coming soon to take me away?*

"And they are sure that this woman, you say Herr Dressler's wife, was involved?" The Nazi Major whom Jonah had met a few weeks ago was questioning the assistant.

"The guards questioned the young one before they took her

away. She said nothing. They cannot be positive, but the older woman's injury and behavior were very suspicious; there was a lot of blood for just a cut on the hand. We're not even sure they were really sisters. It would be just like these kikes to lie and protect each other."

The Major stroked his thick black mustache and wrinkled his exceptionally large nose, lost in thought for the moment. It is too bad. I would like to have saved their lives. His knowledge and influence would have been valuable to us."

Then he tapped his desk and said, "But this I cannot tolerate." He stroked his mustache, thinking. "We have assigned about eighty Jews to Ponar Forest to cut trees for big fires. Take them there. The wife can assist with the cooking. They will be disposed of when that work is finished. Now go!" And he dismissed the German with a flick of his chubby hand.

CHAPTER 36

Cape Town, South Africa
March, 1942

Ben and Joe Ramsey were standing at the deck railing, watching the tugs pull the Queen Mary into the harbor. The plan was to be here only as long as necessary to load more supplies and fuel and rest the crew before complete the last leg of the 40 days and 40 nights journey to Sydney. The temperature was near eighty degrees with no rain in sight. Captain Hawthorne was not in command at the moment, but would return to the wheelhouse for the last part of the voyage to Sydney. He joined them now. "Good morning, lads. How's my medical staff getting along?"

"It's been reasonably quiet, sir," Ben answered. "I'm not sure you even need us around," he joked. "The only real medical work we've done is stitch up a couple of guys who got into a fight over a bet." Then remembering they weren't supposed to gamble he said, "I mean a bed, sir."

"Of course. A bed. They do sometimes get into fights over a bed." Then addressing Joe Ramsey, the Captain asked, "How much do you know about Cape Town?"

"Very little, sir."

"Let me educate you. It has a history that should be familiar to you, Joe." Dr. Ramsey eyed the Captain. Maybe he hadn't dropped by on happenstance. "Both of you are free to go ashore, if you choose. I insist that you take your identification papers with you, just keep them safe. Cape Town is not friendly to indigenous blacks. Since the early part of the century blacks have been denied housing, education and jobs and considered heathens by a majority of the whites who live here."

"Are you saying we would be in danger?"

"Probably not during the daytime on crowded streets. You may have difficulty getting waited on. Ben won't have a problem, so if you two stick together you should be fine."

"Thank you, sir. Ben and I will talk it over."

"Carry on, then." He disappeared down the nearby stairs.

The black doctor and the white doctor stood side by side, arms resting on the railing, watching the boats in the harbor, each waiting for the other to say something.

"I can take care of myself," said Dr. Ramsey.

"I did some boxing in college," added Ben. And off they went.

The city surprised them. So many cars. They weren't expecting that. Double-decker buses. They weren't expecting those either. They saw tall modern buildings and stone buildings with elaborate iron railings enclosing the balconies. They read a sign directing them to the train station, where one could go by rail to Johannesburg. And yet as they walked along Adderley Street—the main thoroughfare in the middle of this modern city—they saw carts drawn by horses plodding along with a rhythmic clop-clop sound. Miles away Table Mountain curled around the city providing a picturesque backdrop to this city of mixed cultures where past met present. The scene was not at all what either one had expected.

Conveniently, the British pound was the money used in South Africa and the pair stopped in front of an interesting small diner just off the street. They could see through the screen door that a few men were seated around small bare tables. Ceiling fans chased themselves slowly overhead. A menu posted on the window beside the door listed soups and shepherd's pie among other British offerings. They entered the restaurant intending to have a bite of lunch. That never happened.

Moments after seating themselves at the only unoccupied table, a coarse scream and a stream of cuss words came from the open grill.

Ben saw flames. Smelled singed hair. Heard the scream. The man behind the grill with the long hair was yelping in pain, shaking his head and wrapping his hand in his grease-stained apron while patrons in the small restaurant stared in the man's direction, waiting for someone to do something. Ben *wanted* to do something. He thought he *should* do something. But he sat there. It was the Cocoanut Grove all over again—the seated dinner guests staring at people on fire. The screaming. The smoke. The smells. The scene now and the scene then blended together behind his eyes and he just sat there, unable to move.

Another shorter balding man wearing a matching stained apron was running around behind the counter throwing baking soda on the grill and shouting, "Get back! Get back!"

Joe Ramsey glanced in Ben's direction first, saw his state, and wasted no time in taking charge. He spotted a white kitchen towel, cleaner than the others and without explaining anything he grabbed a nearby pitcher of cold water, poured it over the cook's head and soaked his blistered hand. Then he doused the towel with more water and wrapped it carefully around the man's hand. The flames on the grill were surrendering to the baking soda, and the bald man, thinking that the emergency was over, stopped shouting. With a commanding tone Joe said, "This man needs medical attention. How can we get him to a hospital?"

Baldy turned his attention from his cook to the large black man and his manner changed dramatically. Not many black men came into the diner and certainly not one who would dare come behind the counter and take charge. He glared at the intruder and moved into his personal space, his two hairy arms crossed in front of his chest. "Who the bloody hell are you and whadda' think yer doin'?" His tone was blatantly hostile.

Joe Ramsey pulled himself to his full height, ignored the hostile tone, and asked again, "What is the fastest way to get him medical aid? Your man is in extreme pain." Then realizing the man could not know he was a doctor, he added, "My name is Dr. Joseph Ramsey. I'm a doctor from the Queen Mary ship in the harbor," he said. Then realized after the incident in Rio. maybe he shouldn't have mentioned the Queen Mary. Too late. "We're both doctors," he said motioning toward Ben hoping that by including him—a white man—baldy might be quicker to cooperate. Then a better thought struck him. "Ben, there are supplies on the ship. Help me get him there."

The bald owner acknowledged Ben for the first time. He had been preoccupied when the two doctors arrived, and while putting out the fire he had not recognized that the two men had come in together. He looked from one to the other. "Hey, If the two of you want to get him help, fine." Still maintaining his hostile attitude, he took a small step back and allowed Dr. Ramsey to guide the man to a seat.

Ben looked around, hearing his name. He saw Joe. He heard the cook moan. He shook his head in a physical attempt to clear the memories that had hijacked him. "What? Did you say the ship?"

"Yes. Go outside and find a taxi or cart driver. Someone who can get us down to the harbor. I'll stay here and keep ice on his burns. Hurry!"

The burned man's name was Henri Wallace. He was a rough looking man in his early forties. His scruffy beard resembled a Brillo scouring pad, and his hair probably hadn't been cut or washed in weeks. One side of the long hair was now singed and gave his head a lop-sided appearance. He had been cleaning the grill when he knocked over a bottle of whiskey he had opened intending to sneak a drink. The alcohol flared up igniting his long hair and the hand that was near the grill. Thanks to Joe's quick response, his injury though painful was not life threatening. At worst he might have some scar tissue on his hand, maybe his ear; his hair would grow back.

Back onboard the Queen Mary, Joe had quickly given Henri some pain medication. Ben was silently bandaging the cook's hand with gauze coated with petroleum jelly, and desperately trying to avoid thinking of all the times that tortured night he had administered this same treatment.

"You need to see a local doctor here in Cape Town. You will need to be checked for infection," Dr. Ramsey explained to Henri, an English-speaking Australian; but the English Henri spoke was like a foreign language to the two doctors. Henri nodded that he understood. "You need to do it right away. When that pain medicine wears off you *will* want more." The two were walking toward the gangway, Henri giving assurance that he knew how to get a ride back to the city.

Joe Ramsey watched him as he left the ship, but he was thinking of Ben, not Henri, as he turned and walked back the way he had come. He and Ben had filled some of the long boring hours talking together, sharing stories of their lives. Stories of growing up. Stories of medical school. Humorous stories. Case studies. Joe had other stories too difficult for him to share, and after today he suspected Ben did, too. He shook his head and kept walking.

Ben had remained behind in the infirmary, sterilizing things and putting away supplies. He wanted to distance himself from Joe right now. Embarrassed? Oh, yes. Angry and confused, also yes. Now, once again he hadn't risen to the occasion. Angrily, temper flaring, he slammed drawers, tossed towels into the laundry bag and then sat on the edge of the bed his elbows on his knees. He ran his hands through his hair as he took deep breaths trying to bring his emotions under control. *Joe had to have noticed my reaction or lack of it,* he thought. *He was so in control. Knew just what to do. He must think I'm an idiot; that I've never experienced a crisis before.*

When his stomach rumbled, he realized they had forgotten all about lunch. The infirmary was back in order and Joe had not yet returned. He went in search of food, wrestling with what to say to Dr. Ramsey. Afternoon tea had been served, and a few sandwiches and sweets remained. In a few minutes several thousand American soldiers would fill the room for the final meal of the day. He clenched his jaw as he relived the afternoon. His chair scraped the floor as he rose to rinse out the empty cup.

Dinner was over and the two doctors were on deck enjoying the perfect weather of Cape Town—late summer. The shimmering night sky was beginning an evening performance that had delighted audiences for thousands of years. Marring the perfection was a slight breeze carrying the smells of fish and ocean and the foul odors of thousands of unshowered men.

They had been standing there for some minutes, when Ben broke the silence. "Joe, I need to tell you a story." Joe Ramsey turned slightly, giving Ben his full attention, and noticed the white knuckles wrapped tightly around the railing. "Last November—" A southern drawl interrupted Ben.

"Ah heard there was a nigger on board." The two turned from the railing to see a young blonde man in an army uniform, tossing a cigarette overboard as he approached. "Who do you think you are swaggering around in that doctor garb. Niggers aren't smart enough to be doctors." Ben's emotional equilibrium was still off and this guy's attitude tipped the scale toward anger. His training took over and with no thought, he bent his knees, straightened his back and spread his feet, fists clenched at his side.

"Apologize," Ben said.

"For what? He's a nigger, right? Oh, I get it. You're a nigger-lover. Yeah, man. You look like a nigger-lover."

"Last time. Apologize to him."

"And last time. I don't apologize to no nigger."

Ben's lead arm shot out with an up jab and his knuckles connected with the soldier's nose sending a spray of blood down his face. The guy wasn't prepared for such a sudden reaction, and stumbled backward before managing an amateur swing in Ben's direction. Ben deftly maneuvered right on the balls of his feet, then moved in for another jab, grazing the guy's ear. Ben was preparing for an upper cut to the jaw when Dr. Joe stepped between them placing an arm on each one.

"Whoa, gentlemen. Ben, take it easy." Turning to the soldier, "I'll forgive you for the racial slurs; probably that's what you were taught. Your blue button indicates you are out of your assigned zone. That infraction carries serious punishments, however, I'm not reporting you. But heed this warning. Don't you *ever* throw anything else overboard. That could get us all killed. Do you understand? Now, go get some ice for that nose." Cupping his bloody nose and glaring once more at Ben, he wisely stalked off. "Ben, I appreciate your noble gesture, but don't you think it was a touch overreactive?"

The encounter did nothing to defuse Ben's anger. He was angry earlier because he hadn't taken control. Now he was angry because he lost control. He turned back to the railing, shaking the pain out of his hand. The mood of the evening had changed radically. "He deserved it."

"Do you need some ice?" Ben shook his head. "You started to tell me something."

"Yes. I thought you deserved an explanation about today." He brought his elevated heart rate under control before continuing. "I was engaged to a lovely, intelligent woman named Laura for all of 45 minutes. We were at the Cocoanut Grove in

Boston, with family and friends. In the middle of our celebration the lounge caught fire. It was a death trap. In fifteen minutes, it was fully ablaze." He stopped and took a deep breath.

"Hundreds were burned. Many died, including Laura. I tried to find her; to help her. But I failed her and so many others. That's why I'm here and not practicing medicine in Boston. I'm not sure medicine is where I should be. And today's performance. . .need I say more? I thought maybe walking away from the familiar; changing my perspective would help me figure things out. Today when I smelled the smoke, the burnt hair; saw the people sitting at the tables, I flashed back to that night. I froze." Ben stared out across the water, gripping the railing.

Joe turned toward the water, his elbows on the railing, his chin resting on his folded hands. Neither spoke for a moment. "Doctor or no doctor that's a horrible experience for anyone," he said. "If you were a lesser doctor, you wouldn't still be struggling, searching. Sometimes, Ben, our best is not good enough. People die. There are good men on board. Young men. A few with biases." And he nodded in the direction the soldier had taken. "Some of them won't be alive a month from now. But there are good field doctors out there who will save some. Will they wish they had saved them all? Of course. But they saved some.

"Your future is your decision, and yours alone; no one else can decide it for you." They were silent for a time until Joe spoke again this time with a rich southern accent. "When I was 'bout fifteen. "T'was grown big for my age. I hung out with black boys older'n me." He had deliberately slipped back into the speech of his childhood. It made his story real. "One night we was kickin' cans in front of ma's house and the KKK came walkin' down the road. They was maybe five of them. Torches held high in the night air." He looked up at the stars. "A night not unlike tonight. We stopped what we was doin' to watch. They kept a-comin' up the road toward us and then stopped in front of my friend, Willie. 'Hey, boy,' one shouted through his white hood. 'We saw what you did.' Willie looked around. The whites of his eyes was shinin' in the dark. First, he began shakin'. Then he began a-runnin' Never had no chance. Never did know what those KKK boys thought he did, or if he ever did anything. He was so scared of what was comin' he ran. We were helpless to stop them so we just stood there. We was 'fraid they would come after us, too. I've seen too much hate. And you know what, Ben? Hate is not overcome with more hate."

"What happened to him?"

Joe's speech changed back. "They caught him, carried him off. They poured hot pitch on his back and stuck chicken feathers in it. The burns never healed right and he carried burn scars and emotional scars the rest of his short life. That's when I decided to do whatever it took to become a doctor to Negroes. That became my purpose, my passion." He moved his gaze from the harbor to Ben and gave his shoulder a brief squeeze, "I hope you find your purpose, Ben."

Ben had given the story his full attention, incensed at the violence, pain and injustice. He struggled with the proper response. His exposure to hate consisted only of a bit of playground bullying. "What happened to those men?" he asked.

"Nothing. They went home. Took off their white hoods. Maybe had a drink together. Slept like babies. More than likely, one of them was the town constable."

"Were they ever punished?"

"Not by man. But the Almighty is a just God. Sooner or later they'll face Him." Ramsey removed his pocket watch, opened the cover and checked the time. "I'm heading off to bed. See you in the morning."

"Yeah, see you in the morning," Ben answered but continued leaning on the railing appearing to anyone noticing that he was watching the activity in the harbor; but his thoughts shifted from the fire in the diner, to a black boy running for his life and then to Boston, thousands of miles away.

For the first time since he left Boston he missed home and Mom. The winter snows were probably beginning to melt. That meant the loamy rich smell of Mom's garden would be filling the air. Tender green shoots would be pushing through the nearly thawed ground determined to proclaim that spring had arrived. Soon the nuthatches would be scuttling up the big maple tree in the front yard looking for newly hatched larvae. Robins would be cocking an eye to the ground as they listened for earthworms wriggling around in the warming soil, breaking it up, and thereby assisting those tender green shoots. He never could figure out how those birds could hear worms buried in the ground.

He missed Laura. All of her. The little toss of her head as she laughed that made her dark curls shimmer. The smile when she saw him that silently conveyed, 'I love you.' He missed the soft curve of her breast against him and how beautiful she was in that green dress the night they danced together, his last memory of her. And again, anger wound its way into his thoughts. This time he was angry because it wasn't fair. They should be together. He realized his hands were tight fists and he had a strong urge to punch something or someone again. He rubbed his knuckles then slowly flexed and unflexed them letting them drop to his side.

Absently he looked out as two dockhands placed the last wooden box into a lorry and its engine sputtered to life, the sound drifting up from the pier. The wooden pier rattled as the truck moved away, its two tiny red tail lights blending in with the lights in the city until his eyes and ears could no longer distinguish it. He had been traveling for weeks now—the Caribbean, Rio de Janeiro, and now South Africa. Really, halfway around the world. Trying to put his failure behind him. He rubbed his forehead. How could it have happened again?

CHAPTER 37

Vilna, Lithuania
March, 1942

Jonah and Ana were being marched along with several other men. All they had been told was that they were being sent to the Commandant of Ponar Forest. Ponar. A memory that now seemed a million years ago flashed through Jonah's mind. Samuel running through the labyrinth of Scots Pine trees being chased by two boys from their synagogue as the trees cast an ever-changing shadow pattern around them. All three boys were laughing as Ana called them to the picnic lunch spread out on a blanket on the floor of the forest. He glanced at Ana walking tall and straight beside him and wondered what she was thinking. The stress, exhaustion, loss and pain of the past few days had wrapped around her like a death shroud. She was staring straight ahead, her mouth a grim line, not speaking a word as they were marched along.

No one had picnics in Ponar Forest now. No children ran and laughed and played games. Rumors about Ponar were circulating around the ghetto. No one who went to Ponar came back alive, it was said. Jonah knew it was an accurate rumor. But he had a secret. Something he had not yet shared with Ana. He had made an amazing discovery.

Jewish tailors often sewed hidden pockets in men's coats and trousers. It was a common practice. As he and Ana were re-packing their few remaining belongings, Jonah had gone through the pockets of his long black woolen coat checking on the papers and cash he had placed there weeks ago. They were still safe. But tucked away absently and forgotten was the official paper he had picked up in Kaunas months ago. He had put it in the hidden pocket and forgotten about it. When he took it out and read it he was astounded. Before anyone could read the astonishment on his face, he re-folded it and placed it in another secret place in an undergarment. It must be protected at all costs. It was hope.

Their walk continued for nearly an hour until they arrived at the edge of Ponar Forest. There was no commandant to greet them, but their escorts appeared to know what to do. Without a doubt they had done this before. Following a rough footpath, they were led to the very same stone-lined, unfinished pit that Jonah's firm had helped design and build. Now against one of the rock walls was a crude building, more of a hut. He could see and smell wood smoke issuing from the left side and two Jewish women sitting on wooden stools preparing food nearby. There were other German guards stationed at the top of the pit. In the distance he heard wood being chopped.

One of their captors lowered a wooden ladder into the pit and ordered them to climb down. Ana gathered her long skirt. She noticed that the hem was frayed and dirty. She would never ever have allowed that, but now it seemed inconsequential, even laughable. Laughable? Was she becoming hysterical? Jonah guided her as she navigated the rickety ladder.

"Put your things in the hut," one of the guards said. He pointed at Ana. "You should stay," and pointing to Jonah, "Come with us." They used the same ladder to climb out of the pit and pulled it up behind them. Jonah guessed they walked about a kilometer before he saw many Jewish men cutting trees and stacking wood. "Get to work," the guard said.

Another Jew, close to Jonah's age but more muscular and thinner, had just picked up a crosscut saw and Jonah joined him. "Why are we cutting trees?" Jonah whispered with a backward glance at the two guards. The man also checked the location of the guards and said in a low voice, "No one will tell us. We have asked that question—many times. We get nothing." The two men positioned themselves alongside a nearby twenty-foot pine tree and soon the rhythmic sawing sound and sweet pine scent filled the loamy forest signaling the end of life for the tree.

The sounds of sawing and chopping continued for the remainder of the afternoon. Soon the March daylight began to dwindle away and the cold air became colder. One of the Nazi guards approached the men and in a loud voice shouted, "Aufhören!" Stop. The men began stowing the saws and hatchets and fell in line behind the guards. Jonah followed suit and soon the group were back at the large pit. As Jonah was descending the ladder one of the guard's heavy boots slammed into his shoulder. He lost his footing and would have tumbled to the ground had there been no one in front of him. He snagged his elbow around a rung of the roughly hewn log ladder and flinched as he twisted the same shoulder. The guards were laughing as they pulled up the ladder. One guard reminded the men that there were land mines and soldiers positioned in the woods nearby. "Don't try to escape," he said as they left.

Jonah grabbed his shoulder and looked around the pit. The guard needn't have bothered with his reminder. Without the ladder there was no way to scale the smooth rock walls. He turned his attention toward the hut just as Ana reached his side.

"How bad is it?" she asked, her expression a mixture of anger, concern and frustration.

"Nothing broken. It'll be bruised and sore tomorrow. Makes using the saw more painful."

"I will place a piece of clothing near the fire. The warmth will make It feel better."

She gestured for him to join her around the fire as other men moved toward the light and warmth of the burning logs. She spoke softly with the other women making it obvious she had spent the afternoon getting acquainted with them while preparing an evening meal for the tired men.

The laborers having ceased their physical activity for the day donned sweaters and coats to ward off the chill of the March evening. At least they could talk among themselves. The guards were far out of hearing range, apparently confident that escape for their prisoners was impossible.

Pieces of log had been brought into the hut for seating and Jonah sat down alongside the man he had worked with earlier. For the first time Jonah noticed the man's refined bearing; his cultured speech. His beard, like all of the men, was unkempt. Jonah watched as he located his glasses, adjusted them on his broad nose, extending a hand to Jonah. "I am Rabbi Shuler." His voice strong.

"I'm Jonah Dressler. My wife, Ana," he said with a look in her direction." Before the Germans came, I had an engineering company. Ironically, we built this pit for the Soviets, but they left before it was finished. How long have you been here and what is happening here?"

"I was in the Yiddish library at Vilna University when the Germans came for me. Jews from our synagogue had already been taken to the ghetto. We were in the ghetto only a short time, then brought here—time is difficult to judge— but maybe a month has gone by. Maybe more. Each and every daywe cut wood and stack it for big fires." He pointed in the direction they had cut wood today. "And near there is a strong stench of death and decay. You may have noticed. We suspect it is many, many murdered Jews. We have talked and we think we are cutting wood for burning corpses. You have heard the rumors about Ponar, yes?"

Jonah nodded. "No one comes back from Ponar. It is a death sentence."

"We are convinced that when this task is completed—whatever it is—we will be killed." He rubbed his long beard, lost in thought for a minute, then said. "You could be of great help. We have been working on a plan. Later I will show you."

Ana brought the two men plates of rice and beans, served with a crust of bread the women had baked over the outdoor oven that afternoon. The Rabbi stood and with a loud voice commanded everyone's attention. Then, bowing his head he blessed their meager allotment. There weren't enough utensils to go around, so some scooped the meal with the bread or their fingers. The food was depleted long before appetites were satisfied.

Jonah wanted to speak further with the Rabbi, but another man called out 'Rabbi' and he moved his exhausted body across the compound. Jonah studied the group. He counted 75 men and four women, all Jewish.

The fire helped quell the cold, but still Ana moved closer to her husband. "This is a bad place," she said, her voice low and filled with anguish. "I feel much sorrow and terror here." She turned her head and spit on the ground three times, followed by a whispered "Pooh, Pooh, Pooh!

Jonah knew from experience that his wife's sixth sense was uncannily accurate. She seemed to always know when a letter from Samuel was about to arrive. Never a demonstrative husband in public, tonight he felt her deep need to be comforted. He placed an arm around her shoulder and she leaned heavily against him. These past weeks had been filled with fear, loss of home, friends, comfort and dignity, and heavy labor. A small sob that wouldn't be stifled any longer broke free from within her. He touched her cheek and gazed out beyond the flickering fire.

The moon had not yet risen and the dense forest blocked out any light except the fire. As he watched the fire he was overcome with the feeling that the darkness of the night surrounding them was infused with a much deeper darkness of hate in men's hearts—an unprovoked hate. A hate so profound that evil found fertile ground within it giving birth to a vile and malevolent cancer that threatened to choke the life out of everything he found beautiful. As if he could see into the future—Ana's prescience giving him eyes—he knew that far worse days were ahead for them. Jonah had serious doubts that Ana's ritual to ward off evil spirits would work in this place. The evil was much too monstrous. "Ana, let us say the Shema together. The words of the Jewish prayer, recited morning and evening and in times of danger, floated into the sky: *"Hear, O Israel, the Lord is our God, the Lord is one. . ."*

Now they lay side by side on the makeshift bed that Ana had invented earlier. It did little to keep the cold ground from seeping into their bones. Ana thought back. She realized this was the only time she had slept outdoors in her life. She shivered. The ground was frozen. In no time the sleeping mat was also frozen and the deep freeze moved into her clothes. She moved closer to Jonah, finding comfort and hoping for warmth. The camp had quieted now as the exhausted men made futile attempts to find comfortable spots for sore, cold bodies. A sudden rustle in the dried leaves startled her. Icy tendrils shot through her chest. Was it a snake? A rat? Or worse a human rat come to bring harm. Now she had *two* reasons to shiver.

She tensed. Eyes wide. She peered into the dark, her eyes sending imaginary visions to her brain, visions conjured up by the breeze, trees, and. . . music? Like someone singing and harmonizing? And yet, not quite. Way in the distance. She focused on the sound. The pitch changed and it became more mournful. Singing a song for the dead? Then—a snarl like a cymbal clash. She recognized the voice of a wolf, or two. "Jonah." She clutched his arm. "I hear wolves." No answer. "Jonah!"

Drowsily, "Yes, yes. We saw them today. Gray wispy shadows as they circled among the trees and watched us working in the forest. A group this large will keep them away. Besides, the ladder is gone. They can't climb down into the pit. We are safe here near the fire." His voice drifted off.

Jonah was right. Wolves couldn't get into the pit; and they are afraid of fire. "I'll try to think of things besides snakes and wolves," she whispered, more to herself than Jonah. She concentrated on thoughts of Samuel. He would be so worried about them by now. They hadn't been able to write him in months. He would know something was wrong. Think of happier times. The day of his bar-mitzvah came to mind. That was a good day. They had given Samuel his own *siddur,* prayer book. It was given to Jonah by his parents at his bar-mitzvah and he wanted to pass it along to his only son. They had also given him 18 litas, as did some of their friends—eighteen being a significant number within their faith. It was a lot of money for a thirteen-year old, but they made him promise to save most of it. Her mind sifted through other precious memories as if she were thumbing through photographs. Hannakuh, and Seder dinner celebrations. Sabbath rituals at the synagogue. Cooking challah and baked apples with honey for her family. She thought of the one cup and saucer carefully wrapped and protected at the bottom of her satchel. Only one cup and saucer remained from the tea set she had cherished. But she had *one*. Already that life felt like another life she had lived years and years ago. As her mind dwelt in the past she forgot the snakes and wolves. Her eyes grew heavy. In spite of the harsh conditions, exhaustion won, and she slept.

Jonah felt someone shaking his shoulder and the sudden pain woke him immediately. His first thought was Ana needed him, but she was asleep next to him. "Jonah. Wake up." The hushed voice failed to clear his foggy brain and he struggled to focus on where he was. He rubbed his hand over his eyes and reached for his glasses nearby. Illuminated by the fire, he saw it was the Rabbi standing over him and he took the extended hand pulling him to his feet. Still, softly hushed, the Rabbi said, "We want to show you something."

The living area was centered around a large wooden hut, built so that the rock wall of the pit served as the back wall of the hut. The men had used scrap wood to build a cupboard for storing dishes and assorted cooking utensils. This cupboard stood in the back of the hut, against the rock wall. Now it was pushed away from the wall and as Jonah watched, a man crawled out of the opening holding a candle in one hand and a cup of dirt in the other. He nodded to Jonah and the Rabbi, emptied the cup, and smoothed the small amount of dirt out with his shoe.

"What is this?" Jonah asked.

Rabbi Shuler spoke. "I told you earlier that we are all certain we will be killed when we're finished here. There is only one way out of here. A tunnel. We take turns digging each night after the guards leave. Some men sleep. Some dig. Some watch the fire. It is a slow process. We only have cups and spoons to dig with; but it is our only hope. You said you know engineering. We could use your help. The soil is sandy and dry and a collapse would set us back many weeks. You can help us avoid that."

While he spoke the man with the candle returned carrying another cup of dirt. Jonah moved past him, knelt, and peered into the opening—into the darkness that was their only chance for escape.

CHAPTER 38

Boston, Massachusetts
March, 1942

There were many long narrow windows letting in the dwindling afternoon light. The soft rays they created streamed across row upon row of tables filling the large room. Women in snow white uniforms sat side by side, each facing a black sewing machine. White silky fabric lay in soft folds all around the immaculate floor. The gentle purr of a hundred sewing machines, while not particularly unpleasant, was relentless all day long.

Ziva took her foot off the pedal of her machine, stood and stretched. She looked across the room and caught her mother's eye. In just a few minutes a loud buzzer sounding like a hundred angry bumblebees would signal the end of the work day and it would be time to board the bus back to Boston.

After the fire at the Cocoanut Grove and the bombing of Pearl Harbor, Ziva's brother, Monroe, had put his education on hold and enlisted. He was still in Louisiana, but would be leaving soon. He didn't know where. Monroe was gone. Camille was gone. Samuel was busy at the hospital. Ziva was at loose ends. The days were monotonously the same. Then one day in late January her mother, Rose, received a telephone call. It was brief, but as Rose hung up the receiver, she called, "Ziva! We're going to work. On Monday." That was news to Ziva, but Monday morning both were on board the bus that brought them to this factory.

Rose had been a seamstress for many years, altering frocks for wealthy women and making baby clothes. She had a steady clientele. As Ziva got older Rose taught her to sew. It wasn't Ziva's favorite activity, but her mother insisted. When Rose's delivery schedule was tight, she would enlist Ziva's help.

Now they worked together five days a week stitching long sections of the filmy nylon fabric together, adding cords and harnesses until a new parachute was finished. Some days she worked at the sewing machine all day. Other days she worked as half of a two-woman team inserting the cords and harnesses and metal or bone strips into the chutes. Only men worked in another part of the factory folding the newly made parachutes by hand into the pack that would be strapped onto the paratrooper's back as he prepared to jump into the hellish world below. This job took a lot of skill and concentration. A sloppy job could mean death for an unlucky service man. Ziva thought women could do as good a job as the men, but the thought of one of "her" chutes not opening stopped her protest.

The bumblebee buzzer sounded and Ziva closed up her work area, gathered her purse and lunch box, threw her coat on over her white uniform and joined Rose as the women lined up for the bus. This was good work. She liked it. It made her feel like she was making a difference. Sometimes in the newspaper she would see pictures of the paratroopers and she would wonder if any of them was wearing a parachute she had helped make. That thought was what had motivated her to place a little note inside some of the chutes she completed. Short little notes that said "Godspeed," or "Come home soon," or "Many are praying for you." A few times she'd written, "Hey soldier. Give 'em hell over there."

Their day started at 6:00 a.m. and ended at 2:30 p.m. The one-hour bus ride dropped them off within blocks of their house allowing them to arrive home before dark. With Monroe away now, it was just Ziva and Rose. The money they made, the money

Monroe was able to send home and the money from the insurance settlement allowed them to meet their financial obligations, but little more.

The bus stopped at an intersection and Ziva caught sight of several young women standing in front of a small department store protesting—of all things—the shortage of nylon stockings. Dupont, the largest manufacturer of nylon, had changed from making stockings to producing nylon for airplane cords and parachute material. Silk was no longer available from Japan so nylon had become the best substitute.

Watching those young women waving placards and pointing to the bus made her wonder if they knew that this was the bus from the parachute factory or was it just a coincidence they were there when the bus passed by? The bus began to move and the women disappeared from view. Ziva looked away. *I could have been in that group a few months ago,* she thought. *Actually, I do miss nylon stockings.* The bus braked and Ziva steadied herself with her hand on the seat back in front of her. She glanced over at her mother. Rose's brown eyes were closed, her hands clasped loosely in her lap. She had shared her dark hair with Ziva and it was tied at the nape of her neck, a few tendrils escaping here and there. "Worry lines" had begun to appear on her forehead now that Monroe had joined the war effort.

Ziva looked down at her own hands. Her nails used to be long and manicured with bright red polish. Now they were short and hadn't seen polish for weeks. Ziva sighed and turned again toward the window consciously filtering out the quiet chatter on the bus. She could see her reflection superimposed over the countryside and she let her mind drift while the landscape clicked by, scenes in a toy view master. So much had changed. She had changed, she thought. Not just manicures and nylon stockings. Everything. She and Samuel had talked. Really talked. With Monroe going off to fight, she understood his concern. He had been right to worry about his parents. He had heard nothing from them in months. After trying every resource to reach them . . .nothing. The news coming out of that part of Europe was dire. Thousands of Jews were being rounded up, killed or sent to work camps. Samuel was certain if they were alive they would have found a way to get word to him. He was convinced they were dead. She felt sorry for him, but nothing she said helped. God knows she had tried.

Not that they were together that much. Her long factory hours and his long hospital hours left little time for socializing. When they did see each other, they were both tired. Margaret fixed dinner for them sometimes, always including Rose. The two women had found a common bond, both having sons away from home for the first time. In fact, she and Rose were invited there for dinner this evening to celebrate Margaret's birthday. Avery would be there, too. He was spending a lot of time with Margaret during Ben's absence; but then, he *had* promised to look after her while Ben was away.

She looked at her mom again. A nap might be good and she leaned back and closed her eyes as the bus jerked along.

Margaret's dinner was delicious. She had fried a chicken, made pan gravy. mashed potatoes and green beans. Samuel had arrived halfway through dinner and was just finishing.

The birthday cake—chocolate of course—was in the middle of the kitchen table yet to be cut. Margaret was busily assembling the dessert plates, silverware and candles when Avery placed his hands on her shoulders and gently guided her to a chair at the table. The dinner guests noticed and became attentive. Earlier he had hidden a wrapped box on the kitchen counter and he placed it in front of Margaret now. "Happy Birthday," he said as he bent and kissed her on the cheek. She touched his arm and looked up at him.

"How sweet, Avery. Should I open it now?" He pulled the

chair out next to her and sat down, nervously wiping his hands on his trousers. "Yes, yes, open it."

Slowly and gently Margaret removed the pink wrapping paper and laid it aside. The exposed box was about the size of her recipe file box. She removed the lid and discovered an exquisite porcelain music box. It was light blue decorated with violets around the sides and had gold accents. She turned it over to wind it and something clinked inside. "Oh, Avery, did I break something?" she said.

He grinned. "No. Turn it back over and remove the top."

She did and peeked inside. Immediately she closed the lid and placed the music box back on the table. "I'll cut the cake now," she said, pushing back her chair and standing.

Avery, along with everyone else, was confused. "Margaret, should I have gotten down on one knee? I would have, but the image I had of Samuel helping me back up didn't seem very romantic."

"Wait! What's inside?" Ziva asked, her eyes bright with excitement and she reached for the music box.

Before Rose could stop her, Ziva had the box open and was removing the ring. It glittered under the overhead light. "This is so exciting. Avery it's so-o-o beautiful."

Avery wasn't listening to Ziva; he was watching Margaret. "Margaret?" he said. "Say something?"

She turned from the sink to face him, drying her hands on her apron. "Avery—

Rose cut her off. "Margaret, you and Avery find someplace to talk. Ziva and I will cut the cake and make some coffee."

Margaret nodded. The sun porch was too chilly now so she led Avery into Peter's old den. After his death she had added some plants, changed the draperies, reupholstered the big chairs, but it still reminded her of him and she needed that right now. She motioned Avery into one of the overstuffed chairs and she took the other. *This wasn't how it should have gone*, he thought. *They should be dancing around the kitchen, laughing, everyone congratulating them. What had gone wrong?* There was an awkwardness between them now that hadn't been there before. "Did I do something wrong?" he asked. He stammered on. "It's just the war. The uncertainty of life. We're not getting younger. I should have—"

"Avery, I'm very fond of you," interrupted Margaret. "This. . .tonight. . . just took me by surprise. We haven't really talked about an engagement or. . . anything. Besides, Ben isn't here. I couldn't possibly make an important decision like this without talking to him."

"Is that what's wrong? Ben isn't here? Margaret, Ben is a big boy. He's living his own life now. You need to make decisions for you. Maybe your answer is no, but it needs to be a decision you make for you, not Ben." Then his tone a bit softer, "Regardless of what you decide, I'm not going anywhere. I care about you very much. Ben is expecting me to be here for you while he is gone and I'm not going to let him or you down."

She placed a hand on his knee. "I need time, Ave."

"Take whatever you need. I'll still be here; just up the street." He stood and helped her to her feet. "That cake and coffee should be ready now, birthday girl." He raised her chin to look into her face for a moment, thinking better of giving her a kiss and they started back toward the kitchen.

"Wait." Margaret spoke. "What do we tell them?" She gestured toward the kitchen.

"Good question."

Ziva leaned toward Samuel using a subdued voice. "Well, that was uncomfortable." She was still holding the ring. "My gawd. This is gorgeous." She held it up to the light, staring into it as she spoke, examining the small round diamond surrounded by rubies.

"Ziva, put it back in the box," irritation in Samuel's voice.

"What do you think it cost?"

"Put it back!" More irritation.

"Okay, okay." Carefully she slipped the ring back into the music box. "What's her problem, anyway? I mean Avery is really a nice guy and you can see he loves her. I don't get it. She should have been thrilled."

Rose made a stern face at her daughter. "Ziva! Let's concentrate on celebrating her birthday. They'll work this out between them. When they come back no mention of the ring. I mean it."

Ziva pouted. Samuel was withdrawn and quiet. Rose busied herself with the cake and coffee.

The three looked up as Avery's slight cough caught their attention. He and Margaret were standing in the doorway. "My attempt at surprise seems to have backfired," he said. "We've had a talk." Then, nervously, "She didn't say no, so there's still hope. Right? Yep. I think she may need some proper courting. Okay then, let's have a party and enjoy some of that great chocolate cake, what do you say?"

Margaret deemed it necessary to put her guests at ease, so she gave Avery a quick kiss, smiled at him and took over her hostess duties, with no explanation of her earlier behavior. Avery's out of tune rendition of 'Happy Birthday' as he grabbed a wooden spoon and conducted an imaginary orchestra changed the mood and sparked some laughter. The cake was delicious. The ring was put aside. And the small talk centered on other things.

Margaret had much to think about; and her first thought was that she needed to write Ben.

It had become customary now for Samuel to drive Ziva home. As he pulled up to the curb Rose said, "Samuel, please, won't you come inside?" Samuel had been in Ziva's home before but only briefly when picking her up. Most times she took a bus and met him somewhere, often close to the hospital. He accepted and now he and Ziva were seated on the clean, slightly threadbare pink and blue flowered sofa in a parlor-type room. A braided rug covered the dull hardwood floor scuffed and worn from years of traffic. It brought Samuel memories of home. Two blue side chairs and a coffee table completed the room. An oval picture of a man and woman was the only wall ornament. He could see the stairs to the second floor and hear kitchen noise as Rose busied herself making a pot of tea.

"Are you comfortable? Do you need anything?" Ziva asked nervously. Before he could answer she continued. "What an evening. Why do you think Margaret didn't say yes? That ring was fantastic! I mean, he loves her. And I think she loves him. Why not get married?" Finally, she took a breath giving him a chance to respond. She was dizzying sometimes. The way her mind raced was part of her appeal. . .but annoying at times.

"Marriage is a big step, Ziva. I think she needs to figure things out."

"What do you mean? That doesn't sound very romantic."

"In Lithuania parents arrange the marriage. You marry the person they choose, always within the faith, and over time you grow to care and love one another. Here *you* can choose who you marry. Maybe it's for money; friendship or companionship; or a need to take care of someone. Maybe it's for love. Or even a combination of those reasons. That's what I meant."

Rose brought in the tea things and excused herself, saying she was retiring. Ziva grew silent for a moment as they sipped the hot beverage. "Samuel, if we ever—I'm not saying we will—but if we were ever to get married, which of those reasons would it be?" Her question caught Samuel off guard and he choked on the hot tea.

He set the cup on the low table and avoided looking at her. She did have a point. They had been seeing each other for over a year and a half now. *Is that where they were headed. Marriage?* Marrying outside his faith was not permitted at home and would never have been an option. But here? While still uncommon, it did occur. He knew she was looking at him. Those large dark eyes framed in thick black lashes were focused on him. *How had this conversation gotten so serious?*

"Okay, Samuel. Which one?"

He squirmed. Picked up the cup again. *How did he feel toward her?* He swallowed the last of his tea replaced the cup and said quickly, "Combination."

A smile lit up her face. "I rule out money. That leaves friendship and love." She kissed his cheek, but then she grew unusually serious. She drew in a quick breath before blurting out, "Has Monroe ever spoken about our father?"

"Just that he had passed away."

"Yeah. I figured. We don't talk about it." Samuel wasn't sure how to respond, so the two sat silently for a long moment. He had to strain to hear Ziva say, "I want to tell you about it." She turned toward him, but slid away on the sofa. "Do you remember once when you brought me home, you told me that you could never think of anyone as. . .uh. . .as not good enough?"

Samuel searched for the memory, and nodded.

"Did you really mean that?"

He studied her serious expression and her tenseness, but still wasn't sure where this conversation was leading. "What do you want to tell me?"

She moved further away and fidgeted with her skirt, her eyes avoiding his. "Okay, then. A few years ago our father was severely injured at work. The pain never went away. It made him mean and bitter and angry. He couldn't work and we had to take care of him." She stopped, not sure how much more she should tell him. He might not understand. But then, again, he was a doctor. She plunged ahead, anyway. "Mom and I came home one day over a year ago, and I went to check on him. He was dead."

"Ziva, how difficult for you."

"There's more. I screamed for Mom and when she came into the room she hid his bottle of pain tablets in her pocket. We've never talked about it. I don't know for sure what happened." She stopped talking and took a long breath.

"I'm guessing the tablets were strong and maybe she wanted to secure them," Samuel said. 'What did his doctor say was the cause of death? I doubt there was an autopsy."

"Samuel, that doesn't matter! Did he just die? Did he accidently take too many? Did he commit suicide and did my mother help him?" And what does that say about—" She folded her arms across herself and gave a shiver, tears beginning to slide down. "I haven't ever told anyone before. You being a doctor, I probably shouldn't have said anything to you."

He took a minute to figure out the right words. "It's true. As a physician and as a Jew, suicide and euthanasia are considered illegal. But it's okay that you told me. This has been a terrible secret for you to keep. Ziva, let's talk about this. First, and probably, your father may have died of natural causes; and that is what the doctor decided, right?" She nodded. "Second, your mother could have *accidently* left the tablets in the room and if your father was simply tired of living in pain. Of having no life. Of being a burden to his family, then. . . We don't know what it's like to live in extreme pain day after day after day. I see great pain sometimes in the hospital, especially with cancer patients who suffer much. Life is very hard for them. Maybe he was someone who just couldn't do it anymore. Third, Ziva, even if your father did convince your mother to leave the tablets, it was still his decision whether or not to take them. This must be difficult for your mother, too. You should try and talk to her."

"Do you have to report this, or anything?"

"No. I wasn't treating your father or attending him in any way. I didn't even know you then. You don't know for sure what happened. Could be that your dreams are confusing what really happened. So, no. The way I see it, your father died because his body's will to live died, however it happened."

Ziva's tears were now flowing freely and she buried her face in Samuel's shoulder, softly sobbing and sniffing. He held her close until she sat back and rubbed her nose with the back of her hand; then he grabbed his handkerchief for her. "Thank you, Samuel. I mean for listening." She raised her tear-stained face and smiled. "You will make such a good doctor one day," she said.

CHAPTER 39

Sydney, Australia
March 28, 1942

The Sydney Harbor Bridge loomed before them. Made of steel and labeled the largest arched bridge in the world it had just celebrated its tenth anniversary. Overhead a canopy of brilliant blue sky crowded with flat-bottomed clouds covered the harbor now painted with the triangles of sailboats and other small craft welcoming the Queen Mary to Australia. An array of tall buildings rimmed the docks. Tug boats puffing dark gray smoke came alongside the ship. Soldiers lined the decks waving to spectators on the banks and pointing out various landmarks as they neared the docks. Their long voyage from the New York harbor was ending. Fragments of comments were overheard as soldiers lined up to disembark.

As the 9,000 plus troops filed off the Queen Mary, Ben caught some of their comments as they raced down the corridors toward the waiting launches. "We're finally here." "Where are you going from here?" "Think we'll see any kangaroos?" "I am so glad to be off this stinkin' ship, and I mean 'STINKIN!'" And, frankly, so was Ben. 'Stinkin' was being kind. *Forty days and forty nights onboard with over 10,000 souls crowded together, some throwing up, others smoking cigarettes, most not showering, created a disgusting mélange of odors unique in human history*, Ben thought. He pitied the crew that had to clean the ship.

They would be docked for nearly a week in Sydney before sailing back to New York. Compared to this trip the ship would be empty going back. Only a few passengers and the crew of 800. The ship would make three stops, Freemantle, Cape Town and Rio and it would still take a month to get back to New York.

He and Dr. Ramsey were watching the disembarkation from an upper deck. Sydney was a big and busy harbor made even busier by the number of troop transport trucks lining up and loading the American soldiers. Mixed in with the American vehicles were some trucks with the Australian military insignia on the side, a golden rising sun with a banner underneath. The Queen was also the transport for Australian soldiers wounded in North Africa and then flown to Rio for treatment and convalescence. Now they were returning home to a heroes' welcome. Their jaunty brown hats, curled up on one side with a wide chin strap and their shorts made them easy to spot—that and the wide smiles at being home again. Some had family greeting them. He saw reporters snapping pictures for the local papers and angling for interviews.

"Greetings," lads. The two turned at the sound of the captain's voice. As he approached he nodded toward the ramps full of hurrying men. "Can't say I blame them for scurrying off my ship. I'm ready to leave her for a bit myself. I think I mentioned that my wife and daughter were evacuated to Sydney months ago and are staying with my sister and family. I spoke with Lizzie—that's my sister— and asked if she could stand a couple of extra houseguests for a few days. There's a spare room available if you would like some home cooked food and a floor that doesn't move under your feet all the time." Ben gave an enthusiastic yes; but Dr. Joe's expression said something else. The Captain thought he understood.

"Joe, while it is true the indigenous people here are, should I say 'looked down' on by much of the population, colored men from America are held in much higher esteem. My sister and her husband are quite comfortable extending an invitation to you and that goes for my wife and daughter as well. Have you shared with Ben why Cunard decided to hire you?" Joe shook his head. "May I?"

"Of course. But first allow me to explain to Ben how I heard about this ship." He turned back to Ben.

"There's a publication well-known to Negroes called *The Pittsburgh Courier*. It covers many items of particular interest to us. I had made plans to enlist, but through the *Courier* I learned there was a good chance my training as a doctor would not be put to use. Most coloreds were being assigned as mess boys, or other low-level jobs. When the Queen Mary was in Boston it was big news everywhere. The *Courier* reprinted an interview with you, Captain, and you casually mentioned that finding medical staff had become a bit of a problem. I gave it considerable thought and then sent a letter." He paused.

The Captain turned toward Ben. "When the United States was thrust into the war Cunard was still struggling to find qualified medical staff for the Queen Mary. It was after all, an obscure assignment. We weren't really advertising for positions. We had you, Ben, and Dr. McHenry lined up. Then I received Dr. Ramsey's letter offering his services. He told me in his letter he was a Negro. It set me to thinking. Cunard and I were not certain who was going to be transported aboard the Queen Mary. Your President, Mr. Roosevelt, had put the discrimination order in place and we didn't know just what that meant for transporting soldiers. And in addition, we carry nearly 1,000 crew members of varying ethnicity. It seemed practical to have Dr. Ramsey on board. Chaps, I'm being frank, here. In the event anyone did have objections to treating a Negro, a Negro doctor on board could be beneficial."

Ben searched for an adequate response. He hadn't given any thought to how Dr. Joe came to be aboard. "I never thought about any of that." He started to add more but loud raucous laughter interrupted them and they turned their attention back to the men exiting the ship.

It was late afternoon when Cunard's private car stopped in front of a large white clapboard house supporting a bright red roof that extended over the front porch. While the Captain spoke with the driver, Ben and Dr. Ramsey unloaded their small bags. The location was ideal. The home was situated on a high piece of land and Ben correctly guessed that the upper floor had a glimpse of Sydney harbor. He pointed out the flower beds still blooming with delphinium, Singapore orchids, and calla lilies, remembering here it was late summer. Large shade trees reached out to the house on two sides capturing the strong breeze that lived here. A winding flagstone walk wandered up to the front door that was flanked by leaded glass panels.

Suddenly the front door burst wide open and a blur of gray and white fur came bounding down the flagstone path followed by Kate her bright red curls flaming behind her. The breeze tossed her yellow sun dress around her knees. In the open doorway stood her mum, Norah, and the Captain's sister, Lizzie. "Papa! We've missed you so much!" Kate's father dropped his bags to catch Kate as she propelled herself into his arms. "You've been away so long this time." The dog wriggled around both of them, tongue out, competing for attention.

"I've missed you, too, Poppet," he said, using his pet name for her. He kissed the top of her head then turned her toward their guests. "Look who I brought with me. You remember, Ben, right? And this is Dr. Joe Ramsey. Joe, this is Kate, my daughter. They'll tell you how they met, later, after I've introduced you to the rest of my family."

Ben reached down and rubbed the dog's ears, feeling its silky blue-gray fur.

"That's Miki. It means moon," Said Kate. "Down, Miki." Immediately the dog came to attention by her side.

"Is he, uh, she very old?" Asked Ben

Kate laughed. "No, No. Miki's a two-year old male; that's why he's so energetic. The blue-gray is called blue merle, not old age. We're still training him. Grab your bags and come on inside."

The house was large with five bedrooms. Their hostess, Lizzie, guided Ben and Joe to their shared room and the Captain dropped his bags in Norah's and his room. Lizzie explained that her husband, Bertram,—everyone called him Bert—was in Melboune for a couple of days on business and their two children were still away at school.

Presently they were all seated on the large wraparound porch at the back of the house, sheltered from the persistent wind. It was a brilliant afternoon—the temperature hovering in the high seventies, a rich floral aroma rising up around them. What a contrast to the aromatic ship. In this place it would be easy to forget the war. A glass pitcher of lemonade was being shared among them as they all became acquainted and re-acquainted.

Kate's version of Ben's fall and their first meeting told for Joe and Lizzie's benefit was not at all how Ben remembered it. He was certain he was more in charge of the situation that day than she had been.

Norah sat next to her husband, their fingers intertwined, hands resting in her lap. She showed him the most recent letter from Robin. Their son was ecstatic about flying, always skipping over the danger for his mum's sake, but she knew better. Either or both of her men could be gone in an instant. That thought was always with her.

The Captain went upstairs for a nap. Lizzie moved off into the kitchen beginning dinner preparations and Norah left, too, presumably to help. They didn't notice her slipping up the stairs.

"I think I'll just go unpack and write a couple of letters," Joe said as he stood, stretched, and yawned.

"That yawn says maybe a nap, too?" Ben queried with a wink. He and Kate remained on the porch, silent for a moment or two. Then, Kate spoke softly.

"Papa wrote us about the fire and your fiancée. It was certainly a horrible experience for you. I'm so sorry, Ben."

This conversation was still so difficult, he thought. "Thanks, it was." He looked away. "So, it must be nice living here with your aunt and uncle. It's beautiful here. Safe. What have you been doing?" He sipped his lemonade watching Miki frisking around on the lawn throwing a small ball up and then dashing to catch it. Kate was sitting across from him, her chin propped up on her hand, watching him, noticing the change of subject.

"It's boring," she said. "I miss home. I miss my work as a nurse. Mum's busy with our Auntie Lizzie and it's a big house to take care of—I mean, I help, too—but I want to do more. My brother is doing his part. Papa too. I feel like I'm not doing anything important. Tell me what it's like aboard the Queen Mary now? When Papa comes home he doesn't talk about it."

Ben should have realized that Kate's father didn't talk about it for a reason, but he didn't. So, he told her about Rio and the near miss with the U-Boat. He told her about the incident in Cape Town (leaving out his part of that story). He shared how the ship had changed; how it had guns on it now and how crowded and smelly it was. He talked about the soldiers—how young they were; how energized, but how bored they got on the long voyage. He told her a little of Joe Ramsey's story, too. She asked questions and he answered. Quickly the afternoon was gone and Lizzie was calling everyone to dinner. Despite his aversion to fire, Ben's narrative had innocently fanned a flame in Kate that had been smoldering for weeks.

After dinner and dishes, everyone gathered in the spacious main living room and Lizzie, an accomplished pianist, filled the room with the music of Liszt and Chopin. Kate's mind, however, was not on the music.

The warm weather held and the following day a trip to the Taronga

Zoo was on the schedule. The group included only Ben, Kate and Dr. Ramsey and when the trio crossed the old rustic bridge at the entrance they were immediately transported into a new strange world. Many of the unique, weird wildlife creatures housed here could only be seen in Australia. Gray teddy-bearlike Koalas clung to the branches high in eucalyptus trees.

"Koalas' only food are those eucalyptus leaves," Kate pointed out.

"Yumm," Ben replied smacking his lips noisily. She punched his arm and wrinkled her nose at him.

Kangaroos, some females complete with a 'joey' safely ensconced in her pouch, bounced along on those enormous hind legs. Overhead the Kookaburra chortled its eerie laugh as they walked along following the winding paths lined with a colorful array of uncommon flowers and trees.

And then they came upon the platypus. The unusual appearance of this egg-laying, duck-billed, beaver-tailed, otter-footed mammal baffled them at first. They couldn't figure it out. "It looks like someone took a bunch of different animals and sewed them all together," Ben said twisting his head to the side for a better viewing angle. Kate laughed. "Crikey! Plus, I think he surely must have been a bit bladdered when he did it." The men looked at her, brows furrowed. "Chaps—you know—he had tipped the bottle too many times when he did it?"

Their teasing and laughter lasted all afternoon. *Being with Kate again was like a breath of fresh air,* Ben thought. *I'll miss her when we leave Sydney.*

"No, absolutely not, Kate!"

"Papa, you don't understand!"

A note of discord filled the same room where they so recently had enjoyed Lizzie's melodious harmony.

"I do understand. You don't know what you're asking. Your

mother would never agree and I don't either."

"Papa. Maybe I should bloody well remind you that I don't need your permission. I am of age, you know. I could contact Cunard myself and put in an application, or enlist as a nurse, or. . . or something. This is not a whim. I've given it thought. *Much* thought."

"The answer is no. And don't swear."

"This isn't the end of this discussion," Kate stated. She stared her father down for a minute and with a flip of her red hair stomped from the room. He watched her go. *So young,* he thought. *So naïve.* She didn't believe him, but he did understand. What if she did contact Cunard directly? With a deep sigh he went to find Norah.

He found her upstairs folding laundry. "Norah, we need to talk about Kate."

"I know. She's been restless. I need to encourage her to find something else to do. I'm sure she can find nursing work in Sydney."

"It's more than that. She wants me to take her with me on the Queen."

Norah laughed. "That's absurd. Where did she get an idea like that? Why would she even think that?" She folded a towel and laid it aside. "Of course, you said no."

"I did. Then she reminded me she's of age. She threatened to speak to Cunard, directly. Norah, listen. I have an idea. You know from the beginning how passionate she's been about this war. Robin is serving. I am serv—"

"James." *Bad sign when she used James and not Jimmy,* he thought. "About Robin. We had this same discussion when he joined the RAF. You always side with them. When will you think about how I feel?"

"Now, hear me out. I am thinking of your feelings. . . and hers. She thinks she's not doing her part. When we leave in a couple of days we're going back to New York through Rio again."

Norah opened her mouth to interrupt again but he placed a finger on her lips. "What if I allow her to work on the Queen—just for one trip. She could get this desire to help satisfied. There is a real need for her skills. We won't be carrying troops so there'll be no nurses onboard until New York; but we will still have a full crew that needs medical support. This will be a safe trip. South America is safe and we will be in the United States part of the time. We'll only be gone six or seven weeks. Think about this. If she gets hired through Cunard she commits to six months and might not end up on the Queen with me." He was watching his wife as he talked. She had stopped folding clothes and turned toward him.

"Jimmy," *Jimmy. That was better.* "Are you out of your mind?" *Maybe not.* "Don't you realize that any moment I could lose you or Robin or both! I think about that every day. Do you want me to think about losing our Kate, too?"

"Norah, you may not be able to stop her." She wasn't looking at him any longer. Her eyes focused beyond his shoulder. He turned. Kate was standing in the doorway.

"Mum. Please. I'd prefer going with your blessing."

At Captain Hawthorne's request Cunard arranged a larger car for them. Bert had returned from Melbourne and stood with Lizzie inside the doorway; Miki wriggled by Bert's side. The warm weather from earlier in the week had been replaced by rain and much cooler temperatures. Luggage was stowed, thanks were extended to their host and hostess, and Ben and Dr. Ramsey were seated in the car while the family's goodbyes were said. The Hawthorne family were standing on the porch, Norah tightly holding her husband. "We've done this so many times," she said. Her stomach knotted up and her mouth went dry. She reluctantly released her husband and turned toward Kate.

Kate was dressed in her white nurse's uniform and cap, white hose and shoes. A dark navy woolen cape over her shoulders would protect her from the rain. Her curls fell around her shoulders and Norah touched them softly. "Rain always makes your hair curlier," she said and then adjusted Kate's cape. There were so many things she wanted to say, but the words refused to be spoken.

"Mum. It's okay. I'll be back before you can say 'Jack Sprat.' I'm safe with Papa."

The Captain nudged everyone along. "Norah, we need to go." He spoke over his shoulder. "Lizzie. Bert. Thanks for your hospitality. Look after my wife for me." He opened the umbrella for him and his daughter and they sprinted to the waiting car.

They didn't see the tears falling from Norah's eyes. "Lizzie, I may never see them again," she breathed. She shivered in the damp air and watched until the car was out of sight.

CHAPTER 40

~

Ponar Forest
Early April, 1942

The ladder was in place and a German soldier waited at the top. Jonah and Rabbi Schuler along with the other seventy-four men approached. This wasn't the usual beginning of their day. This German was not one of their guards. When they were assembled, he spoke; the big rifle across his chest. His German was clipped. "Achtung! The Ponar Commandant is on his way here. You are ordered to follow me." One by one the men climbed out of the pit lagging behind the brisk pace of the soldier. They had walked about two kilometers when they began to notice a smell, slight at first but increasingly pungent. Decay. Human decay. They looked at one another, the fear they continually lived with clutched them. *Was this it? Are they finished with us?* Ahead they saw more soldiers clustered around a large depression in the ground. There was a noticeable absence of Lithuanian soldiers. The Jewish men's German guide raised his gun. "Haltestelle," he announced.

Jonah gave voice to their fears. "Rabbi, we are dead, no?" he whispered.

"Maybe not. If they are shooting us they would not wait for the Commandant."

They stood for a long time before they heard a vehicle approaching. The German driver sprang from the front, opened a rear door and stood at attention. Jonah stared as the Commandant walked their way. "Rabbi, I know this man. We have met before." A chorus of 'Heil Hitler' was raised along with the salute and the snapping of boots as the leader approached.

The Nazi leader stopped several feet from the Jewish men, his strong German accent filling the morning air. "I am the Ponar Commandant and I am here to tell you a story. Your Lithuanian brothers have been executing Jews and burying them in these surrounding pits. We have word that Russian soldiers may soon be at our borders. It would not be good for them to know about the atrocities your country has committed. We need you to clean up their mess. The wood you have been cutting is for fires. These corpses are to be dug up and burned beginning immediately. He pointed to the German guide. This is Ober Schar Führer Schneider. He will be in charge of this operation. You will take orders from him." He looked around at the soldiers. This part of his message was directed at them as well as the Jews. Again, a chorus of 'Heil Hitler' and the snap of boots was directed at the Commandant as he turned back toward his military escort.

Herr Schneider watched him exit the forest then turned toward the men. "Shovels will be arriving soon."

April, Weeks later

He dug furiously. Dig during the day. Dig at night in his sleep. The smell and the carnage were always with him. Every day they uncovered more bodies. Many naked. All in various states of decay. Men, women and children. Even babies. Jonah thought he recognized Soske and Rebekah. It was hard to tell. The clothes looked familiar. The German soldats ordered them to remove any gold teeth from the corpses and drop them in a bowl. *They don't need them anymore*, the soldiers laughed. In this first pit Jonah estimated there were more than 15,000 bodies. This was a horror no sane person could recover from. What kind of depraved mind could do such a thing to innocent human beings? Children. What have we done other than be born Jews?

As the crematory fires were built, nowhere could the captives escape the smell of burning flesh, day or night—possibly ever. They hauled the stacked logs they had been chopping for weeks and laid them side by side in layers. They carried or dragged the decomposed remains to the logs, placing about 200 bodies on each layer. The gasoline stunk as they doused each layer of bodies and set it on fire. An inverted V-shaped ramp was built to reach the top of the pyre as more and more layers were added. The fires burned hour after hour. When a pyre finally burned itself out the men mixed the ash with the surrounding sandy soil and re-buried the cremated remains. They repeated this day after day. The scene was hellish.

The men washed and washed their hands in an attempt to not only cleanse them from the smell and decay of their work but also to cleanse them in an act of forgiveness to their Jewish brethren. Neither was successful. The smell still clung to their bodies and they found it impossible to forgive themselves.

In spite of the heavy labor the men's sleep was troubled now. The images they saw all day haunted their dreams at night. There was no escape from the grisly horror they lived with. *Sreyfe, Sreyfe,* the Yiddish word for fire, shattered the silence of the night as a man's nightmare ended with a scream. Many had seen neighbors, friends, business associates among those in the pits. One man recognized his wife's body and had fallen on his knees, sobbing, until a Nazi soldat saw him, struck him with his rifle and ordered him to keep digging. Rabbi Schuler had sat with him later saying prayers, but the man's eyes were vacant and he had a hollow look. The Rabbi was concerned that he might curl up and die in the night. Hell, itself, could not possibly be more macabre than what they were seeing—what they were doing. Their only hope was the completion of the tunnel.

Jonah came out of the tunnel and stretched. The cramped position in the tunnel after lifting and digging all day made his shoulders and neck stiff and ache. Another man took over for him. "These men can't go on much longer," he said to Rabbi Schuler. "Food isn't adequate. Sleep is tortured. We're all exhausted. Many will die soon if we don't get out of here. We need help."

The help came in the form of heavy rain during the night. The hut provided little shelter, but the rain kept their captors from appearing the next morning. They had a full day of rest from the grueling task forced upon them. They used the extra time to work on the escape tunnel. Some slept. Some dug. Daylight created the need to be ever vigilant for the Nazi guards. The digging continued throughout the day and into the evening. Jonah's engineering expertise and especially his knowledge of the soil—gathered when his firm designed these pits—prevented a collapse. It was nearly his turn to dig again. He was so tired. The toilsome digging was taking a heavy toll on all of the men. The stronger ones picked up a larger share of the digging which cost them more of their sleep.

A subdued shout from the mouth of the tunnel caught the attention of Jonah's sluggish mind. The Rabbi was signaling to him. "We have broken through," he said. "The digging is finished." Euphoric relief surged through the group. Before the celebration became too loud, Rabbi Shuler motioned everyone together. "Let us gather and make our plans."

The success of their exhausting efforts was an elixir to the group. With renewed energy they discussed what would come next. After saying the *Shema,* Rabbi Schuler led the discussion. "There is little moonlight now and the rain clouds may fill the sky for a few more days. I suggest we make our escape in two days. My best estimate is that it will be Passover then when the angel of death killed the firstborn in Egypt but passed over the homes of the Jews, freeing them from slavery. It is time for us to be free. Surely God will help us." The men nodded silently as he spoke.

A shaky female voice was heard. "What about the mines?"

"We've watched. Those of us who have worked in the forest. We paid attention to the guards, and they seem unconcerned about mines. We think it is only a scare tactic." He saw the men nodding. We will go at midnight two nights from tonight when it is darkest."

Jonah looked from one man to another as the Rabbi finished. Some were so weak and malnourished he was certain even two more nights' rest would not help them survive this journey. *Would he and Ana be among the survivors? Would they ever see these people again?* He rose and walked around the group, gently touching each man on the shoulder. It was his way of acknowledging the brotherhood they shared; a brotherhood stretching back centuries strewn over and again with blood and sacrifice. As bright as the funeral fires a thought burned in his mind: *What we have witnessed here should be told to the world so it will never happen again. Some of us must survive and make that our mission.*

CHAPTER 41

Atlantic Ocean
April 1942

K ate shared Ben's earlier amazement at the transformation of the Queen Mary and walked nearly every inch. When they came to the dining room, she was stunned. Her eyes roamed the large room while moaning, "Where are the chandeliers? And the exquisite paintings?" She remembered the night the two of them had danced on the parquet floor. She had given him a tour that next day and now the tour he was giving her was of a completely different ship. When she saw the cannons and big guns she grew quiet, aware for the first time the extent of the danger her father and the Queen Mary faced.

As Ben showed Kate around he noticed with delight that the cleaning crew had done an admirable job. There were no soldiers on board for this trip just 800 crew, several Red Cross workers and a few newspaper correspondents returning to the States. The medical needs were minor—a kitchen cut that needed stitches, pills dispensed for headaches, some dysentery. The dysentery was a concern for a few hours, with Ben noting that the condition sometimes runs through a ship's crew? The word choice 'runs' provoked an eyeroll from Kate.

Only once did they have an alert that a U-boat was in the area causing them to intensify their zig-zag course and increase their speed. Every activity on board was stopped, including speech, keeping the ship as silent as possible. If a German sub was in the area that day they were able to outrun it and no one saw it. One day they did sight a ship and it turned out to be the Queen Elizabeth with troops aboard. Many went on deck to wave and cheer and the two sister ships saluted each other with blasts from their horns.

It would have been a boring trip except for Kate. For her everything was an exciting new adventure and her enthusiasm was infectious. Now they were berthed in Rio de Janeiro for two days for supplies.

Ben and Kate had gone ashore, posted the mail from the ship, including a letter to his mom letting her know when he would be home, and sampled the South American food, music and beaches. Then Ben decided to have a bit of fun with Kate.

"I don't know, Kate. It looks pretty rickety to me." He and Kate were standing in line for the cable car which would take them to the top of Sugarloaf Mountain, 1,299 feet above the city.

"What a lot of tosh. Come on, Ben. I'm sure it's not wonky."

"Ok. But don't say I didn't warn you. Wonky?"

He and Joe Ramsey had ridden to the top when they were here and he knew what to expect. He helped Kate into the enclosed wooden car and it swung slightly as the other cars were loaded. Kate was next to the window and watched the ground below. With a low growl the cable began its long crawl through the wheels toward the summit. As their car approached the first wheel, it gave a shudder and then a jerk and stopped for an instant swinging wildly. Kate's blue eyes opened wide and she moved closer to Ben, fiercely grabbing his elbow. Then with another jerk the car moved upward toward the next wheel and continued with that shudder, jerk, swing pattern all the way to the top.

Ben kept watching her as the car ascended. Kate had been holding her breath still gripping tightly to his elbow and staring straight ahead. As she gradually got used to the ratchety pattern of the ride she turned her head to look at the beach and water as it receded below. The car slowed and stopped at the top and Kate jumped from the car, a bit wobbly. "That was smashing, really. You thought I was nervous, right?" she giggled.

"Well, you could have fooled me. My elbow thought you were. It may never be the same."

"What an absolutely grand view," she said, scampering away toward the railing. The strong breeze tossed her curls into her face and she tacked them behind her ears. Far below them the warm blue Atlantic water in the bay sparkled merrily as it cozied up to the glittering sand of Ipanema Beach littered with colorful umbrellas and sparsely clad bathers. Across the bay on Corcovado the white 125-foot tall Christ the Redeemer statue gleamed in the sun. Its outstretched arms appearing to pronounce a sweeping blessing while welcoming everyone to the paradise below. "I've never seen anything like this. Even Seté in France wasn't this bloomin' beautiful."

Back on the ship that evening Ben was in his room. His journal sat open before him, the page empty. His intention was to record the recent events, but his mind kept wandering. To Kate. They had spent such a grand day together. His face gathered into an involuntary smile as he thought of how she tried to cover her anxiety during the cable car ride. Her enthusiasm and high spirits were so exhilarating and contagious. Everything was a grand adventure to her. There it was again. The word "grand". She said it a lot. Now he found himself using it. Lately he tracked Kate down more and more, making up flimsy excuses to talk or have a cuppa' together.

He tried to picture Laura on the cable car and realized that wouldn't have happened. Unlike Kate, she wouldn't have ridden to the top. It had been five months since he proposed, but so much had happened it felt like five years. He knew he shouldn't compare the two women, but he did. Laura would have been loyal and steadfast. A good match for him. And Kate? She certainly made life exciting.

He closed the journal and turned off the small light he was allowed, relegating the room to complete blackness. He lay stretched out on his back, hands behind his head, and as sleep wandered in, he asked himself if he should invite Kate to come with him to Boston.

The Queen Mary pulled out the following day. Ben and Dr. Ramsey studied the harbor activity pointing out items of interest from the railing as tugs towed them out of the bay. The two men paid particular attention to the ship that was berthed next to them. It was similar to the one they saw here last time. Neither spoke but both had the same sobering thought. Those men died and we lived. It was supposed to be us.

They were headed for Trinidad and Tobago where they would skirt around the Windward and Leeward Islands and head up the eastern coast of the United States, berthing in New York City.

As the British ocean liner pulled out into the Atlantic moving silently up the coast of Brazil many miles east of them an early season tropical storm was beginning its counterclockwise rotation, churning up the vast Atlantic waters. There was plenty of open water for fuel as it began its southwesterly trek. It was in its infancy and presently undetected.

And down on "D" Deck in the steward's quarters, a 28-year old British steward named Reuben felt a bit nauseous. He had been crewing for several years and nausea was unusual for him. He returned to the kitchen intending to ask the docs for some pills at his first opportunity.

CHAPTER 42

Ponar Forest
April 1942

There was no moon. The group actually wished for rain. It might make their planned escape easier—cover any noise they made by forcing the guards to remain sheltered. But the night sky was not shedding any tears for them. They gathered in the hut, each one carrying what few remaining belongings they had. Jonah's long woolen coat was snug around him and he and Ana each carried their cloth satchels. Rabbi Schuler was giving last minute instructions. "We will enter the tunnel one by one, but no one will exit until the tunnel is full. We live together or die together." As he whispered to the assembled group, Ana looked around. They had left a fire burning purposely to give the appearance of normalcy. The flames flickered and cast shadows into their squalid living quarters. *How strange*, she thought. *As much danger as we have been in, as much evil as is here, it is difficult to leave. Here we know what to expect. Out there, who knows what awaits us. If we survive.* The Rabbi's words broke into her thoughts. "God be with us. Let us say the *Shema* together before we leave." Their combined hushed voices rose into the night along with the smoke from the fire—woven tendrils of prayers ushered to God on the night wind. The first man entered the tunnel. One by one they followed until as many as possible were stretched along its 130-foot length. The Rabbi, Jonah and Ana were last.

Then rapidly they were scrambling on hands and knees out of the escape tunnel into the dark night. At first it seemed they had made it, scattering in all directions hearing only the night sounds. But suddenly Haltestelle! Haltestelle! broke the stillness followed by the staccato bursts of gunfire. They knew it was the end. Screams of pain from the lead runners slammed into those still in the tunnel, but they resolutely forged ahead, preferring death by a gunshot to one more day of the gruesome job they had been doing, the end being the same anyway. At least they had a choice.

Ana covered her ears and pressed against Jonah. "They will kill us. What should we do?"

"We are going. We aren't living now anyway." Rabbi Schuler nodded his agreement.

Jonah and Ana exited the tunnel, running, breathless, adrenalin-laced hearts pumping violently. Gunshots exploded around them. They could hear screams and bodies falling when suddenly Ana screamed, slipped and fell. Her momentum carried her down a small ravine filled with dried leaves and debris. Jonah scrambled after her, searching frantically for her in the darkness. He realized at once if he couldn't see her neither could the Nazis. He risked a low whisper. "Ana, Be very quiet. Don't run. Cover yourself with the leaves." He prayed she could hear him. He burrowed down, covering his skin and face with his dark coat blending in with the moonless night. He wanted to locate her. To know that she was alive and not injured. But the least movement or sound would give them away. It took all of his will power, but he stayed where he was, blood pounding in his ears.

Over and over staccato bursts of gunfire from the Nazi MG42's lit the night until finally becoming fewer and more distant. He could hear the sound of the running Wehrmacht boots crunching the leaves and their sharp shouts to each other, but the shots were now only sporadic. Then one last burst of gunfire sliced the night, undoubtedly ending the life of a wounded Jew or shooting at a distant runner who, unknowingly, was leading the guns away from Jonah and Ana.

It grew quiet. He listened. Either Ana had heard his instructions or she was unconscious or . . . Suddenly voices. Two voices belonging to the German soldats. They appeared to be hurrying back toward the pit, one saying to the other, "Those *drecksau! Kikes!* Dirty pigs! I don't want to be the one who reports this to the Commandant! What *should* we tell him? Hey! Kazimierz! Pay attention! We'll make up something—how they overpowered us but we killed them anyway."

Then a deeper voice not German, Lithuanian. "I thought they were too dumb to try to escape. Well, we shot a lot of them, even the one they called Rabbi."

"We should tell the Commandant that we killed *ALL* of them. None escaped." The rest of their conversation was lost as they hurried back toward the pit.

Jonah waited, wondering if they were gone or if it was a trap. He flattened himself staying hidden in the dead leaves, fallen brothers just feet away. and the smell of damp earth and moldy decaying leaves filling his nostrils. And now more dead bodies. These dead bodies he knew. These dead bodies he had labored with for weeks. These dead bodies he had prayed with just minutes ago. Jonah took a shallow shuddering breath but stayed buried. He still had not heard a sound from Ana. Then a new thought. *Maybe she's waiting for me to make the first move. Maybe she thinks I'm dead!* Desperately he wanted to raise his head and look around. *Was it safe yet?* Tentatively he uncovered one ear and listened intently. He heard the faint rustle of leaves. *Was it the wind or the monsters?* His gut tensed. *How long should I lie here?* The minutes ticked by. Still nothing from Ana. And nothing from any of his Jewish brothers. He hoped he and Ana weren't the only ones to escape. *But then we haven't actually escaped yet, have we?*

He kept listening trying to filter out the forest noises from human noises. *How long had it been? Ten minutes? An hour?* Then a rustle. But different, somehow, from the other noises. Closer. It was just ahead, off to his left. His mind had been working on two levels. *The soldats may be gone, but they will be back with others. And soon. So, if he and Ana were going to get away they had to time it perfectly.* Okay. He slowly lifted his head and looked to his left. The moon which had been slow to rise was just beginning to throw a little light through the tall trees. There! That mound of leaves moved slightly! He inched his way along toward the bunched-up debris, still remaining buried. "Ana," he whispered hoarsely. Whether from fear or the forest mulch he spit out, his voice had become raspy. Then faintly he heard her. The voice was weak and shaky, but she was alive. He crawled faster until he reached the spot where she lay. He brushed some of the leaves from her face and she spat out some sandy soil. "Are you hurt?" he asked.

"I'm not sure. I haven't tried to move since I fell."

"You weren't shot then?"

"At first I thought I was. Now I'm not sure. My ankle hurts. And you, Jonah. Are you hurt?"

"No. But, listen, Ana. They will be coming back. We must move further away from here. The moon is rising. It won't be so dark soon. Can you walk?"

"I'll try." Carefully, Jonah helped Ana to her feet. They both stood a moment, letting the blood rush into their legs. Jonah remained alert to any sounds out of place in Ponar, but heard only wind and rustling leaves as some forest animal came out of hiding and tentatively began foraging around. The two moved their limbs and felt for broken bones thanking Yahweh they had escaped serious injury. Ana had a slightly sprained ankle, but managed to put her weight on it. Her satchel had tumbled several feet away when she fell, and its weight had carried it down into the leaves. She picked it up, brushed it off and they were ready to leave. *But where to go?*

"Ana, we must be very vigilant. Up ahead about two kilometers is a train track. Remember? It runs along the edge of

Ponar. The train to Kaunas uses that track." Then a thought he chose not to mention. *The Germans also use that track to bring carloads of Jews to Ponar Forest to be exterminated.* "I have a contact in Kaunas. A Lithuanian, sympathetic to the Jews. He may be able to help us if we can get there." Weeks ago, when Jonah heard about the escape tunnel, he thought about where he and Ana would go, what they would do, if they were successful in getting away. He pulled his coat tighter. It was time to put that plan into action. They had a chance, but the odds were very much against them.

CHAPTER 43

Coast of Venezuela
April 1942

Captain Hawthorne was on duty and had taken control of the ship from Captain Merriwether. "Ay, Sir. Canna' say the weather's lookin' too good. Seas are a bit choppy and a brisk wind's a' been increasing," Merry informed him. "Aye. Been through much worse, though. She's all yours, Captain." They shared a nod and Merry went below.

Although the wind speed had picked up to 25 knots and the seas were choppy as a result, this wasn't a concern for a ship the size of the Queen Mary other than sudden gusts might rock it a bit. The Captain called the First Mate and his Chief Navigator together, directing them to give him course corrections if conditions deteriorated further.

Ben and Kate were in the infirmary treating a crewman's persistent nosebleed. Kate was packing his nose with Vaseline-covered gauze after Ben had taken his blood pressure and listened to his heart. "Kate, place a compress across his nose and pinch it firmly." Turning to his patient, "Arthur, right? You'll need to sit here for a few minutes until we get the bleeding stopped. You're going to be just fine. It seems like a lot of blood, but I've never had anyone die from a nosebleed," he joked.

"Funny, doctor," Kate said sarcastically.

Unexpectedly the ship quivered and lurched at the same time

the eight-inch cannon boomed—testing again—startling Kate, causing her to lose her balance. She grabbed at Ben to steady herself and found herself wrapped in his arms.

"Aha!, that's what you get for not appreciating my humor. See how easily one can fall when a ship does that?" Ben teased.

"Aha! I *didn't* fall like you did." She wrinkled her nose at him, pushing away playfully.

"No, because I was here to *catch* you."

Dr. Joe's entry interrupted Kate's comeback. "Children, play nice. Thought I would check if we are having high tea later."

Their light banter was in direct contrast to what was happening in the wheelhouse. The Captain was reading a coded wireless transmission containing recent weather information. His directions to the crew were terse.

On Deck "D" the room steward named Reuben was still battling nausea, now attributing it to the increased rolling motion of the ship. He was taking the medicine the doctor had given him, but the nausea still nagged him; and today he had a persistent pain in his stomach. He decided to go to his quarters for a lie-down.

Three hours later conditions on board were worse. Because the rolling of the ship was constant now with wind gusts heavier and more frequent, high tea was cancelled. Kate and Ben were on their way to the wheelhouse. They could see immense gray clouds blocking the horizon and the wind buffeted them as they climbed the stairway using both hands to tightly grip the handrails. Quickly they pushed into the wheelhouse.

"Papa. It's bloomin' windy out there," Kate said, pushing hair from her eyes and patting the curls back in place.

"Kate, Ben, greetings," acknowledged her father. "I'm going to make an announcement soon. We are receiving regular weather updates from other ships and land weather stations in the area telling us that this storm has every indication of becoming a hurricane. They're rare this time of year and a bit of a surprise, but an unavoidable part of life on the sea. I need to alert the crew to secure as many loose items as possible.

"Dinner will be served early before the seas get rougher. From your point of view be thankful only 1,000 seasoned crew are on board instead of 10,000 blokes who've never been at sea before. However, from my perspective more is better. The extra ballast helps mitigate the roll. You are probably going to be overwhelmed with minor injuries and sickness. Get prepared."

They had a good view now off the bow and could see the towering waves as they crested in front of the ship. The Queen Mary had changed course pointing the bow into the waves in order to better absorb their impact and ease the pitching motion. Even so, the pitch and roll were becoming more unpleasant each hour.

Ben watched the surging ocean for a minute more. "Sir, hurricanes are rather dangerous, right? Sometimes ships. . .get sunk?"

"We're working on charting a course around it, if possible, but these storms can be very unpredictable. I wish we had better weather information but we'll take what we can get. This is a big ship and she can take a lot. Even so, it's going to be a rough few hours. Now I would suggest heading down to the dining room soon and getting a bite to eat. It may be hours or longer before regular meals will be served again. Secure the infirmary. Check supplies and equipment. Alert Dr. Joe for me. I have a strong feeling the three of you are going to get very busy."

Reuben lay doubled up on his cot. No position was comfortable. First, he felt hot, then cold. He heard the Captain's announcement about the weather, meals, and safety procedures but he wasn't hungry anyway. He just wanted the pain to go away.

As the ship maintained its course and the Atlantic became a fierce force against them, the fine dining experience became a challenge. The ship would ride the crest of a wave and then drop into a trough, causing it to tilt. Dining room chairs slid away from the table. Cutlery bounced into a diner's lap. And if your plate of food wasn't securely held down it might end up in front of the person next to you, or worse on the floor. It was a meal like none other.

"Blimey! My dinner roll just took off down the table," Kate laughed.

"Here. Have mine," Ben said. "My stomach isn't feeling so good right now."

"Where do you suppose Dr. Joe is? I thought he was joining us."

"Maybe his stomach's jump—"

With no warning the ship took a hard bounce and Kate slipped off her chair. Ben grabbed for her but the ship's momentum threw him on top of her instead—followed by two plates of pasta. The couple lay in an intimate heap splattered with the creamy white sauce, noodles lodged in Kate's red curls. Ben attempted to push himself off her, his hands ending up where they shouldn't be. He felt himself turning red and scooted away. "I'm so sorry. Are you hurt?" he asked. A nearby server rushed to their aid and helped them up. "I'll fetch more serviettes for you," he said.

Gingerly, Kate pulled a long white noodle out of her hair. "Why do we keep ending up on the floor together?" she asked. If an element of fear hadn't been residing in the background they would have laughed harder.

At the same time, below them one deck, Reuben made a valiant effort to get to the steward's washroom. When the ship bounced he fell to his knees, collapsing just inside the doorway unable to stop the vomit rising in his throat.

And above them in the infirmary, Dr. Joe was on his way out the door to the dining room when he remembered he hadn't locked the supply cabinet he had been stocking. He turned back removing his hand from the door handle. The sudden bounce of the ship jolted him. He planted his feet grabbing onto a nearby railing, but his glasses fell from his face and slid across the room out of sight.

CHAPTER 44

Ponar Forest
April 1942

Jonah and Ana's progress was slow. Her sprained ankle and their need to remain hidden resulted in a slower pace than Jonah wanted. Thankfully, clouds scurried across the sky, subduing the moon's light. They stopped each time a rustle of leaves or a sound in the wind reached them. Jonah wanted to have a plan worked out before they got to the tracks. He didn't have a train schedule and the train only stopped here if it was unloading Jewish prisoners. He had been considering a way to stop the train, but he discarded every idea as either too dangerous or physically impossible.

Both he and Ana were dirty, him particularly. The smell of death, decomposition, and decay would take hours of scrubbing with strong soap to completely remove. They had brushed off most of the debris from the ditch, but bits of twigs, leaves and sandy soil clung to them. They were exhausted, thirsty, and hungry. Jonah was still working on a plan. *Maybe we won't get out of here after all. No.* He thought. *There has to be a way.* Over an hour had passed since their desperate escape from the tunnel. The tracks were just ahead.

"Ana, we need to find somewhere we can hide and rest."

There were no hiding places along the track, but a trestle had been built over a deep ravine. Large boulders were stacked beside the pilings providing some cover. Jonah helped Ana down the incline and they inched in among the shadowy shapes. The random-shaped rocks provided a secure hiding place. As the adrenalin rush left the fugitives' bodies it was replaced by the enormity of what they had just endured. Sobs began to shake Ana and she smothered the sound in his shoulder. He held her close until she quieted. The anguish he felt for the men and women gunned down around him eclipsed his anger for now and he prayed for their souls.

As hungry as they were they rationed the small amount of food from Ana's satchel and tried to rest while Jonah thought about a plan.

They had stayed hidden long enough now that their legs were beginning to cramp and Jonah still had no plan. Ana tugged on his sleeve. "I need a klozet."

"I'll give you some privacy." He moved a few feet away while Ana relieved herself.

It wasn't daylight yet, but Jonah knew it wouldn't be much longer before the safety the darkness provided would be gone. A noise. Louder. A vehicle? He made a shushing noise to Ana and pulled her down with him as he crouched lower. It was a vehicle. A German armored vehicle. Headlights bounced along through the trees and the car braked to a loud stop several yards ahead on the opposite side of the track at the far end of the train trestle. Car doors slammed and Ana's body shuddered with fright. Two Germans climbed from the vehicle and began talking but the words were indistinguishable to Jonah. He risked a peek around the piling. There were only the two, one taller than the other. Both Nazis lit cigarettes and looked around. Jonah was careful not to make a sudden move. He wished he could hear what they were saying, but they were too far away. They weren't searching the area. They seemed to be waiting for something. What? Why here?

He puzzled about it. Could this help them? Could he overpower them and steal the auto? No, that was a stupid idea.

They had guns. Could he trick them somehow? He was still analyzing that when he heard a low clatter in the distance. A train? He peeked out again. The Germans heard it, too. They turned on a bright light and directed it down the track. Jonah had already retreated back into the rocks but he crouched down further. The clatter of the wheels and the singing of the rails grew louder but the engineer had seen the light and applied the brake. The train slowed as it entered the trestle, brakes making a metallic squeal and steam spewing from the funnel. It stopped short of the men on the track. Jonah could see that the train contained only four or five cars. And the last car interested him.

The train engineer climbed down and accompanied the two soldiers to the first car. They slid open the large door and one of them jumped inside. After a quick look he jumped back down. That process was repeated for each of the other cars. Jonah understood then that they were searching this train for any escapees from earlier in the night. They must not have believed the soldats that all of the Jews were killed. *Good,* he thought. *Maybe others got away, too.*

The Germans continued around the back of the train passing within feet of the couple's hiding place. The taller one looked their way and tossed his cigarette toward them. It lay feet from Ana, its glowing end slowing dying. Jonah thought for sure they had been spotted and held his breath. He could hear them clearly now and he was right. They were looking everywhere for any Jews who had escaped murder earlier. Slowly the two, still accompanied by the engineer, continued around the rear of the stopped train looping back toward the engine.

Jonah was interested in this train. It was short. Only four or five cars, mostly empty. Why? There wasn't time to figure it out. The engineer was climbing back in. The train would be leaving in a minute or two. He turned to his wife keeping his voice barely a whisper. "I have a plan. The soldats have searched the train and are leaving. The train will move in a minute. See the last car with the platform and the two steps facing us? See the short wall around the platform? I've seen those cars before, usually on longer trains. It's risky but as soon as the train begins to move we'll climb onto that car's platform and lie down. The trestle noise will drown out our movements. I'll cover us with my black coat; the short wall will hide us. We must do this quickly and as quietly as possible. Understand?"

By now Ana had been through so much stress, hunger, physical exhaustion and fear that she was numb. She merely shook her head to indicate she understood. The train began to slowly move across the trestle. As quickly as they could the two scrambled up the ravine with Jonah pulling Ana along. He grabbed Ana's satchel and threw it onto the caboose followed by his own. The train began to gather speed. "Ana, grab the railing!" He tried to keep his voice low hoping the train noise would cover it. "Grab it!" She tried to pull herself up, but her ankle had stiffened and swelled. It wouldn't hold her and buckled. She began to fall backward off the stairs as the train gathered speed. Jonah reached from behind and gave her a push causing her to fall onto the platform. She cried out in pain. The delay left him exposed for a moment just as the taller of the two Germans looked his way. Had he heard them? Jonah saw his face for the first time. It was the Ponar Commandant.

He continued to look in Jonah's direction. His driver was standing at attention, holding the door open for him. The Nazi leader hesitated a moment still watchful, then slowly ducked and climbed into the vehicle. Jonah moved closer to Ana on the platform, heart beating wildly, and spread his coat over them. The train was nearly at full speed now and passed the car as the driver turned it around and drove back the way they had come. Jonah's heartbeat began to slow. The Commandant had looked right at him. Why didn't he raise an alarm? Maybe he hadn't seen them. Or maybe he had. Regardless, Yahweh had helped them this night. Of that Jonah was sure; and he prayed a prayer of thanks.

In place of the train whistle the cold wind whistled over them as the train creaked and rocked through the shortened night. They didn't know where it was going only that it was taking them away from the death in Ponar Forest.

The caboose door wasn't locked, and Jonah and Ana found shelter inside. While not warm it was out of the wind. There were benches along each side and using the satchels as pillows they were able to get a very short nap before Jonah noticed the cadence of the track changing as the train slowed down. "I think we are approaching the train station in Kaunas," he told Ana. He had been here many times. With no passengers on board he assumed they wouldn't be stopping at the station. And he was right. The train passed the station and veered left onto a siding track, eventually coming to a stop.

"Jonah. The train has stopped. What will we do?"

"We're in Kaunas, but not at the station. Slide under that bench as much as you can. Your satchel, too. I don't think they will search this train again, but we need to stay hidden." Jonah knew that Germans sometimes rode the trains checking for Jews; but obviously, not this train or the Commandant wouldn't have checked it himself. He couldn't see or hear any movement around the train making it difficult to know if the engineer and any other railway persons were nearby. He whispered to Ana, "Stay down. I'm going to see what is happening."

He wriggled from under the bench, duck-walked to the door and opened it just a crack. No one was behind the train. He slipped out the door onto the platform, laid down like before and waited a moment. Nothing. But he couldn't see anything either. He inched toward the steps on the left-hand side of the platform and looked around the side of the train. He could make out a small shed several meters away. He could see two men walking away from the train toward the two tracks to his left, both with train cars at rest on them. Quickly, he ducked back into the car.

"What did you see?" Ana asked.

"I think the railway men are gone. Ana, we need to go now. Before daylight. Before the terminal opens."

"Jonah, I'm so thirsty. I still feel dirty. And I need. . . ."

"Ana. It's time to go. One more thing. Remove your arm band. Here, I will help you. We need to be as inconspicuous as possible."

"But Jonah, Jews without arm bands are shot on sight. We've seen it before."

"How does your ankle feel?" He ignored his wife.

"Better, maybe. It's rested."

"Before—the Rabbi—he told me there are ghettos in Kaunas, same as Vilna. A few Jews have escaped, but not many. Patrols are concentrated around the ghettos to watch for any escaping Jews. It will be very dangerous for us. My friend, Adolfas, may not want to help us, if we make it that far."

Jonah stuffed the bands into one of the satchels. "We shouldn't leave anything behind." In the darkness he couldn't see the tears in Ana's eyes.

In a hushed tremulous voice that gave away her tears, she said, "I trust you, Jonah. I just wish I could see Samuel one more time."

He sat down beside her and took her hand. "Yes, Ana. I do, too."

Ana pulled her scarf tighter around her head and staying close to the train, they silently crossed the yard toward the shed Jonah had seen earlier. There were some maintenance workers two tracks over. When the workers moved to the far side of the train cars, the fugitives scurried toward the next bit of shadow. The shed was still several meters ahead, lit only by a faint bulb over the small door. During the final few meters they would be completely exposed.

They waited impatiently, crouched in the shadows. Jonah could see the men but couldn't hear their voices as they ambled off into some trees on the edge of the trainyard. He could see two glowing dots for a moment and realized they were smoking. "Now Ana. We go." Moving as silently and quickly as they dared they darted into the shallow light of the shed and continued behind it. Jonah had not been sure what they would find on the back side and with no weapon, they would be defenseless. No one was there and a quick peek toward the glowing dots told him they had not been seen.

A metal and wood scrap heap lay behind the shed. Beyond lay trees and low buildings, dark and closed for the night. They hurried into the trees away from the train yard and toward Kaunas. Now to find Adolfas' house. But that didn't happen. A Lithuanian Police Colonel found them first.

CHAPTER 45

The Atlantic
April 1942

The storm was really upon the Queen Mary now. The attempt to change course had not fully succeeded and the waves had increased to the point that the ship was now tilting from twenty-five degrees heeled on one side to twenty-five degrees heeled on the other in a matter of minutes.

Wind battered the empty decks and howled around the corners. The lifeboats swayed precariously, and though properly secured with thick cables they were at risk of being ripped away into the frothing ocean. Nausea plagued many well-seasoned crewmen who had not been through a storm of this magnitude.

Ben and Kate were again on the floor, this time on hands and knees in the infirmary. They were helping Dr. Joe find his glasses. "They have to be here somewhere," Kate said. The rolling and pitching motion of the ship was making the simple task much more difficult.

A cry from the open infirmary door interrupted their search. "Please help. Reuben, very, very ill. Help me." Two room stewards stood in the doorway, one supporting the other who was doubled over in obvious pain. Evidence of vomit—something they had seen a lot of—stained his uniform.

"Seasick?" asked Ben "I recognize Reuben, what's your name?"

"George, sir. No, he says lot of pain. In stomach."

"Help me get him into a bed." Ben came along the other side of Reuben and struggling against the bucking ship the two men managed to get him onto the secured cot-like bed bolted to the wall.

Addressing Reuben, Ben said, "I'm going to take your temperature and your blood pressure and do an examination. But first I'm going to strap you down. We don't want you leaving unexpectedly. Kate, could you get some gloves, sterilize a thermometer, and find my BP kit, please while I wash up."

The initial examination yielded results Ben did not like. Joe Ramsey stood by analyzing the results as well—his missing glasses forgotten for the moment. The two doctors were talking outside the infirmary. "Reuben's temperature is 103.2 degrees. He has had vomiting and the lower right quadrant is very painful plus his stomach is slightly swollen. I think it may be appendicitis," Ben said.

"I agree, Ben," Dr. Joe said.

"Good. Now we need to find your glasses so you can operate."

"Ben, there isn't time. We've looked all over this place for them."

"Well, do you need them to operate? Do you have a spare pair?"

"Yes, to both. Close-up work is blurry without them. And with the ship's movement right now, need I say more. I do have another pair, but it's an older prescription. I would not be comfortable wearing them to perform surgery in a hurricane. You're going to have to do this."

"Whoa, I've never performed an appendectomy on a real patient, just cadavers; and only observed during my surgery rotation."

"Ben. It's a fairly simple procedure. I've done it many times. I can guide you through it. You may know more than you think."

"No. We can't do surgery during a hurricane. We're bouncing around like a damn cork right now."

"The longer we wait the greater the risk of rupture and then we'll still have to operate in this storm. His chances of survival will be even less. We can't risk doing nothing."

The words 'doing nothing' resonated in Ben's mind. He grew silent. "What if I freeze?"

"I'll be right next to you. We can do this, *You* can do this, Ben."

The great ship rose on the crest of one of the tallest waves yet and plummeted into the trough, sea water crashing across the decks. The ferocious wind wailing along the decks. Both men planted their feet and grabbed the railing. "I need to talk to Captain Hawthorne," Ben said.

The news wasn't good. Weather reports from other ships and weather stations indicated at least several more hours before they passed through the second wall of the storm. One transmission gave hopeful evidence that they might soon encounter a period of calm water for a short time, but when was a big question mark. So far the ship's engines were powerful enough to keep them steering on a determined course instead of being pushed around by the fierce waves and wind. If that changed, the ship might not survive. It would be broken apart by the constant battering and pounding of the surf against the hull.

Ben replaced the receiver that connected him to the wheelhouse. "Can you handle the anesthetic?"

"I can prepare the cone and gauze if you double check the measurement of the ether," Dr. Joe replied.

They stood silent, looking at each other for a moment. Then Ben said, "Kate can assist as surgical nurse. Let's prep the patient."

Kate had remained with Reuben while the two doctors contacted her father. "How's the pain now?" she asked him. He slurred a few words at her and nodded his head. "The morphine is taking affect," she told him. Her feet were planted and she was holding on tightly to the metal support at the foot of the bed as the ship continued to sway violently. It seemed to her that the motion, while steady, wasn't getting worse, maybe even a bit less— at least that was her hope. While she waited she was mentally reviewing parts of her training, ticking off what she knew about surgical procedures. It wasn't a lot, and it didn't include hurricane conditions. She wondered what Ben had learned from her father.

Ben. I've rather changed my impression of him. Before, I thought he was a bit of a tosser; papa didn't think so, but I did. Now he seems like only half a tosser. Actually. . . he's quite likeable. We've had some good chuckles together. Quite a handsome chap, too, if you like the—
The momentary respite from the rolling motion was over and Kate grabbed onto the bed again scarcely managing to remain on her feet.

Ben was ready to make his first incision. The anesthetic cone and ether-soaked gauze had done its work thanks to Dr. Joe. Kate placed antiseptic in a deep steel bowl to minimize it sloshing out as the ship rolled and bucked. She sterilized the hemostats, retractors, grabbed swabs and suture and placed them in a tray with deep sides to prevent them sliding onto the floor like her pasta had done earlier. Everything was laid out on a surgery table bolted to the wall and Kate was positioned so she could assist Ben, keep everything in place, and use the table for support. Or so they hoped.

The mid-ship location of the small operating room was allowed lights even during the blackout times. They kept flickering as the ferocity of the storm invaded every part of the ship. "Deep breath, Ben. You can do this," Dr. Joe told him.

He felt shaky. Lacking confidence. He took a cleansing breath and forced himself to concentrate on the surgery. He tried to feel a rhythm to the movement of the ship. It seemed that after crashing into a trough there was a half-minute maybe a full minute before the ship tilted again. If he timed the incisions carefully. . .

With Dr. Joe guiding and encouraging him they turned Reuben onto his left side, found McBurney's point and Ben cut through the subcutaneous tissue, facia, peritoneum, and external oblique, attempting to make those cuts between jousts of the ship. Dr. Ramsey kept close watch on the anesthetic and blood pressure. Kate was carefully listening for Ben's instructions as she handed him scalpels, retractors and swabbed the wound clean. She could feel his tension but could see that his hands were steady and his mind focused. Everything was going well. Until it wasn't.

CHAPTER 46

B en was dividing the two parts of the appendix when the rhythm of the ship changed. She lurched into a trough and antiseptic sloshed from the pan. Kate had a firm grip on the instrument tray or it would have sailed onto the floor. But the jostling caused Ben to nick the appendix artery. Immediately blood began filling the cavity and covered his hands. He couldn't see where the nick was so he couldn't ligate it properly. The rolling, heaving ship became a bigger adversary. As did the flickering lights. "Kate, swab the blood as fast as you can. We have to get this stopped!" panic rising in his voice.

"Ben. Don't panic. You either, Kate." Dr. Joe kept his voice even and low. "It happens. Even when not in the middle of a hurricane, it happens."

And suddenly, miraculously, everything was quiet. No wind. No noise. No creaking. No tilting. Just calm.

"What happened?" Ben asked fingers still inside the incision searching for the cause of the bleeding. His own blood pounding through his ears.

"Probably in the 'eye'. While living in the southeast I went through one or two of these, except I was on land. If we're passing through the center there's no wind. No rain. Just very quiet. But it's not over yet."

With the storm temporarily at bay the surgery became a bit easier. Kate was able to sop up the blood and Ben was able to find the arterial bleeder and tie it off. Then Ben could remove the diseased appendix, suture the layers, close and dress the wound while the sea remained remarkably placid.

"Excellent job, Ben." Dr. Joe was slowly decreasing the ether, checking the blood pressure again, and would soon be bringing the patient around.

Ben was cleaning up and removing his bloody scrubs. "Thanks. Those sutures won't win any awards, though. If we hadn't entered the eye when we did I think old Reuben would not be with us."

"I doubt very much if Reuben will care about the sutures. And he's alive, thanks to you. I'm certain he'll care about that." They both turned their attention to Kate. "And he's alive because you did such a marvelous job, too, young lady. Thank the good Lord you knew the names of the instruments."

It was suddenly too much for her. With the tension broken she deflated like a one-day old party balloon. She tried to hold it together, but the tears spilled over and ran down her cheeks. She started to shake and hugged herself hoping that would help. "I've never even watched a *live* surgery before," she whispered. Ben understood fully what she was feeling. He had been in that same place. Quickly removing the rest of his operating garb he went to sit beside her. She leaned against him, displaying a fragility he hadn't seen before. She suddenly sat up. "This is bloody stupid." Then realizing how that sounded. "Sorry, poor choice of words. It's just having someone depend on you for his life is frightfully scary. Ben you were magnificent. I don't know how you did it, really. This has been a real thumping heart afternoon. I'm exhausted. Would it be alright if I went and had a lie-down?"

"Or course. Take your time." Ben helped her stand.

When Kate opened the door into the infirmary to leave, the outer room was filled with pale crewmen enveloped in the sour smell of vomit. Hours of sickness had left them dehydrated and in need of IV therapy. Another older man was holding a cloth to his head, a trickle of blood escaping down the side of his face. Taking advantage of the calm seas they had all hurried to the infirmary. Turning back she called to Ben and Dr. Joe, "Chaps, I don't think any of us will be havin' a lie-down for a bit just yet."

Ben was back in the OR checking on Reuben. The steward was awake and Ben dosed him with more morphine. The incision looked good and he was returning to the infirmary just in time to hear the Captain's voice in the outer room.

". . .still in the eye, but probably not much longer. The next few hours will be worse than we've seen once that passes. I'm planning a bit of a lie-down. Merriwether is in the wheelhouse. Thought I would check on you chaps. You had a bit of excitement in here? Right?"

Ben entered in time to hear Dr. Joe say, "Ben did an admirable job under extreme conditions. Maybe it was for the best I lost my glasses.

"Thanks, Joe," Ben said. "But it was your support and Kate's able assistance that saved Reuben's life. I would not have succeeded without either of you. And what? Captain. You're saying there's more storm to come?"

"Afraid so. We still need to navigate the outer wall. Sometimes these storms weaken and fall apart, not likely for this one, though. I'm concerned that our fuel may run low if we're thrown off course much more. This calm may last for a bit. You should get some grub while you can. Where's Kate?"

Dr. Joe spoke up. "She's gone to lie down."

"Very good. Carry on, then." Kate's father was out the door.

One hour later winds and monstrous waves were lashing the ship again as it struggled to keep its directional control. The force of the water broke through one of the bolted porthole covers with a loud explosion and the round glass window shattered casting glass shards across the deck and flooding the interior. It sounded like the cannon, Ben thought, then quickly realized it must be storm damage. He just hoped it wasn't serious and kept working. The infirmary was the busiest place on the ship.

All night and into the early morning the ship heaved and tilted. Hours of loud creaking and squealing as her joints were tested convinced those onboard that surely the Queen Mary was breaking apart. But the mighty ship fought this war and won. By mid-morning the worst was over. There was mopping up to do and damage to be reported and repaired if possible. Lifeboats, firepower, safety equipment, all needed to be inspected. But it was over. They were way off course, but they were safe.

Captain Merriwether addressed the crew: "Good mornin'. Ay dare say this bucket of ours has a mighty will to live. We've suffered only damage to one porthole and we'll all be doin' some moppin' up today. Our great scullery folks'll have a hearty breakfast a-waitin' for us in a bit in case you have your appetite back. Good job our doctors did performin' surgery on one of our fine stewards in the middle of that mighty storm. I understand the fella's gonna' be okay. Ay, more announcements later. Get on with it."

And they did, all the way into New York harbor, fuel dangerously low, a day and a half late.

CHAPTER 47

Kaunas, Lithuania
April 1942

"Sustabdyti!" Halt!" the policeman commanded. Lithuanian, Jonah registered instantly. The two large men in front of them had even larger guns pointed at them. One was considerably younger than the other. The older one was thicker around the middle. Both were clean-shaven. Although it was dark, he could see their coats were longer and the knee-high boots different than the German uniform. Lithuanian police.

"Papers," the older one called for sternly.

This was the end, Jonah knew. Their papers identified them as Jewish. Their arm bands still in their satchel. He reached for their papers. "We are Jonah and Ana Dressler from Vilna. We are Jewish. He handed the papers to the older policeman.

"How is it you are here, in Kaunas, and not Vilna? And late at night, unescorted? This is not permitted. And where are your arm bands?"

Jonah had no ready answer.

"What will we do with them?" This was the younger policeman speaking. "Shoot them, now?"

"Yes, this must be dealt with. I will take care of it. Go toward the road and watch for any other escaping Jews. There may be others with them. He waited, leveling the rifle toward them as the younger man walked back up to the road. "You two. Move back into the trees." He prodded Jonah with the rifle and took Ana's arm shoving her along in front of him until they disappeared from view into the forest-like growth.

"On your knees," he shouted loudly. Jonah helped Ana down onto her painful ankle. He took her hand. Neither of them spoke. They knew this day would come. They had been fortunate to make it this far. He heard Ana's quiet sob. *I wish I could have saved her*, he thought, and began to breathe a soft prayer as they waited for the bullets. *Samuel will never know what happened to us. He made the right decision going to America. He will be safe.*

He squeezed Ana's hand, felt her shiver. "Ana, I love you." He sensed the policeman directly behind him. *What is taking him so*—. Two shots rang out. "Any more kikes?" he called to his partner who was still out of sight.

"Nein, sir."

"Keep watch while I hide these bodies. These *drecksau Kikes*—dirty pigs." He bent down and began scattering debris around. "Have you heard of the *Lietuvos laisvés armija*, LLA?" he whispered.

Jonah's mind was still processing the fact that they were alive. "No, sir."

"It is a resistance movement against the Germans. I am Colonel Markas Kazlauskas, a member. I must go now. Hide here and I will come back for you. There is a training camp on the edge of Kaunas. They can help you. Are there others, escaping?"

"No."

I will tell Bronius, then, that we need to go to headquarters and make a report about escaping Jews. I will distract them to another area. They will send out more patrols. I will tell them I need to return to remove your bodies. This may take some time. Hide here until I return. Now, I must go."

"Colonel, do you need help?" Bronius called.

"No. I am finished. Go to the auto," he called over his shoulder. Then to Jonah, "Hide. I'll be back."

The two heard the automobile drive off, neither one speaking as their heartbeats began returning to normal. Death had been so imminent that now all words failed them. They spoke very little as they crouched in the darkness of the trees, Ana still quivering, Jonah holding her close. He considered their options. *We could leave now. Try to find Adolfas' house. What if we don't? Or he can't help us? Ana is exhausted. The colonel. He could have killed us, but he didn't. Can we trust him?*

"I must leave you off here. The camp is about two kilometers to your right. Ask for Antonio and give him this card. Remember, don't speak of this to anyone or our lives will be in more danger."

"*Toda raba,*" Thank you very much, Jonah responded. The men shook hands and the colonel left.

Daylight was replacing darkness when Ana and Jonah saw lean-tos and tents ahead. Cautiously they approached, still uncertain that what they were seeing was safety. They could see two guards patrolling the perimeter but not much else. The rain Jonah had predicted was beginning to fall producing a muted patter as it targeted the tree branches and soft ground. Surprisingly it was Ana who took the brave first step into the line of sight of the guard.

"Sustabdyti!" Halt!" The same sharp words they had heard only a few hours ago. Ana kept walking. The guard kept his weapon directed at her.

"We are sent by Colonel Markas Kazlauskas. We have a message for Antonio," Ana called out. The guard still did not lower his weapon. Jonah, a step behind Ana, reached out and grabbed her elbow.

"We are Jonah and Ana Dressler. We have escaped from Vilna and need help," he said. Then with a small cry, Ana slumped to the ground in a pitiful heap. The guard rushed forward and helped Jonah carry her into the camp. Immediately Antonio was awakened and ordered food and water be brought to the struggling refugees.

Jonah helped Ana to bed in one of the smaller tents before joining Antonio in the camp leader's headquarters. The gas lamp in the tent gave enough illumination to see that it was sparsely furnished. A cot. Two chairs and a table that held a shortwave radio, maps and other papers and a stack of some type of newspaper. A short clothesline held two or three Lithuanian Police uniforms, shiny boots paired up underneath. A small cabinet held several guns except the one Antonio always kept close by. Beside the cot a small square table supported a wash basin, shaver and comb. In a corner on a perch sat a small bird with a hood over its eyes, apparently sleeping. "Your wife is very ill. She has a fever. Medical supplies are very limited but we have potions and treatments that may help her," Antonio said.

"I thought she was shivering from fear and cold only. Not fever, too," Jonah said.

"You will stay with us while she recovers. We have clean clothes for you, and washing—you need. Now, tell me your story."

Antonio gave full attention to Jonah. The camp leader was a small and wiry man, Jonah's junior by 20 years. He had not bothered with a full uniform when awakened simply pulling on his woolen pants and a heavy shirt. His uncombed short brown hair stuck out at odd angles around his ears. The gas lamp in the tent cast shadows on his clear features and furrowed brow as he absorbed Jonah's story, interrupting occasionally with questions as Jonah related their grisly days at Ponar Forest, the painstaking work of digging the escape tunnel, and their frightening escape by train.

"We have many recruits from Vilna. You may know some. We have heard rumors of a Ponar Forest massacre and that all were killed. No one else has made it to our camp. Your bravery may have disrupted things there for a time. You are very tired. We have cleared the tent where Ana is and prepared a bed there for you so you can watch over her. Breakfast at this camp is at 0600 before training exercises begin, but today they will make special meal for you when you wake up. After that you will eat with the other recruits. Now go. We will talk more later. You may be able to help us with your knowledge of Vilna. We try to help as many Jews escape as we can but we ask for something from them in return, whatever they are capable of providing—some have money, some have information, and some have a special skill. A few have all three. When that happens it is *labai geras,* very good," and he laughed.

He rose, a signal for Jonah to leave. They shook hands and agreed to meet later for a tour of the camp. Jonah was eager to check on Ana. A farmer's wife from nearby made regular visits to the camp and had just looked in on her. "I medicated her fever and will do a check on her later. You sleep, sir. She left them. Jonah let Ana know he was nearby, but he couldn't tell if she sensed his presence. He settled into a warm dreamless sleep so deep he didn't hear Ana's feverish moaning, calling to their son over and over.

The rain had stopped when Jonah awoke in the afternoon. Ana's fever was lower but she was very weak, able to eat and drink only small amounts at a time. Jonah's meal though still meager was the most substantial food he had eaten in months. Antonio escorted him through the camp with the sleeping bird from earlier now wide awake and perched on his shoulder. The epaulets on his uniform protected him from the needle-sharp talons of the small falcon.

"I'm surprised how large the camp is," Jonah said.

"About one hundred men are in this camp. In every way we make attempts to disrupt the Nazi communications and mobility. We have dynamite to blow up roads or bridges. We use wire cutters to cut telephone lines, he said pointing to an unusually large scissors-like apparatus. "These are mines that we place in strategic locations. Our members are trained to use all of this equipment. I also help other commanders plan our operations." They continued their walk around the camp, Antonio stopping from time to time to address his men.

"The *LLA* has developed a network of Lithuanians who help us pass information from camp to camp. We have others who help us print and distribute a newspaper called *Karinés ir politinés Žinios* (Military and Political News) giving information to the commanders and other sympathizers. We have a recruit in a wireless office near Kaunas who also helps us when it's safe for him.

"When we find Jews hiding, running for their lives, such as you, we feed them and find them safety. We have told the farmers that they must help us. They know it would not go well for them if they refuse. They give us milk, eggs, grain, clothing, blankets. They hide Jews and help us get them out of the country."

"And why do you do this? You are not Jewish? Why do you risk your life for us?"

"It is not right what has been done to your people. And we want to see Lithuania liberated. We want independence from German and Soviet control. We are tired of the occupation of our homeland by these two countries. For too many years we have been at the center of the tug of war between them. It is time for us to fight for a free Lithuania. And now let us talk about you, Jonah. How can we help you and how can you help us?"

CHAPTER 48

New York, NY
April 1942

Kate was seated in her cabin, fountain pen in hand. A beautiful new journal was open on her lap. Pages empty. She had promised to write in it every day. That hadn't happened; this was her first entry:

> *April 25, 1942*
> *Tomorrow we dock in New York. I would adore seeing more of the city, but Papa can't. Too busy this time. And Dr. Joe needs to see about new glasses after we found his broken ones. Sort of boring—doing walkabouts by myself. Ben invited me to Boston to stay at his house and see some sights. I'd rather see New York, but. . .*

A knock on the door interrupted her. "Kate, you're wanted in the infirmary," a passing steward called through the closed door. She snapped the journal closed and looked for her shoes.

Boston, MA

"Kate, it's so good to see you again," Margaret said and gave her a hug. "Here, let me take that case." She handed it to Ben. "Son, I've put her in your room and I made up the sofa on the sunporch for you. Would you take her things upstairs, please? I made some sandwiches and cake whenever you're settled. Kate, please, consider this your home. If you need anything, anything at all, just tell me."

Her eyes settled back on Ben. Fearful that she would demand even more hugs from him, he scurried up the stairs with Kate's travel cases.

Moments later in the kitchen Ben had a thousand questions. "When will Samuel be home? Is he still seeing Ziva? And how's Avery? The mail never seems to catch up with us. I haven't had a letter from you in weeks, Mom." He and Kate had made the plate of egg salad sandwiches disappear along with generous pieces of chocolate cake. Margaret and Avery had been saving sugar ration coupons.

"I don't know what Samuel's schedule is like today. Yes, he and Ziva are still friends, I think." She paused. "Avery is. . ." then settled with, "well, Avery. He has been a wonderful neighbor and friend while you have been away. But I want to hear about your adventure. I haven't had many letters from you, dear prodigal son. And Kate—you must have much to tell, too."

While Ben shared with his mom his experiences aboard the Queen Mary, Kate took in her surroundings. She had expected Ben's home would be much like this. Warm. Cozy. Suppers in the kitchen. Big trees in the yard. The sunporch to enjoy when warmer weather arrived. It reminded her of her home in England and unexpectedly a wave of homesickness caught up with her. She wasn't certain her house was still standing or in one piece after more recent bombings. She thought of the big hawthorn tree in the yard and the daffodils and tulips that Mum planted every spring. She missed her room with the chintz curtains and the antique doll collection that she never had an interest in, but that Mum wanted—

"Kate? You must be very tired, my dear." She didn't realize how far away she had drifted until she heard her name.

"I apologize, Mrs. Stuart. I must be more tired than I thought."

"Dinner won't be for a while yet. Why not take a nap? And please, call me Margaret."

Kate had napped, bathed, washed her hair and dressed for dinner. She had chosen a deep blue cashmere sweater, a black mid-calf length fitted skirt and black pumps. As her hair dried she twisted it into ringlets and tied them back with a blue ribbon. A gold locket ringed her neck. She stood before the mirror applying a small amount of makeup and smiled at her reflection; then blushed. "What am I doing?" she said aloud.

Ben and Margaret were still in the kitchen when Kate came back downstairs and Ben turned from the sink as she entered. Recently, he had rarely seen her in regular clothes since she wore her nurse's uniform aboard the ship most of the time. She was stunning. He hadn't thought of her as such a desirable woman. A nurse, yes. The 'girl next door, kinda". But not this.

"Am I dressed appropriately for dinner?" she asked.

"You are dressed appropriately for anything," Ben said, his eyes moving from her head to her feet, slowing down in between.

Margaret wiped her hands on her apron, observing her son's expression, then said, "You look absolutely lovely, Kate. Feel better now?"

"Yes, thank you. How can I help?" she asked, continuing into the kitchen.

The doorbell rang and before Ben reached the front door Avery had let himself in. He dropped the expensive ham onto the table and gave Ben a bear hug. "Glad you're home, Ben. If you only knew how excited your Mom has been knowing you were coming home. She's hardly stopped for a breath—planning meals, cleaning, shopping. What a whirlwind it's been around here." He let out a low whistle as he turned toward Kate. "You must be the captain's daughter. Kate, right? I'm Avery. Live down the street. Maybe Ben's mentioned me?"

"Yes, sir. He has. He's said several times that's it's a relief knowing you are close by."

He glanced at Margaret before responding. "I promised him I would look after her."

"Ben, show Kate around. Avery can give me a hand here."

CHAPTER 49

Boston, MA
April 1942

Samuel didn't make it home for supper, but called. Said they'd see each other in the morning. Now after a long evening of talking and catching up Ben lay awake. The familiar tones of the grandfather clock struck twelve times. He was tired. Why couldn't he fall asleep? It felt good to be home. But strange, too. He wondered if his internal clock was messed up from all the time zones he'd traveled through. That couldn't be it. That would have happened long before now. Things felt different, and it didn't have anything to do with time zones.

When he left a few months ago his motive wasn't to serve on that ship. People thought him so altruistic, temporarily sacrificing his career. Maybe his life. He knew better. He was simply running. It was an escape. But now the surgery, under extraordinary circumstances and Reuben's recovery had revitalized him. It gave him hope that maybe he could be a physician his Dad would be proud of.

Afterward he had told Captain Hawthorne it was a team effort. And it was. Joe Ramsey had believed in him and that had made the difference. Even when he hadn't believed in himself, Dr. Joe had believed. His thoughts were back onboard already. The Queen Mary had become a part of him in a way he couldn't have imagined. This time, when he returned, it would be because at least some of those things people thought of him were true.

And Kate? Something was different. He rolled over on the not-very-comfortable sofa bed and groaned. She stirred feelings in him that until now only Laura had owned. The two were so different. Laura had been there, quietly in the background, agreeable. More like Mom. Kate had a stubborn streak, was argumentative at times. But adventuresome, inquisitive and funny. It's only been six months. *Too soon*, he thought. As the clock chimed once, sleep finally came, bringing dreams he didn't remember.

"So, Ben tell me what it's like being a doctor on a cruise ship," Samuel asked. He blew on the hot cup of strong coffee. It was just the two of them in the kitchen.

"It's not a cruise ship."

"Yes, it is."

Ben scowled at his friend, then laughed, realizing Samuel was teasing him. "Well, for one thing you get to operate in the middle of a huge hurricane." And Ben repeated for Samuel's benefit some of the stories he told last evening of medical conditions and treatments on board the Queen Mary and places he'd seen. Kate arrived then, a big yawn escaping the back of her hand and poured coffee. "Kate, meet Samuel." Another yawn.

"Mornin' to you. I'm a bit daft before my first cuppa'. Please, carry on." Kate listened in as the two friends caught up.

"Any word from your parents?" Ben asked.

"Nothing. Every day I pray for word. Something. But I hear nothing." His dark Jewish features mirrored the worry he carried inside every day. "What is so difficult is if they are dead there is no one to tell me. I wouldn't be able to know where they are or how to give them a proper Jewish burial. Sometimes it is too much."

"I'm so sorry." Ben couldn't find any other words that might comfort his friend so he remained silent, shaking his head as Samuel spoke.

"I must finish dressing and catch the bus. Are you bringing Kate to hospital today?"

"If she wants. Our visit has been cut short because of the arrival delay into New York, so our time home is more limited. We'll see you later."

Kate had been observing their exchange and as Samuel left the room sat down beside Ben, coffee cup in hand. "I would jolly well like to visit your hospital—you know compare it to surgeries in the UK. Would it be alright?"

"Yes. Of course." Ben was thoughtful. After a minute, "You know I wish there was some way I could help Samuel. I was thinking about how I would feel if it was my own mom who was missing. Maybe dead. I admire him—carrying on with his studies and work while every day he hopes for word from them. I can't imagine. . ." Then his mood lightened. "Enough. Let's see what Mom has planned for breakfast and then drive over to the hospital. You will be astonished when you see an *American* hospital." While he was waiting for Kate to dress, he spent some time in his father's den. Thinking.

Ben's colleagues were delighted to see him and hear about his weeks on the transport ship and meet Kate. And yet again he told the story of the 'surgery in the hurricane', impressing everyone.

The day was mild and because Boston's history is tied to England Ben decided to take Kate to the site of the Boston Tea Party. The two strolled Boston Common, the oldest city park in the United States. Kate told him she and her Papa had been to a baseball game in New York, so they visited Fenway Park. No game was in progress but they walked around the stadium grounds. It felt natural to Ben to reach for Kate's hand. But his increased heart rate was a surprise when her fingers weaved around his. They discovered a frankfurter stand; bought two; found a bench; and ate while they talked. They joked around; Kate maintaining her allegiance to England; Ben standing up for the American rebels. They both tried to ignore the feeling that their camaraderie of the past weeks was becoming something more.

The afternoon was winding down and Ben pointed the car toward home. He hadn't intended it, but there it was. The corner where the Cocoanut Grove lounge had stood. The land had been cleared of debris, but still sat vacant, looking like a parking lot.

Kate noticed the change in Ben as they passed by. "Is that it? Where the fire was?"

Ben nodded, keeping his eyes ahead. "Kate, it's been such a wonderful day, let's not end it on a sad note. I didn't come this way purposely, it's just my usual route home, okay," Ben said.

"I understand. It's been a lovely day for me, too." They were silent for a moment. Kate gently touched his shoulder. "I know you loved her. Please, don't think you can't ever talk to me about her. About this." He glanced across the seat, catching the earnest look in her blue eyes. He choked up.

"Thanks, Kate." He turned his eyes back toward the road.

When they arrived home, Samuel was seated in the kitchen, eyes brimming over with tears. *Oh no, bad news*, Ben thought. Quietly he sat down beside his friend. Samuel was holding a piece of paper in one hand.

"Ben, they're alive. They're alive," he said through a mist of tears. He handed Ben the paper.

```
NLT MARGARET STUART=
4343 RIDGEWAY LN BOSTON(MA)=
SAFE FOR NOW NEAR KAUNAS. LEAVING
HERE SOON.
```

The joy and relief on Samuel's face said everything that needed to be said. Ben touched his shoulder, tears springing to his eyes, too; then wiped his cheek with his hand. What he had considered earlier that morning came to mind and he went into action. "Let's go look at something. I've been thinking and I may have an idea."

In his father's old study was a large world globe. The two of them studied it together for a few moments. "Look here. This is Lithuania, right?" Samuel nodded. "Over here is Denmark. While onboard I've learned a lot about the war in Europe. There is much more news reported there than here. Denmark is a semi-neutral area. If your parents can get to Denmark and from there to Leith, which is the port at Edinburgh, Scotland, there just might be a way to bring them here to America." He thought about what he was going to do next. He knew it was against the rules, but he wanted to give his friend some hope. He walked over and closed the den door. "We are instructed *never* to tell anyone the itinerary of the Queen Mary. Never. To no one. It must remain secret for the protection of everyone on board. I'm telling you this in very strict confidence. You must not tell anyone. Not my mother. Not Avery. Not Ziva. No one. I wouldn't tell you, but I trust you completely. Physicians know how to keep a secret. Are we clear?" Samuel nodded.

"Okay. When we leave New York in two days we're going to Gourock, Scotland to unload the troops. We will be there just long enough to unload troops and take on supplies before returning to New York. Then he outlined his plan to Samuel. "I promise, Samuel, I'll do the best I can to help them. Now, we need to go to the telegraph office, find out where this telegram came from and send one back to them."

He didn't tell Samuel that their plan had very little chance of succeeding.

CHAPTER 50

LLA Camp near Kaunas, Lithuania
Late April 1942

"Ana, we sent it. Antonio's person in the telegraph office sent a message yesterday to Samuel. He knows we are still safe, for now. It is good you remembered his American address."

Ana smiled from the cot where she was still recuperating. "Thank you, Jonah." She took his hand and kissed it gently. "Did you tell him we love him?"

"He knows." He returned her kiss, placed her hand back under the ragged blanket tucking it securely around her. It seemed to him her recovery was very slow. She was still so weak; certainly unable to travel yet. "I am meeting with Antonio again and must go. Rest now."

He had been relating to Antonio everything he knew about the infrastructure of Vilna. The information he possessed about the sewer tunnels, water systems, bridges and roads was valuable to the LLA and Jonah prayed that his knowledge would help the LLA defeat the Wehrmacht. He had spent his life trying to live in peace with everyone, but after losing everything, after the ghetto, and Soske and Rebekah and after seeing the depravity of Ponar now he would do whatever he could to destroy these animals, even though there was nothing left for him and Ana in this country of his ancestors.

Jonah spent most of the afternoon with Antonio. When he returned to his and Ana's small shelter he was surprised to see Ana up and about. The rest, decent food and other care were beginning to make a significant difference. "Ana, should you be up?" Jonah moved to her side, supporting her.

"I'm feeling much better. The farmer's wife has been very good to me. I need to be up to get my strength back. Help me take a walk, please." She seemed frail to him as she leaned her small frame against him taking a few tentative steps. He knew she needed more time before they could leave the camp, but her marked improvement was a good sign. He and Antonio would talk tomorrow about an escape plan for them.

He slept better that night knowing Ana was improving.

After washing up, dressing, and morning prayers, Jonah and Ana shared some brown bread, cheese curds and raisins together then he went to find Antonio.

About mid-day, while they were talking they heard the rumble of a horse-drawn cart bringing supplies from a nearby farm. Within minutes a tall husky bearded man in dark coveralls and muddy boots appeared in the tent's doorway. "Benas, come in," Antonio said turning toward the visitor, the bird on his shoulder giving Benas a wary eye.

"I have paper for you. In Kaunas I checked for messages." He held out the paper to Antonio. "He told me to tell you he cannot do this again soon. Germans are watching him. Are suspicious. Putting him in danger now. Maybe after a few days he can help again.

"Thank you, Benas. Your help is appreciated."

"I help only because you could cause problems for me if I don't. I don't want to fight these Germans. I just want to run my farm." He cast a stern glance at Jonah as if all of his problems were his fault and backed out of the doorway.

Antonio turned his attention to the paper he was holding. It was a telegram. From the United States. He used a code name when sending communications so the message was addressed to that name in Lithuanian:

```
NLT DARIUS VITKUS=
17 ZEMACHIA G.=
KAUNAS LITHUANIA

JONAH.COPENHAGEN  CAN  HELP.  AND
EDINBURGH.  WILL  CONTACT  YOU
THERE BY 6 MAY. SAMUEL
```

"Does this make sense to you, Jonah?"

"No. These places are far away and travel is impossible for Jews."

"Let me think on this. We'll talk again later."

They walked out together. Jonah going to check on Ana. Antonio joining some of his men.

Ana was steadily improving, now being able to take short walks around the camp. The farmer's wife, Gracel, no longer needed to bathe her and instead of using the chamber pot she walked the short distance to the field latrine. Jonah gave a prayer of thanks for her recovery.

Now that he was more rested and fed he was becoming restless. This was the first time in months that he wasn't doing heavy physical labor every day or running from the Germans. The afternoon evolved into evening and Antonio appeared at their entrance. "Jonah. Come with me." The two men walked back to the main tent and seated themselves around Antonio's small table. "I have some maps I have been studying and I may have a plan for you and Ana.

"Our country has been bandied about between the Soviets and the Germans for decades. As you may know, the Soviets worked a deal with the Germans. Germany gave up Klaipedá in exchange for Kaunas and Vilna. I have heard that, at least for now, that port city is reasonably secure. The Soviets are not as hostile to Jews as the Germans are. Also, word is that Denmark is somewhat neutral in this war. That doesn't mean it's safe but, German presence is less. From Copenhagen you might find passage across the North Sea to Leith, which is the port at Edinburgh. I have a possible way to get you to Klaipedá but the rest will be up to you."

Jonah listened but didn't say anything for a minute or two. "There is something I should show you. I'll be right back."

It took only a minute to retrieve a small paper from his tent and return. "I have saved this in case I would need it someday." He handed it to Antonio. The camp leader unfolded it. The evening light was nearly gone so he held the document under the gas lamp. "This is a blank signed travel visa. However, did you come by this?"

"I was in Kaunas months ago, and a Japanese gentleman was throwing papers from the train. I picked one up not realizing what it was. It looked official. Is it helpful?"

"Yes. It is helpful. I know this man. He has left Kaunas now, but he was the Japanese ambassador. He helped thousands of Jews escape with these travel visas. This piece of paper may be able to get you from Klaipedà to Denmark to Leith. We will need to get you different clothes and immigration papers. I have resources that can do that. But understand. It will still be a long and dangerous journey. If this telegram is correct, you will need to be in Edinburgh by 6 May."

"I do not know what day it is today."

"30 April. That gives us six days. It will take me two days at least to get proper papers and new clothes. Is Ana able to travel?"

"Perhaps another day or two. When the papers are ready."

"It possibly might work. You are very fortunate to have this paper. You were there on the day he left for Japan. He was throwing as many signed visas as he could out the train window. He was a good man. He saved the lives of many Jews."

CHAPTER 51

Boston, MA
April 1942

I t was Ben's last night at home. He and Kate would catch the
first train to New York tomorrow. It was a balmy evening for
late April and they were alone on the sunporch, sitting
together on the sofa. Margaret had gone up to bed early and
Samuel was at the hospital. This was one of the few times they had
been alone here. Kate was bringing her journal up to date,
recording her time in Boston. "Ben, is it Boston Common or
Commons?"

"It's Common."

"Thanks."

"You're welcome."

Their conversation was banal. They both felt the sexual
tension that had been building between them. Neither one wanted
to step off the cliff, so they were playing it safe. But Kate being
Kate said, "Ben, we should talk."

"Sure, what about?" He fidgeted. Rubbing his hand on his
knee. He knew Kate. He knew how direct she could be and he had
a slight hunch where this was going. "Wait. I'll make a cuppa' tea
for us."

She reached out and took the hand that was on his knee.

"How do you feel about. . .us? I mean me. I know it's only
been a few weeks, but we've been together constantly." She turned

slightly to face him as she spoke.

He didn't withdraw his hand. Instead he used the other one to rub his other knee. *This is stupid. I'm not in high school anymore.*

"Uh, what do you mean. . . us? Us. You mean us." *I sound like an idiot! Why did she have to start this? I don't know how I feel. What can I say?* Kate moved closer to him, those intensely blue eyes searching his face.

"It's just. . . I thought I felt something between us." She slipped her hand further into his. Ben stayed silent. She pulled her hand away. "It's so soon after Laura's death. I understand."

Ben studied her for a moment seeing flashes of noodles in her hair; the jerky cable car ride; the way they worked together to save Reuben's life; this week. Her enthusiasm and, yes, her stubborn streak. All the things that made her Kate. He felt a definite attraction, but said only, "Yes, it is soon—"

"Ben, I'm sorry." She turned away.

"But. . ." He cupped her chin in his hands. He wasn't sure what he was doing but her nearness was irresistible. He pulled her to him and kissed her, tentatively. Her lips were soft and he moved closer, feeling her response, their kiss deepening. He nuzzled her hair, her cheek. She kissed him again, her arms around his neck pulling him closer still. His arousal was sudden but here. . .this. . . what was he doing?. He pulled away. "Kate, I can't. . ."

She stood up, those blue eyes flying wide open. "What? Did you think I. . .?" She stood up, smoothed her hair. "I'll go now and make us a proper cuppa' tea," and she left the room. Ben ran his fingers through his own hair and thought, *What just happened? What is she thinking? Did I just mess up?*

After a minute he followed her into the kitchen. Now it was his turn to say, "Maybe we should talk. . .about what just happened. I didn't mean for us to—"

She turned to him and interrupted. "Ben, did you think I wanted a romp in the hay? Wait. Don't guys usually get accused of that?" Sarcasm in her voice. "I simply wanted to know if we were more than friends. Are we?"

She busied herself with the tea preparation, china cups and spoons clinking. Kettle whistling. "You know, when I first met you—seems like ages ago now—I thought you were a bit of a dolt, actually." She pointed a spoon at him. "Papa disagreed. Well, maybe I was wrong. When I saw you take charge and do surgery on Reuben, I saw another side of you. One I hadn't seen before. It took a lot of courage, or I suppose could be arrogance—I prefer to think courage—to do what you did. Maybe they're the same thing. Anyway, it seems I've come to like you a bit. Quite a bit, actually. You're rather a loveable chap after all."

She stopped talking, waiting for him to say something, but any further conversation between them was halted when the front door opened and Samuel called from the foyer, "Anybody here?"

"We're in the kitchen. Come have a cuppa' with us," Kate called back. Ben sat there not saying anything else, his head in his hand, watching her.

Flummox. That's what she did. She flummoxed him. A dolt! Really?

Samuel was still euphoric after the telegram. The three of them sat around the table and talked until it grew late. Kate and Samuel retired and Ben was settled on the sunporch, reading a month-old medical journal that he couldn't stay focused on. Kate was on his mind as well as the plan he and Samuel had worked out. He was so absorbed he wasn't aware that his mom had come back downstairs, pulled up a chair and was talking to him. ". . . to say doesn't come easily. Adding someone to the family is a big decision, don't you think?"

Now he was alert. "Yes, I do. Absolutely." He put aside the journal.

"It takes a lot of thought, right? How will each person adjust? And what will change? It's a very emotional decision, I think."

"I understand completely."

"You do? Then that makes this so much easier, I—"

"Sorry to interrupt; but, Mom, that *is* a big decision. Marriage is a long long way off, if ever.

"What do you mean?"

"Weren't you talking about me and Kate."

"You and Kate? I adore her. She's lovely. No. That wasn't what I was talking about. Avery proposed a few weeks ago. I didn't handle it very well, sorry to say. I wrote to you but—getting a letter to you takes forever! I thought we should talk about it before you leave again." She sat posture-perfect with her hands folded in her lap twisting her lace handkerchief.

"Mom, that's great! Avery's great. He already seems like part of the family." He paused. "I mean, do you think it's great?" She relaxed a little.

"I don't know, Ben. Avery is a good man. A very good man. He's funny, gentle, kind. I can see he cares a great deal for me. I just don't know if I can be the wife to him that I was to your father. We went through a lot together. . ." Her voice trailed off and she looked away.

"Mom. I know I don't have the life experience you have and all. But I lost someone too, don't forget. Someone I was prepared to spend my life with. It still hurts. But what I'm learning is that every relationship is different. Kate and Laura are two different women—two very different women. Two very different relationships. Avery could never take Dad's place, you know that; but he could very well make a place of his own. I think he's smart enough to know that. And I think you are, too. You're happy when he's around. Comfortable. You'll make the right decision."

Her eyes rested lovingly on her only son. "How did you become so wise?" She stood and bent down kissing her son's cheek and tweaking an ear." I wish you weren't leaving again. It seems like you just got home." Then she thumped his head. "You must write your dear mother more often."

"Ow! I love you, Mom. I'll try. Really, I will." As his mom left the room he wondered why she hadn't quizzed him more about Kate. He shrugged.

He went back to his reading, then began parsing the earlier exchange with Kate. This was his third night of troubled thoughts. He remembered that he had never answered her question. There was no denying an attraction to Kate; but he still felt loyalty to Laura or—no—to her memory. When the tug of love had occurred between them and everything felt perfect, he had been dealt a devastating and painful blow. *First, Claire, then my father, and Laura. Are love and pain always inseparable? I'm not sure I'm ready for more pain.*

The lengthy tearful good-byes had been said and Ben and Kate's train was chugging steadily toward New York. Kate had seemed her normal self at breakfast and spent most of the morning dressing and packing. Kate was reading the current Pep Comics issue and Ben moved it away turning to face her. "Kate, I need to talk about last night. It's just that—"

"I understand, Ben. It's okay."

"Please. Let me finish. It's just that I didn't think I could have feelings again so soon." He weaved her fingers into his own. "The pain's still so real, and I wouldn't do anything to hurt you. . ."

"I appreciate your honesty, Ben. I do. I should listen to Papa's advice more often and think before I leap. Let's take it a day at a time and see what happens." She leaned over, kissed him lightly and went back to her reading. Ben felt an unmistakable sense of relief, but, surprisingly, a deeper attraction. Comfortable conversation filled the remainder of the trip.

CHAPTER 52

Aboard the Queen Mary
May 1942

The scene at Pier 90 in New York was a repetition of the one in February with the exception that this time the Queen Mary would transport 16,000 troops, a complete division. The first time in history that one ship had carried that many soldiers. The hurricane damage was repaired, and Dr. McHenry's hip had healed enough that he was accompanying them on this one trip; but when they reached Gourock he was retiring to his home in Edinburgh, Scotland. Dr. Joe was already onboard when Kate and Ben arrived, and they shared stories from their brief vacations.

Because of the increased number of troops, loading supplies and military personnel took the entire night. Captain Hawthorne repeated his welcome speech with the additional restriction of no chewing gum after they found it stuck on the bottom of almost everything. And as the sun decided it was now the morning of May 1st, the great ship moved slowly from her berth out into the Atlantic. This would be an historic crossing.

Could have been the rougher seas or nearly twice as many American troops were on board, whatever the reason, the infirmary was busy night and day with medical problems. Seasickness resulting in dehydration. An impetigo outbreak caused by the close quarters. A couple of busted noses when fights broke out over gambling. Ben and Dr. Joe were immensely thankful to have Dr. McHenry on board. However, over half of the twenty-five nurses heading to field hospitals were too seasick to be of much use, so Kate worked, too. Although crowded before, 16,000 soldiers on board the Queen Mary left very little vacant space anywhere.

Conditions gave Ben and Kate little time alone or opportunities to explore their new relationship. A few stolen moments here and there gave them a glimpse of what could be as their attraction and intimacy grew. Kate's father was too busy to notice the change, but Dr. Joe did. He saw the secretive glances. The smiles they threw at each other. The more frequent touching as they moved about the surgery. He suspected. And he was happy for them. It meant Ben was beginning to heal.

Often the Queen Mary was accompanied by an escort ship, sometimes a full flotilla of ships. On this trip the Curaçaó was assigned to accompany her into Gourock. It was early morning as the Cunarder approached Tory Island off the coast of Ireland, and the helmsman in the wheelhouse spotted the old World War I cruiser. The Queen Mary had become a symbol of victory for these men and many others who spent their lives on the sea, and they took great pride in her successful patriotic efforts. There was much cheering from both ships as the cruiser moved into position with some men waving British flags, raising fists in recognition and singing "God Save the Queen."

Six smaller destroyers assumed flanking positions several miles off port and starboard. keeping watch for German U-boats. The Queen Mary, now carrying a full military division, was under intense protection until her cargo was safely delivered. For several hours the ship continued her zig-zag course as the convoy moved steadily toward Scotland. The decks were full and thousands of eyes searched for German U-boats in the steady wind that buffeted them.

It was mid-afternoon and Captain Hawthorne had just come into the wheelhouse, relieving Merriwether. The First Officer directed his attention to the escort ship. "Captain. We're traveling faster than the Curacaó. We've been steadily gaining on her all morning. You can see she's only a few hundred meters off our bow. What do you suggest?"

After a moment's thought he said, "Let's increase our zig-zag course. That can slow us down, some. I'll be on duty the rest of the day. We can make further adjustments if necessary."

Several hours from Gourock Ben and Kate had a few free hours. Eager to be alone together and away from the infirmary they settled back in Ben's cabin. He went to grab tea for them. While he was gone Kate melted into the one chair, removed her shoes— stockings had gone by the wayside long ago—and propped her legs on the bed. She leaned back and closed her eyes. In no time Ben was back with the hot tea, set it down, and plopped onto the bed. He studied Kate, her eyes still closed. Funny, he hadn't noticed those seven pale freckles across her nose before. He reached over and began massaging her feet, working away the soreness. "Ah. That is smashing," she cooed and opened her eyes. "This is the first break we've had in. . .how long?"

"Awhile." Ben's hands slowly moved up to her ankles and then her calves, massaging gently, enjoying the feel of her smooth skin. His hands moved higher and her eyes softened giving him an unspoken okay. She removed her feet to the floor and stood in front of him. He no longer held back his desire for her

She knelt down and leaned toward him, her hands braced on his thighs, lightly brushing his lips with hers, "I want—" she never completed that sentence. A loud explosion and a sudden jolt sent her toppling onto Ben's lap.

"My God! We've been hit!" Ben cried out. They both scrambled off the bed and he grabbed Kate's arm pushing her toward the door. She pulled away and ran back slipping into her shoes and grabbing life vests. The wind, laden with the smell of acrid smoke and oil, hit them in the face as they climbed onto the top deck. What they witnessed was unbelievable.

The zig-zag course earlier had not worked and the Captain had ordered the helmsman to make another evasive maneuver. The escort ship, the Curacaó, had unpredictably continued into their path. The Captain immediately ordered a hard-a-port which at first appeared to work and those in the wheelhouse and those watching below breathed a sigh of relief. Then to their horror, the Curacaó cut back in front of the Queen. There was no chance to change course again and in just a minute the Queen Mary rammed the Curacaó, slicing it in half.

The Queen Mary struck the cruiser just behind the bow, spinning the ship and slicing through it as easily as a sharp knife through a roll of salami. Billows of black smoke were filling the air from the fires on both halves of the vessel as Ben and Kate arrived on deck. Men who had been waving and cheering the transport ship only hours earlier were now jumping into the icy oil-slick water trying to stay afloat, their earlier cheers transformed into screams of horror.

In disobedience to the strict regulations, American soldiers were throwing life belts, deck chairs, life preservers, anything that would float off the side of the Queen Mary. They screamed instructions at the drowning men at the top of their lungs. Instructions that were whisked away on the strong wind. The scene was chaotic. Already the rear half of the ship was steadily sinking beneath the waves. All of this in the space of only five minutes.

Ben quickly assessed that the soldiers' efforts were ineffective. He decided he could be of more help elsewhere. "Kate! We need to go ready the infirmary. We're going to be overwhelmed with patients who need us." He turned to go below, then noticed something strange. The Queen Mary hadn't slowed. Hadn't changed course. The ship was plowing ahead as if nothing had happened. Men were still in the water but many had already disappeared beneath the frigid oily surface. "Why aren't we stopping?" He leaned over and looked up. "Why aren't the life boats being lowered? Those men are dying! We have to help them! I'm going to the bridge to see your father. Are you coming, Kate? Kate!" She had been speechless since the sound of the collision. She nodded and followed Ben.

"We've alerted the destroyers. They will act as rescue ships. That's all we can do," Captain Hawthorne explained to Ben.

"What do you mean, 'that's all we can do.' Those men will die out there before those ships arrive. It'll take 20 or 30 minutes! We have to help them, now!" Ben's voice had risen an octave.

"Ben, Ben. I understand you don't agree with my decision." He placed an arm on Ben's shoulder meant to defuse his anger. It didn't work. Ben shoved it away. Hawthorne's voice became sharp and authoritative. "My orders are and have always been that this ship does not stop for anything. My job is to get her and those soldiers down below safely to their destination. Stopping can put us in great danger."

"It can't put us in any more danger than we're in already. Can you not understand that I am a doctor! That I took an oath to *save* lives. The idea of leaving those men to drown when we could save some of them is inhumane. Delaying our arrival by an hour or two to save countless lives is the right thing to do." He made no attempt to control the tone of his voice. The wheelhouse crew discreetly disregarded Ben.

"As Captain of this ship my decision stands. We are not stopping. I'm waiting on a damage assessment and I'm asking you to leave. I don't want to make that an order." Ben knew his anger at the Captain was out of control. He had vowed again, after the Cocoanut Grove fire, to control it. But this inhumane decision was beyond belief. He knew he was going to say things he would regret later but in his very core he believed leaving those men to die was wrong.

"I misjudged you, Captain. I thought you had a conscience." He spun around and left the command center unaware that Kate remained behind. He moved outside to the stern of the ship pushing his way through the crowd of soldiers. The Queen Mary was already well past the wreckage. Both parts of the Curacaó had disappeared now and fewer men's screams reached his ears, begging for the ship to stop. To turn around. That same enormously helpless feeling grabbed him as he watched the brave men of the Curacaó sacrifice their lives for their country, one by one. Tears fell unchecked. Tears from anger? Compassion? Helplessness? He kept his fists clenched around the railing, watching the receding disaster, vision blurry. And just as he feared, the destroyers had not arrived in time to save most. He would find out later, much later, that only 101 men survived. Two hundred and thirty-eight men died in front of him as the Queen Mary, ordered by her Captain, moved on, ignoring their final pleas for help.

"Damage report." Captain Hawthorne was in communication with the damage control officer.

"Sir. The collision stove in the stern below the waterline and the speed of the ship is forcing great amounts of water inside." The Queen Mary like all ships her size was built with a bulkhead designed to prevent water rushing into the main part of the hull. "I'm afraid, sir that if the entire forward section floods, the weight of all that water and the speed of the ship could cause the bulkhead to fail. If that happens, sir, and the main part of the hull is breached we would be lookin' *up* at one of those German subs, sir."

Captain Hawthorne quickly gave the order to reduce speed to ten knots.

Speaking again to the engineer, "Get the crew in there with collision mats and bring in the water pumps. Now! Give me a report when that's done." As the ship began to slow, the reduced force of the incoming water allowed the damage control crews to cover the hole with the collision mats and reinforce them with timber. The pumps began working reducing the amount of water inside. The ship began to stabilize.

Captain Hawthorne had several concerns. First and foremost was the serious damage to his ship. But equally serious was the loss of the escort ship and the destroyers that out of necessity had now become rescue ships. The Queen Mary, loaded with a full division of soldiers on board, was unprotected. Quickly he contacted the gunnery crew and anti-aircraft men and instructed them to be extra vigilant. "We're on our own, fellas'. Our job is to deliver this damaged ship and cargo to its intended destination. The Queen is a warship and we follow warship rules."

The Queen Mary's speed had been her greatest asset against the German submarines. That was gone. The flotilla of ships searching the waters around her, protecting her, were now rescue ships for the Curacaó. They were gone. She limped slowly toward Gourock, alone and vulnerable, leaving bodies in her wake.

Kate's eyes had followed Ben's angry exit from the wheelhouse. She remained behind watching and listening as her father dealt with the crisis. Everything had happened so fast. One minute she and Ben were sharing an intimate kiss that had quickened her pulse and created a deep ache for more; then the loud explosion that jolted the rhythm of her already pounding heart. Then smoke, fire, and the hideous scene of burning, screaming men choking and dying before her eyes; and now Ben was accusing her father of being inhumane when he had so much to deal with. She understood Ben's reaction—she was a nurse. Like Ben, a part of her questioned her father's actions. However, unlike Ben, she knew there was no way her father was inhumane. Ben's public condemnation of her father hurt and angered her. He had no right!

Her love and loyalty for her father ran deep and her new exhilarating feelings for Ben held that same promise. But now she was confused. With so much happening all at once, a storm of emotions gripped her—horror, sorrow, anger, disappointment, each taking a turn, pulling at her. Leaving her dazed. Like the Queen Mary, she stood there alone and vulnerable.

CHAPTER 53

Near Kaunas
May, 1942

It was smelly. It was noisy. It was way beyond uncomfortable. Jonah and Ana were hidden in the false bottom of a Lithuanian farmer's chicken truck. Stacked above them were crates of chittering chickens destined for the market in Klaipedà. Antonio had given them new immigration papers, some clean clothes and together they had completed the travel visa. Thanks, and good-byes were exchanged. There was little doubt they would ever see one another again, even if Jonah and Ana were successful in their escape. Jonah had explained the plan to Ana and laced it with as much false hope as he could, but she knew him too well. They were embarking on a perilous journey with little hope of success, and she knew it.

The farmer had picked them up early for the nearly three hours of torture to the port city of Klaipedà. The noisy, jarring ride of the truck and its load of fowl made speech impossible. The satchel beneath Ana's head did little to cushion her from the ceaseless bucking of the truck. She closed her eyes, but that failed to subdue her claustrophobia. The panic attacks made her heart pound more and the bile in her stomach rise. *I can do this*, she kept repeating to herself. *I can do this.* She took a corner of her mitpachat, her head scarf, and covered her nose. Besides the 'fowl' smell there were bits of chaff, chicken feathers and dust in the air they were breathing. Sneezing at the wrong time could be deadly. The air grew thicker and warmer as the truck bobbled along.

Antonio told them they would pass through one German checkpoint just outside Klaipedà. There was no border crossing, only the passing into Soviet occupation. After that the farmer would take them as close to the docks as he could safely, for all of them. He had done this before—never near the quays—putting his own life in danger each time.

Ana was at the point of screaming, *Out, let me out!* when the truck began to slow. The Dresslers took a deep breath, cleared their noses as they had been told and lay perfectly still. Jonah took Ana's hand. He had been praying to Yahweh.

They could clearly hear the German guards ordering the truck to halt. Heard the German word for 'Papers.' The rustle of paper from up front. "Where are you going?"

"The market in Klaipedà. I have chickens to sell." The hidden husband and wife heard the crunching of boots as the German soldier walked around the truck. Just thinking about not sneezing made her want to sneeze. She pinched her nose, eyes closed. Unexpectedly the soldat pounded on the side of the truck startling Ana's eyes open but she made no sound. The sudden noise and vibration set the chickens squawking and the guard left, seemingly losing interest. He must have waved them on because the truck began to move, then suddenly the guard's sharp command, "Haltestelle!" The truck jerked to an abrupt stop. What was wrong? Had he seen or heard something? Ana was certain the loud pounding of her heart must have alerted him, and now it was pounding louder than ever. They could hear the boots crunching alongside the road again. "You have a low rear tire. Should fix it. Soon."

"Danke, sir. I'll do that." The truck began to move again, gathering speed this time. Relief spread through Ana like a summer breeze. The first danger point was passed. But how many more were there before they would be truly safe, she wondered.

Klaipedà's harbor was ice-free, so this was the busiest seaport in

Lithuania. As they walked along they smelled the docks before they saw them. Oily diesel fuel, salty sea air, and pungent iron smells were unfamiliar to them. But the smell of dead sea life brought back recent memories of death and decay for them both. Three more turns on the narrow, cobbled streets brought them in view of the seawall and the bay. They passed fishermen hawking their morning catches on small wooden carts. An assortment of ocean-washed fishing boats danced along the piers, each one rising and falling to the cadence of the ocean. Gulls and pelicans competed for the scraps of fish left behind on the boats, their raucous calls coloring the morning air. The large pier for the overnight ferry was obvious, though empty this early. The ferry would arrive soon to be cleaned, loaded with supplies, and then boarded in late afternoon. They entered the small wooden building.

"And again, what is your purpose for traveling to Copenhagen and when are you returning?" The harbormaster was examining their papers and the travel visa Jonah had laid in front of him. He placed his lopsided spectacles on the end of his long nose and hunched over the papers as if he were examining diamonds. The glasses balanced precariously and he needed to keep repositioning them as he read. The nails on his hands were ragged and ink-stained.

"We are visiting my son and family. He was re-positioned there a year ago. We will return in a month."

"Travel is difficult, you understand?"

"We know we are living in dangerous times. That is why we want to see our son."

"I saw many of these visas months ago. Not so many recently. This Sugihara is still ambassador?" He pointed to the signature.

"Yes. He was called back to Japan recently but still holds that office." These questions were beginning to unnerve Jonah, and Ana could feel her stomach turning into a knotted mass.

Working up some authority in his voice, Jonah said, "Sir, we would like two passes for the overnight ferry to Copenhagen. Now, danke."

"One moment." The harbormaster glared at him and then left his chair to confer with another man, dressed in Soviet attire in a small office off to the side. They both studied the papers, heads bent low over the desk.

Jonah studied the building while he waited. The ferry terminal was an old low wooden structure with small high windows so coated with salt spray that even on a rare sunny day they did little to lighten the room or provide warmth. The wooden floor was blackened and stained from the passage of years of dirty boots. Hard wooden benches lined two walls and yellowed schedules and posters decorated the back wall—a large one indicated men's and women's clozets. Otherwise the room was empty except for one other man. If the ferry passes were purchased he and Ana would be staying here for several hours.

"Two passes. Four rubles, please." The conference had concluded, and the harbormaster had returned. "The ferry leaves from Pier D at *keturi valanda dienos*, 16:30 hours, and arrives in Copenhagen at *dešimt valanda nakties*, 10:00 hours, tomorrow. There are no rooms available, only seats. The pass includes a small meal for each of you. You can wait here." He indicated the wooden benches and handed the passes to Jonah along with his papers, still eyeing him with suspicion.

Jonah wished for another place to wait, but walking around would be more dangerous, and Ana still needed rest. They had a small amount of food with them. That would suffice until they boarded.

Jonah walked to the men's clozet, so Ana took a seat. The benches were more comfortable than the chicken truck; and the smell was slightly more tolerable. There was still risk, however. At any minute they could be accosted and arrested. She seated herself as inconspicuously as possible on the hard bench. Jonah returned and sat down beside her, stroking his chin where his long beard had been, partly out of nervousness; partly because it felt strange. His yarmulke was in the satchel and he felt half-naked without it covering his head. Ana kept glancing up at him, squinting her eyes and wrinkling her nose trying to adjust to his new appearance. Her mitpachat was around her shoulders instead of covering her head.

"Jonah, I am using the clozet." She gathered the scarf around her, smoothed her new long skirt and lowering her head, walked across the room to the women's clozet. The bathroom was minimal, but did include a small mirror. She hadn't seen herself in a mirror in months and when she caught her image she gasped. She was surprised at the pallor of her skin. The hollow cheeks. The deepening wrinkles. *And, oh no! My hair is so gray.* She covered her hair with her scarf and finished freshening up from the chicken truck ride as best she could in the tiny sink and returned to Jonah. She sat down beside him and brushed his hand, refusing to look at him. "Jonah, I am old," she murmured.

He took hold of her hand, "Ana, we both are."

They shared the remainder of the food Antonio had provided and waited. Fearful that the harbormaster would send an alert, Jonah lowered his head, pretending to doze, but through half-closed eyes he divided his attention between the man and the terminal door. If Jonah noticed anything suspicious, he and Ana would quickly leave. There was little doubt that a Soviet soldier would appear before the departure of the ferry.

CHAPTER 54

Atlantic Ocean
May 5, 1942

Ben paced. His cabin was small so he paced in a tiny circle hands clenched at his side. His stomach churned and he felt nauseous. In a sudden fit of anger he jabbed his fist into the door. It didn't make him feel any better and his fist felt worse.

This was worse than the fire. That night he had eventually swung into action, focusing on the injured, taking charge, making decisions. Today all he could do was pace, still seeing before him horrifying images of those men struggling for their lives in the burning, oil-covered icy water and he could do nothing. His eyes rested on the bed where only a few short minutes ago he and Kate had shared a lingering kiss, urgency building between them. It seemed like hours ago. *Kate? Where had she gone?* He had been so angry, so frustrated, he had forgotten about her. *She had stood there, silently, listening, as he yelled at*— "Oh, no," he groaned. He rubbed his eyes with his hand and slumped onto the bed.

The knock on his door was so quiet he didn't hear it at first. "Ben. It's me—Kate. May I come in?" He crossed the small room in two strides and pulled open the door. The distraught look on her face slowed him down; and he stood aside as she entered. His eyes followed hers to the bed. "We should talk."

He reached for her hand, but she moved away. The room was

small and the distancing was inadequate, but Ben got the message.

"Kate, if you want me to apologize, I won't. To you or your father. What happened out there didn't need to happen. Those men did not need to die today. We should have stopped, turned around. How did the collision happen, anyway? Did your father say?" Even a semi- neutral tone required much effort.

Kate moved further from him. "Are you blaming my father? Yes, you should apologize. That was a difficult decision for him." She stared at him a minute, then looked away. "I also came to tell you that I think maybe we've moved too fast. That we should take a step back. We should take time to—"

"You agree with your father, then? He did the right thing?" His angry tone was spoiling for a fight.

Kate bristled, her emotional equilibrium shook up. "You are just such a bloody pig-headed sod! Why can't you see more than your view of things?" And, what? Do you think the accident was my father's fault? My Papa has more integrity in his little finger than you have in your. . . your. . .Oh, never mind! Coming here was a mistake." She didn't know if the tears that were threatening were from anger, disappointment, sorrow—or probably all three. What she did know was that Ben was not going to see her cry. She fled through the open doorway and made a valiant but losing effort to slam the door. "Cabin doors do not slam effectively," she said defiantly as she ran down the corridor, allowing the tears to blur her vision, nearly running into Dr. Joe.

Joe Ramsey saw the tears but assumed they were the result of the collision. He had not been privy to the scene in the bridge. He continued down the corridor and rapped on Ben's door, "Ben, are you in there? Some men were injured during the collision. We need to go."

"Be right there," he called out, stuffing his anger only to have it resurface as he berated himself loudly. "I should have thought of that!" Quickly he pulled on his white coat and left his cabin. "She'll never understand me," he said, failing, like Kate, to slam his door.

Ministering to the injured in the infirmary was a temporary remedy for his emotional crisis. The three doctors and several army nurses—Kate noticeably absent—treated cuts, a dislocated shoulder and possible concussions. The most serious injury was a punctured lung. Dr. McHenry inserted a hollow needle into the pleural space and withdrew the air, stabilizing the patient until he could be treated in Gourock.

Later, back in his cabin, Ben was stretched out on his bed. *So, Kate thinks I'm pig-headed. Just because I have convictions. I understand her loyalty to her father, but if she cared for me she would see my side, too. I doubt we can get beyond this. I can never un-see what happened today nor ever condone it. I can't work for a man who would leave hundreds to die in such a horrible way. I can't do that. I just can't.*

After their argument, Kate had fled to her cabin. Her short bout of tears purged her and then restlessness set in. The small room felt confining, suffocating almost. She needed some hot tea and she needed to talk with her father. The tea she could find. But not her father. She knew he would be busy for several hours. She was sitting alone in the dining room when Dr. Joe walked in.

He poured coffee from the bottomless carafe and sat down beside her. "Want company? he asked. She smiled at him. Weakly. But a smile. "Been a hard day, hasn't it," he said.

"I can't get those men out of my mind. Their horrible deaths. I think about their wives, children, maybe girlfriends. They don't even know yet." Her voice broke. "We didn't stop, you know. Ben blames my father. Told him he had no conscience. How do you feel about that? You're a doctor."

Joe considered his answer for a moment. "Your father faced a very difficult moral dilemma. I can't imagine how troubling this day has been for him. His decision might break a lesser man." He held the coffee mug in both hands and took a sip.

"It's easy to pass judgment on what we don't understand. This may sound strange coming from me—a black man—but Ben is thinking in black and white right now. I'm not faulting him. That's where principles originate. He has yet to learn that life has shades of gray. War has shades of gray. The line between right and wrong can get very blurred. There are times when there are no good choices; so, we make the best ones we know how. He'll learn that; but, Kate, he may never agree with your father's decision. You should understand that, and just hope that he can learn to respect the courage it took for your father to make it."

Dr. Joe left and Kate was alone with her thoughts again. The dining room was mostly empty at the moment, as the kitchen staff cleaned up debris before beginning meal preparations. Her crowded emotional state had exhausted her and as she finished her tea, her mind shifted back to the night she and Ben danced in this room. She had thought him to be a bit of a twit, actually, even though she had enjoyed showing him around the ship and the wheelhouse, delighted by his excitement. No way could she have known he would be a part of her life again—like this. That she would have these feelings for him. It occurred to her if she had stayed in Sydney like Mum wanted she wouldn't be struggling with any of these feelings. Was being aboard the Queen Mary a mistake?

CHAPTER 55

Klaipedá, Lithuania
May, 1942

"I see him," Ana whispered. The Soviet lieutenant had arrived to check out the ferry. Soviet occupation in the past brought recognition of various uniforms. The black cap, black boots, khaki jacket and blue pants indicated a Junior Lieutenant. A very large male German Shepherd dog accompanied him.

"We wait," her husband whispered back. And they continued to sit on the hard, wooden backless benches that had been their resting place for five hours now. Other passengers had arrived over the afternoon and now about 25 or 30 people filled the benches.

In Lithuanian they heard, "The ferry to Copenhagen now boarding at Pier D." A long line of assorted vehicles had been lining up perpendicular to the pier and began inching forward on the ramp after the announcement. Trucks loaded with fragrant timber and fuel oil, personal autos, and military vehicles moved slowly on board. The fugitives continued to wait.

"Why are we waiting?" Ana asked quietly.

"I want to board toward the last. By then others behind us will be hurrying him along. He might give our papers only a quick check."

"But if he detains us, we'll miss the ferry."

"Yes. That is the risk."

Boarding of the vehicles continued. "Now, Ana." They

gathered the two worn satchels, stood, and walked with a confidence they didn't feel toward the boarding area and the Soviet Lieutenant.

"Papers." Despite the different uniform, the man was a carbon copy of the many soldiers they had encountered so far. His dog sniffed around both their shoes, probably catching scents of chickens. The uniformed man eyed the scruffy satchels suspiciously.

Jonah handed over the papers and the travel visa. The lieutenant studied them, reading every word. "Why are you going to Copenhagen?"

"We will catch a freighter to the UK. We have family there."

"This travel visa is most unusual. Most travel is restricted now. How did you come by it?"

Jonah hated lying, but sometimes you had to do what you had to do. "It was given to me personally by Mr. Sugihara. He has been recalled to Japan but still retains his office in Kaunas. This visa is a valid document. . .sir."

"We will see. You and your wife need to come with me. We will need to verify this."

"The harbormaster has already validated it. We will miss the ferry and there isn't another one for two days. I assure you these documents are in order," Jonah exclaimed. A final boarding call was given and the ferry gave two short blasts on its horn. All but a few vehicles were now boarded.

Another traveler was witnessing the exchange between Jonah and the lieutenant. He attracted the lieutenant's attention and walked in their direction. Spotting the Soviet's last name, he said, "Lieutenant Schumann? This is a new assignment for you, no? I ride this ferry regularly for business. I have not met you. I am Steponas Matas and I own a company that supplies great amounts of lumber products and fuel oil to the Soviet army. Actually, I am quite well-acquainted with Justas Paleckis, the Lithuanian President. I can assure you that I have seen many of these visas and they are quite legitimate. There is no need for validation. When I see President Paleckis again I will mention you to him—how diligent you are, Lieutenant Schumann."

The Soviet Lieutenant knew that the Lithuanian President was heavily aligned with the Soviet army. Being mentioned to him by a successful businessman was indeed good fortune. He tapped the papers against the palm of his hand. Considering. Even though they did appear to be valid, he thought he should look somewhat suspicious. So, he squinted and re-read them, twice. Slowly he handed the papers back to Jonah. "These seem to be in order. You may board."

The dockhands were pulling the enormous ropes from the dock pilings as the couple and their new benefactor hurried aboard the ferry that would take them away from the only country they had ever known.

Once onboard Jonah was quick to thank Mr. Matas. "Your comments to that Soviet Lieutenant were very helpful. Thank you. We are very grateful. We are Jonah and Ana Dressler. I owned an engineering firm in Vilna until the Germans arrived. But I must ask, why did you find reason to intervene?"

"I know Ambassador Sugihara. I have been a guest in his home. He is a fine Japanese gentleman and when you said you knew him—"

"Excuse me. I must interrupt. I am only barely acquainted with him."

"Yes. What I was going to say was Mr. Sugihara distributed those travel visas to Jews, mostly. Like you were, I am a businessman. I sell and ship timber, lumber, oil, among other things, to whomever gives the best price. I harbor no ill-will toward Jews, and when I can, I help my fellow countrymen. What is your cabin number? I can assist you in locating it."

"We have no cabin, only seats."

"I see. Well, then, I am traveling alone and would appreciate the company for dinner. Please be my guests."

The waiter placed the plate in front of Ana. Chicken, leeks, carrots, and brown bread. Chicken. She idly wondered if it was one of the chickens they had shared a ride with today. *The bird going to its death, she going to. . .what?* She picked up a utensil and ate some vegetables. Jonah and Mr. Matas were talking business talk. Today's stress had exhausted her and she only picked up a word or phrase of their conversation. "We don't know," and "Sakansia," and "give them this."

After all they had been through, she knew she should be grateful for the chance to be waited on, sitting at a table and eating a hot meal. And she was. . .thankful. This was the safest place she had been in months. But this vision of normalcy brought greater feelings of loss.

She knew now. In the face of everything they had endured, hope had still existed. Hope that she would return to her home. Hope that their life would return to what it had been. That hope was gone now. She would never see her home again. Never sweep the floors. Never prepare a meal in her tidy kitchen. She would never be able to visit the graves of her ancestors and never again worship at the Great Synagogue. That life was over. She knew. She sighed, soundlessly. *And my hair is gray.*

Ana had opened her satchel earlier. Wrapped as it was in a heavy brown head scarf, the little cup and saucer had miraculously survived. That was her only possession from the life she and Jonah had built. Everything before them was unknown and uncertain. *We are Jews. We will always be Jews. Jews are never safe.* She stabbed a bite of chicken.

CHAPTER 56

Gourock, Scotland
May 6, 1942

The crippled Queen sat in her berth, 16,000 soldiers still filing off the ship into slow rain. Somber. If the men hadn't seen it firsthand, they knew the story of the crew on board the Curacaó. Whatever joviality and comraderie had existed among them before was replaced with solemnness and reverence.

Dr. McHenry's valise was open on the bed and the Scottish doctor was emptying the small dresser. He heard a light tap on the open door as Ben called out, "May I come in?"

"Aye, lad. Just doin' some packin'. Leavin' tomorrow."

"I know. I heard. I'm sorry you're leaving us. It's been a real pleasure working with you."

"'Tis a sorry day. I'm gonna' miss this ol' tub, but my old body donna' work so good now."

"How are you getting to Edinburgh, doctor?"

"Me brother is bringin' a càr for me."

"If possible, I'd like to ride along with you. I'll pay you, of course."

"Wanna' see Edinburgh, eh?"

"Yes. I do."

"Why, Laddie? It be a dangerous road. You should stay here. It's safer. Luftwaffe bombed us in '40, striking the fuel depots. But we don't hear the planes as much now. The bombing was why I stayed on in New York. But now I'm ready to go home."

"I made a promise to a friend. I'd really like to ride along, sir." The Scotsman looked Ben in the eye and saw his resolve.

"Be ready in the morning, then."

"Thanks. I will."

It was late evening. The ship was secured and Captains Hawthorne and Merriwether had gone ashore to discuss repairs and their subsequent delay with Cunard Line marine engineers and the Royal Navy. They had concern whether the Queen Mary could continue its transport mission. After analysis, they made the decision to pump cement into the bow of the ship. This temporary repair would require an extra two days in Gourock. They also decided that remaining in Scotland for permanent repairs was too risky, so the ship would undergo final repairs in Boston. The two Captains returned to the Queen Mary.

"It's been a pleasure having you on board, Mac. Stay safe during this god-awful time."

"Aye, Captain. One more thing. Ben is riding with me to Edinburgh. He's a good mon. He needs some seasoning. He'll come 'round."

"Thanks, Mac. He and I haven't spoken yet, but I'll talk to him."

The Captain closed the door behind Dr. McHenry and sat on the edge of the bed, slowly untying and removing his shoes. He stretched out on the bead, hands behind his head. It had been a grueling day. He had successfully completed his mission. The 16,000 troops were on their way to the field. His ship, though injured, was repairable. *Then why do I feel so wretched?* Now that the immediate crises were resolved and his mind wasn't consumed with getting his battered ship and American cargo into Gourock, his thoughts turned back to the collision. *What will the investigation show? Was I at fault in some way?* His heart was heavy.

He hadn't shared this information with anyone, but the Admiralty had decided to hush up the collision. There would be no news release until after the duration. The thinking was that the collision would be a prime piece of propaganda for the Axis.

And Ben. He replayed the words in his head. *I misjudged you. I thought you had a conscience.* "Ben, if you only knew," he whispered. He sat back up on the edge of the bed, stepped back into his shoes and re-tied them.

Ben was alone in his cabin packing a small bag, his back to the door, when the Captain knocked. "Ben, may I come in? It's your Captain." He deliberately chose those words—a choice Ben took note of. The young doctor steeled himself before answering.

"Door's open." He kept his back to the door.

"I know it's late, but I thought you might like a drink. I know I would. I really think we should talk."

"Thanks, but I want to finish this."

"Mac told me you were going with him to Edinburgh. May I ask why?"

"It's personal, sir."

"Did you hear my announcement earlier." Not a question. "No one has been allowed shore leave this time. It's too dangerous. You understand that the Luftwaffe are still bombing the UK. Scotland was bombed heavily earlier in the war, especially Edinburgh because of the huge amounts of fuel stored there. It has slowed in recent months, but that doesn't mean it isn't still dangerous. You must have a very powerful reason for making this trip."

Ben hadn't invited the Captain to take a seat, implying their conversation be brief. He considered explaining his reason, telling him that sometimes you have to put *yourself* in danger to help others. He felt his anger returning, but this time it was tempered by his emotional exhaustion. "It's a long story. I'm helping a close friend. It's something I need to do. Promised to do."

"Come on, then. Let's have that drink and you can tell me the story." Ben looked up from his packing, straightened his shoulders, and looked directly into Captain Hawthorne's eyes.

"I'll have a drink with you, but that doesn't in any way mean I've changed my mind about what happened today. I'm not apologizing. I will always disagree with your decision to leave those men behind."

"I understand. And I will never feel the need to explain my decision to you."

CHAPTER 57

Copenhagen, Denmark
May 4, 1942

Ana's strength had not fully returned and she was very tired. She drifted in and out of a shallow sleep, leaning against Jonah during the long overnight sea ride to Copenhagen. Exhaustion accompanied Jonah, too, but his conversation last night with Mr. Matas had yielded exhilarating information, making sleep more difficult. He remembered Antonio telling him that Copenhagen was so far neutral. Copenhagen offered a degree of refuge at a time when nowhere was safe for Jews.

In the morning after a porter brought around coffee, tea and rolls, Jonah and Ana walked outside on the deck. It was a beautifully sunny morning. The ferry was entering the narrow inland waterway and the two watched as tall brick buildings came into view. Colorful little shacks seemingly glided by as the ferry moved along. Soon they could see cranes stretching out over the water that were even taller than the buildings. And pleasure boats and small fishing vessels. "Be ready to disembark," the unseen voice announced.

The Dresslers gathered their pitifully inadequate, worn out satchels and Ana asked Jonah, "What do we do now?"

"We had a stroke of luck last night. Mr. Matas gave me the name of a cargo ship, the Sakansia, and a paper giving us priority to a cabin. Steponas didn't know the ship's schedule, only that he uses it frequently for shipments to and from Leith. He said that Edinburgh was beginning to rebuild after the bombings and building supplies were coming into Scotland frequently from many sources. Good lumber from Lithuania was in constant supply. So even if the Sakansia isn't available, there might soon be another. That's what we'll check on."

The Copenhagen harbor was very large with many piers spread out like long fingers lined with huge cargo ships and naval vessels. Jonah ended up needing to ask for directions, and not knowing any Danish, showed the dockhand the paper with the ship's name on it. They followed the seaman's pointed finger but could not decipher his directions. After several more attempts they stumbled onto a truck driver who made deliveries every day to the docks. Fortunately, both spoke German, making conversation much easier. He instructed them how to find the harbormaster who had a schedule and from whom passage could be purchased. Alas, it was in the opposite direction. They must have passed it.

The booking agent, speaking in German, did not have good news. The Sakansia was traveling to Rostock, Germany not due back until late the next day, 5 May. After loading and refueling it would leave again on 6 May due in Leith the night of 7 May, a twenty-two-hour trip. There were four cabins total, but only one remaining. Otherwise, steerage was available. Jonah purchased the remaining cabin. The money he had hidden in his coat many weeks ago plus the few rubles Antonio had given them were disappearing quickly. Antonio had changed his Lithuanian Litas into German marks before they left the camp.

Ana spoke up. "Jonah. I need to sleep. It has been many hours since we have rested on a bed." Jonah turned back to the agent.

"Wie bitte, sir. Where could we stay?"

"I know of only one place close by. A lady I know rents out a room." He gave them instructions for the trolley, where to get off, and walking directions. He scanned Jonah's appearance. "You should know. She does not rent to Jews."

"Danke," Jonah replied. They knew of nowhere else to go so they began walking toward the trolley stop. If she wouldn't rent to them, perhaps she knew someone who would.

They had never been in such a large city and it was overwhelming. People everywhere. Noisy streets. Every building was tall. Ana thought it was like a forest made of bricks. Jonah was attentive to everything, insuring they could get back to the docks.

They found the house by the agent's description. It was a small two-story brick structure with square windows. Enclosing the small yard was a four-foot wall of large, smooth colorful stones snuggled into a bed of pink and white flowers. A locked iron gate opened off the street with one hinge pulled loose from the rock wall. Beside the gate was a bell.

The bell was answered by a middle-aged woman, wearing a kerchief over her hair and a long colorful printed skirt. She was wiping her hands on her white apron while inspecting them with a keen eye. When her Danish wasn't understood, she switched to German. "May I help you?"

"We would like a room for two nights, bitte."

Her eyes darted to their sparse luggage, took in their haggard appearance, and was about to wave them away when Jonah said, "I noticed your gate needs repair. I can do that for you."

She hesitated, then, "Are you Jews?"

Jonah didn't like lying. It had never been part of who he was. Accepting the risk of an honest answer, he said, "Yes. We are. We have lost everything. We have been running for days and we are very tired. We need to rest. Two nights. That's all. I have money to pay you."

She continued to scrutinize the man who was begging her. "Jews usually mean trouble." She continued to stand there. "But I need the money. Only two nights? You can fix the gate, you say? Five weeks! My nephew promise to fix. He is lazy dumbkopf." She took in Ana. "I may have some better clothes for you." She moved to unlock the gate. "My name is Helgesen, Clara Helgesen. Come. Come."

When settled in their room, Jonah quietly said to Ana, "I don't trust that woman. She could take our money and then sell us out to a German friend or relative for some additional income. If we knew where else to go, I would leave."

"Jonah, I am so tired, please?"

Ana's strength had not fully returned and Jonah saw she needed rest. "We will stay," he said. And to himself, *Mrs. Helgesen bears watching.* Ana slept soundly all night, but Jonah lay awake, listening.

CHAPTER 58

Gourock, Scotland
May 6, 1942

"I thought this was a dry ship, Captain," Ben remarked sarcastically. The two were seated in the Captain's quarters.

"When the soldiers have disembarked and the ship is secure, I allow myself a drink or two. Today I'm definitely having two. But I brew the coffee first so it's on call. Now, tell me why you are so eager to trot over a dangerous strip of motorway. I've not known you to want to get into the thick of it before. What's changed?"

Ben had never been much of a drinker and the good Scotch whiskey was going straight to his head. His words tumbled out in a mostly coherent account of how his Jewish Lithuanian friend, Samuel—Kate had met him—came to be living in Ben's home. Samuel thought his parents were dead only to discover last week that they were alive. "We wired them to secure passage to Leith by May 6th. Have no idea if that was possible for them. This delay for repairs gives them more time. My plan was—is—to arrange a car and pick them up in Leith, bring them back to the Queen Mary and take them to Samuel in Boston. At the time I thought we would be going back to New York, but you said we're heading to Boston for the repairs. Fortunately, there's an immigration office in Boston. I figured I would hide them in the isolation ward rooms. Unfortunately, I have no way of knowing if they even made it as far as Edinburgh."

"Were you planning to disobey the 'no shore leave' order?"

"Yes, if I had to."

"What were you planning to use for transportation to Leith?"

"At first I didn't know. Then I remembered that Dr. McHenry was going to Edinburgh. I asked to ride along."

"How were you planning on getting back?"

"I don't know. But, I'm resourceful. I'll figure something out."

"Have you driven on the left-hand side of the road yet?"

"No. But can't be too hard. They do it in movies all the time."

"Can you do it and dodge bombs?"

"Yes. I can even shoot them down with one-hand and drive with the other." He pointed his index finger at the Captain and let off with a popping sound. The scotch talking.

The Captain failed to be impressed. Instead he was deep in thought. *If I helped Ben I wouldn't be aiding and abetting the enemy. In fact, I would be aiding and abetting the victims of this senseless war. When we leave here, it will be with a very minimum crew because of the lengthy repairs in Boston; no soldiers will be on board. There will be some German prisoners, however. Cunard won't care about Jews on board. Hundreds of Jewish soldiers have been transported. And this isn't smuggling. Samuel's parents will go through immigration.*

His decision made, he said, "Ben. Listen to me. If I accompany you we can bypass the 'no shore leave' order. It applies to everyone but the captain. Instead of riding with Mac, you and I can drive to Leith. Cunard gives me access to transportation in every city we stay in. I can have an automobile or lorry in a day or two. I know the area. I know the driving rules and the rest; plus, I can get you back."

The Captain's surprising offer cleared Ben's head a bit. "Why? Why do this? It's not your problem. You don't even know Samuel. . .or his parents. Not only that, it's a covert operation. You run a clean ship. Can't let you do it, sir."

The Captain smiled at Ben's alcoholic-tinged, spy-like comments. "Covert operation might be a bit dramatic, Ben." He was silent for a moment—then added—his tone serious, "You may dismiss this as so much self-indulgent twaddle, but honestly, I need to do this. For me. I left hundreds of sons, fathers, brothers, nephews behind today. It was a bloody rotten thing to do; but it was my mission. My decision. The vision of those drowning men will stay with me for a long time. Helping save your friend's parents, victims of this tosser's war, might prove to you that I do have a conscience. Can you understand?" Ben was silent and the Captain took that as a 'yes'. "Okay, then. Come on. We need to find Mac."

May 7, 1942

Cunard arranged for a maroon 731 Vauxhall GL model that had a commanding 25 hp engine and a good heater. May in Scotland can be quite chilly. Mac contacted his brother and canceled his ride. Even though there was no plan from this point on, having Mac along with his knowledge of Edinburgh would be very helpful. The three men discussed options and possibilities as the car consumed the 130 kilometers.

They agreed that if Jonah and Ana Dressler had made it as far as Leith or Edinburgh they would go to a synagogue for shelter, food and local assistance. That's where the trio would look first. Mac knew of only one synagogue in Edinburg, The Salisbury Road Synagogue. He would direct them once they arrived.

Fewer bombings had allowed crews to make temporary repairs in the main roads, so they stuck to those with only minor detours. The motorway traveled along the ocean inlet for ten or fifteen kilometers, then veered inland. The landscape changed to small farms, rock walls, green fields and trees. A light drizzle produced a mistiness to the countryside making it appear as if they were driving through an impressionistic painting. Three hours later they were nearing Edinburgh.

They drove down Princes Street and The Royal Mile filled with Scottish history, with Dr. McHenry pointing out places of interest. The street was filled with uniformed military, women shoppers dressed in suits, hats and walking shoes. Hairdressers, millineries, cafes and bars lined both sides of the street. Double-decker buses ejected streams of passengers. They passed the Palace cinema and Ben laughingly pointed out the F.W. Woolworth's next door.

It was late afternoon by the time they checked the synagogue with no results. "Ben, I must be back to the ship no later than tomorrow evening. The Queen leaves for Boston early the next morning," the Captain said. "Let's drive down to the docks in Leith and ask about ships due in today or tomorrow from Copenhagen."

"Good idea," Ben answered. They drove down Market Street into Leith and found parking. A few questions later they got answers from the harbormaster and the immigration office. No one named Dressler had passed through in the last week. They learned that Jews would automatically be given asylum and directed to the synagogue. A freighter named *The Sakansia* was scheduled in tomorrow or the next day, but schedules were really only loose estimates of arrival. Weather, enemy detour delays, and loading delays played havoc with schedules. They left a message for the Dresslers with the immigration office.

"My brother opened my house. Ye can stay with me for the night and enjoy some Haggis in honor of my return. And *neeps* and *tatties*. And wash it down with a good Scotch whiskey."

Ben looked at the Captain for the translation. "What is haggis?"

"You may not want to know. I can tell you *neeps* are turnips and *tatties* are mashed potatoes. "And what is haggis?" Ben pressed.

"Aye, Laddie, the cook takes the heart, liver and lungs of a sheep and minces them. After, she adds onions, carrots and spices and cooks it a wee bit. It is a celebratory dish. And a proper house guest usually has two helpings to be polite."

"You're right. I shouldn't have asked."

Mac's home was larger than Ben had thought. The living room was furnished with a salmon-colored large print sofa and two large chairs grouped around a stone fireplace. Surrounding the fireplace were built-in shiny dark wood cabinets. Mac lived alone and the only knick-knacks on the shelves were large china farm animal figurines and a collection of pipes and tobacco. A reddish-brown carpet covered nearly all of the hardwood floor. An eclectic assortment of lamps and tables were scattered around.

Introductions were made to Mac's brother and wife and the group gathered in the farm-like kitchen around the long plank table to enjoy the Haggis. Ben wasn't a polite house guest. He scarcely got two bites down after watching the preparation.

Tonight, though, he placed limits on the excellent Scotch. He was restless after dinner. Everything felt strange. He was in limbo, and he wasn't good at limbo. He called back to his host who was laughing and catching up with his brother. "Mac, I'm going to take a walk. I remember we're not far from the synagogue. I'm going to leave another message with the Rabbi."

"Aye, laddie. Keep your peepers open. The streets canna' be chancy. Lots of military will be cruising' the bars and cafes. At times, if they've had a bit too much whiskey, they canna' be hammered. Donna' want you punched up. And don't forget the curfew."

"Thanks for the reminder. I'll be careful. I know boxing, remember?"

Ben did want to check in with the Rabbi, but he also wanted time to sort out all the thoughts buzzing around in his head. He wasn't sure where things stood with Kate. He still wasn't sure what to think about the help from the Captain, and his mind was wrestling with what to do if Samuel's parents weren't on that ship tomorrow.

In the twilight evening he could hear revelry from the taverns a few short blocks away. He had not gone far when without warning a brilliant light flashed behind him followed by a thunderous explosion.

A number of bombs the Axis and Allies were using were constructed with delayed detonators that often malfunctioned. Their purpose? To hamper reconstruction efforts. Sometimes they never exploded. And sometimes weeks, months or years later an unexpected detonation would occur. Buried in the vegetation, rubble and the hole it had created weeks ago when it was dropped, this one lay in wait. Until tonight.

CHAPTER 59

The Scotch whiskey had done its job of relaxing the Captain and he was thinking of sleep when he and Mac heard the muffled blast. Mac was out of his chair in seconds, "Bomb!" he said and began searching for his medical bag. The sound of sirens screamed into the sky within minutes of the explosion, a response perfected through repetition. The Scottish Police, Ambulance and Fire Service tore off in the direction of the blast.

"Wait! I'm coming with you," Captain Hawthorne said, downing the last of the Scotch.

By the time they had shoes, jackets, and Mac had checked the contents of his medical bag, they could hear sirens chirping in the distance. Rushing out the door, they ran in the direction of the sirens. Within a block or two they could smell the acrid air and see people milling around. Twilight would not succumb to darkness this time of year, so they could clearly see what was before them.

"Oh my God, Ben! Hurry!" Hawthorne cried out. Mac's slight limp and still healing hip slowed them down. They could see people gathering near a large blackened area deep in a copse of short pine and oak trees. The stand of trees and the fact the bomb was buried, had likely minimized the bomb's explosive power reducing damage to surrounding buildings; but the house closest to the trees was on fire and fallen trees had buried another building. Other homes and buildings had roof damage and broken windows. Two autos parked on the street were overturned and burning.

There were casualties, but the curfew saved many.

The sirens were loud now as both medical and fire vehicles began arriving, spilling trained workers into the devastation. "Do you see Ben anywhere?" Mac shouted. The two searched for Ben in the crowd hoping he was among the curious. Neither one spotted him.

Some British soldiers were in town and suddenly one of them yelled out, "Hey! There's an injured bloke over here!" Elbowing people out of the way, Mac hurried in that direction while the captain quizzed another group.

"I'm a doctor. Let me through, please." The bloke was Ben and he was just picking himself up off the ground. "Ben, it's me, Mac. Don't get up. Let me check you out."

"What? My ears are still ringing. I'm fine. What happened?" He continued to brush himself off as he stood up, unaware of the large amount of blood beginning to soak the arm of his jacket, and obviously in shock.

"It was a bomb. Delayed detonation. You were lucky, but some others weren't. If you're sure you're okay, I'll go see if I can help," he said and disappeared among the bystanders without seeing the blood on Ben's arm.

"Yeah. I'll go with . . .y—" The initial shock began wearing off and he began to react to the scene before him. The sirens became louder. The devastation around him clearer. Trees were shredded. The blazing house and two or three smaller fires produced an eerie glow. What had been garden plots moments ago were now charred blackened earth.

Stone and brick debris, twisted tree branches, yard implements and decorations were flung in all directions. Already emergency workers were triaging the wounded and searching for any other victims. Firemen were preparing the long hoses. His legs got a little wobbly as he began to grasp how fortunate he had been.

From around the side of the burning house, he caught sight of a dark shape that stumbled and fell. With little thought he ran toward the fully engulfed house to give assistance. When he lifted the man, he felt a stabbing pain in his left arm and could give only one-armed support. Pointing back to the house Ben tried to mime if everyone was out. The injured man seemed to grasp the question and breathing heavily, replied in English that he was the last one out. Ben shifted his hold on the man and it was then that he saw the blood.

A fireman spotted them and rushed to help, half carrying the man to a triage area. Ben stood there, his brain still foggy from shock, trying to decide what use he could be, but the language, protocol, and foreign medical procedures were a big problem. Anyway, there were numerous emergency workers present who seemingly had things under control.

"Ben, you're bleeding." The Captain had found him. "Let's get you checked out."

Ben nodded.

Later he lay in bed at Mac's, staring at the ceiling; his arm sore, as much from stitches as injury, and wrapped in a thick bandage. He had been lucky. Only the one deep laceration and multiple bruises from flying debris, plus a dull headache. A couple of minutes later and he would have been lying in the street waiting for help. Or worse. The thought brought a shiver and touch of nausea.

Tonight's scene took him back yet again. Flames lighting the acrid smoke-filled sky. Sirens blaring. Emergency workers rushing to assess injuries and rapidly administer immediate aid. People weeping. . .moaning. Himself a victim, too. But this time it was different. He was different. This time he had actually run toward the fire to help. The fact amazed him. No flashback. No state of frozen animation. He just saw the injured man and rushed to help. It was a good feeling. He wondered about the man's injuries and prognosis, but knew he wouldn't be able to follow-up.

The Captain appeared in the doorway. "How are you feeling?"

"Not too bad. The tablets Mac gave me took the pain down.

"You were very brave tonight, you know. Rushing in to help that man." He sat down on the other twin bed, laying watch, keys and money clip on the bedside table and began untying his shoes.

"It was just instinct. The right thing to do." Then realizing how that might sound to the Captain, he added, "I mean it felt good after all we've been through." Then he changed the subject. "I wonder if there's any chance at all that Samuel's parents will be on that ship tomorrow. Or if the ship will even get here tomorrow. He'll be so disappointed if our plan doesn't work."

The Captain nodded. "We'll wait here as long as we can. But traveling that road late at night is extremely dangerous. We were fortunate getting here with no interference. Might not happen again."

CHAPTER 60

On Board the Sakansia
May 7, 1942

After seeing the steerage accommodations Jonah and Ana realized how thankful they were to Mr. Matas for their cabin. Even though tiny, it contained two small beds. The head was shared with the three other cabins. The passengers in steerage, many of them Jewish refugees, were crowded together and, if lucky slept on bunk bed benches attached to the wall; otherwise, they slept on the floor. All were required to bring their own bedding and eating utensils. They were required to remain in the bowels of the freighter allowing them no fresh air or sunlight. The motion of the ship below was intensified, and many became quickly seasick creating a noxious, slimy, sour -smelling floor.

Stories ran rampant of freighter crewmen stealing from passengers, roughing them up and sexually molesting the young women travelling alone. Captains were known to single out a woman and with brute force manhandle her into his cabin where she would be locked in during the entire voyage and forcibly raped. Although the conditions in steerage were disgusting, the Sakansia Captain did not permit abuse aboard his ship. But it still occurred. All passengers received the same food—a warm bowl of watery flavorless bean soup, brown bread, dried fruit, and water with a peculiar smell.

The creaking sounds, the unpleasant odors and the rocking

of the boat made sleeping only a word, so Jonah and Ana were up early. They spent most of the day on deck walking and watching instead of in their confining room.

Today was overcast, a bank of clouds off to the north. Jonah was concentrating on the clouds when he noticed a dark something moving near the horizon. It appeared at first to be a flock of birds until it grew larger and he could see it was a plane. It circled out over the North Sea, searching, drawing closer and closer. A loud squawk echoed out of the speakers, and then in Lithuanian, "Clear the deck! Clear the deck! Incoming! Incoming! "The fighter plane banked and was close enough now to make visible the swastikas on each wing. It was a Messerschmitt Bf109, not a bomber, but its three machine guns could still inflict much damage. This one seemed to be just cruising around, searching for some target practice.

It came in low over the freighter, bursts of fire and the staccato beat of bullets hitting metal and wood effectively ending the tranquil morning. Jonah and Ana had not had sufficient warning to return to their cabin and took refuge between several large wooden water barrels. The strafing lasted only a few seconds as the plane swooped back up to return for another pass—attempting a deadlier approach. Jonah watched, his eyes squinting, as the dark plane banked. The human psyche can take only so much abuse before it either turns inward or outward. Something in him erupted. The long months in the ghetto, the weeks of burning thousands of murdered Jews, days of running for their lives, all of that fused into an anger that was ignited against that plane.

As the pilot made the turn and came straight toward the freighter, Jonah stepped out from behind the barrels and raised both fists high above his head. A guttural scream that came from the dark side of him spewed into the air. Beside him Ana's scream combined with his as she tried to pull her husband back into the shelter of the barrels. The Messerschmitt pilot aimed the plane at the barrels, the screaming engines adding the third strand to the braided scream.

Suddenly Jonah heard a different droning sound. Looking back over his shoulder, he saw another plane approaching. Emblazoned target symbols on the wings identified it as an RAF Spitfire V and it was rapidly approaching from the port side. It came low over the bow of the Sakansia, moved along the starboard side and then entered a steep climb. The Spitfire distracted the German pilot's machine guns, but a short burst of fire still pierced the water barrels and the leaking water slowly became tinged with red. Bursts of fire and tracers cut through the air as the two planes approached each other. The Spitfire banked to the right passing over the Messerschmitt. Both planes maneuvered for another pass, the Spitfire successfully drawing the German pilot away from the freighter.

Those who train fighter pilots extol the superiority of the Spitfire. But beyond that they say that a superior pilot in an inferior plane can often prevail. In this case it was a superior pilot in a superior plane. As the German pilot chased down the RAF plane, the British pilot was calculating. He knew that the German planes had increased their armor and were equipped with self-sealing fuel tanks. But he had learned their vulnerability. He knew what he needed to do to take down this bastard. He banked hard to the left and then dropped, coming around just as the Luftwaffe plane came over the top of him, a dangerous maneuver. He tore loose a barrage from the 7.7mm machine guns ripping into the German plane from underneath near its tail. Then he put the Spitfire into a steep dive getting as far away as possible. In just seconds the Messerschmitt exploded above him into a fireball, a black smoke cloud spiraling upward as the plane sputtered and corkscrewed into the blue ocean, splashing down and disappearing.

The Royal Air Force pilot circled back over the top of the cargo ship, tipped his wing and headed back in the direction he had come. The red-headed twin in the cockpit raised a fist in victory.

Ana was sitting with Jonah's head in her lap, slapping his face, panic driving her sobbing. Her husband sat up, shaking his head to clear his ears, blood pouring down his arm. "Ana, Ana, it's okay. I'm okay. Don't cry." Relief replaced her panic. "And please don't hit me anymore! When I jumped back I lost my balance. Took a whack on my head. Looks like I have a sliver from that wooden barrel in my arm. He stood up and helped his wife up with his good arm. "We need to find someone who can remove it and bandage it for—" An announcement from the bridge cut him off.

"Attention! Our crew has reported no significant damage to our ship from the air strike. However, bullets did puncture one of our fuel oil storage tanks. We must travel slower to conserve the remaining fuel. This will delay our arrival into Leith."

Between the earlier loading delays and this new delay, the Sakansia's arrival was now delayed until 8 May. Samuel's telegram indicated no later than 6 May. Jonah was troubled.

"Arriving late? Jonah, what does that mean?" Ana asked.

"I'm not sure. Don't worry. We've come this far. We'll figure it out when we get there."

CHAPTER 61

May 8, 1942

I t was evening when the Sakansia pulled into its berth in Leith. After the dockhands had secured the freighter and the ramps were lowered and put in place, the passengers began slowly filing off onto the wooden pier. Jewish men, women and children, most exhausted, malnourished or ill, were directed to the immigration office. The Dresslers joined the line trudging along the rough cobblestones up to the top of the slight hill. In stark contrast to the crowd of freighters, oil tankers, and military ships hugging the harbor a centuries-old gothic church became visible amid a stance of large green beech trees emphasizing to the couple how far away from home they were.

The telegram had told them only to be in Edinburgh by 6 May. It was the evening of 8 May. Two days late. Jonah had no further instructions to follow. No more plan.

They stepped into the wooden building that served as an immigration office and after a short wait were summoned forward. A young man, upper lip hidden by a blonde mustache and wearing colorful suspenders, asked for their papers. He read through them, looked up, gestured around and asked, "Is anyone meeting you?"

"Nein," he said.

"Wait. I believe I saw a message for you," he said, quickly finding the note.

Jonah was amazed both that there was a message for him and

that the young man could find anything on the messy desktop. "Read it, please?" Jonah asked.

"Certainly. *Mr. Dressler: When you arrive go to the Salisbury Road Synagogue. I will contact you there. If you arrive after May 7. I may not be able to help you further but I will find a way to contact you. Ben Stuart.*

He handed Jonah his papers. "I have something else for you, too." He grabbed a paper printed in Yiddish and English, and with a smile said, "The paper contains directions to the synagogue. Welcome to Scotland. You are free people now."

Ana and Jonah picked up their satchels and moved away from the window. They stood for a moment looking up the street toward the buildings of Edinburgh, and for the first time since their long journey began a tenuous new feeling of hope began to replace the fear they had lived with for so long. *Even if Dr. Stuart couldn't help them,* Jonah thought, *he would find his own way.* He took Ana's arm as they walked toward the bus stop ahead.

Mac made the final call from his kitchen. He replaced the handset and turning toward Ben and the Captain, shook his head. "The Rabbi said no one by that name has arrived at the synagogue. Aye, sorry, boys."

"We'll gather our things together. We need to start back. I'm sorry, Ben. We did all we could. You knew it was a long shot." Disappointment took over. They completed their packing and bid thanks and good-bye to Mac. Their Scottish host waved as they drove away, sad for them. The phone was ringing when he walked back into the house.

"Yes. This is Dr. McHenry. They are? No. They just left. I have no way to reach them now. Aye, too bad they missed each other. Thank you for calling." Living alone he often spoke out loud. "I'm a poor driver at night, but only one thing to do. I'll drive them to Gourock." He was changing into warmer clothes when he heard a knock on the door. "Coming," he called.

"Mac, it's me, Captain Hawthorne," he heard from the small porch.

Hobbling across the room—one shoe on, one in hand—Mac unlocked the door, "Why. . .what brings you back?"

"I think I left a ring of very important keys in the—"

"Listen. Sorry to interrupt. Remember I gave my phone information to the Rabbi? They called right after you left. The Dresslers are here. I was gettin' ready to drive them to Gourock myself."

"Mac, what a generous and also dangerous thing to do. But, no need. We'll pick them up. Ben will be thrilled. Thanks, Mac."

"Wait. How could you drive without the keys?"

"The Cunard motorcar key was separate from my personal keys."

He hugged his friend, fetched the keys and ran back to the auto.

Captain Hawthorne drove the Vauxhall slowly up Salisbury Road and stopped in front of the synagogue, a two-story red brick building with high arched windows. After securing the vehicle, they entered into a vestibule and were greeted almost immediately by a tall thin man with a long white beard. He was dressed in a traditional black and white striped tallit, or prayer shawl, and a black kippah, or skull cap, that contrasted dramatically with the long white hair.

"I am Rabbi Glasser. How may I help you?"

"My name is Dr. Ben Stuart. I understand you have two refugees here, Ana and Jonah Dressler."

"Yes, they arrived only this evening. Come. I will take you to them." His English was reasonably good. The vestibule opened into the main worship chamber and the Rabbi led them out through a side door into a large multi-purpose room with two long tables. Seated were maybe thirty-five men, women and children, haggard and gaunt.

The Rabbi called to Jonah. Ben could see tension—or was it fear—on the man's face as he stood and joined them. He also noticed that they both had bandaged arms. "Jonah, this is Ben Stuart. He wants to talk with you."

"Rabbi, stay and translate for me, please?" Ben asked.

"Certainly."

Ben shook Jonah's hand. "I'm Ben Stuart—Samuel's friend—from Boston. I'm so pleased to meet you and even happier that you are safe." He took the Captain's elbow and introduced him. "Samuel has been so worried about you. When we get you to the Queen Mary we'll let him know you are safe." The Rabbi translated.

"We say thank you," Jonah said, shaking Ben's hand, then the Captain's. A long string of Yiddish phrases followed, relief registering on Jonah's face, followed by confusion.

The Rabbi turned back to Ben. "He says he was frightened at first when I called to him and he saw men with me. He didn't know what was happening. Fear is a common reaction. These people have lived with it for so long it is all they know."

"He seemed puzzled, too," Ben said.

The Rabbi laughed. "He was. He didn't know what the Queen Mary was. He thought you were taking them before royalty. I explained."

Captain Hawthorne spoke for the first time. "I need to relay some rather bad news. "I can see you are quite exhausted," he said, addressing Jonah. "But we must leave immediately. The Queen leaves tomorrow morning and I must be back tonight." Again, the Rabbi translated and Jonah nodded his understanding. He walked back and spoke to Ana. The couple retrieved their two satchels, stopping to presumably thank the Rabbi, and then followed the two men outside to the large car.

The deep twilight drive in violation of the curfew and imposed blackout created an atmosphere of tension. Violation of curfew was a serious crime. If they were caught and their explanation not accepted, they could be forced to stop, fined or be put in jail. As a result, few vehicles were on the road. When the rare one was encountered, the travelers held their breaths, relieved when it wasn't military police. Jonah prayed most of the way. Ana dozed leaning against his shoulder. The tension plus the language barrier limited most conversation.

Even though this time of year total darkness was hours away, the deep twilight still made the numerous small detours difficult to detect. Fortunately, the Captain remembered most of them from two days ago. The appearance of sea fog further delayed them as it closed in around the Vauxhall. The upside, however, was the welcome cloak of invisibility it provided. Twice they heard the droning of a plane directly overhead, and in spite of the fog, they pulled off the road each time, hiding in the shadows until the droning faded away. The hour was very late when they arrived safely at the docks in Gourock.

CHAPTER 62

~

Onboard the Queen Mary
May 9, 1942

Kate was up and dressed and finishing breakfast when her father strode into the dining room. He had left instructions that Kate not be told about their trip to Edinburgh until after they were gone. Otherwise he was sure she would have pressed to go along.

Her father sat down beside her. "Why didn't you tell me where you were going? I could have been a big help?" she pouted.

"Why? Because it was dangerous. Because we needed the room in the motorcar. Because you were needed her. We did it, Kate. The Dresslers are onboard. Safe. Their exhaustion is extreme. For now, they are in the quarantine area, sleeping. Later today we will find a room for them. Their English is quite limited, but they do speak German. There is something you can do. We need to find a staff member who speaks German.

Kate decided pouting was juvenile. "I can do that. We should let Samuel know. I met him, remember?"

"We've already cabled him."

"Good. I still wish I could have gone, too." Brief silence. "When I found out the two of you left. . .together. I mean I was surprised that. . ." her voice trailed off.

"It was rather an abrupt decision. I saw a way to help. A way to feel better about myself, Popette."

She leaned over and kissed him on the cheek. "I love you, Papa. But I meant. . .Ben. What about Ben?"

"We had a drink. Talked. We're working on resolving our differences. Oh, yes, he was nearby when a bomb exploded."

Her heart raced; blue eyes wide. "What?"

"Before you ask. He's okay. But it was a close call. He can tell you about it. I need to be in the wheelhouse now. We'll talk more later." He rose, kissed the top of her head and left. Kate rushed off to find Ben.

She found him not in his cabin, but sound asleep in the infirmary, apparently staying close to the Dresslers in case they woke up disoriented. What would she say to him when he woke up? Maybe it would be easiest to say what she wanted while he was sleeping. She moved to the end of the bed and looked down at him. Faint circles under his eyes testified to his recent lack of sleep but his facial expression was relaxed. She noticed an ugly purple bruise on his forehead and a thick bandage on one forearm. She thought about what her father had said and decided if he and Ben could come to terms, she should try, too.

Clearing her voice, she said, "Not that this is any kind of apology. You really can be quite pig-headed." Her voice caught and where did that tear come from? Her hand quickly made it disappear. She had meant to remain firmly distant, but as she talked the realization of what could have happened to him impacted her. "This could have had a very different ending. And that's frightfully scary. You and Papa were very brave. . .doing what you did. . .together. I'm glad you're here, safe." Then softly, nearly a whisper, "I love you, Ben."

Kate turned at the sound behind her. A small man with a little skull cap on his head, his right arm bandaged and in a sling was standing in the doorway. The woman next to him was small and shorter and had a black scarf covering her graying hair. Both looked very tired.

"Kate, let me introduce you to Jonah and Ana Dressler," Ben said from the bed, grinning broadly. Kate whirled around, hands on her hips.

"You scoundrel. You were awake! You let me go on. . .You really are a bloody ars." But she grinned as she said it.

Jonah stepped closer. He spoke some English and said to Ben, "We say thanks to you now, but later we will thank you more."

Dr. Joe showed up then and was introduced to Jonah and Ana. "Ben, I'll be keeping an eye on that arm. I'll be your doctor now so *try* to be a good patient," he said, wagging a finger at him. He pointed to Jonah's arm and mimed that he would take care of it, too.

Kate located a German-speaking crew member and he gave the Dresslers a tour of the ship. They were stunned at the amount of food, the hot water for bathing, and the clean sheets and towels. Over the next five days with the help of that crew member, parts of the Dresslers' story slowly unfolded. Jonah told them about the chicken truck, and the miraculous travel visa and he related how he became injured and how the Spitfire came out of nowhere to save the freighter; but other parts of their story, more painful parts, couldn't be told for a long time. Someday though, Jonah vowed, he would tell the world what happened in Ponar Forest.

After two days at sea, Ben was enjoying some time on deck. The day was cloudy and chilly, but the briskness felt good lessened by the woolen blanket wrapped around him.

"May I join you?" Kate's father asked.

"Please, have a seat." Ben motioned to a chair. A moment of silence passed between them before Ben spoke. "Captain, I wanted to talk to you. First, I don't remember thanking you for your help. So, just in case, thank you. Second, I've had some time to think." He looked off in the distance for a minute and adjusted the blanket. "Before being on this ship I was pretty naïve. I used to think right and wrong were absolutes. They never changed. You saw the right choice and you made it. Then this war came along and changed all that. Those absolutes were turned upside down. So, what then? When there are no clear right choices? When choices are gray, not black and white? Where's the compass? What do you do? He turned to face the Captain. "It's 'why', Captain. It's important to understand why. You can live with a decision when you know why you made it, even if no one else understands. Honestly, I don't know if I would have made the same decision as you, but I've come to understand it was yours to make, yours to live with."

"All true, Ben. But that doesn't mean I will ever forget those whose lives were sacrificed that day or that their sacrifice was my decision."

The Captain lightened the mood as he stood. "By the way, you and Kate do look good together." He patted Ben's shoulder as he walked away.

Ben called out to him, "Captain, open invitation while we are in Boston to come for dinner."

"Thanks." The Captain waved over his shoulder and disappeared through the doorway.

Dr. Joe arrived just then and took a seat next to him. "You look better. More rested."

Ben agreed and then a thought came to him.

"Joe, what are you going to do while the ship is being repaired in Boston?"

"Not sure, why?"

"You said Cunard is paying for your lodging, right? Well, I know that Massachusetts General Hospital is doing some innovative work in treating burns and has the latest x-ray machines. I'm confident I could get the hospital to allow you on staff as a visiting physician during the layover. There's much you could learn to take back to Georgia."

"If you can arrange that, I would be very grateful. Thank you."

"We've been through some stuff together, haven't we? You should come to the house while we're in Boston. My mom's a great cook. And you can meet Samuel." Dr. Joe rose, touched Ben on the shoulder. "Thanks. I'll take you up on that dinner, but right now I want to change that dressing on your arm," he said. Ben threw off the blanket and the two walked back to the infirmary. Kate was there, changing the quarantine area bed linens.

"Morning, Kate," Ben said as he pulled her to him with his good arm and delivered a long deep kiss.

"Do you kiss all the nurses like that, Dr. Stuart?" she teased, looking up at him.

"Of course not! Only the redheads this week, Nurse Hawthorne."

CHAPTER 63

Boston, MA
May 14, 1942

Three days later tugs pulled the Queen Mary into a sunny Boston harbor. Arrival details had preceded them, so Avery, Margaret, Samuel and Ziva were waiting expectantly at the docks. Excitement radiated from all four, but particularly from Samuel. When Ben and Kate appeared on the gangway, Margaret rushed forward and gave her son a hug, avoiding his bandaged arm but gently touching the fading bruise on his face. When she did he noticed a new ruby and diamond ring on her finger. That news would come later.

Avery had agreed to sponsor the Dresslers, so he, Samuel and Ziva waited in the customs building while the preliminary immigration process was completed. When Samuel saw his parents come through the door he sighed with relief and reached for his mother's tattered satchel. Ana's eyes quickly took in Ziva and then settled on her son, reaching her arms out to him, exclaiming, "Ah, Zeeskeit"—sweetness. Both parents embraced their son, tears mingling, eventually moving apart—all of them finding it difficult to believe they were finally here, together. Safe. It would take much longer than this five-day voyage to restore them to health, but they had a loving doctor to help them.

Samuel took Ziva's elbow and deliberately speaking in English, not Yiddish, said, "Mama and Papa, I'd like you to meet

Ziva. She saved my life. We have much to tell you."

"We, too," Jonah said.

Kate and his mom were having an animated conversation with Dr. Joe, so Ben walked a few steps away and turned back toward the injured Queen Mary, now moored proudly in the harbor. The Grey Ghost. It surprised him how in this short time she had become such an important part of him. When he left here he was confused, searching—didn't even know for what. This warrior ship and her crew had played a major role in restoring his confidence as a physician; taught him that knowing he had done his best was what brought peace, not necessarily the outcome; and, well, made him grow up. This noble ship had brought Samuel's parents to a new country offering them freedom and unlimited possibilities.

He lightly touched the small scar on his forehead. And the Queen Mary had led him to Kate.

For a fleeting moment he thought of Laura. *I think she would have liked Kate. What was it her father said that afternoon after the fire? 'Sometimes God's plan for your life isn't the same plan that you have.' So much has happened since then it seems like a very long time ago. I remember he also said something about telling me a story. Kate and I should go see him.* His eyes roamed over the stately outline of the ship one more time before he turned away and joined the others. *I can't wait to be back onboard.*

Margaret's loving eyes met Ben's. "Let's all go home. I've a bit of lunch prepared and I'll put on a pot of tea."

Ana's face brightened when she heard 'tea'. "I have cup," she said in halting English.

EPILOGUE

Long Beach, California
July 19, 1972

Standing there, looking at her, Ben realized he had come full circle. The Cunard ship looked the same to him today as that July day in 1939 when he saw her for the first time. She was no longer the 'grey ghost' he had encountered in the Boston harbor that cold February afternoon. It had taken many months of work after the war, but the Queen Mary had been restored to her former luxurious self, ferrying fun-loving passengers across the Atlantic again, until now.

"Ben, are you ready?" the woman at his side asked quietly. The question gradually reached his consciousness drawing him away from the scattered thoughts tumbling in his mind. He turned and looked at her. Her red hair was toned down now with gray. She was dressed in casual west coast culottes and a bright blouse, but he could still picture her in that green gown when they met. And she was still very beautiful. Today culminated a long journey for them. "Are you ready?" she asked again. He nodded and they walked up the ramp, holding hands.

A stocky white-haired docent wearing the official embroidered shirt handed them a map and a leaflet. "Welcome aboard the Queen Mary. My name is Bill," he said, giving them a bright smile. "She is an extraordinary ship as you will soon learn. Fortunately, the city of Long Beach saved her from the scrap heap.

What a travesty that would have been. Do you know anything about her history?" he questioned as they stepped aboard.

Ben and Kate exchanged a smile that engulfed a lifetime. Ben gave her a wink, turned back to the docent and said, "A little. What can you tell us?"

ACKNOWLEDGEMENTS

The idea for this story grew from a visit to the Queen Mary several years ago. I began my research and was astounded to discover that very few books have been written about the history of this great ship, fiction or non-fiction. As I continued searching and learning, the bones of this novel began to emerge. I became fascinated with the role that cruise ships played during World War II. It is my belief that they have not received a proper tribute for their major contribution to winning the war. It was sheer luck that I came across the Nova special about the escape tunnel in Vilna and then later the biography of the Japanese 'Shindler', Chiune Sugihara. Weaving them into a believable story became my mission.

And that leads me to a troubling dilemma that exists for historical fiction writers—maintaining a balance between preserving historical details and creating an exciting and believable story. The following notes identify known deviations from actual events. If you are someone who has lived through one of the events in this story or have relatives or other acquaintances who have first-hand knowledge of the occurrences mentioned here, please forgive me if my research was incomplete or inaccurate. Any mistakes are my own. Please bear in mind that it is a work of fiction. I welcome your input at palynck@gmail.com.

I have beta-readers extraordinaire. Shan Hays and Roberta Gibson deserve considerable credit for slogging through a very early draft, offering their insightful comments, and copyediting experience. I have beta-readers extraordinaire. Shan Hays and Roberta Gibson deserve considerable credit for slogging through a very early draft, offering their insightful comments, and copyediting experience. And congrats, Roberta, on your latest non-fiction children's picture book, *How to Build an Insect,* to be released in early April, 2021.

My husband, Jim, loaded up our RV with supplies and our dogs several times, leaving me home alone to work uninterrupted. Thanks sweetie! My daughter, Lisa Stewart, had the distinction of getting the first look at the first complete draft. My thanks to her for providing valuable assistance and expertise with the publishing and marketing process and her enthusiastic support. Couldn't have done this without you, kiddo.

NOTES

Chapter 9:

On September 3rd, 1939, during a voyage from Liverpool to Montreal, The SS Athenia was the first UK ship to be sunk by the Germans. One hundred seventeen civilians and crew perished. Wartime German authorities denied that one of their vessels had sunk the ship. An admission of responsibility did not come from German authorities until 1946.

The Queen Mary's last voyage before being converted into a transport ship was September, 1939. The itineraries detailed in this book are accurate. It is true that at least one crossing included 16,000 American troops, an entire division, and today the ship still holds the record for the most people transported on a ship.

Chapter 14:

Chiune Sugihara was a Japanese diplomat assigned to Kaunas, Lithuania, for the purpose of providing intel to the Japanese government. The Soviets and Germans were both occupying forces in Lithuania and Chiune's intel assisted Japan in determining where to place its allegiance. Chiune became sympathetic to the Jews and saved as many as 10,000 by issuing transport visas. Some of my information came from a biography entitled *In Search of Sugihara* by Hillel Levine. It is a fascinating story if you want to read more about his life.

Chapter 15:

About 4,000 men, women and children lost their lives when the Lancastria sank 20 minutes after it was bombed by the Germans near the French port of Saint-Nazaire on 17 June 1940. Fewer than 2,500 people survived. The Lancastria was the largest loss of life from a single engagement for British forces in World War II. But it is a largely forgotten chapter in British history, a fact that leaves survivors and relatives aggrieved.

Chapter 20:

The Cocoanut Grove fire in Boston remains to this day one of the deadliest fires in history. The details presented here are accurate, including how it started and its cause. However, it occurred November 28, 1942, not November of 1941. My apologies to Boston. Something called author license is exercised here.

Chapter 33:

On June 7, 1941 Roosevelt issued Executive Order 8802, which declared, "There shall be no discrimination in the employment of workers in defense industries and in Government, because of race, creed, color, or national origin." There was no clear indication of how his order would affect troops. Segregation still existed among the military; however, it was difficult to enforce on the troop transport ships.

Chapter 33:

The Italian Count Edmondo di Robilant was part of a spy ring operating in Brazil. Members illegally accessed secure information, leaking it to the German U-boat commanders and causing the destruction of several merchant marine ships.

In a few years, after the war was over, the hurricane warning system became more organized with coast guard cutter patrols and airplanes monitoring the skies sending reports every six hours to Miami and Puerto Rico. In the mid-1950s the National Weather Service, a branch of the National Oceanic and Atmospheric Administration. (NOAA), defined the hurricane season and by 1970 had become the central location for hurricane monitoring and up-to-date storm information. After the 1954 hurricane season efforts were made to enhance the hurricane reporting network along the gulf coast by setting up a Cooperative Hurricane Reporting Network (CHURN) by supplying anemometers and barometers to members of the public. This effort resulted in monitoring the United States coastline along the Atlantic or Gulf coasts every 25 miles, greatly improving detection. Forecasting intensity and direction was still a long way off.

Chapter 47:

The *Lietuvos laisvés armija, LLA* was one of several resistance movements throughout Lithuania. The LLA did have a camp near Kaunas working with a network of Jewish sympathizers. Lithuania has a complicated history between Poland, the Soviets and Germans and that could become a story itself.

Chapter 52:

The date of the collision with the Curacaó was in October of 1942, not May, 1942. The other details of that incident are accurate, however, including the fact that it was hushed up and the fate of the Curacaó was not announced until four years later. The Queen Mary was partially repaired in Gourock and returned to Boston for permanent repairs. A subsequent investigation found that the Captain of the Queen Mary was one-third responsible for the collision and the Captain of the Curacaó was two-thirds responsible. I discovered some confusion about the correct name of this ship and I have used Steve Harding's book, *Gray Ghost, The R.M.S. Queen Mary at War* (noted below) as my definitive source.

Chapter 57:

In a few years when the Germans tired of their arrangement with Denmark the Danish people would help most of the Jews in that country escape.

Ponar Forest:

In 2017 The Public Broadcasting System produced a Nova special on the Ponar Forest and Vilna, Lithuania, entitled *Holocaust Escape Tunnel*. The atrocities committed there were the earliest of World War II and some of the most heinous. This educational special was the basis for the scenes in Ponar Forest and the daring escape. This same Nova special chronicles the expedition and methods used to locate the ruins of The Great Synagogue which was destroyed by the Germans.

The Queen Mary

Steve Harding's book, *Gray Ghost, The R.M.S. Queen Mary at War*, along with countless internet sites was the source of many of the ship's details used in this fictional account.

Mildred A. MacGregor's journal published by the *University of Michigan Press* contains a detailed look at a nurse's life while aboard the Queen Mary. According to her journal a hurricane did occur and an appendectomy was performed during her trip across the Atlantic.

Besides being one of the fastest most luxurious ocean liners in her day, and still holding the record for the most lives transported on a ship, the Queen Mary also had the joyful task of ferrying war brides to the United States at the end of the war. Hmmm. Let me think about that.

ABOUT THE AUTHOR

This is P. A. Lynck's debut novel. Prior to this her writing consisted of technical writing in the form of personnel and instruction manuals. She assisted with a religious commentary and a doctoral dissertation which was later published as *Emotalerting: The Art of Managing the Moment,* by Carlyle Naylor. She originated and edited a monthly publication in the Arizona White Mountains for six years.

While volunteering at a large Arizona hospital she interviewed patients and created a short life story for each one. The program has received national recognition from The American Hospital Association. According to her: *"This was one of my most satisfying writing experiences giving me the opportunity to experience many different life journeys as I talked with patients."*

She and her husband, Jim, and two very spoiled dogs divide their time between the Arizona southern deserts and the cool White Mountains. Between them they have three grown daughters, a son, and twelve exceptional grandchildren.

CPSIA information can be obtained
at www.ICGtesting.com
Printed in the USA
BVHW040833270522
638300BV00006B/99